Timo
the Adventurer

WRITER
JONATHAN GARNIER

ARTIST
YOHAN SACRÉ

Translated from the French by Lara Vergnaud

ETCH · CLARION BOOKS
Houghton Mifflin Harcourt
Boston   New York

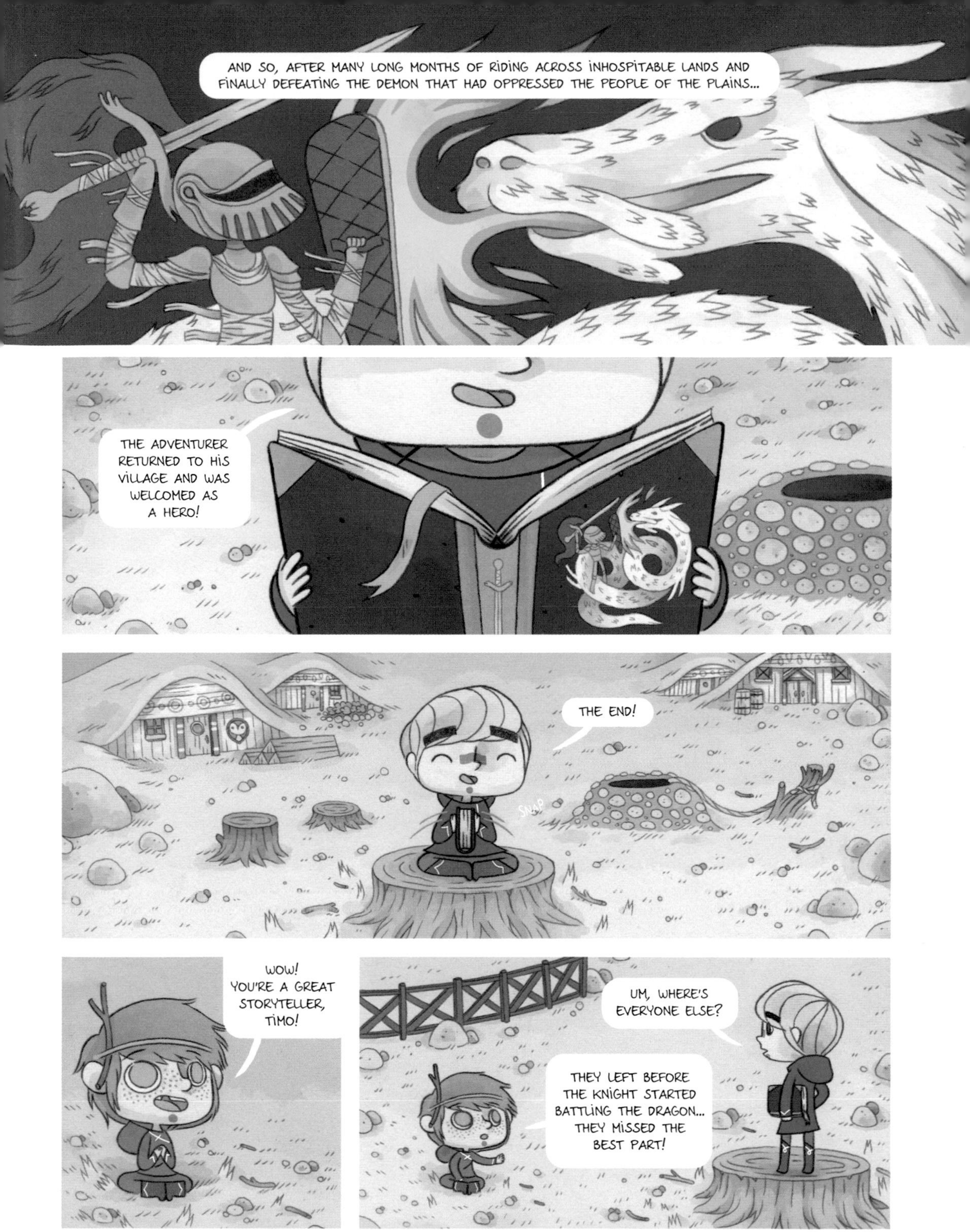
AND SO, AFTER MANY LONG MONTHS OF RIDING ACROSS INHOSPITABLE LANDS AND FINALLY DEFEATING THE DEMON THAT HAD OPPRESSED THE PEOPLE OF THE PLAINS...
THE ADVENTURER RETURNED TO HIS VILLAGE AND WAS WELCOMED AS A HERO!
THE END!
SNAP
WOW! YOU'RE A GREAT STORYTELLER, TIMO!
UM, WHERE'S EVERYONE ELSE?
THEY LEFT BEFORE THE KNIGHT STARTED BATTLING THE DRAGON... THEY MISSED THE BEST PART!

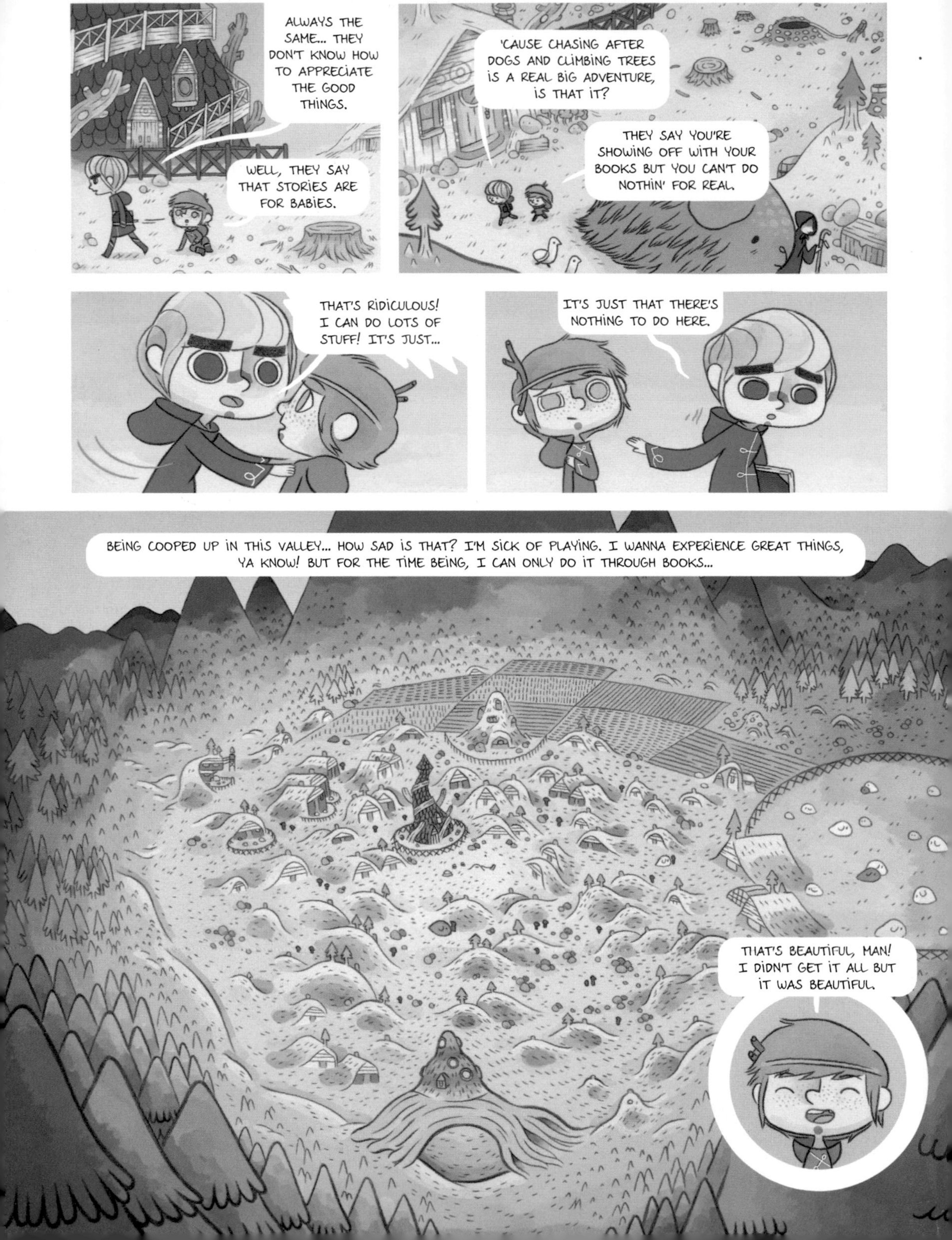
ALWAYS THE SAME... THEY DON'T KNOW HOW TO APPRECIATE THE GOOD THINGS.
WELL, THEY SAY THAT STORIES ARE FOR BABIES.
'CAUSE CHASING AFTER DOGS AND CLIMBING TREES IS A REAL BIG ADVENTURE, IS THAT IT?
THEY SAY YOU'RE SHOWING OFF WITH YOUR BOOKS BUT YOU CAN'T DO NOTHIN' FOR REAL.
THAT'S RIDICULOUS! I CAN DO LOTS OF STUFF! IT'S JUST...
IT'S JUST THAT THERE'S NOTHING TO DO HERE.
BEING COOPED UP IN THIS VALLEY... HOW SAD IS THAT? I'M SICK OF PLAYING. I WANNA EXPERIENCE GREAT THINGS, YA KNOW! BUT FOR THE TIME BEING, I CAN ONLY DO IT THROUGH BOOKS...
THAT'S BEAUTIFUL, MAN! I DIDN'T GET IT ALL BUT IT WAS BEAUTIFUL.

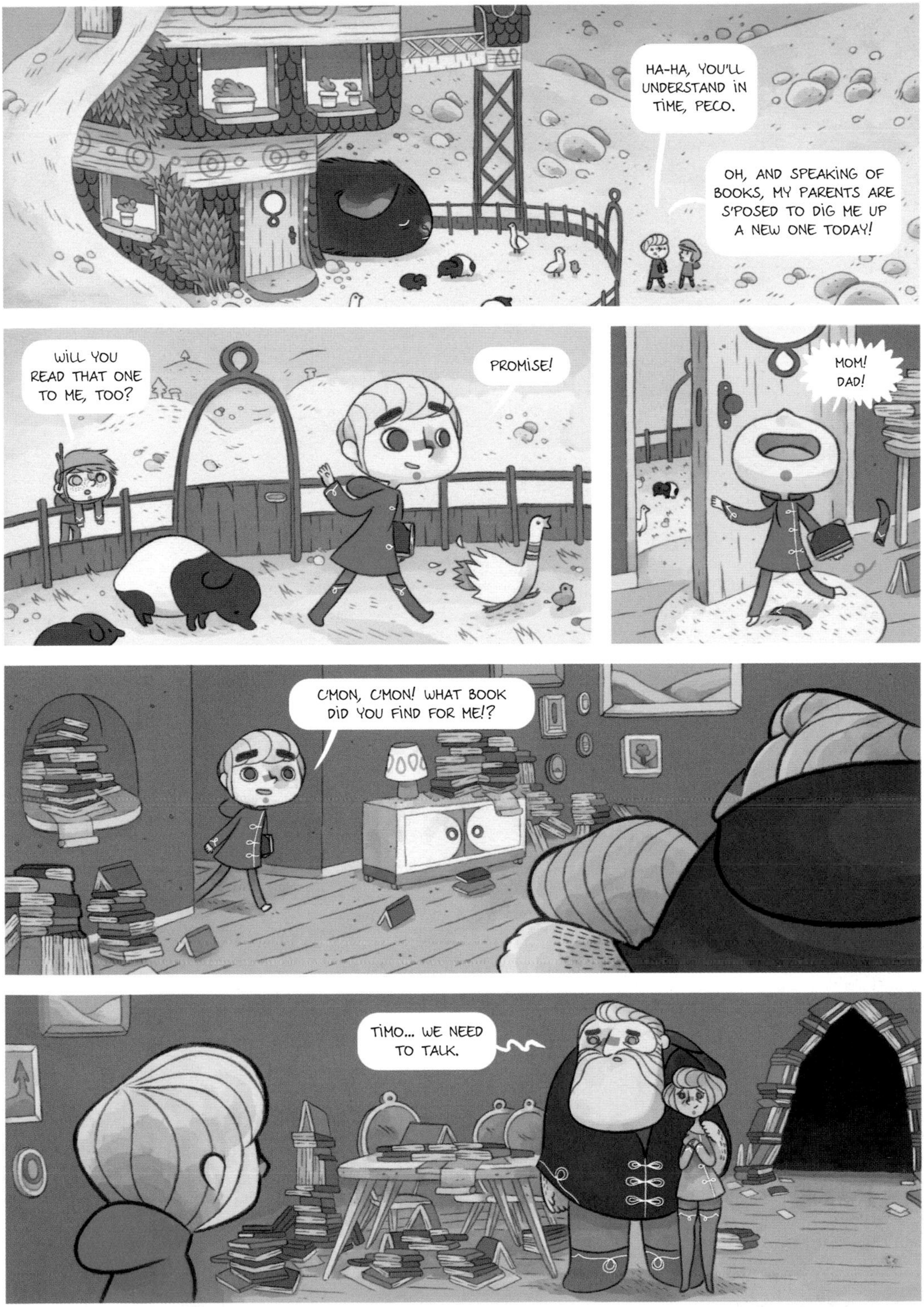
HA-HA, YOU'LL UNDERSTAND IN TIME, PECO.
OH, AND SPEAKING OF BOOKS, MY PARENTS ARE S'POSED TO DIG ME UP A NEW ONE TODAY!
WILL YOU READ THAT ONE TO ME, TOO?
PROMISE!
MOM! DAD!
C'MON, C'MON! WHAT BOOK DID YOU FIND FOR ME!?
TIMO... WE NEED TO TALK.

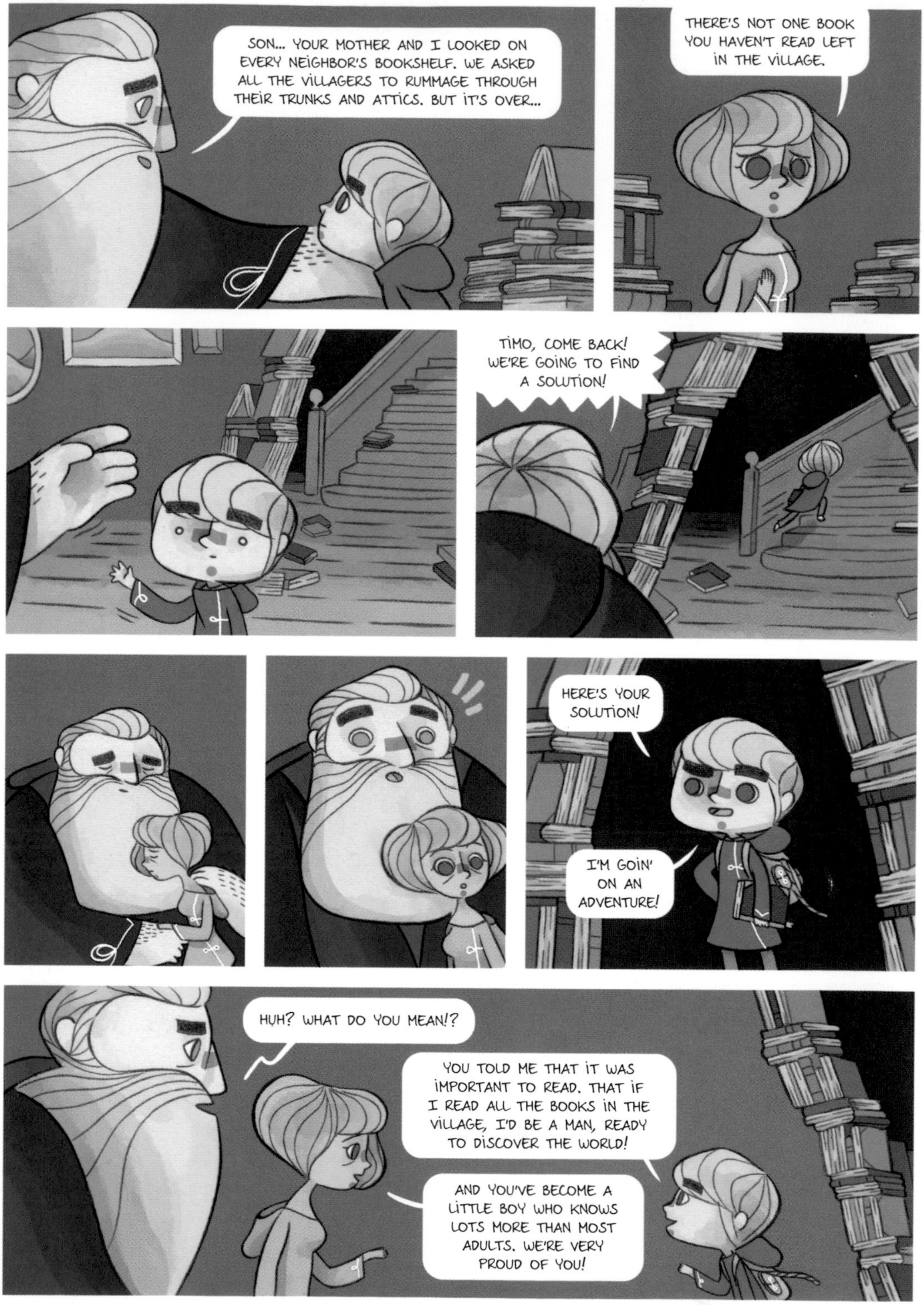
SON... YOUR MOTHER AND I LOOKED ON EVERY NEIGHBOR'S BOOKSHELF. WE ASKED ALL THE VILLAGERS TO RUMMAGE THROUGH THEIR TRUNKS AND ATTICS. BUT IT'S OVER...
THERE'S NOT ONE BOOK YOU HAVEN'T READ LEFT IN THE VILLAGE.
TIMO, COME BACK! WE'RE GOING TO FIND A SOLUTION!
HERE'S YOUR SOLUTION!
I'M GOIN' ON AN ADVENTURE!
HUH? WHAT DO YOU MEAN!?
YOU TOLD ME THAT IT WAS IMPORTANT TO READ. THAT IF I READ ALL THE BOOKS IN THE VILLAGE, I'D BE A MAN, READY TO DISCOVER THE WORLD!
AND YOU'VE BECOME A LITTLE BOY WHO KNOWS LOTS MORE THAN MOST ADULTS. WE'RE VERY PROUD OF YOU!

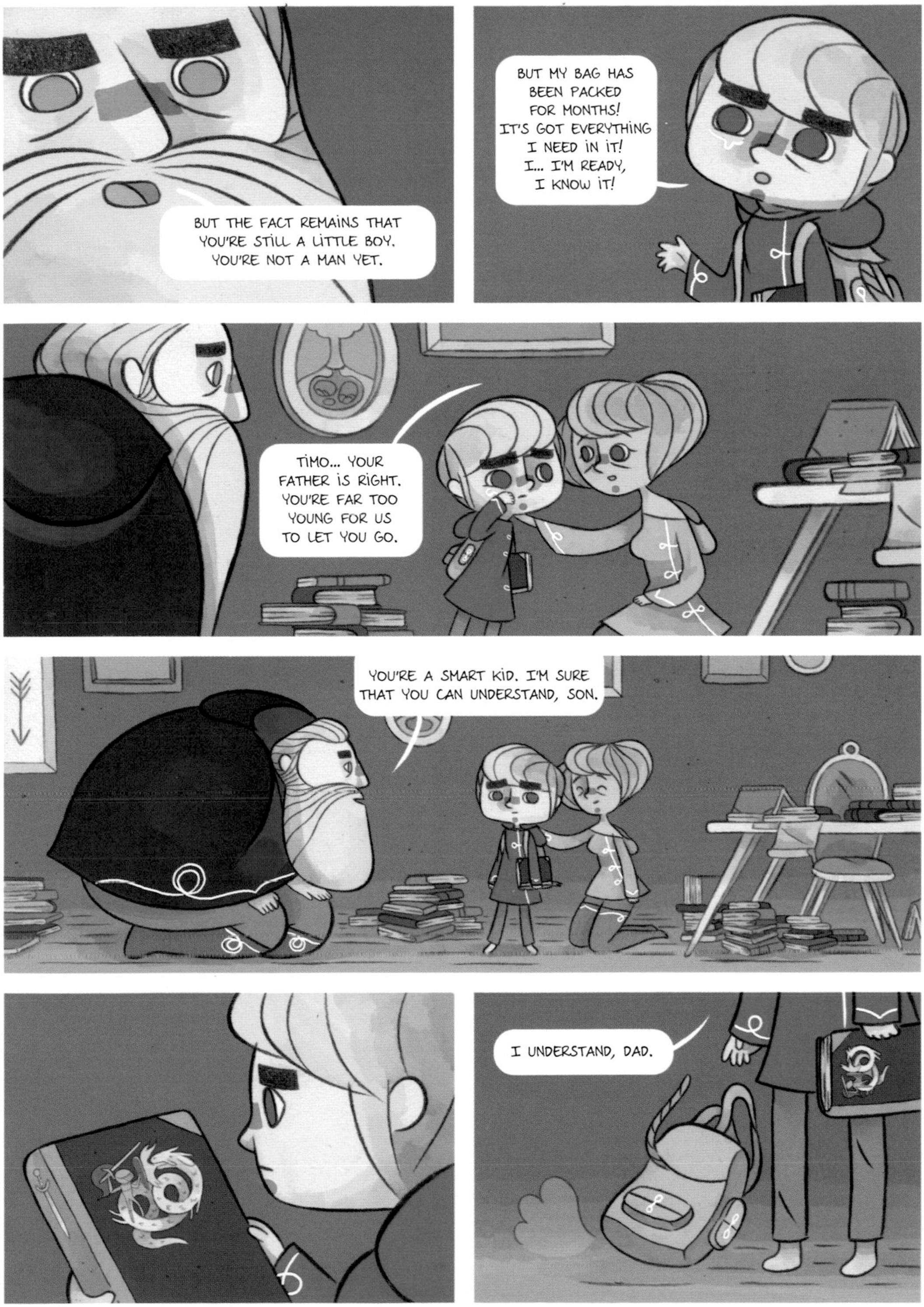
BUT THE FACT REMAINS THAT YOU'RE STILL A LITTLE BOY. YOU'RE NOT A MAN YET.
BUT MY BAG HAS BEEN PACKED FOR MONTHS! IT'S GOT EVERYTHING I NEED IN IT! I... I'M READY, I KNOW IT!
TIMO... YOUR FATHER IS RIGHT. YOU'RE FAR TOO YOUNG FOR US TO LET YOU GO.
YOU'RE A SMART KID. I'M SURE THAT YOU CAN UNDERSTAND, SON.
I UNDERSTAND, DAD.

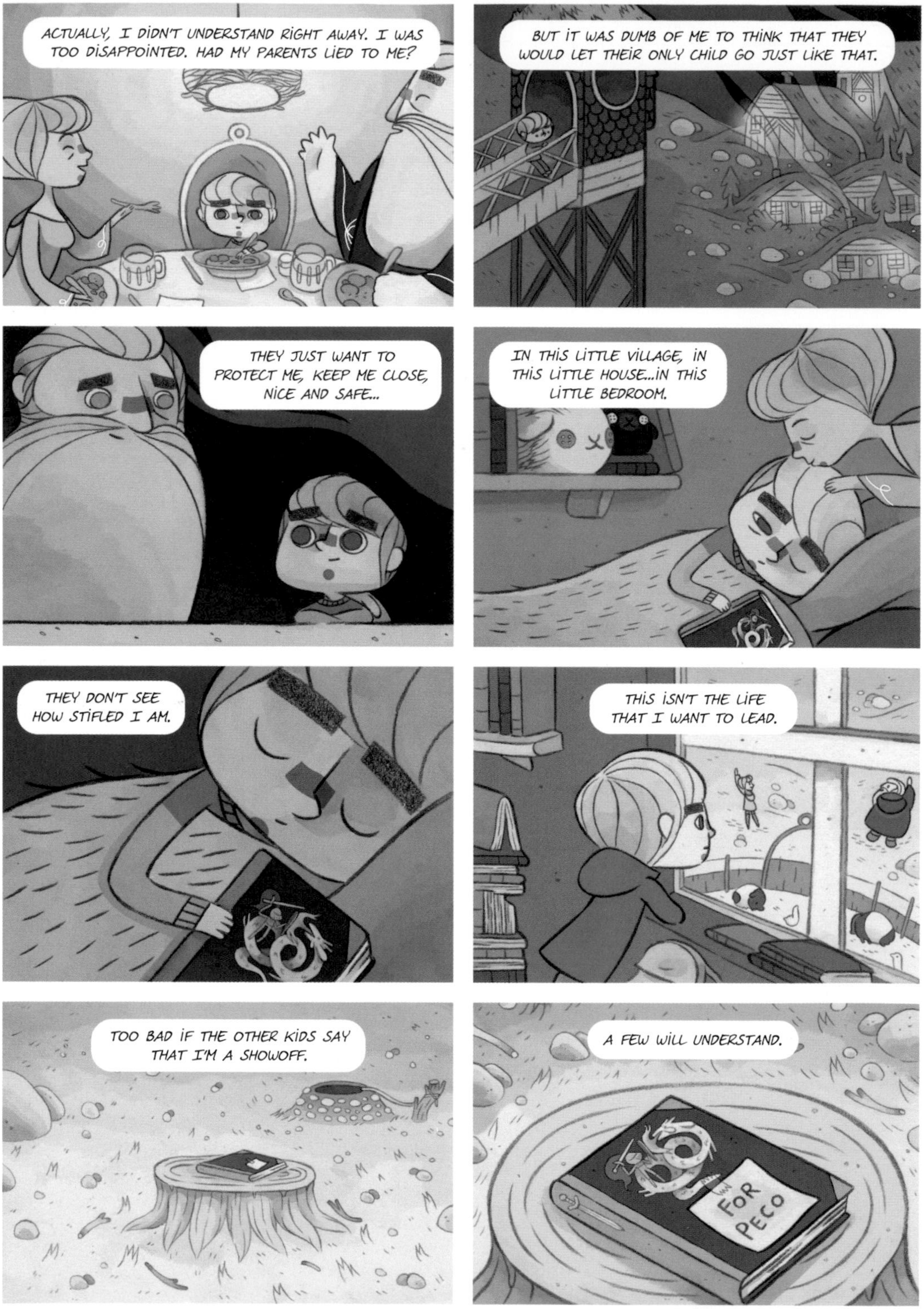
ACTUALLY, I DIDN'T UNDERSTAND RIGHT AWAY. I WAS TOO DISAPPOINTED. HAD MY PARENTS LIED TO ME?
BUT IT WAS DUMB OF ME TO THINK THAT THEY WOULD LET THEIR ONLY CHILD GO JUST LIKE THAT.
THEY JUST WANT TO PROTECT ME, KEEP ME CLOSE, NICE AND SAFE...
IN THIS LITTLE VILLAGE, IN THIS LITTLE HOUSE...IN THIS LITTLE BEDROOM.
THEY DON'T SEE HOW STIFLED I AM.
THIS ISN'T THE LIFE THAT I WANT TO LEAD.
TOO BAD IF THE OTHER KIDS SAY THAT I'M A SHOWOFF.
A FEW WILL UNDERSTAND.
FOR PECO

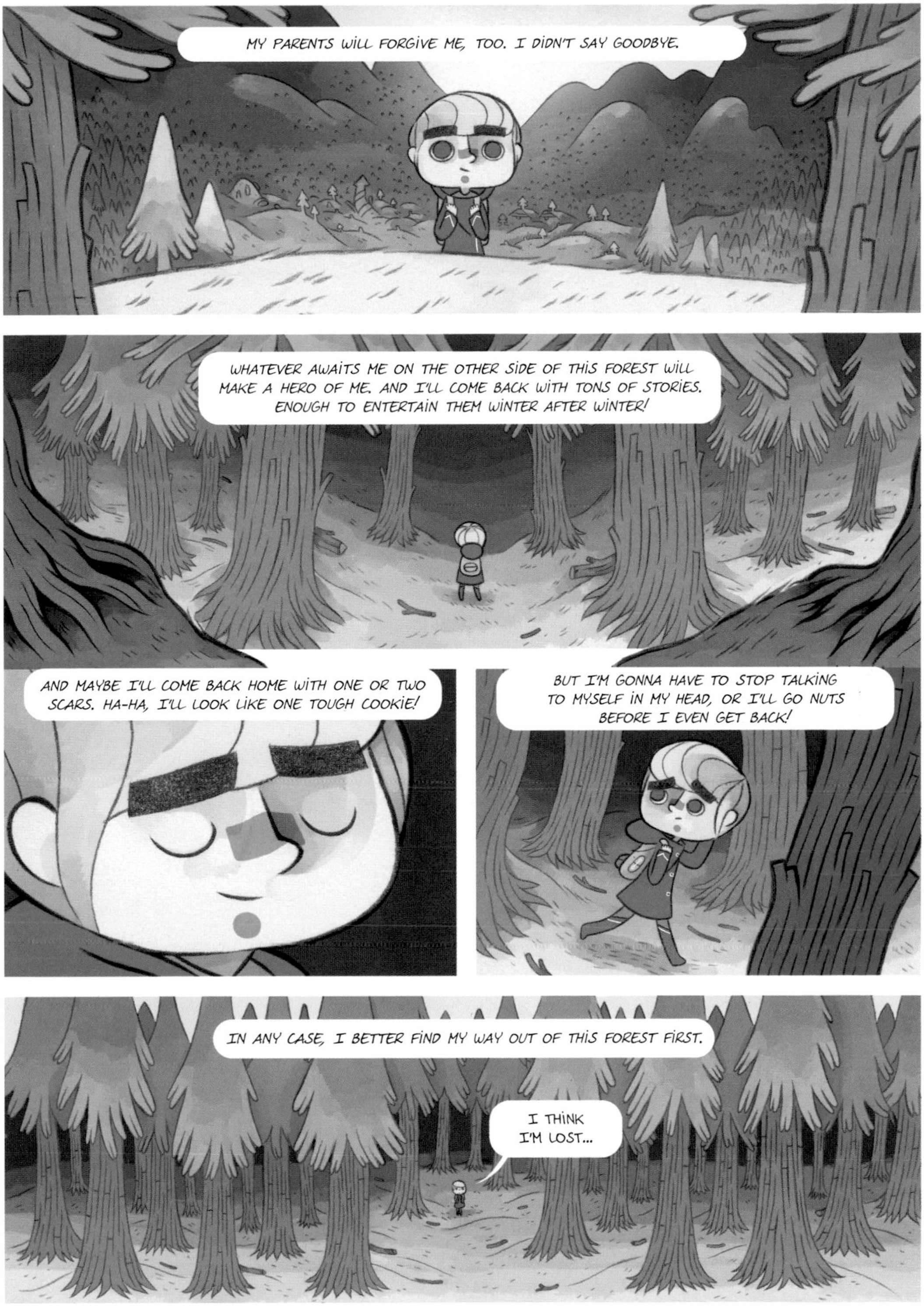
MY PARENTS WILL FORGIVE ME, TOO. I DIDN'T SAY GOODBYE.
WHATEVER AWAITS ME ON THE OTHER SIDE OF THIS FOREST WILL MAKE A HERO OF ME. AND I'LL COME BACK WITH TONS OF STORIES. ENOUGH TO ENTERTAIN THEM WINTER AFTER WINTER!
AND MAYBE I'LL COME BACK HOME WITH ONE OR TWO SCARS. HA-HA, I'LL LOOK LIKE ONE TOUGH COOKIE!
BUT I'M GONNA HAVE TO STOP TALKING TO MYSELF IN MY HEAD, OR I'LL GO NUTS BEFORE I EVEN GET BACK!
IN ANY CASE, I BETTER FIND MY WAY OUT OF THIS FOREST FIRST.
I THINK I'M LOST...

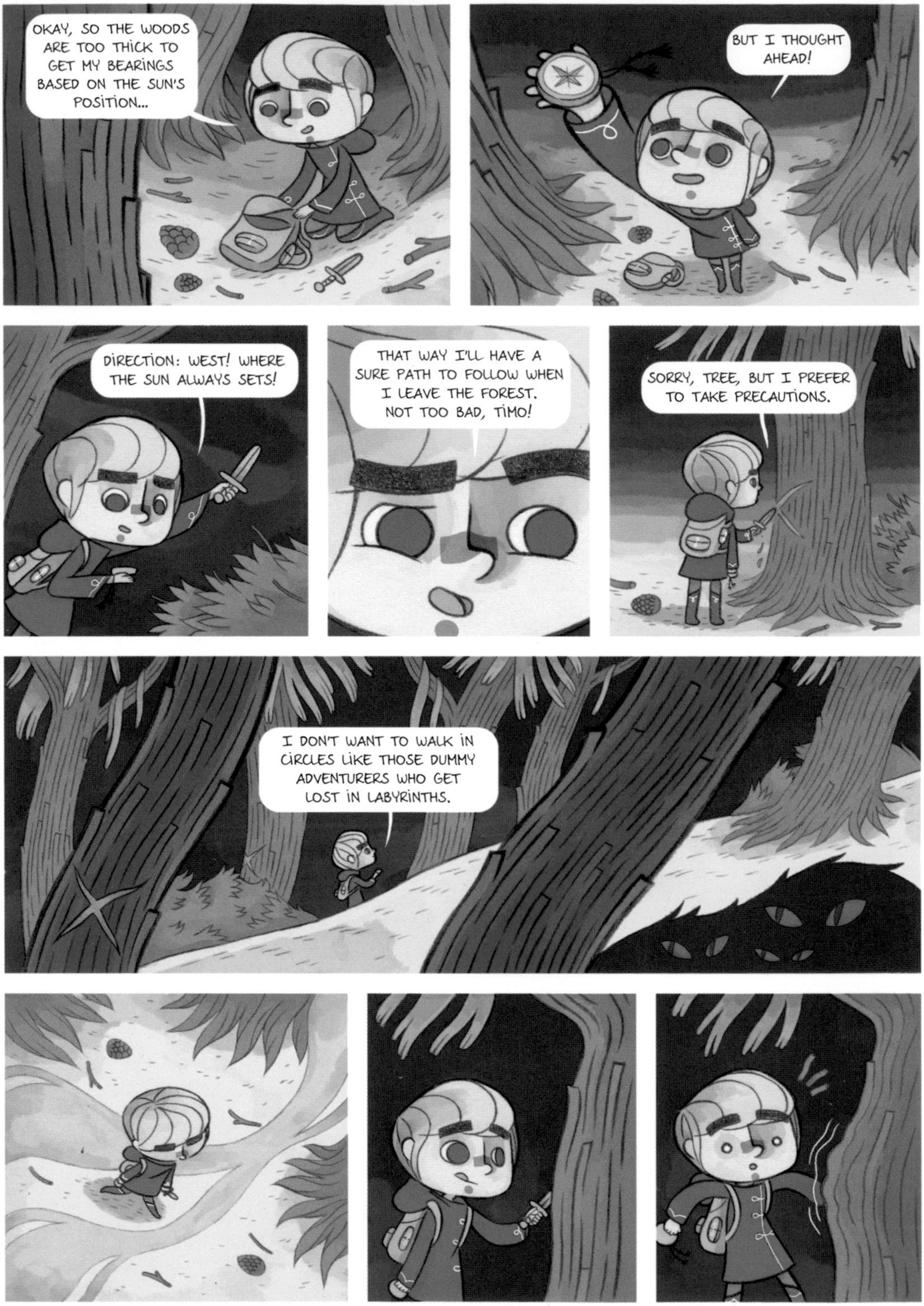
OKAY, SO THE WOODS ARE TOO THICK TO GET MY BEARINGS BASED ON THE SUN'S POSITION...
BUT I THOUGHT AHEAD!
DIRECTION: WEST! WHERE THE SUN ALWAYS SETS!
THAT WAY I'LL HAVE A SURE PATH TO FOLLOW WHEN I LEAVE THE FOREST. NOT TOO BAD, TIMO!
SORRY, TREE, BUT I PREFER TO TAKE PRECAUTIONS.
I DON'T WANT TO WALK IN CIRCLES LIKE THOSE DUMMY ADVENTURERS WHO GET LOST IN LABYRINTHS.

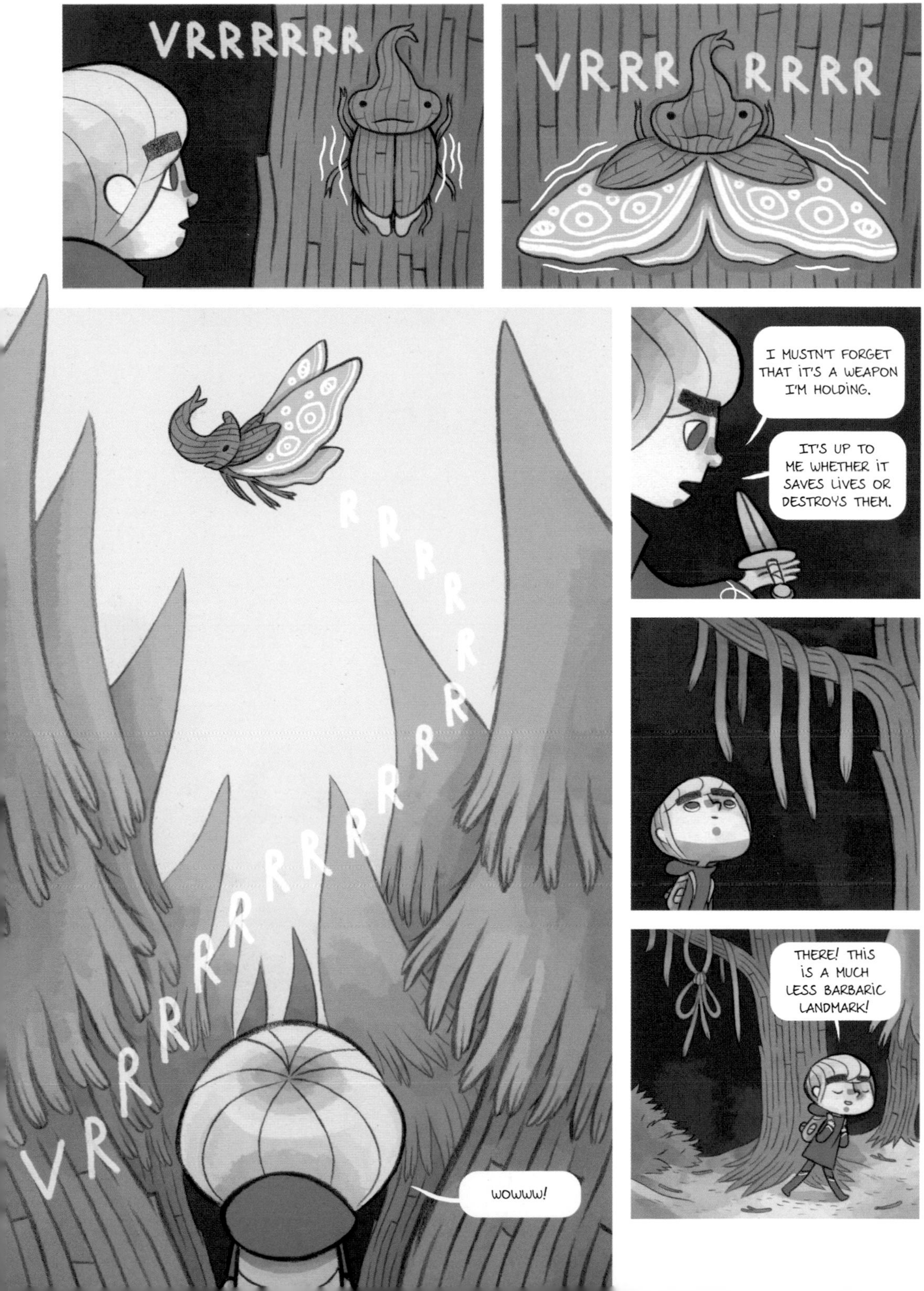
VRRRRRR
VRRR RRRR
VRRRRRRRRRRRRRRRRR
WOWWW!
I MUSTN'T FORGET THAT IT'S A WEAPON I'M HOLDING.
IT'S UP TO ME WHETHER IT SAVES LIVES OR DESTROYS THEM.
THERE! THIS IS A MUCH LESS BARBARIC LANDMARK!

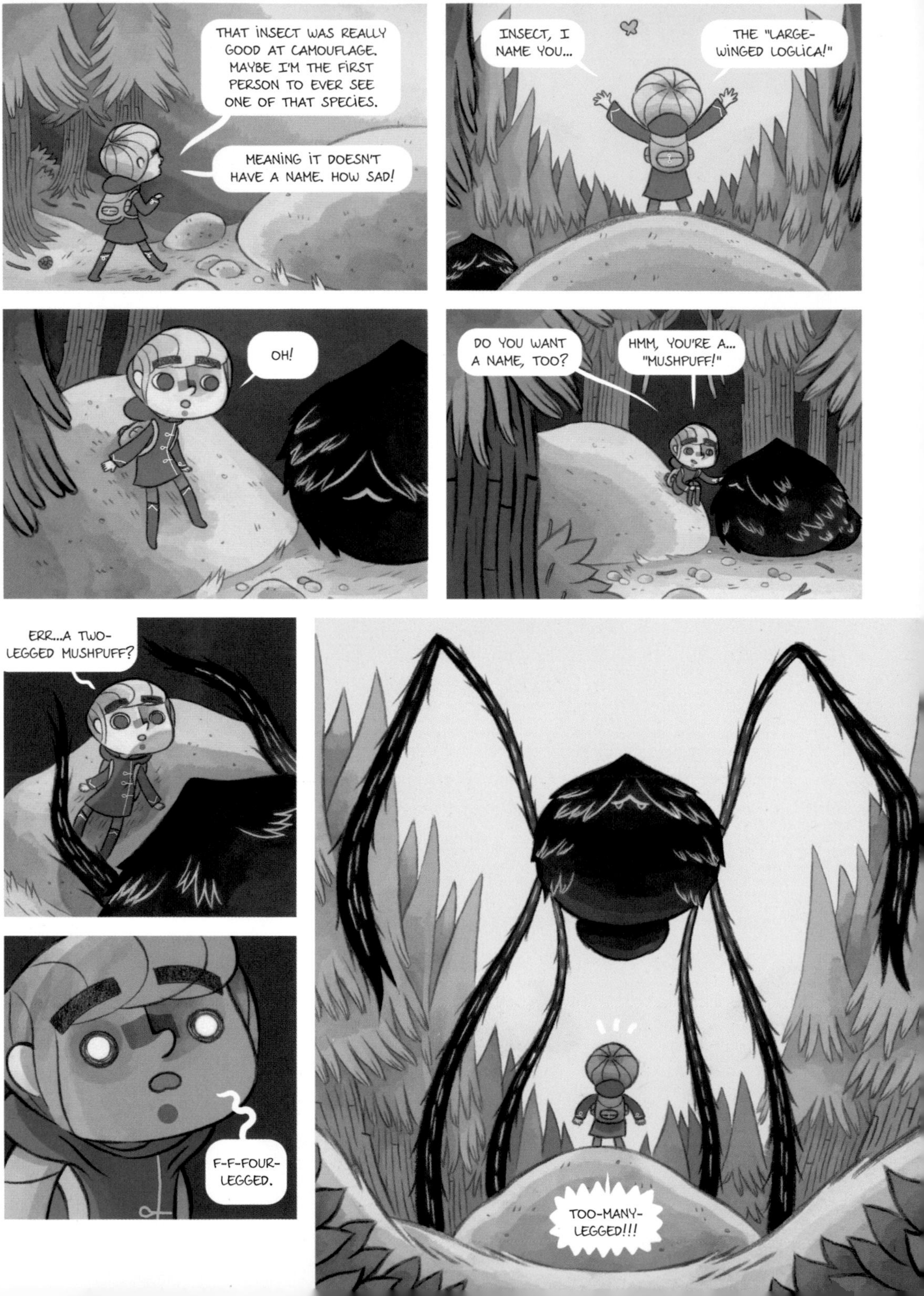
THAT INSECT WAS REALLY GOOD AT CAMOUFLAGE. MAYBE I'M THE FIRST PERSON TO EVER SEE ONE OF THAT SPECIES.
MEANING IT DOESN'T HAVE A NAME. HOW SAD!
INSECT, I NAME YOU...
THE "LARGE-WINGED LOGLICA!"
OH!
DO YOU WANT A NAME, TOO?
HMM, YOU'RE A... "MUSHPUFF!"
ERR...A TWO-LEGGED MUSHPUFF?
F-F-FOUR-LEGGED.
TOO-MANY-LEGGED!!!

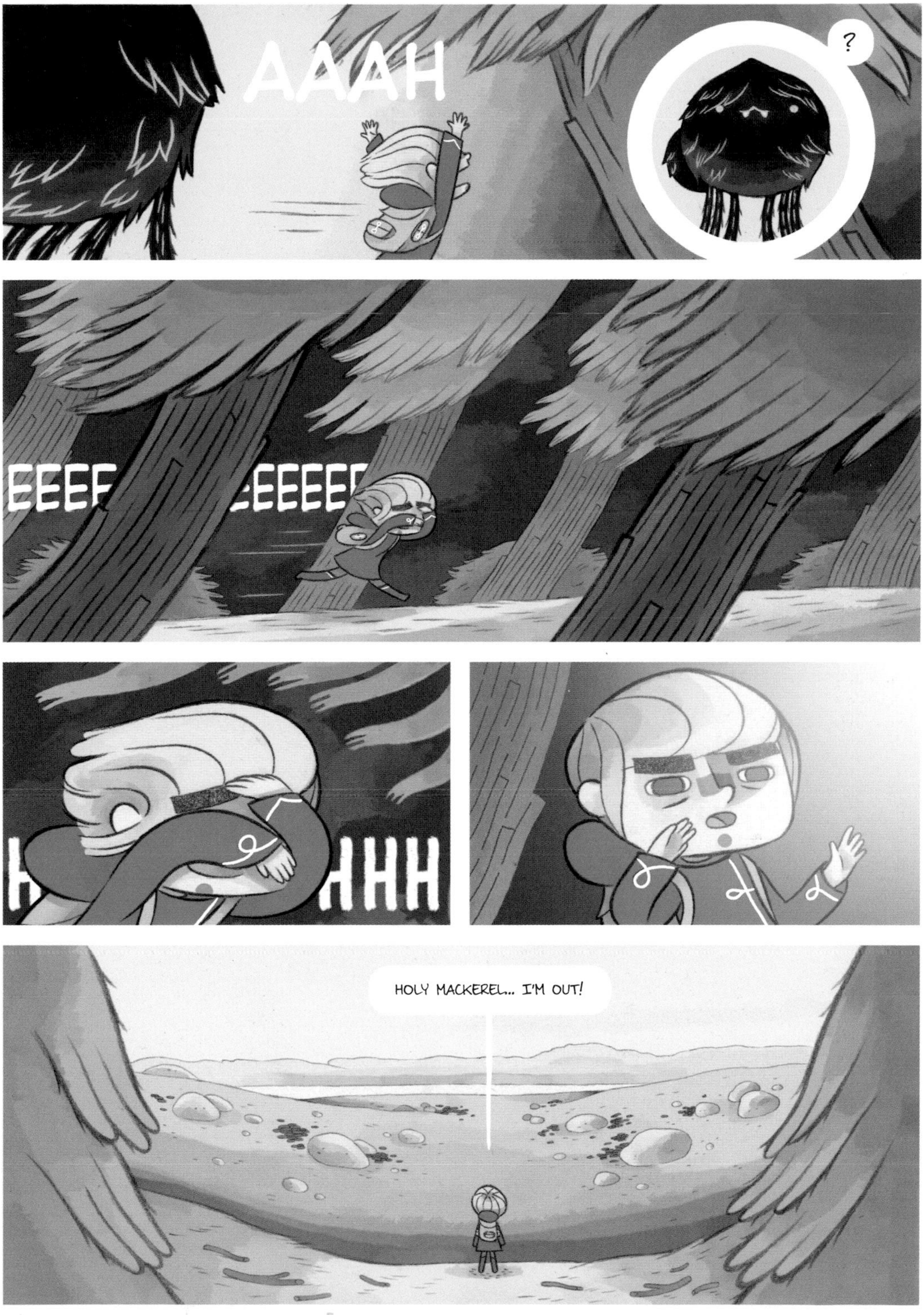
AAAH
?
EEEEEEEEEEE
HHHH
HOLY MACKEREL... I'M OUT!

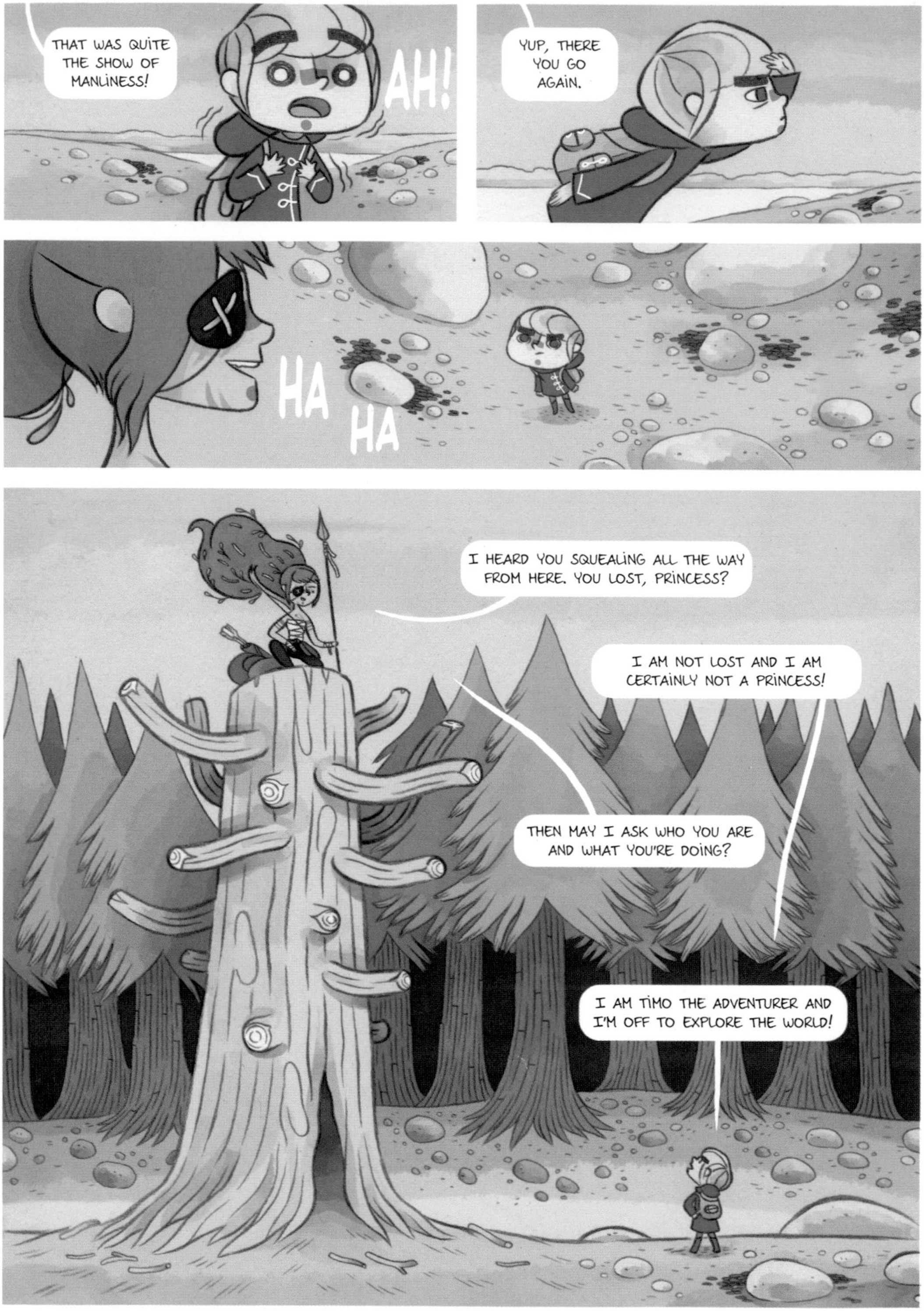
THAT WAS QUITE THE SHOW OF MANLINESS!
AH!
YUP, THERE YOU GO AGAIN.
HA
HA
I HEARD YOU SQUEALING ALL THE WAY FROM HERE. YOU LOST, PRINCESS?
I AM NOT LOST AND I AM CERTAINLY NOT A PRINCESS!
THEN MAY I ASK WHO YOU ARE AND WHAT YOU'RE DOING?
I AM TIMO THE ADVENTURER AND I'M OFF TO EXPLORE THE WORLD!

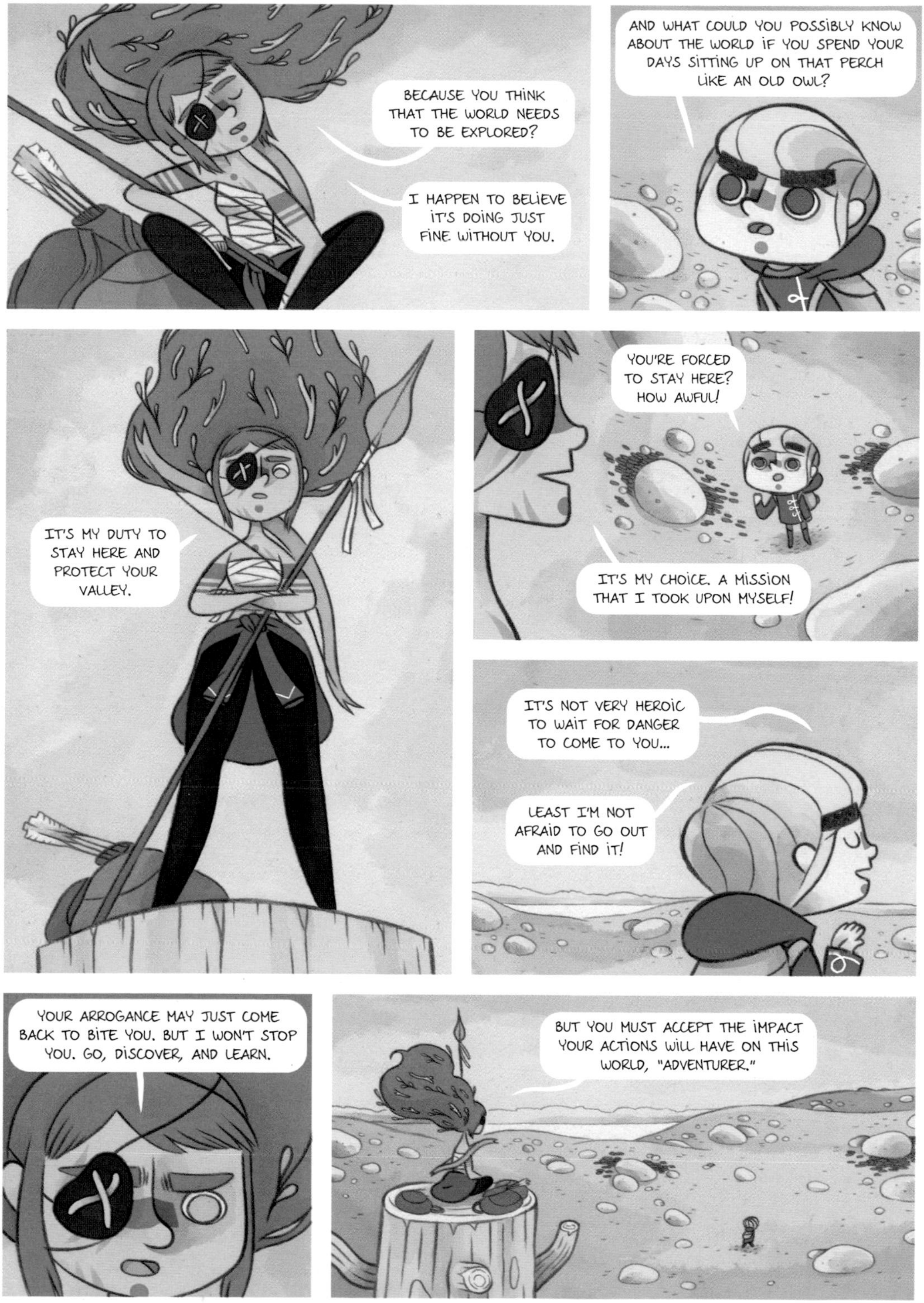
BECAUSE YOU THINK THAT THE WORLD NEEDS TO BE EXPLORED?
I HAPPEN TO BELIEVE IT'S DOING JUST FINE WITHOUT YOU.
AND WHAT COULD YOU POSSIBLY KNOW ABOUT THE WORLD IF YOU SPEND YOUR DAYS SITTING UP ON THAT PERCH LIKE AN OLD OWL?
IT'S MY DUTY TO STAY HERE AND PROTECT YOUR VALLEY.
YOU'RE FORCED TO STAY HERE? HOW AWFUL!
IT'S MY CHOICE. A MISSION THAT I TOOK UPON MYSELF!
IT'S NOT VERY HEROIC TO WAIT FOR DANGER TO COME TO YOU...
LEAST I'M NOT AFRAID TO GO OUT AND FIND IT!
YOUR ARROGANCE MAY JUST COME BACK TO BITE YOU. BUT I WON'T STOP YOU. GO, DISCOVER, AND LEARN.
BUT YOU MUST ACCEPT THE IMPACT YOUR ACTIONS WILL HAVE ON THIS WORLD, "ADVENTURER."

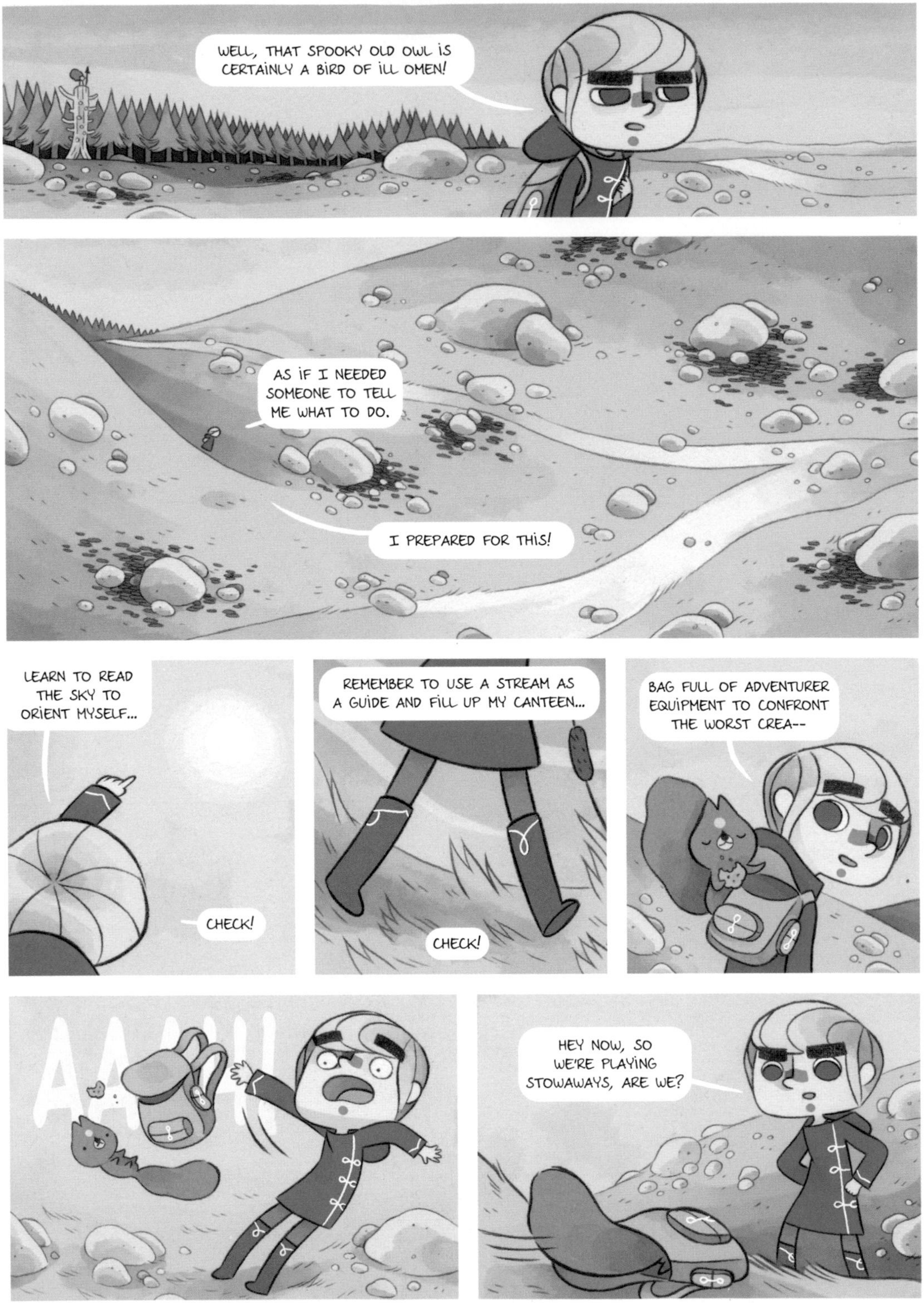
WELL, THAT SPOOKY OLD OWL IS CERTAINLY A BIRD OF ILL OMEN!
AS IF I NEEDED SOMEONE TO TELL ME WHAT TO DO.
I PREPARED FOR THIS!
LEARN TO READ THE SKY TO ORIENT MYSELF...
CHECK!
REMEMBER TO USE A STREAM AS A GUIDE AND FILL UP MY CANTEEN...
CHECK!
BAG FULL OF ADVENTURER EQUIPMENT TO CONFRONT THE WORST CREA--
AAAH!
HEY NOW, SO WE'RE PLAYING STOWAWAYS, ARE WE?

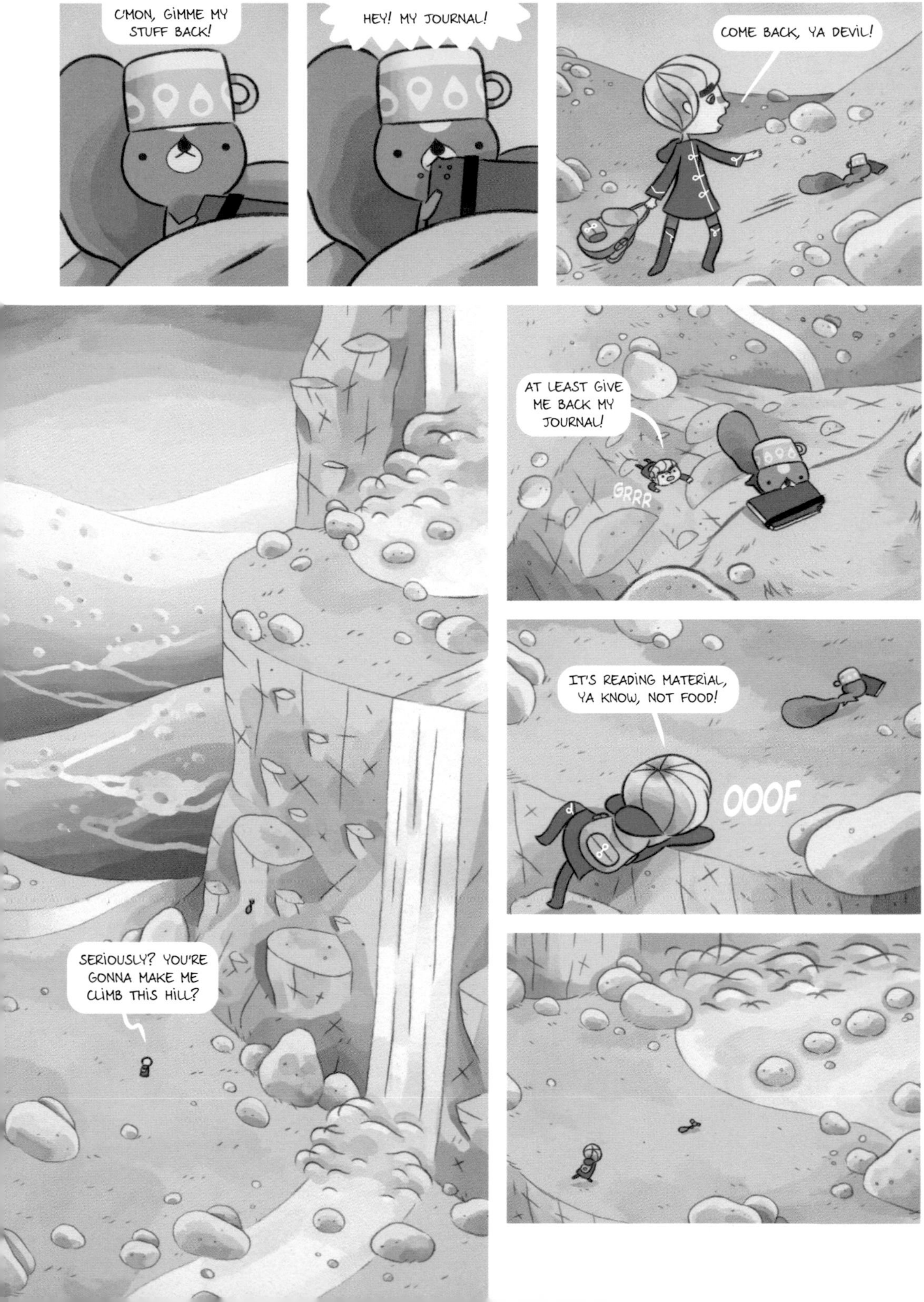
C'MON, GIMME MY STUFF BACK!
HEY! MY JOURNAL!
COME BACK, YA DEVIL!
SERIOUSLY? YOU'RE GONNA MAKE ME CLIMB THIS HILL?
AT LEAST GIVE ME BACK MY JOURNAL!
GRRR
IT'S READING MATERIAL, YA KNOW, NOT FOOD!
OOOF

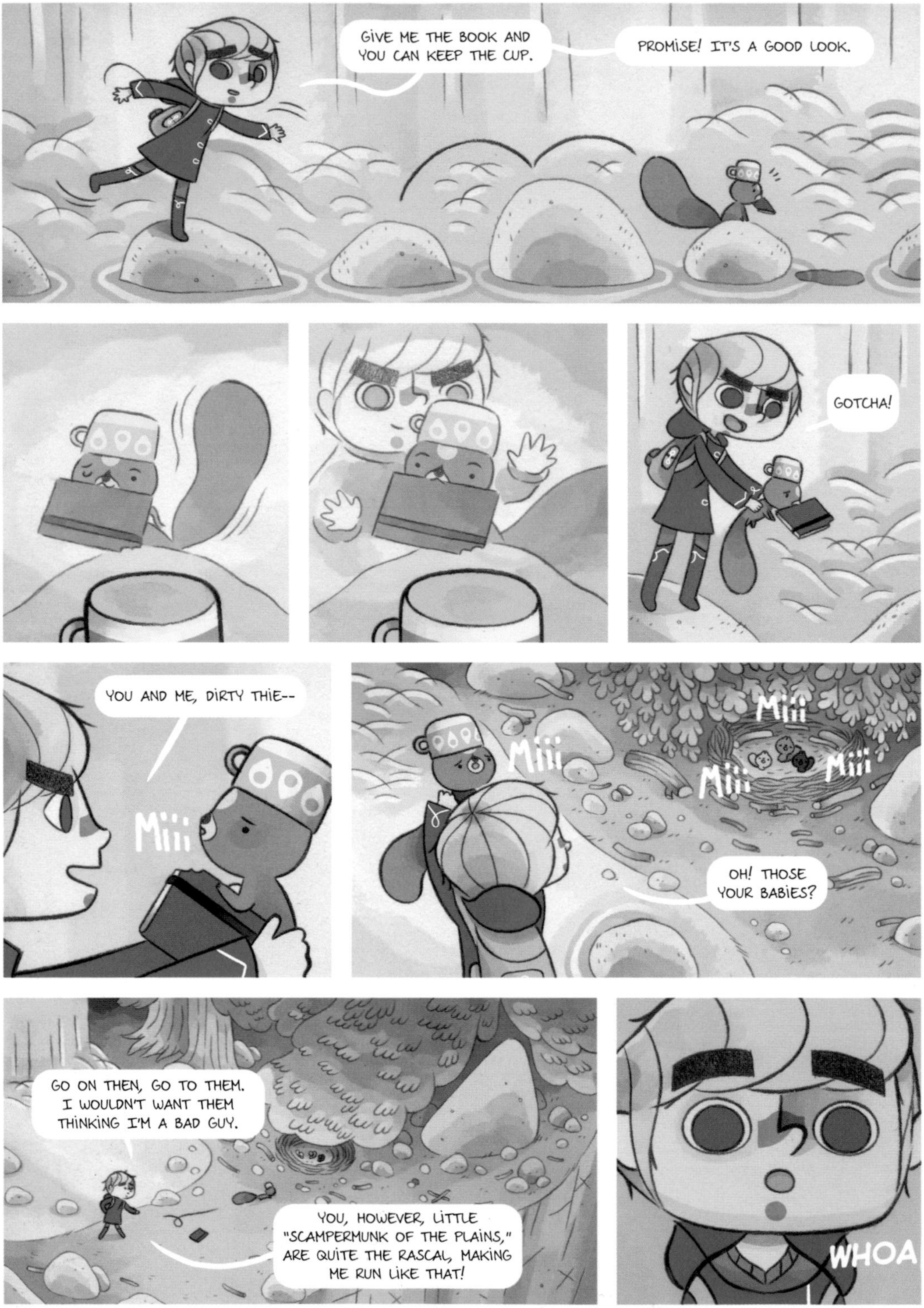
GIVE ME THE BOOK AND YOU CAN KEEP THE CUP.
PROMISE! IT'S A GOOD LOOK.
GOTCHA!
YOU AND ME, DIRTY THIE--
Miii
Miii
Miii
Miii
Miii
OH! THOSE YOUR BABIES?
GO ON THEN, GO TO THEM. I WOULDN'T WANT THEM THINKING I'M A BAD GUY.
YOU, HOWEVER, LITTLE "SCAMPERMUNK OF THE PLAINS," ARE QUITE THE RASCAL, MAKING ME RUN LIKE THAT!
WHOA

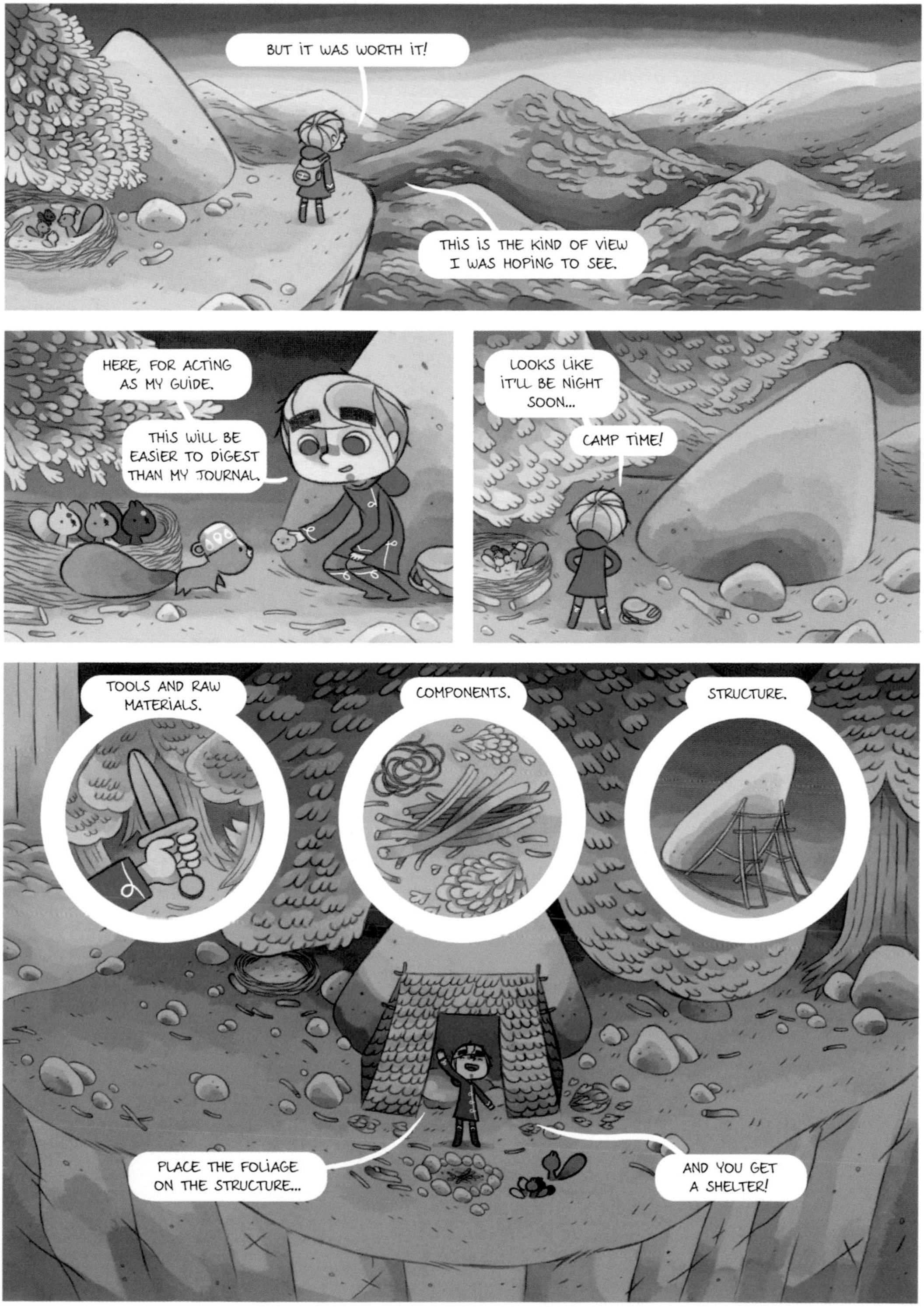
BUT IT WAS WORTH IT!
THIS IS THE KIND OF VIEW I WAS HOPING TO SEE.
HERE, FOR ACTING AS MY GUIDE.
THIS WILL BE EASIER TO DIGEST THAN MY JOURNAL.
LOOKS LIKE IT'LL BE NIGHT SOON...
CAMP TIME!
TOOLS AND RAW MATERIALS.
COMPONENTS.
STRUCTURE.
PLACE THE FOLIAGE ON THE STRUCTURE...
AND YOU GET A SHELTER!

THE ADVENTURER'S JOURNAL

ONCE UPON A TiME THERE WAS A LiTTLE BOY WHO COULDN'T RESiST THE CALL OF ADVENTURE AND LEFT HiS HOME TO DiSCOVER WHAT WAS ON THE OTHER SiDE OF THE LARGE, MYSTERiOUS FOREST SURROUNDiNG HiS ViLLAGE...

Hee hee, I hope that one day they'll write a book about my adventures and that's how it'll start!

In the meantime, I've decided to record everything in this journal, along with my advice and a bestiary, to show you the fantastical creatures I encounter on my journey. Perhaps you'll have the good—or bad—luck to come across them as well, and then you'll know what to do!

The first piece of advice that I'll give you is that you have to be curious. All the things I know didn't come to me just like that, out of nowhere! I learned from listening to people carefully and taking the time to read books! So what do you need to know before you go on an adventure, you ask? (Good, you're curious—that's the spirit!)

Well, it's important to learn several things:
- How to pack your bag (food and water, rope and torch, compass and pocketknife, etc.)
- Where to build your camp (near a water source, in a spot protected from wind)
- How to build a solid shack
- How to identify plants, so you know which ones can nourish or heal you, and which ones are dangerous
- How to cook (yup, you can't settle for sitting back and stuffing your face anymore!)
- How to read the sky to predict the weather and orient yourself using the sun during the day and the stars at night

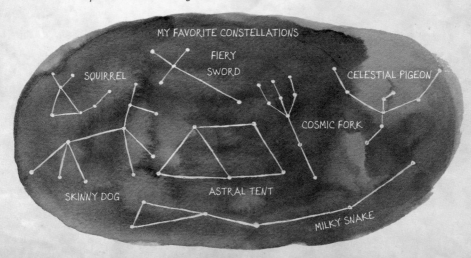

MY FAVORITE CONSTELLATIONS

FIERY SWORD

SQUIRREL

CELESTIAL PIGEON

COSMIC FORK

SKINNY DOG

ASTRAL TENT

MILKY SNAKE

Don't worry—I'll expand on all this later!
But first I wanted to tell you about what makes journeys so fascinating:

meeting new friends.

I say that but...the first person I met

wasn't cool in the least.

PiRATE-WARRiOR

A kind of pirate-warrior perched up in a tree.
Personally, I'm not crazy about pirates. Oftentimes, they're the worst kind of brigands...

I prefer knights. At least the things they do are heroic!

But I have to admit that this warrior was impressive with
her eye patch, flowing red hair, and tough-guy attitude.

And then again, she's not really a pirate. She's a kind of sentry who protects the
valley, though I haven't seen anything very dangerous yet. In fact, she must spend her
days taking naps, but she still thinks she can look down on me...

That's not very nice of you, madame "warrior"!

LARGE-WiNGED LOGLiCA

The first creature that I encountered! A funny little insect whose
back looks just like a tree trunk. A clever way to hide from predators!

So it just looks like a bump on a log when it's not moving. But as soon
as it unfurls its wings, it can fly away while making a funny little noise.

Oh, okay, fine, I could have given a more detailed description...
But I'm a beginner in the study of fauna and flora!

MUSHPUFF

An odd creature that's an unexpected cross between a big mushroom and a spider. I valiantly
managed to escape its monstrous legs thanks to my quick reflexes, but if you're not too fast on
your feet and one day you spot a large puffy mound, don't stop to think... RUN!!!

If that ain't proof that the scampermunk is a real glutton!! →

SCAMPERMUNK

The scampermunk is an impish creature, a bit of a thief but more mischievous than mean.
It can scamper along for miles without tiring, especially when it has babies to feed. It likes
cookies and paper (that's for sure) but I have to admit that I don't know the rest of its diet.
    I would have loved to spend more time studying it, but adventure calls, and starting tomorrow,
the journey continues!

I hope to come across other equally friendly creatures!

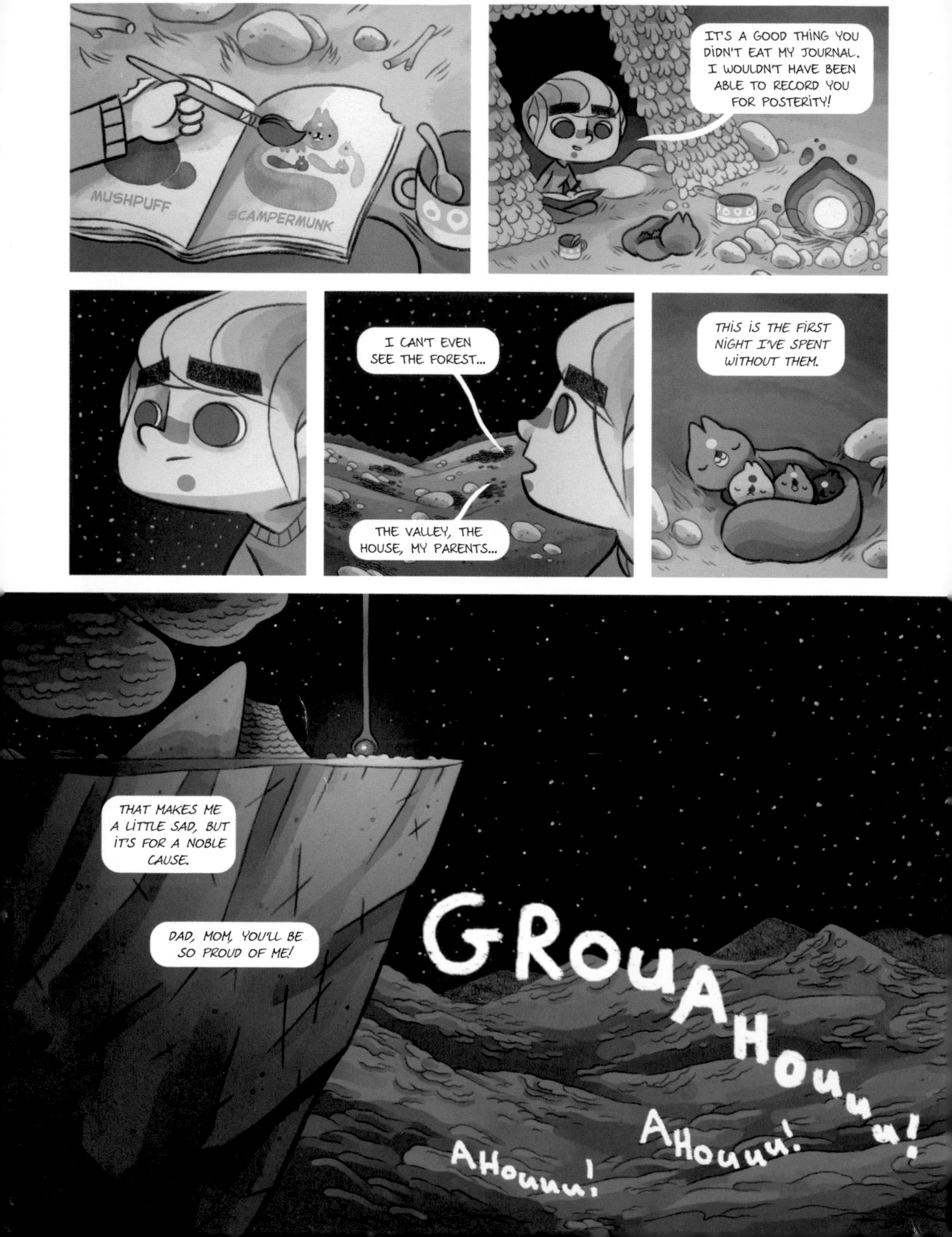
MUSHPUFF
SCAMPERMUNK
IT'S A GOOD THING YOU DIDN'T EAT MY JOURNAL. I WOULDN'T HAVE BEEN ABLE TO RECORD YOU FOR POSTERITY!
I CAN'T EVEN SEE THE FOREST...
THE VALLEY, THE HOUSE, MY PARENTS...
THIS IS THE FIRST NIGHT I'VE SPENT WITHOUT THEM.
THAT MAKES ME A LITTLE SAD, BUT IT'S FOR A NOBLE CAUSE.
DAD, MOM, YOU'LL BE SO PROUD OF ME!
GROUAHOUUUU!
AHOUUU!
AHOUUU!

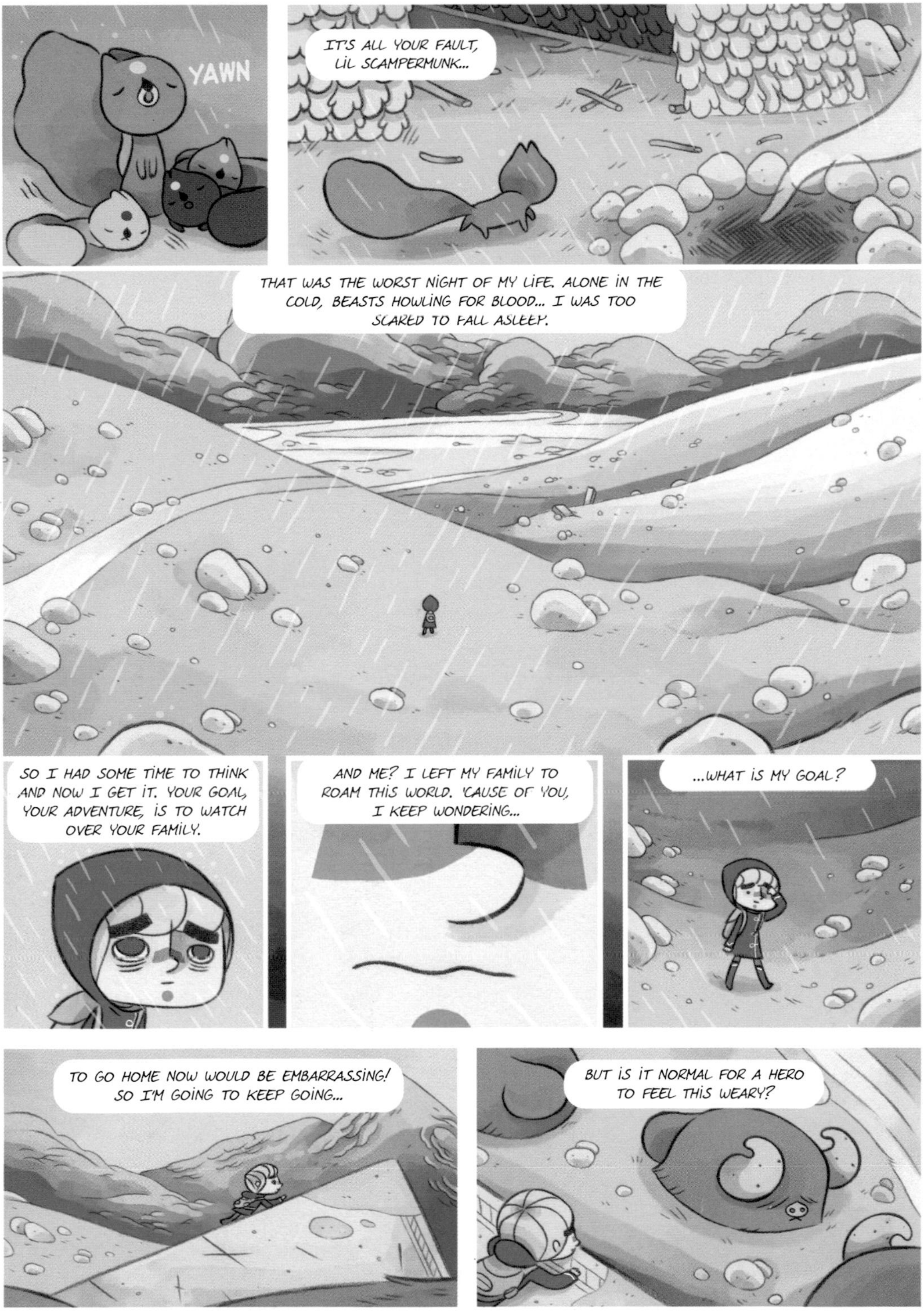
YAWN
IT'S ALL YOUR FAULT, LIL SCAMPERMUNK...
THAT WAS THE WORST NIGHT OF MY LIFE. ALONE IN THE COLD, BEASTS HOWLING FOR BLOOD... I WAS TOO SCARED TO FALL ASLEEP.
SO I HAD SOME TIME TO THINK AND NOW I GET IT. YOUR GOAL, YOUR ADVENTURE, IS TO WATCH OVER YOUR FAMILY.
AND ME? I LEFT MY FAMILY TO ROAM THIS WORLD. 'CAUSE OF YOU, I KEEP WONDERING...
...WHAT IS MY GOAL?
TO GO HOME NOW WOULD BE EMBARRASSING! SO I'M GOING TO KEEP GOING...
BUT IS IT NORMAL FOR A HERO TO FEEL THIS WEARY?

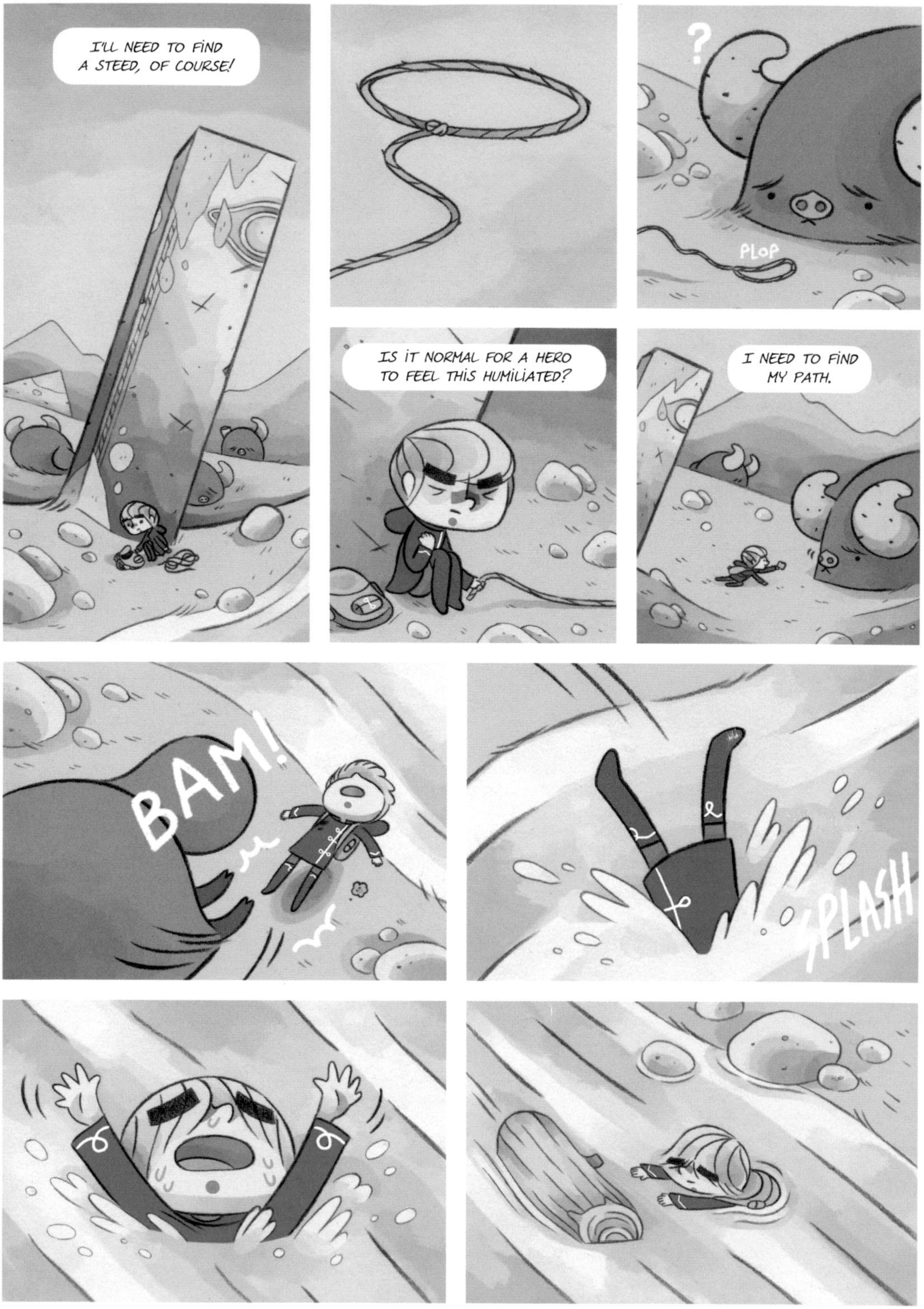
I'LL NEED TO FIND A STEED, OF COURSE!
?
PLOP
IS IT NORMAL FOR A HERO TO FEEL THIS HUMILIATED?
I NEED TO FIND MY PATH.
BAM!
SPLASH

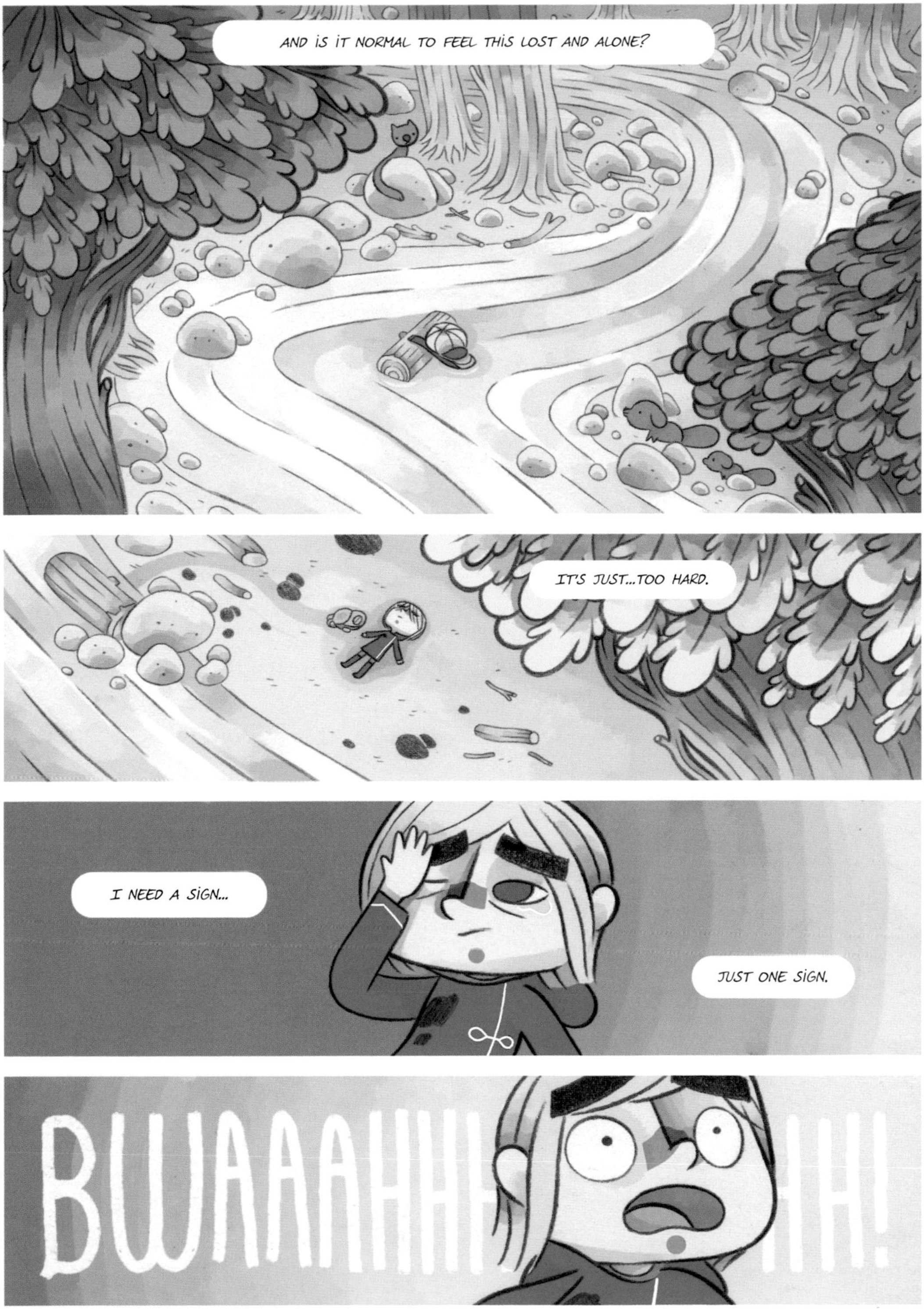
AND IS IT NORMAL TO FEEL THIS LOST AND ALONE?
IT'S JUST...TOO HARD.
I NEED A SIGN...
JUST ONE SIGN.
BWAAAHHH
HH!

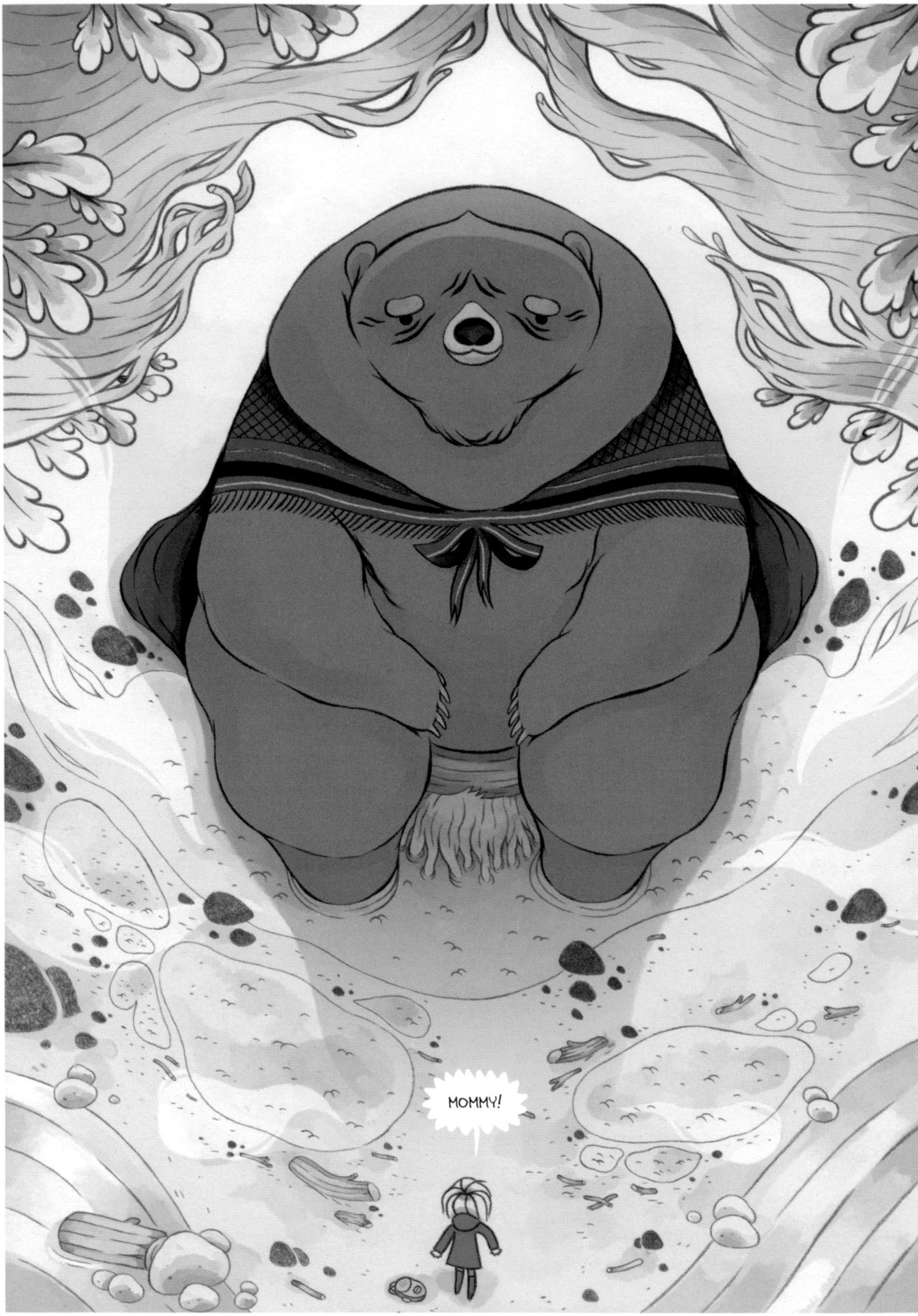
MOMMY!

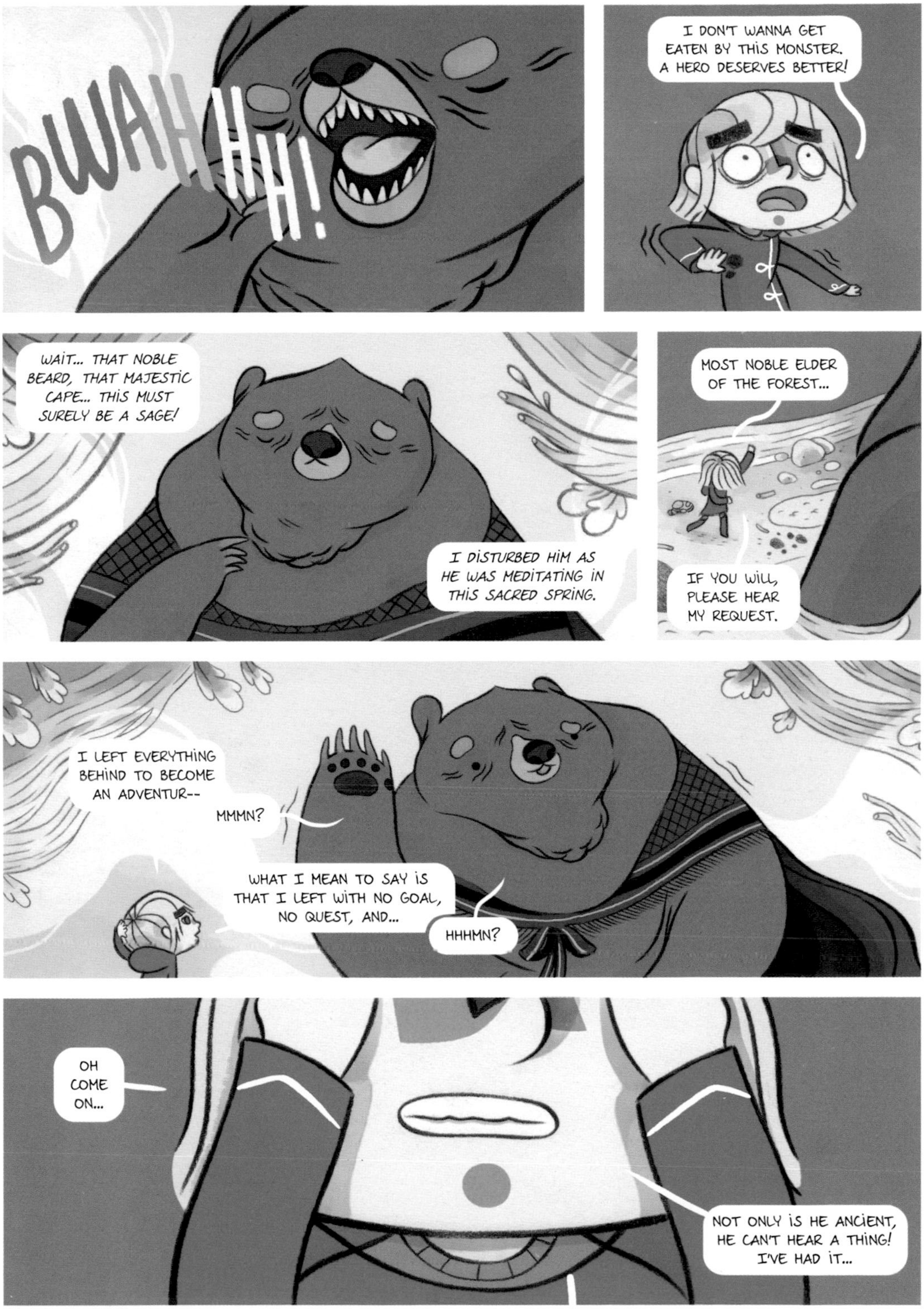
BWAHHHH!
I DON'T WANNA GET EATEN BY THIS MONSTER. A HERO DESERVES BETTER!
WAIT... THAT NOBLE BEARD, THAT MAJESTIC CAPE... THIS MUST SURELY BE A SAGE!
I DISTURBED HIM AS HE WAS MEDITATING IN THIS SACRED SPRING.
MOST NOBLE ELDER OF THE FOREST...
IF YOU WILL, PLEASE HEAR MY REQUEST.
I LEFT EVERYTHING BEHIND TO BECOME AN ADVENTUR--
MMMN?
WHAT I MEAN TO SAY IS THAT I LEFT WITH NO GOAL, NO QUEST, AND...
HHHMN?
OH COME ON...
NOT ONLY IS HE ANCIENT, HE CAN'T HEAR A THING! I'VE HAD IT...

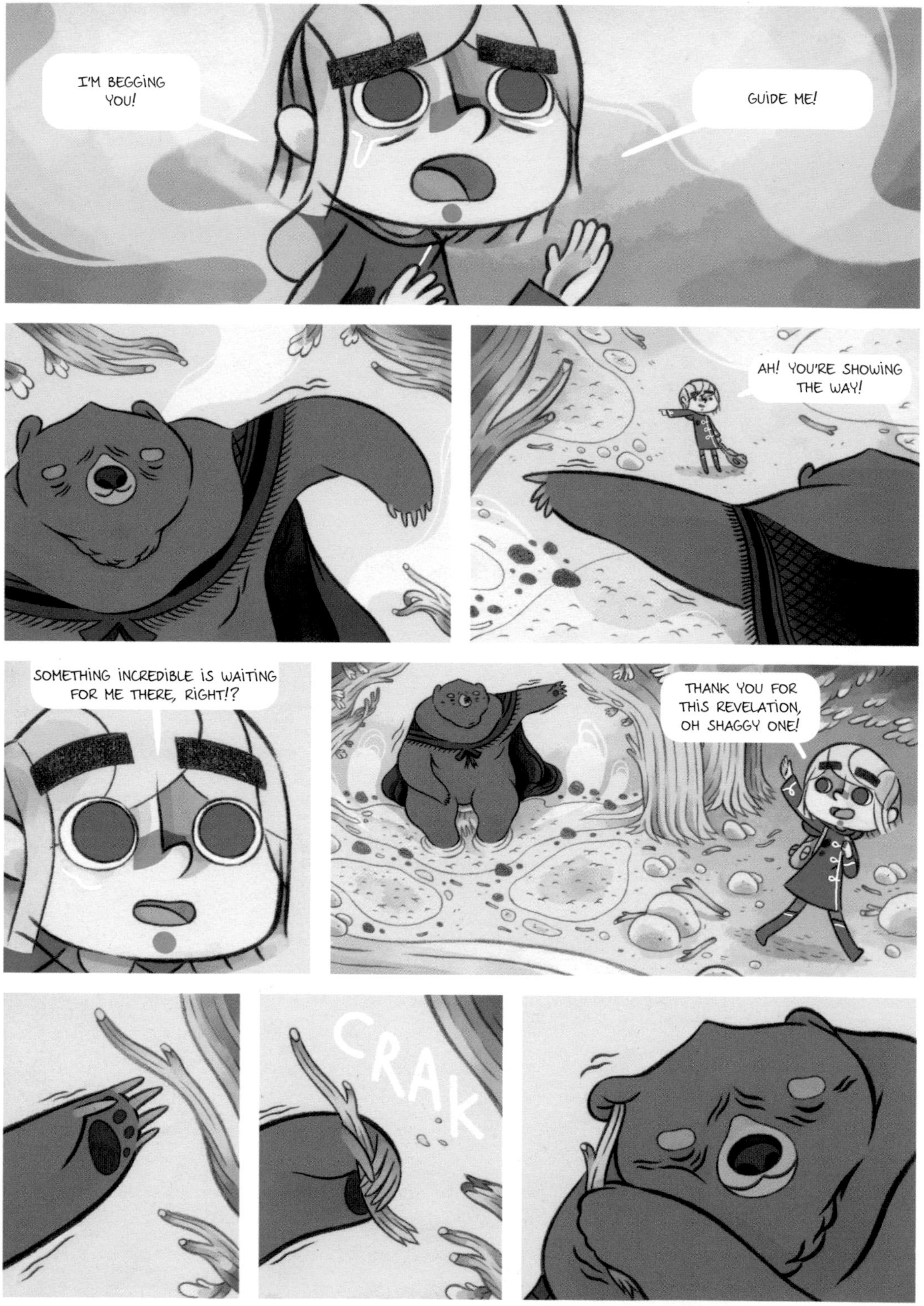

I'M BEGGING YOU!
GUIDE ME!
AH! YOU'RE SHOWING THE WAY!
SOMETHING INCREDIBLE IS WAITING FOR ME THERE, RIGHT!?
THANK YOU FOR THIS REVELATION, OH SHAGGY ONE!
CRAK

POP

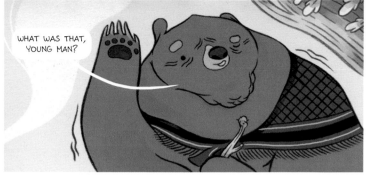

WHAT WAS THAT, YOUNG MAN?

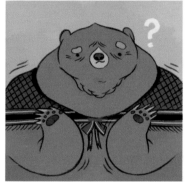

?

GRAMPS!

WAIT, YOU'RE STILL SOAKING YOUR FEET?

LET'S GO. GRANDMA'S WAITING ON YOU TO CLEAN THE DEN!

PAF

BWOOFFF...

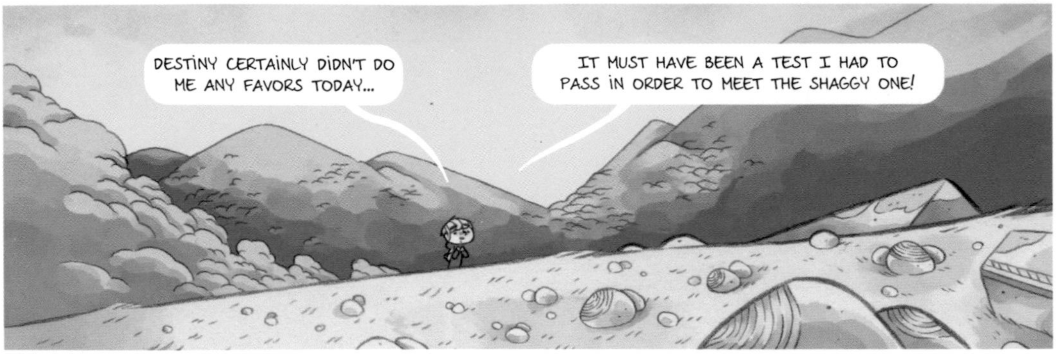
DESTINY CERTAINLY DIDN'T DO ME ANY FAVORS TODAY...
IT MUST HAVE BEEN A TEST I HAD TO PASS IN ORDER TO MEET THE SHAGGY ONE!

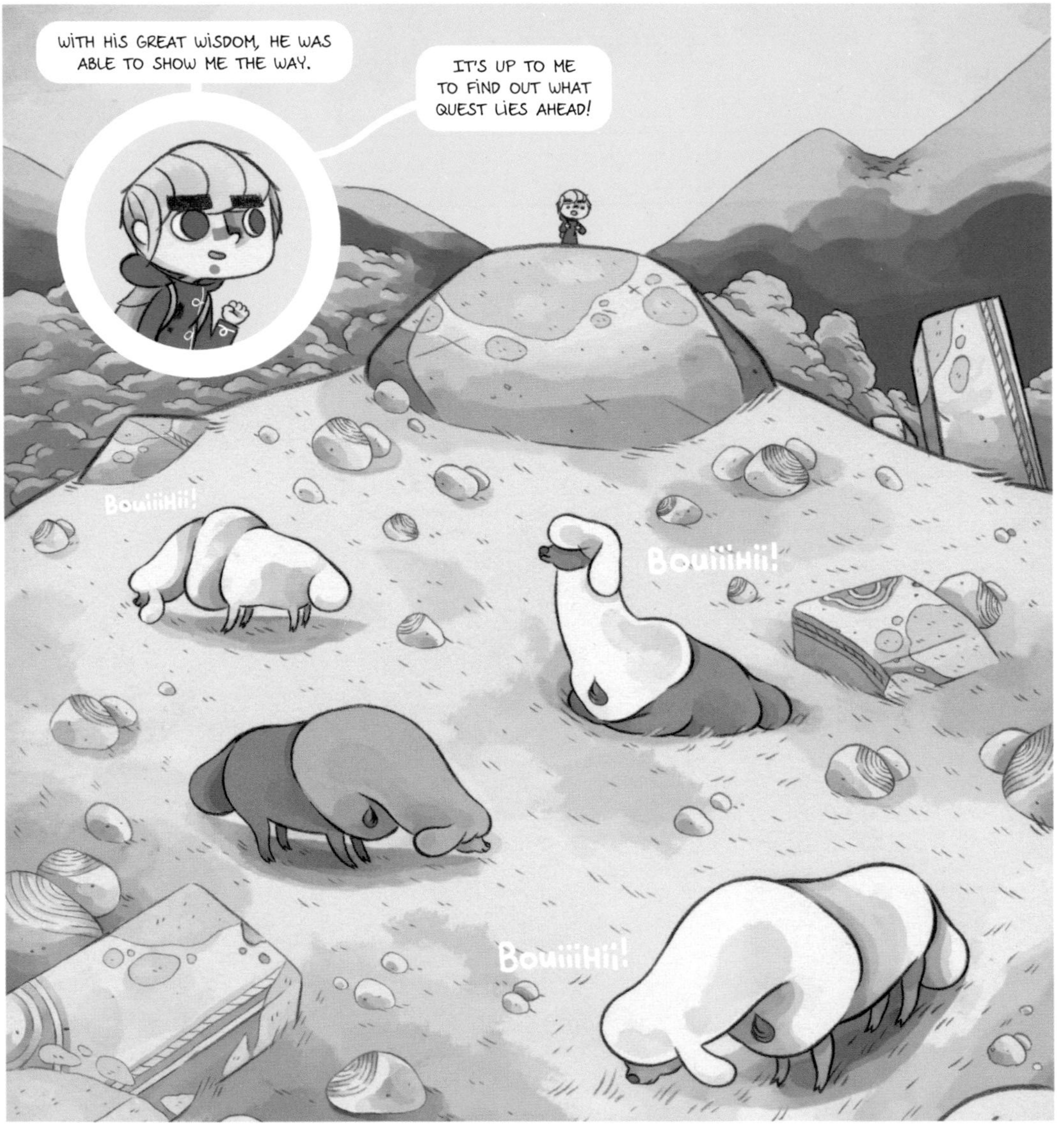
WITH HIS GREAT WISDOM, HE WAS ABLE TO SHOW ME THE WAY.
IT'S UP TO ME TO FIND OUT WHAT QUEST LIES AHEAD!
BouiiiHii!
BouiiiHii!
BouiiiHii!

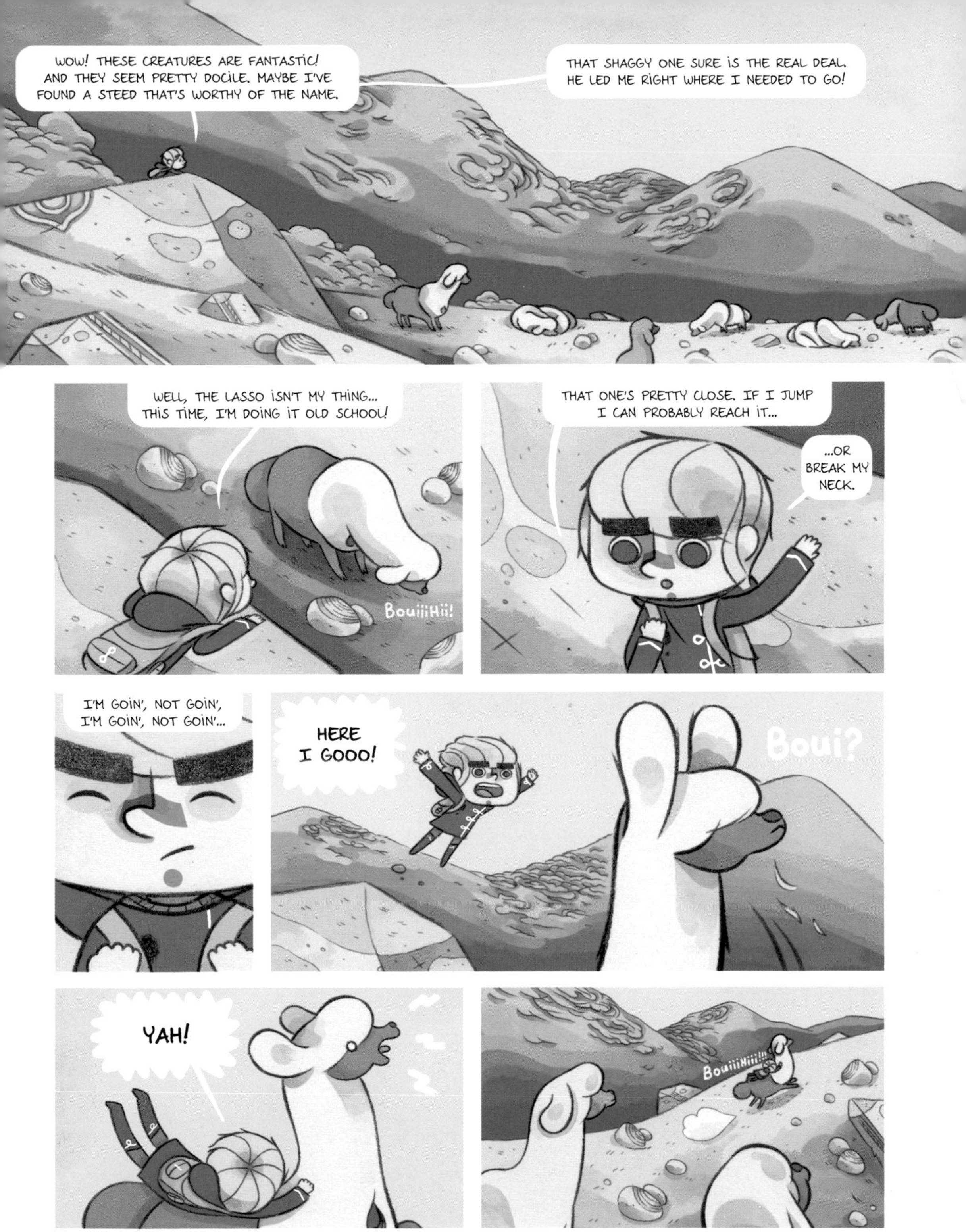
WOW! THESE CREATURES ARE FANTASTIC! AND THEY SEEM PRETTY DOCILE. MAYBE I'VE FOUND A STEED THAT'S WORTHY OF THE NAME.
THAT SHAGGY ONE SURE IS THE REAL DEAL. HE LED ME RIGHT WHERE I NEEDED TO GO!
WELL, THE LASSO ISN'T MY THING... THIS TIME, I'M DOING IT OLD SCHOOL!
BouiiiHii!
THAT ONE'S PRETTY CLOSE. IF I JUMP I CAN PROBABLY REACH IT...
...OR BREAK MY NECK.
I'M GOIN', NOT GOIN', I'M GOIN', NOT GOIN'...
HERE I GOOO!
Boui?
YAH!
BouiiiHiii!!!

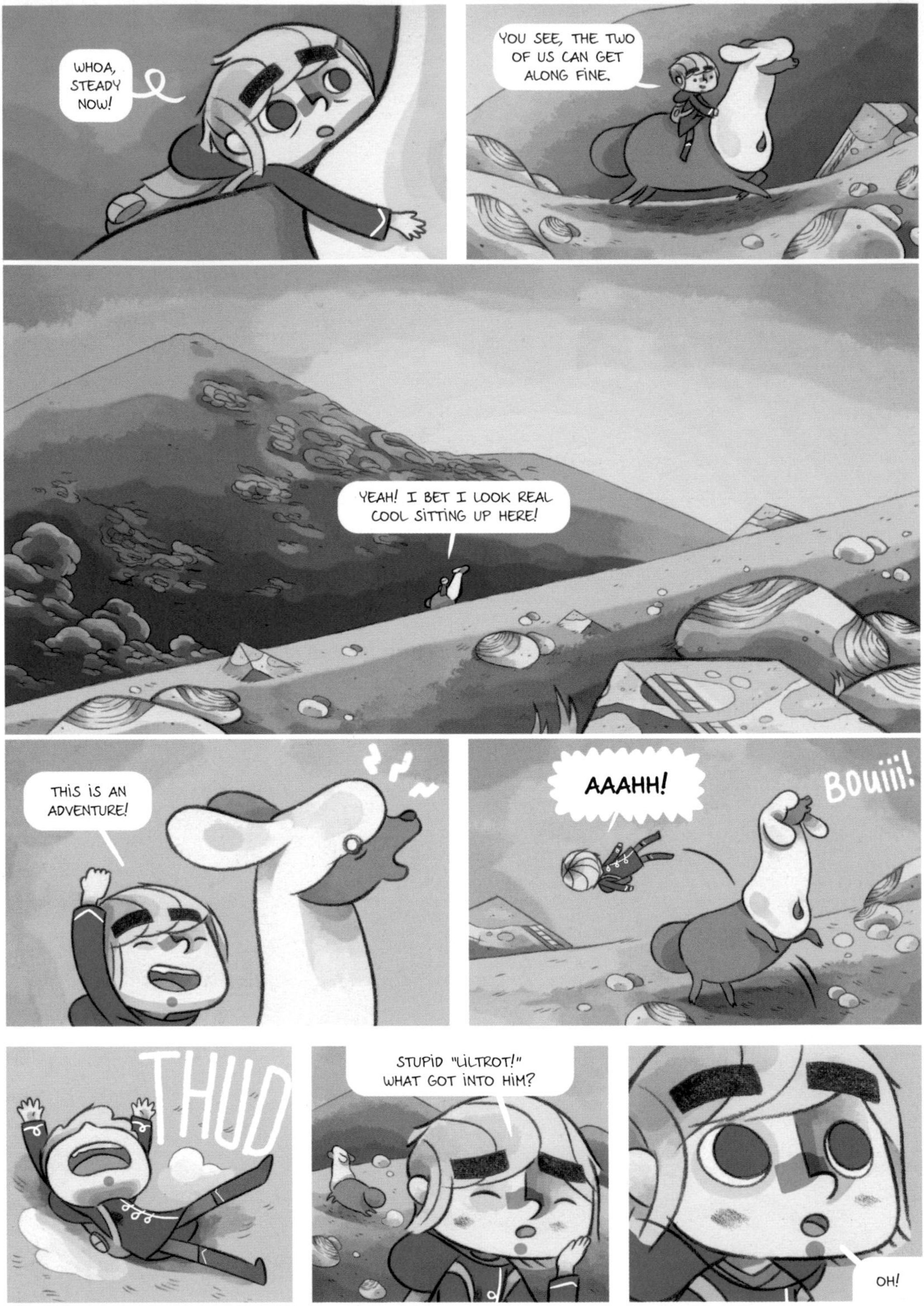
WHOA, STEADY NOW!
YOU SEE, THE TWO OF US CAN GET ALONG FINE.
YEAH! I BET I LOOK REAL COOL SITTING UP HERE!
THIS IS AN ADVENTURE!
AAAHH!
BOUIII!
THUD
STUPID "LILTROT!" WHAT GOT INTO HIM?
OH!

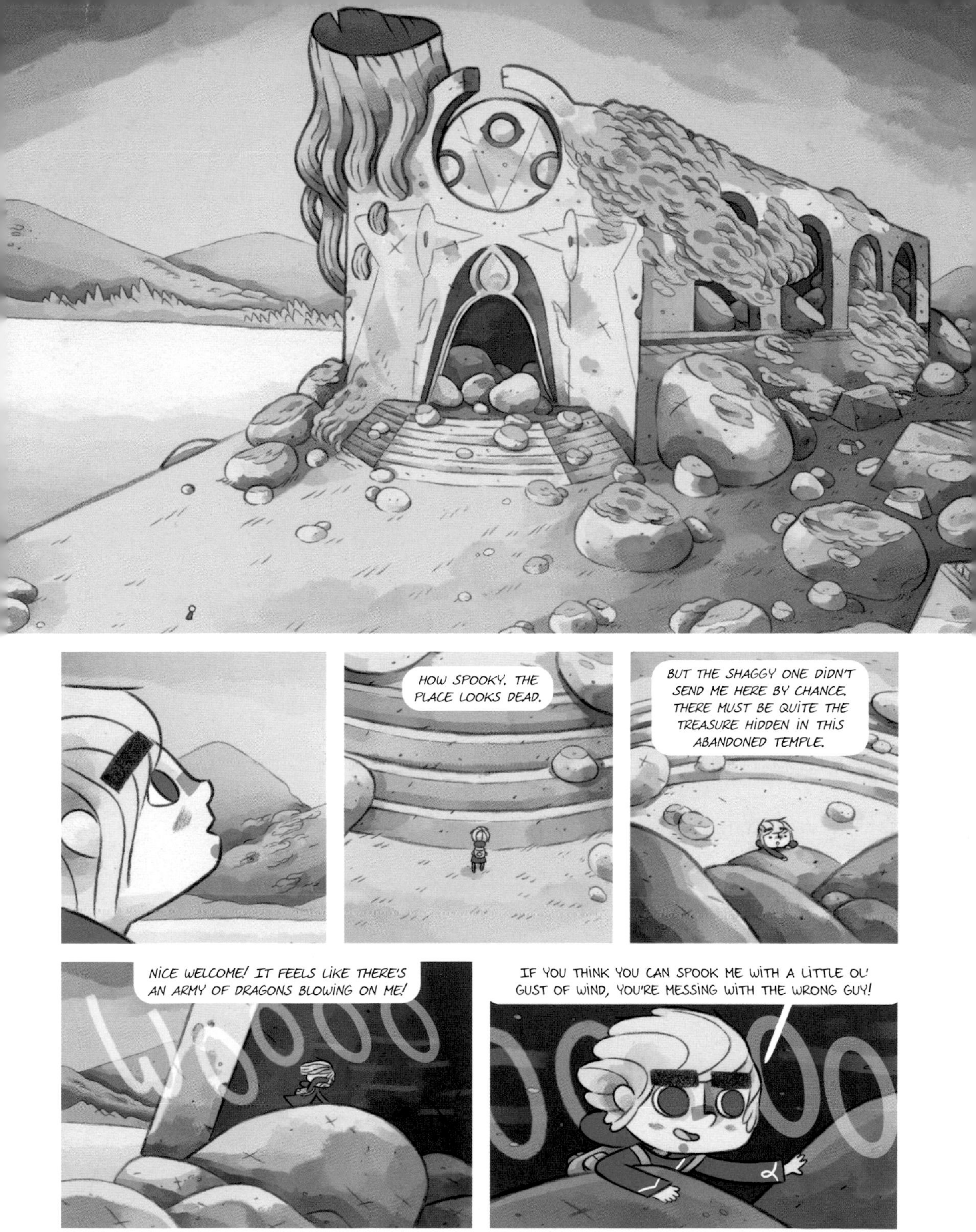
HOW SPOOKY. THE PLACE LOOKS DEAD.
BUT THE SHAGGY ONE DIDN'T SEND ME HERE BY CHANCE. THERE MUST BE QUITE THE TREASURE HIDDEN IN THIS ABANDONED TEMPLE.
NICE WELCOME! IT FEELS LIKE THERE'S AN ARMY OF DRAGONS BLOWING ON ME!
IF YOU THINK YOU CAN SPOOK ME WITH A LITTLE OL' GUST OF WIND, YOU'RE MESSING WITH THE WRONG GUY!

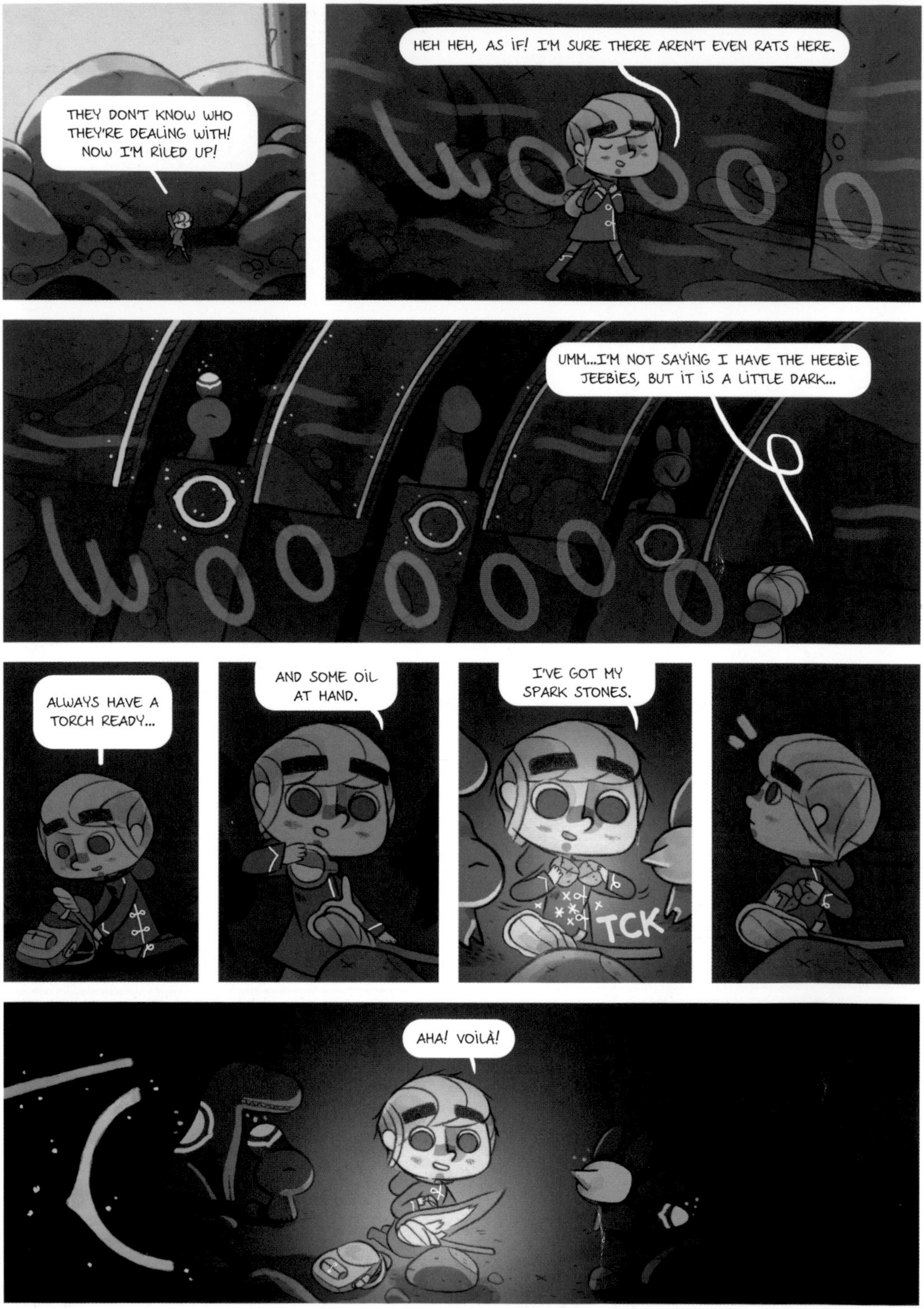
THEY DON'T KNOW WHO THEY'RE DEALING WITH! NOW I'M RILED UP!
HEH HEH, AS IF! I'M SURE THERE AREN'T EVEN RATS HERE.
WOOOOOO
UMM...I'M NOT SAYING I HAVE THE HEEBIE JEEBIES, BUT IT IS A LITTLE DARK...
WOOOOOOOO
ALWAYS HAVE A TORCH READY...
AND SOME OIL AT HAND.
I'VE GOT MY SPARK STONES.
TCK
AHA! VOILÀ!

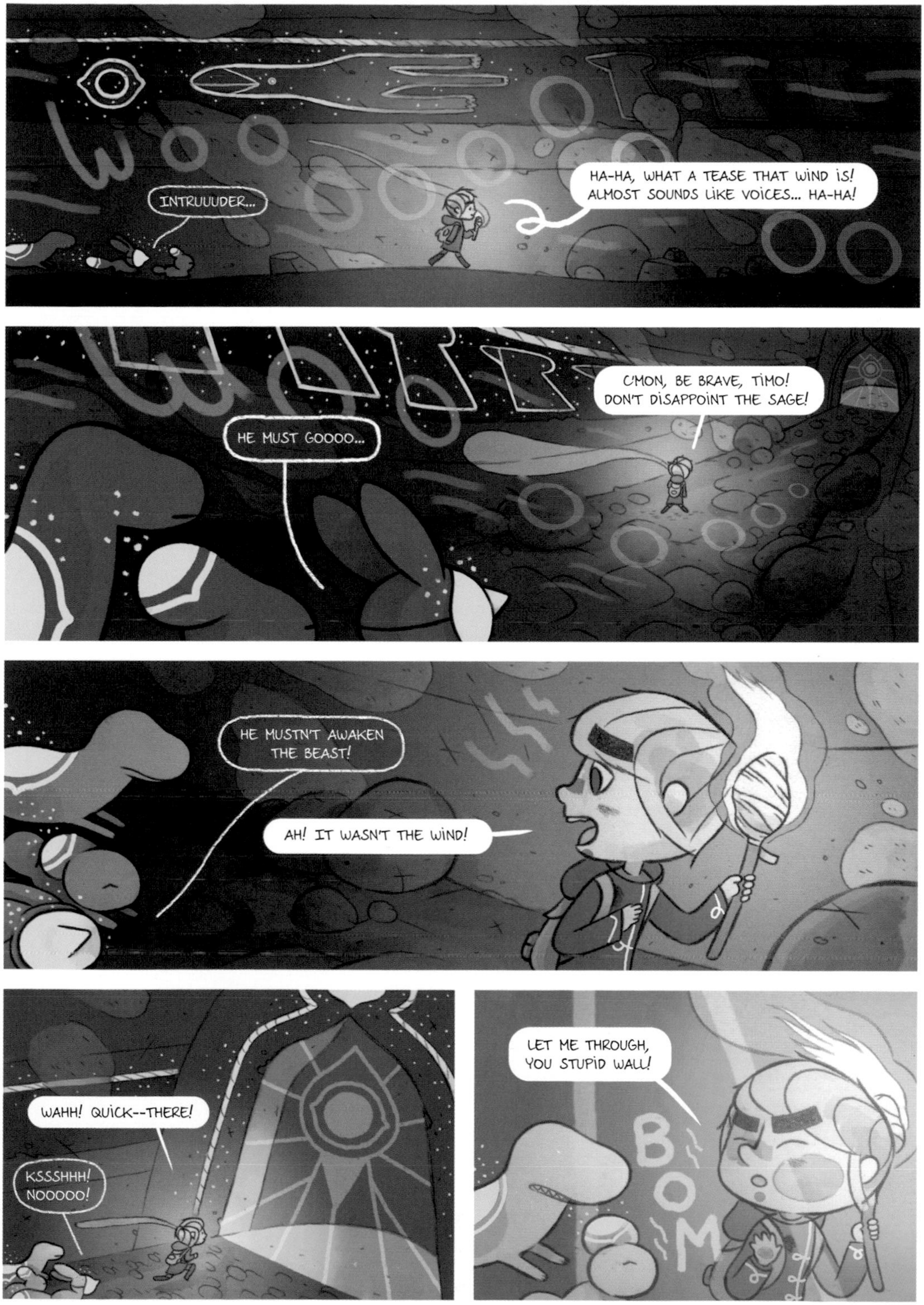
INTRUUUDER...
HA-HA, WHAT A TEASE THAT WIND IS! ALMOST SOUNDS LIKE VOICES... HA-HA!
HE MUST GOOOO...
C'MON, BE BRAVE, TIMO! DON'T DISAPPOINT THE SAGE!
HE MUSTN'T AWAKEN THE BEAST!
AH! IT WASN'T THE WIND!
WAHH! QUICK--THERE!
KSSSHHH! NOOOOO!
LET ME THROUGH, YOU STUPID WALL!
BOM

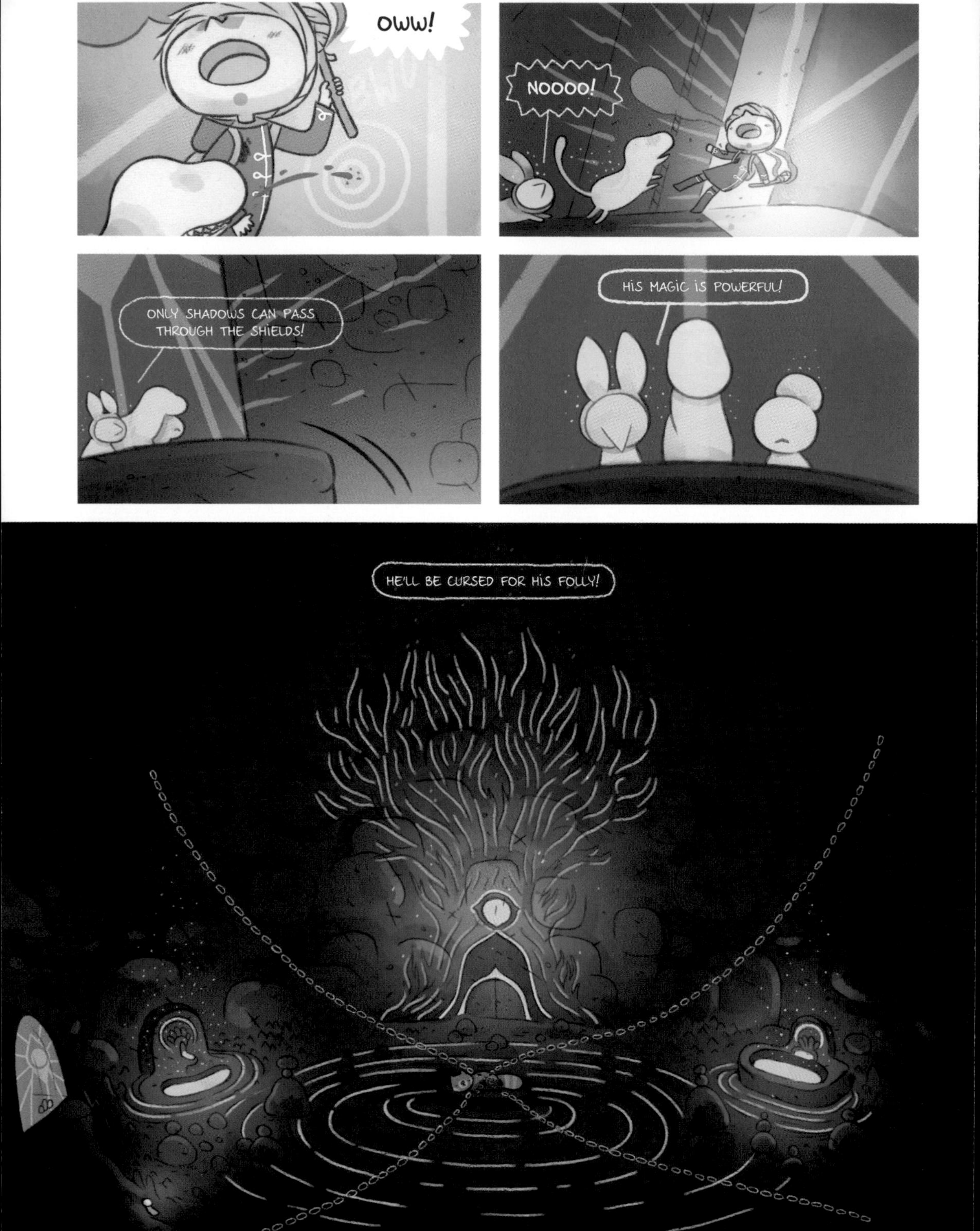
OWW!
NOOOO!
ONLY SHADOWS CAN PASS THROUGH THE SHIELDS!
HIS MAGIC IS POWERFUL!
HE'LL BE CURSED FOR HIS FOLLY!

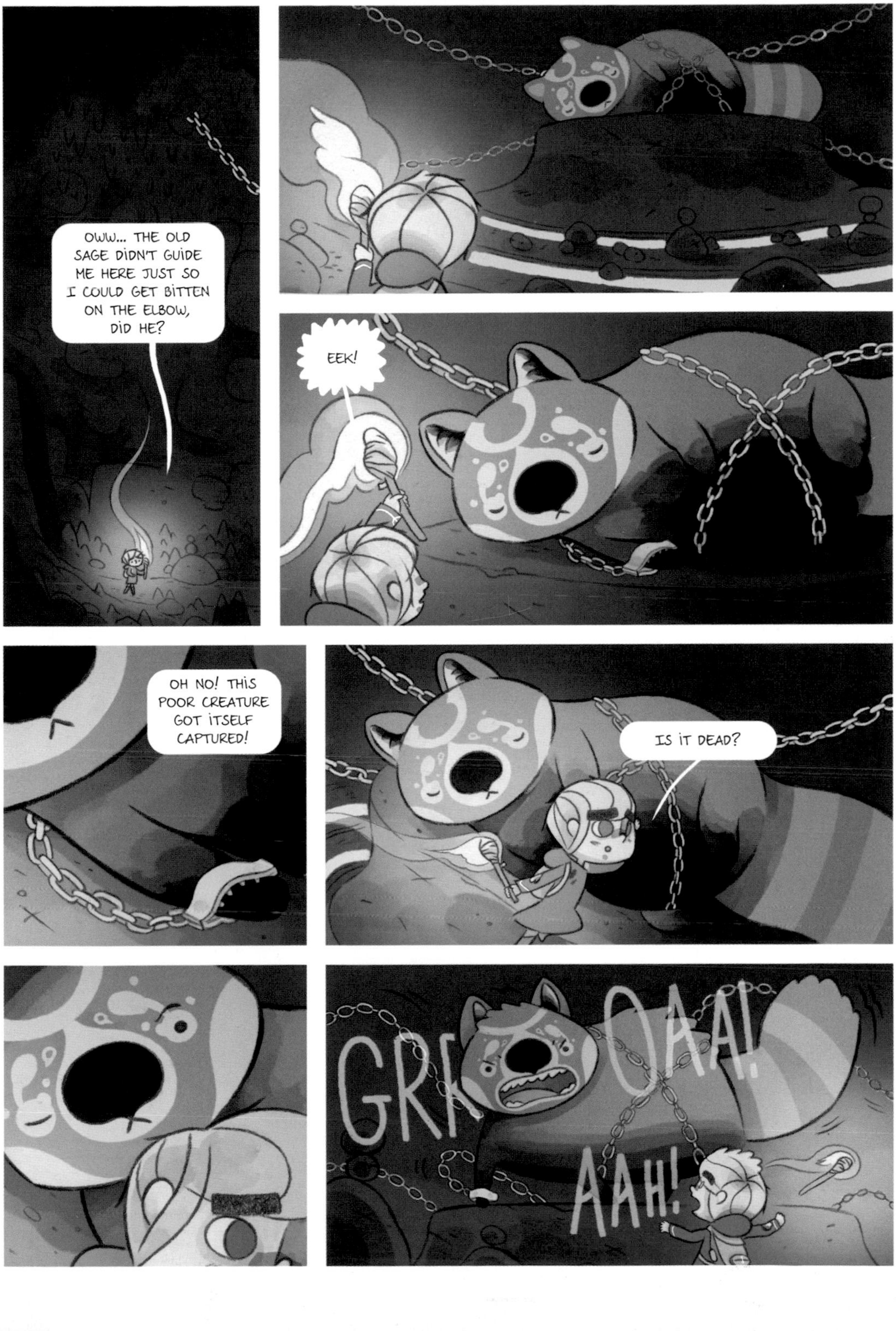
OWW... THE OLD SAGE DIDN'T GUIDE ME HERE JUST SO I COULD GET BITTEN ON THE ELBOW, DID HE?
EEK!
OH NO! THIS POOR CREATURE GOT ITSELF CAPTURED!
IS IT DEAD?
GR OAA!
AAH!

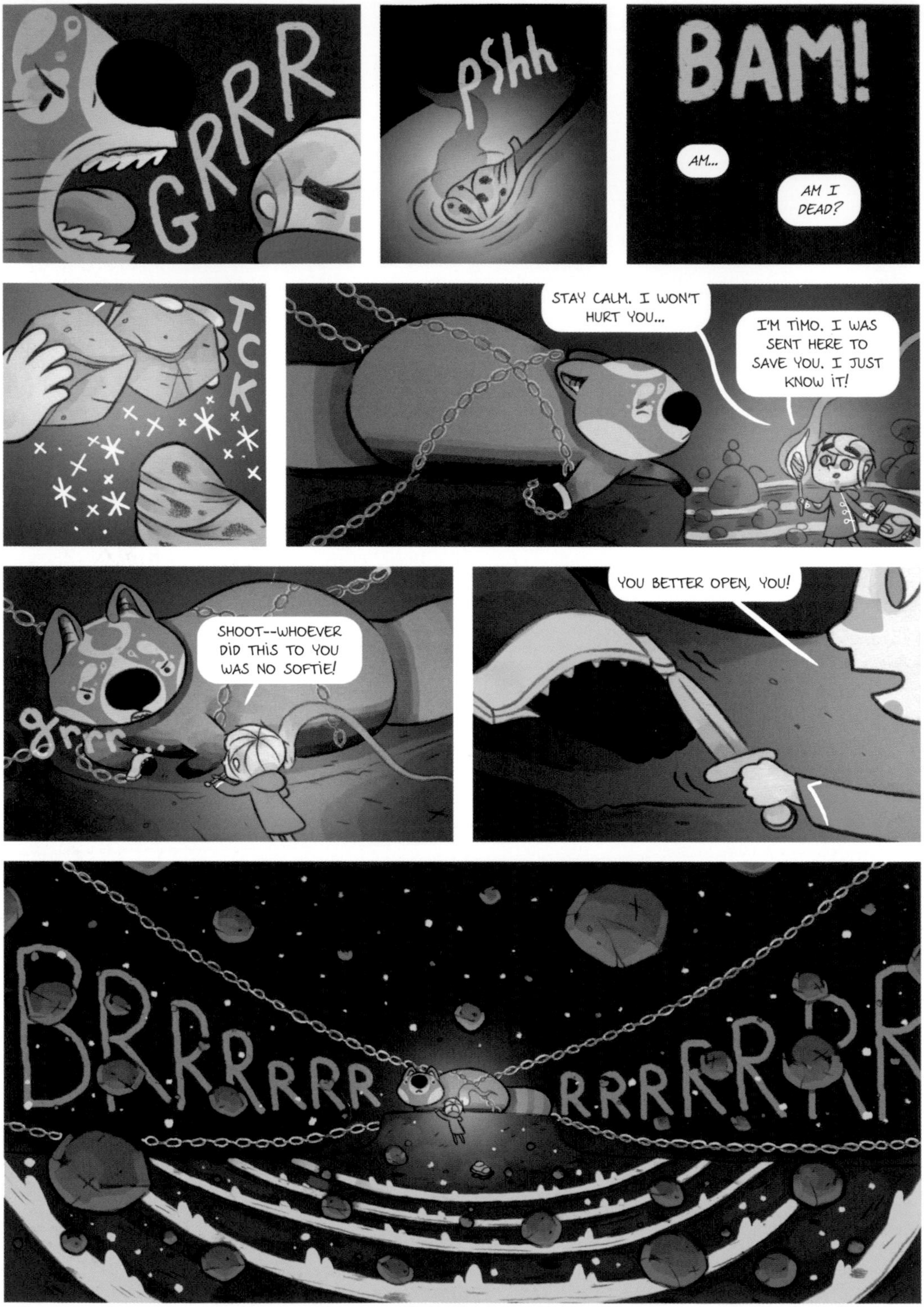
GRRR
PSHH
BAM!
AM...
AM I DEAD?
TCK
STAY CALM. I WON'T HURT YOU...
I'M TIMO. I WAS SENT HERE TO SAVE YOU. I JUST KNOW IT!
grrr
SHOOT--WHOEVER DID THIS TO YOU WAS NO SOFTIE!
YOU BETTER OPEN, YOU!
BRRRRRRRRRRRRRRRR

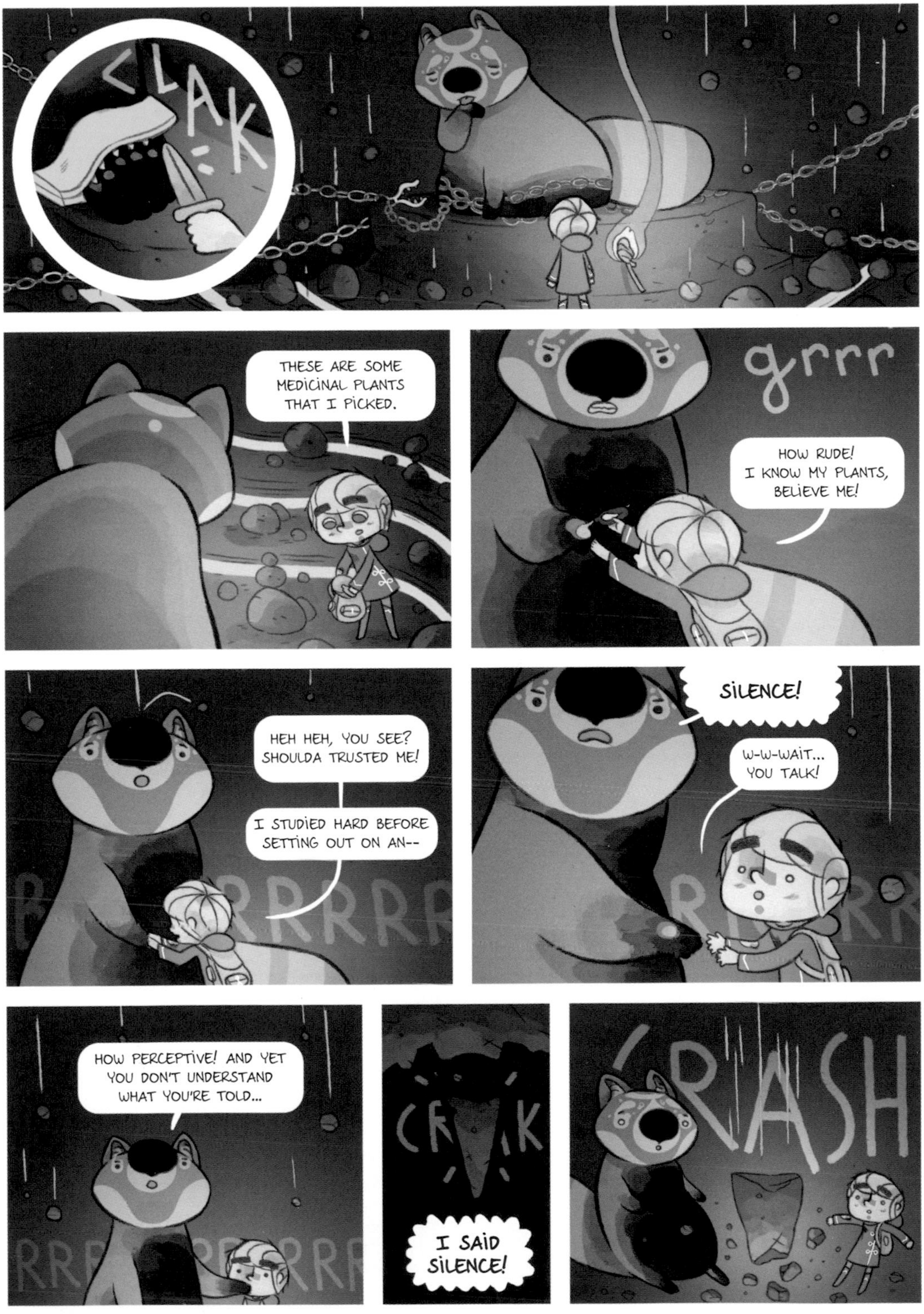
CLAK
THESE ARE SOME MEDICINAL PLANTS THAT I PICKED.
grrr
HOW RUDE! I KNOW MY PLANTS, BELIEVE ME!
HEH HEH, YOU SEE? SHOULDA TRUSTED ME!
I STUDIED HARD BEFORE SETTING OUT ON AN--
RRRRRR
SILENCE!
W-W-WAIT... YOU TALK!
RRR
HOW PERCEPTIVE! AND YET YOU DON'T UNDERSTAND WHAT YOU'RE TOLD...
RRRRRRR
CRAK
I SAID SILENCE!
CRASH

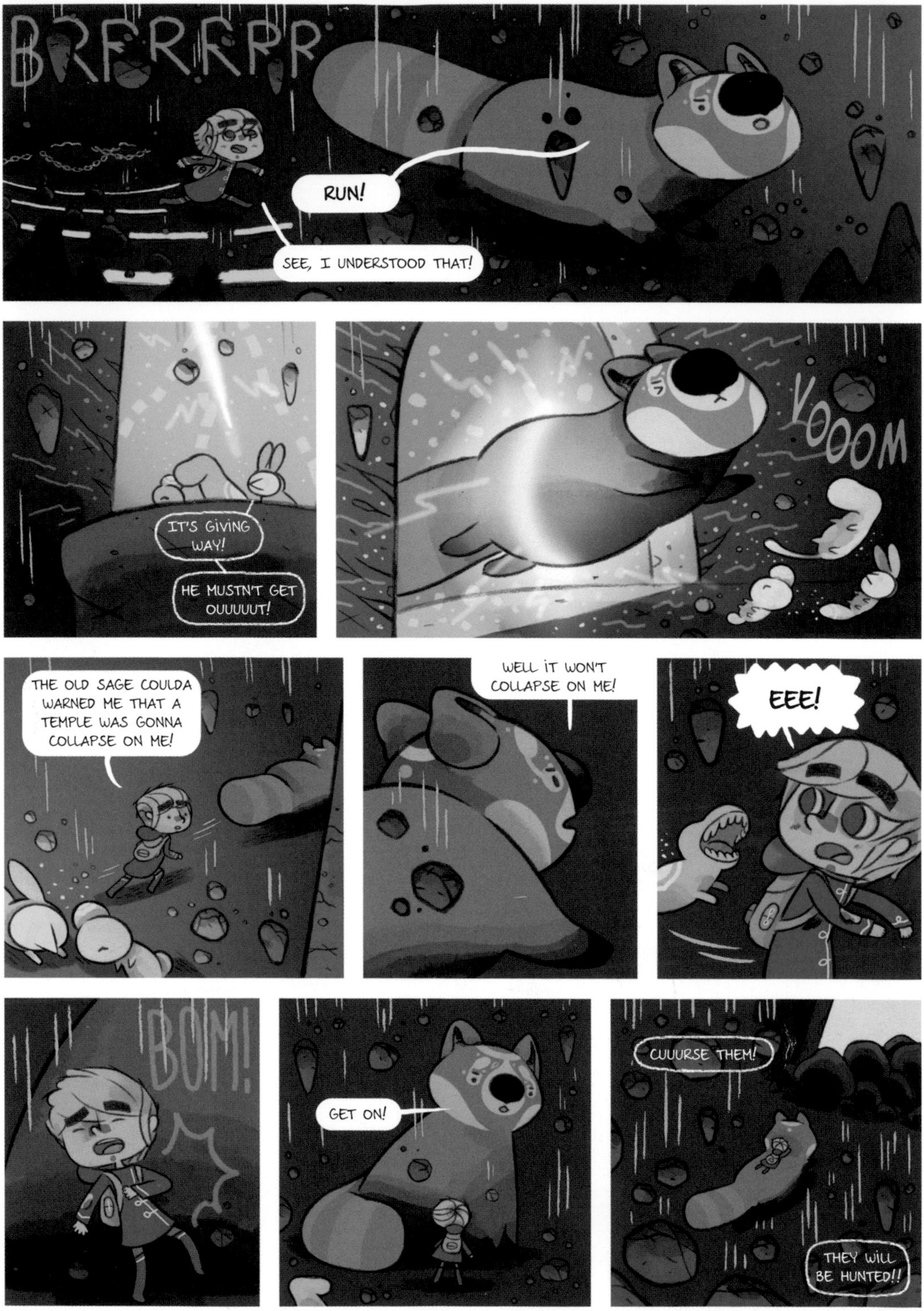
BRRRRRR
RUN!
SEE, I UNDERSTOOD THAT!
IT'S GIVING WAY!
HE MUSTN'T GET OUUUUUT!
VOOOM
THE OLD SAGE COULDA WARNED ME THAT A TEMPLE WAS GONNA COLLAPSE ON ME!
WELL IT WON'T COLLAPSE ON ME!
EEE!
BOM!
GET ON!
CUUURSE THEM!
THEY WILL BE HUNTED!!

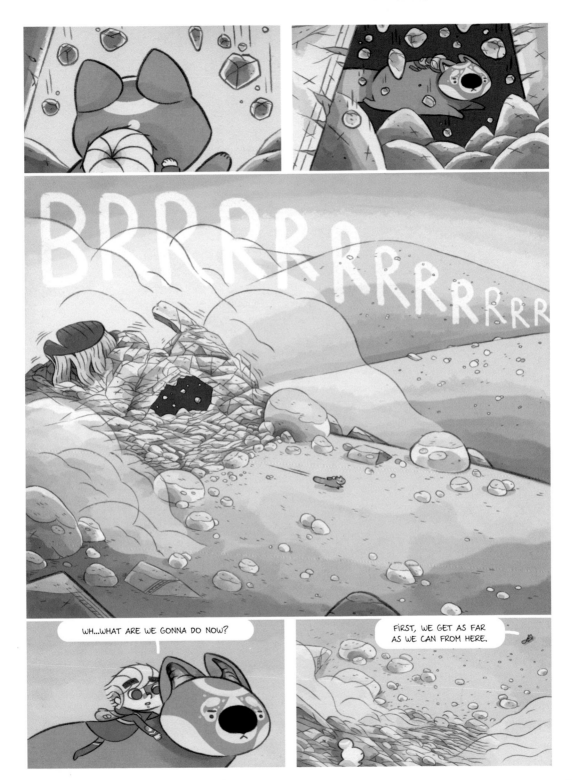

BRRRRRRRRRR

WH...WHAT ARE WE GONNA DO NOW?

FIRST, WE GET AS FAR AS WE CAN FROM HERE.

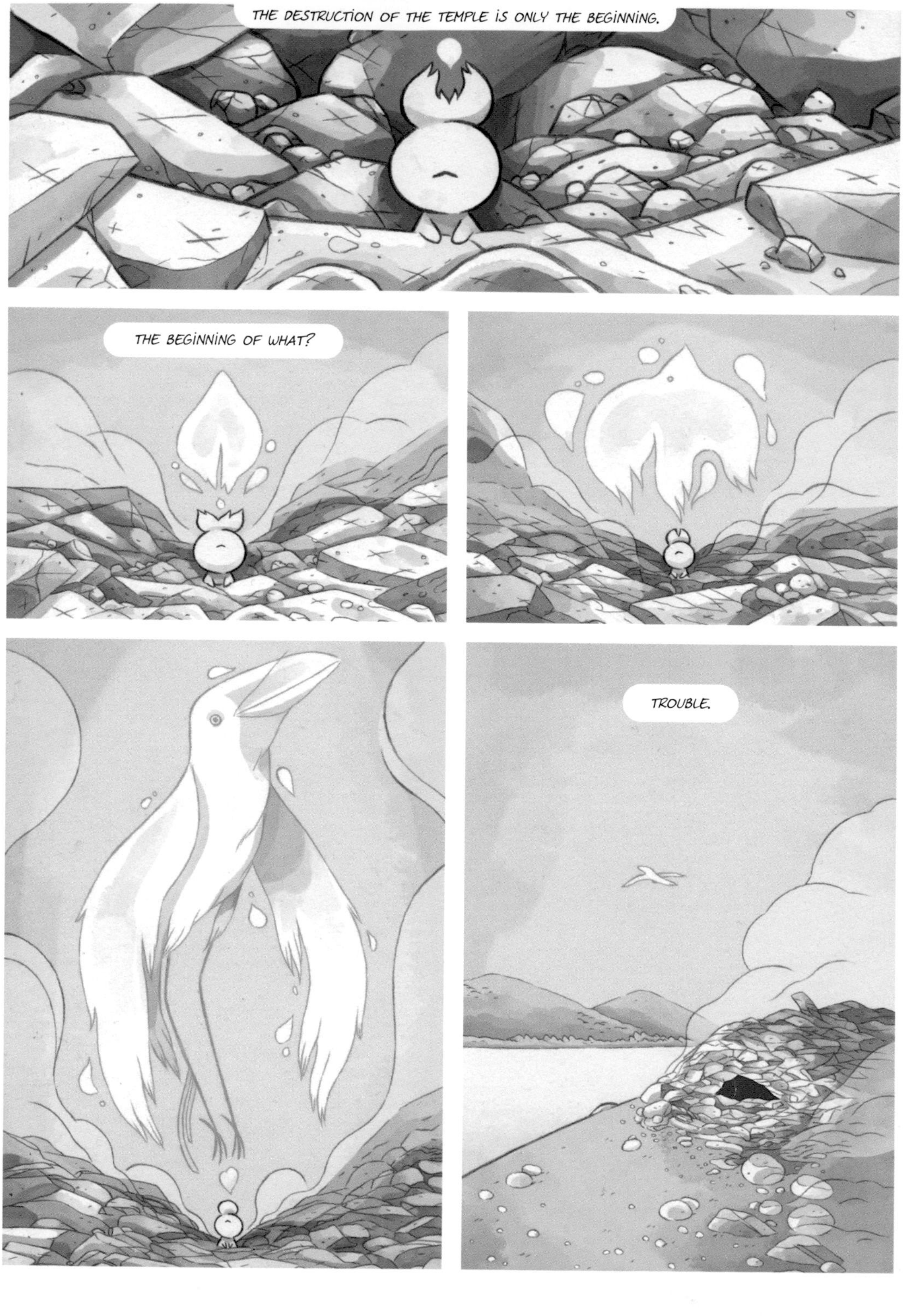
THE DESTRUCTION OF THE TEMPLE IS ONLY THE BEGINNING.
THE BEGINNING OF WHAT?
TROUBLE.

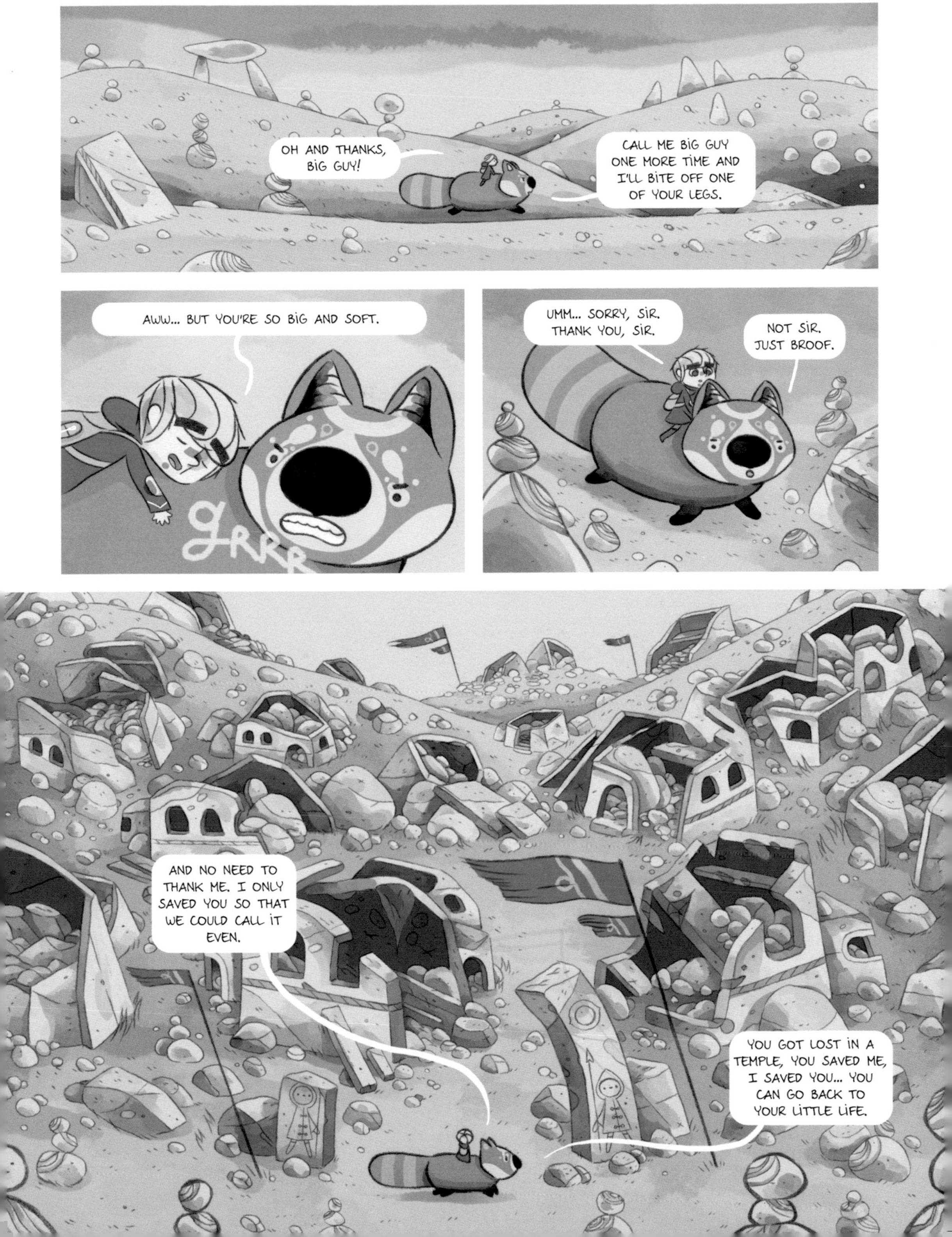
OH AND THANKS, BIG GUY!
CALL ME BIG GUY ONE MORE TIME AND I'LL BITE OFF ONE OF YOUR LEGS.
AWW... BUT YOU'RE SO BIG AND SOFT.
GRRR
UMM... SORRY, SIR. THANK YOU, SIR.
NOT SIR. JUST BROOF.
AND NO NEED TO THANK ME. I ONLY SAVED YOU SO THAT WE COULD CALL IT EVEN.
YOU GOT LOST IN A TEMPLE, YOU SAVED ME, I SAVED YOU... YOU CAN GO BACK TO YOUR LITTLE LIFE.

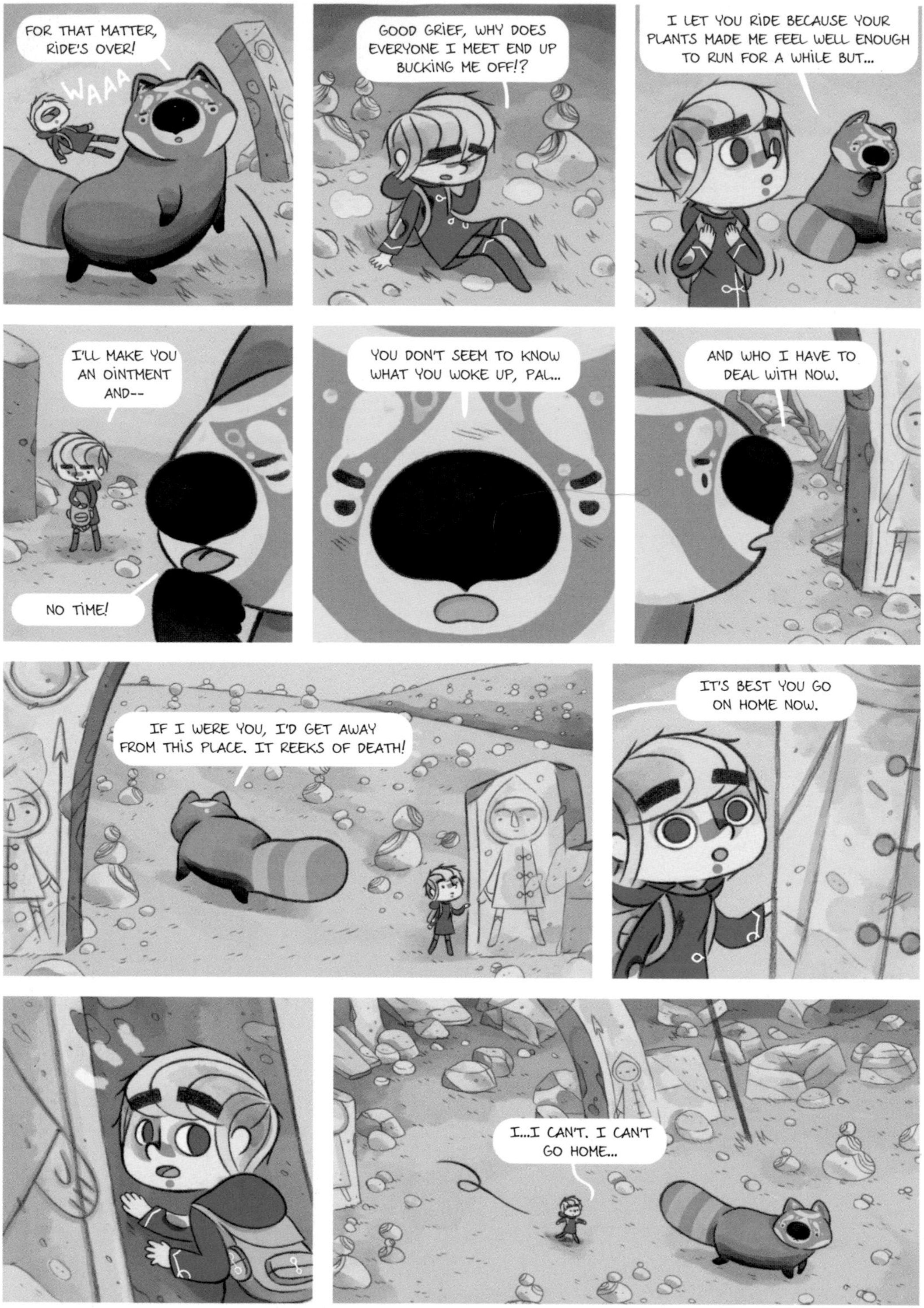
FOR THAT MATTER, RIDE'S OVER!
WAAA
GOOD GRIEF, WHY DOES EVERYONE I MEET END UP BUCKING ME OFF!?
I LET YOU RIDE BECAUSE YOUR PLANTS MADE ME FEEL WELL ENOUGH TO RUN FOR A WHILE BUT...
I'LL MAKE YOU AN OINTMENT AND--
NO TIME!
YOU DON'T SEEM TO KNOW WHAT YOU WOKE UP, PAL...
AND WHO I HAVE TO DEAL WITH NOW.
IF I WERE YOU, I'D GET AWAY FROM THIS PLACE. IT REEKS OF DEATH!
IT'S BEST YOU GO ON HOME NOW.
I...I CAN'T. I CAN'T GO HOME...

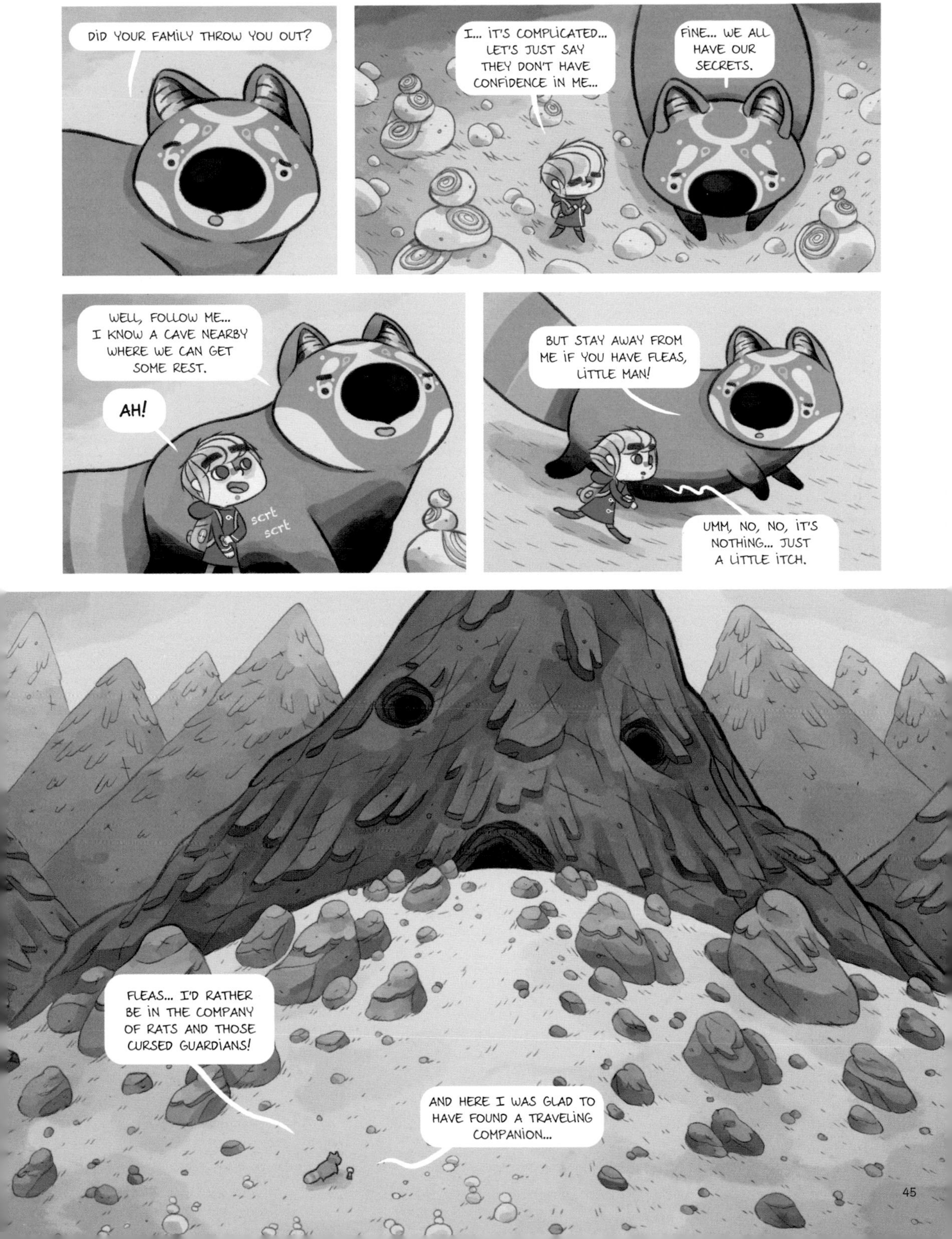
DID YOUR FAMILY THROW YOU OUT?
I... IT'S COMPLICATED... LET'S JUST SAY THEY DON'T HAVE CONFIDENCE IN ME...
FINE... WE ALL HAVE OUR SECRETS.
WELL, FOLLOW ME... I KNOW A CAVE NEARBY WHERE WE CAN GET SOME REST.
AH!
scrt scrt
BUT STAY AWAY FROM ME IF YOU HAVE FLEAS, LITTLE MAN!
UMM, NO, NO, IT'S NOTHING... JUST A LITTLE ITCH.
FLEAS... I'D RATHER BE IN THE COMPANY OF RATS AND THOSE CURSED GUARDIANS!
AND HERE I WAS GLAD TO HAVE FOUND A TRAVELING COMPANION...

BROOF = MEAN

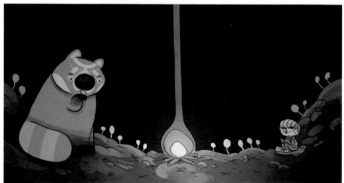

LETTER TO YOUR GIRLFRIEND?

PFF, I DON'T HAVE TIME FOR THAT.

I'M AN ADVENTURER NOW.

BROOF = MEAN

I don't know what to think of Broof...
    I saved him when he was locked up deep down in a temple and instead of
thanking me, he's mean to me. But then, if I were in his situation, I'd probably be
a little grumpy too after being in that prison, and with good reason...

But I was so hoping I'd find myself a travel companion whom I could talk
and laugh with. I can't help but feel a little disappointed that I stumbled
across this temperamental and sarcastic creature...

You want to know the worst part of it? He won't let me touch him, even though it
must be super comfortable to sleep against his big, soft belly! It's downright criminal!

In every great adventure story and every fairy tale, the hero encounters a sorcerer, a sage, who guides him on his journey...

And sure enough, I found mine: The Shaggy One!

THE SHAGGY ONE

He's the guardian of an isolated copse of trees in the middle of the plains. When I discovered The Shaggy One, he was meditating in a spring that's surely magical.

I'm going to be frank: at first, he kind of gave me the willies. He's a massively big bear, after all! But his noble bearing, his beautiful cape, and his shaggy beard revealed to me the venerable sage that was hiding within the animal.

Before I crossed his path, I was depressed, lost. I barely had the strength to keep going. But with a simple motion of his paw, he restored my courage...

I told you: meeting new friends is the most important part of any journey!

I feel more than ever like I have the soul of an adventurer, but I've still got work to do before becoming a "true hero." Because you can't be a hero without a noble steed, and in my case, the noble steed is sadly lacking...

I've certainly tried to tame a few animals in the hopes they'd play the part, but they've all had the nerve to refuse the honor!

There's no reasoning with them: they've thrown me off every time, butt first!

Talk about disrespect...

DOOFHOG

Beneath its calm exterior, the doofhog is a temperamental animal that is easily ticked off. While it has all the qualities of an inelegant but robust steed, it doesn't allow itself to be tamed easily...or at all, in fact!

In any case, lassos and food didn't work one bit.

Maybe I should have tried scratching it.

The pigs in my village really love being scratched.

Watch out:
its rear kick is formidable!

LiLTROT

The liltrot is an elegant creature but only runs at a trot.
(Well yeah, hence its name!)

Though it cut a much finer figure than the doofhog and proved to be more docile, its lack of courage ruled it out definitively as an adventurer's ideal steed.

It's too bad: the liltrot is fast and quite soft. Less so than Broof but soft nonetheless...

Up until now I haven't talked much about the places I've discovered. And while I've seen some beautiful landscapes, today my journey took me to a truly sinister spot.

THE FORGOTTEN TEMPLE

This was an old temple in ruins that looked like it had been uninhabited for a long time. And yet it was haunted by all kinds of ghostly, super-aggressive little creatures! One of them bit me. For now, it just itches. I'm going to put some ointment on it and it should get better... I hope.

I would have really loved to study the engravings on the temple walls. I'm sure they would have taught me plenty of things about the history of this land!

Now that we've finally stopped, tons of questions are running through my head:

Who were those creatures? Did they cast an evil spell on us because we demolished their temple? For that matter, who built the temple? And why was Broof locked up in there?

I'm also wondering what happened to the ruined village we saw.

I wanted thrills, and I got them, all right...

But I didn't expect to find myself diving into so much danger so quickly!

I can't say this to Broof, or he'll think I'm a wuss, but I'm feeling really crummy...

And I miss my family a little.

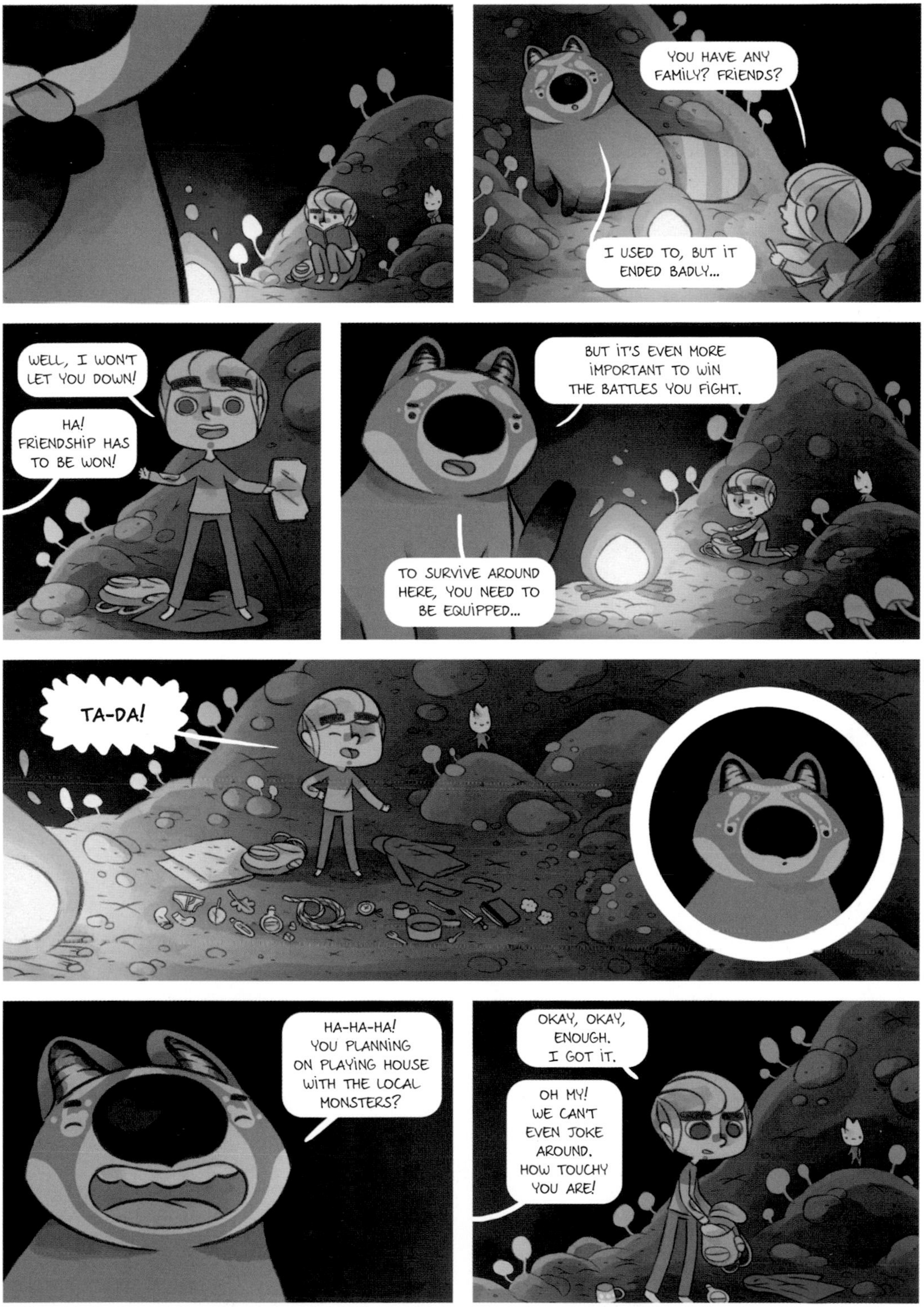

YOU HAVE ANY FAMILY? FRIENDS?
I USED TO, BUT IT ENDED BADLY...
WELL, I WON'T LET YOU DOWN!
HA! FRIENDSHIP HAS TO BE WON!
BUT IT'S EVEN MORE IMPORTANT TO WIN THE BATTLES YOU FIGHT.
TO SURVIVE AROUND HERE, YOU NEED TO BE EQUIPPED...
TA-DA!
HA-HA-HA! YOU PLANNING ON PLAYING HOUSE WITH THE LOCAL MONSTERS?
OKAY, OKAY, ENOUGH. I GOT IT.
OH MY! WE CAN'T EVEN JOKE AROUND. HOW TOUCHY YOU ARE!

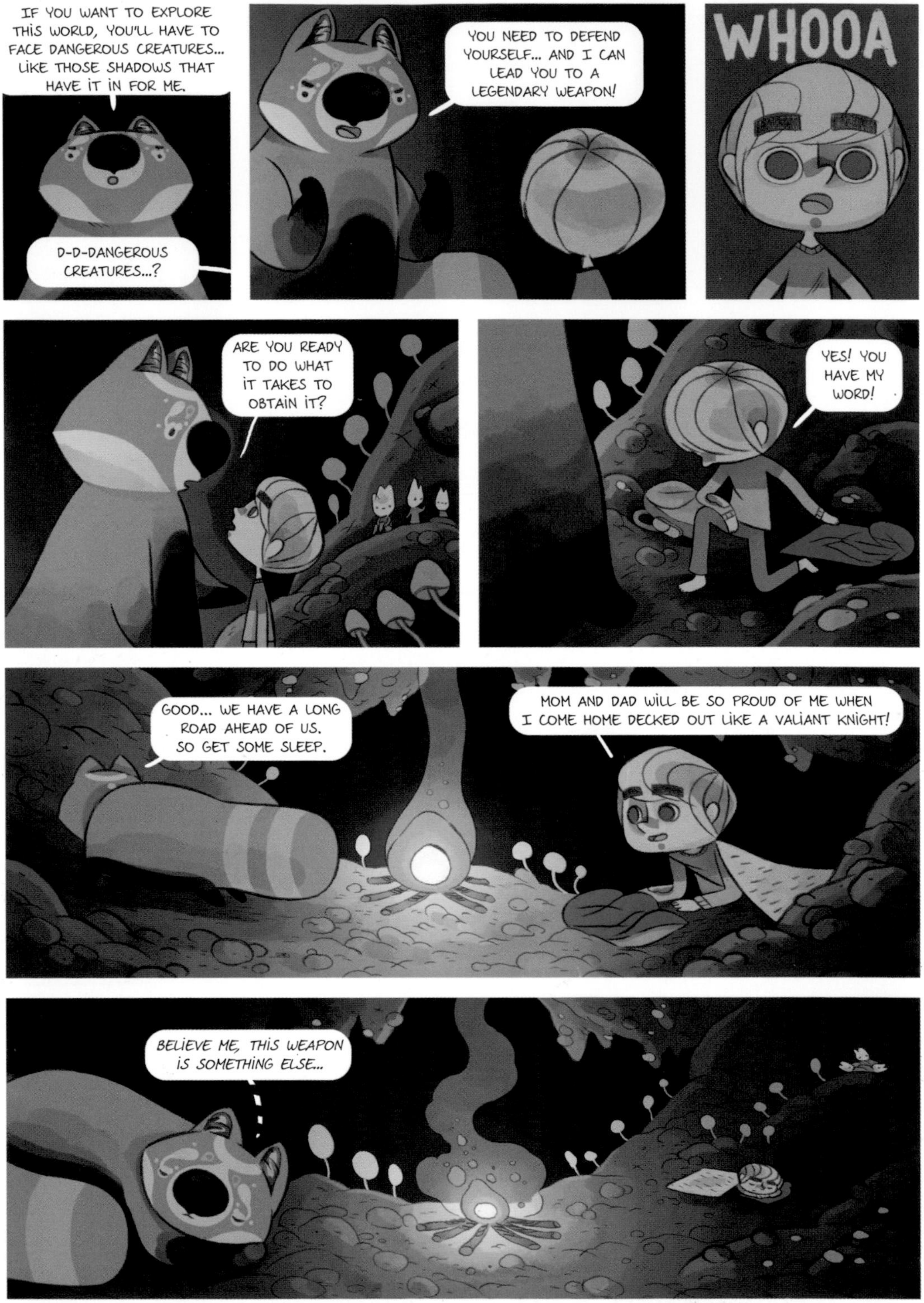

IF YOU WANT TO EXPLORE THIS WORLD, YOU'LL HAVE TO FACE DANGEROUS CREATURES... LIKE THOSE SHADOWS THAT HAVE IT IN FOR ME.
D-D-DANGEROUS CREATURES...?
YOU NEED TO DEFEND YOURSELF... AND I CAN LEAD YOU TO A LEGENDARY WEAPON!
WHOOA
ARE YOU READY TO DO WHAT IT TAKES TO OBTAIN IT?
YES! YOU HAVE MY WORD!
GOOD... WE HAVE A LONG ROAD AHEAD OF US. SO GET SOME SLEEP.
MOM AND DAD WILL BE SO PROUD OF ME WHEN I COME HOME DECKED OUT LIKE A VALIANT KNIGHT!
BELIEVE ME, THIS WEAPON IS SOMETHING ELSE...

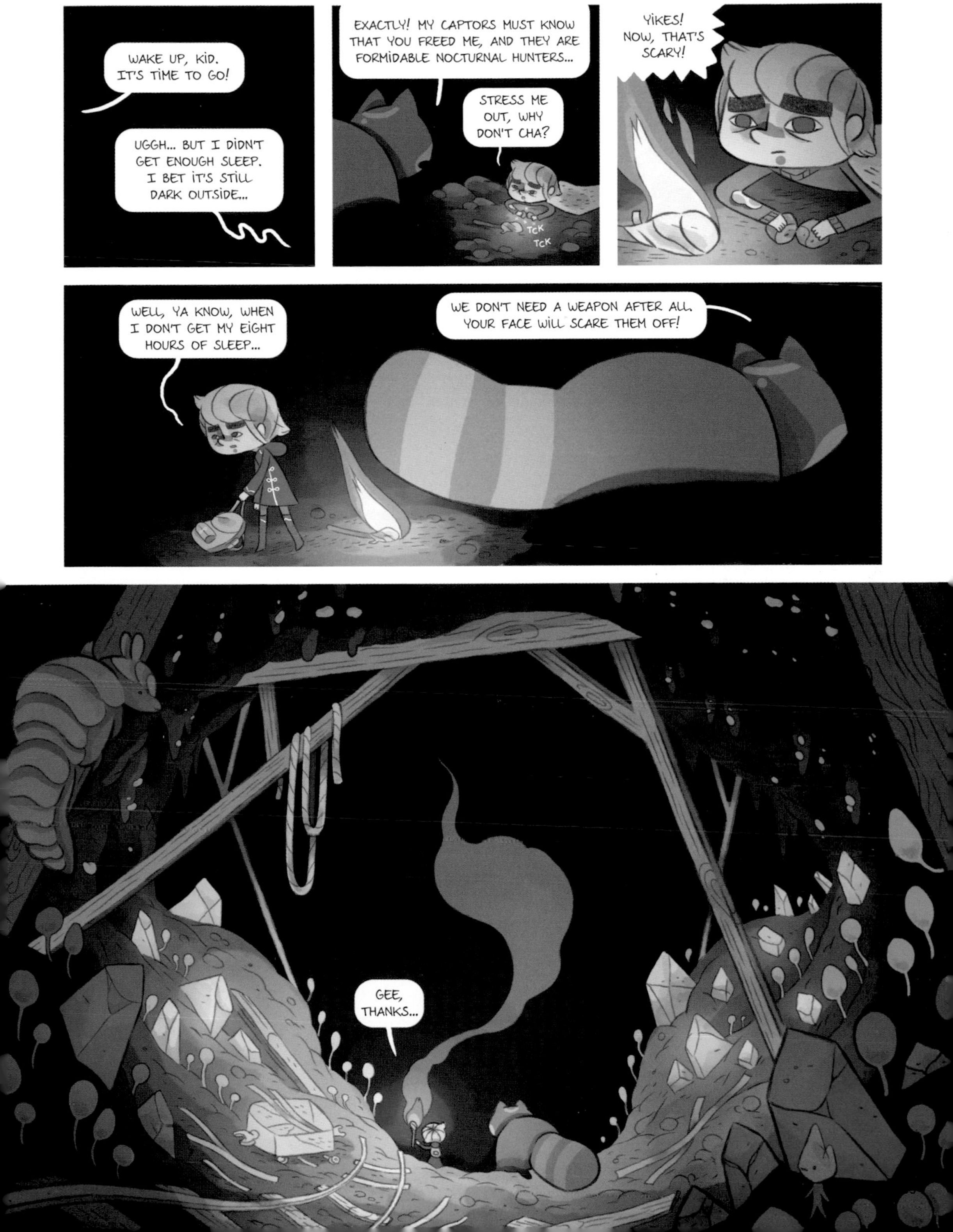
WAKE UP, KID. IT'S TIME TO GO!
UGGH... BUT I DIDN'T GET ENOUGH SLEEP. I BET IT'S STILL DARK OUTSIDE...
EXACTLY! MY CAPTORS MUST KNOW THAT YOU FREED ME, AND THEY ARE FORMIDABLE NOCTURNAL HUNTERS...
STRESS ME OUT, WHY DON'T CHA?
TCK
TCK
YIKES! NOW, THAT'S SCARY!
WELL, YA KNOW, WHEN I DON'T GET MY EIGHT HOURS OF SLEEP...
WE DON'T NEED A WEAPON AFTER ALL. YOUR FACE WILL SCARE THEM OFF!
GEE, THANKS...

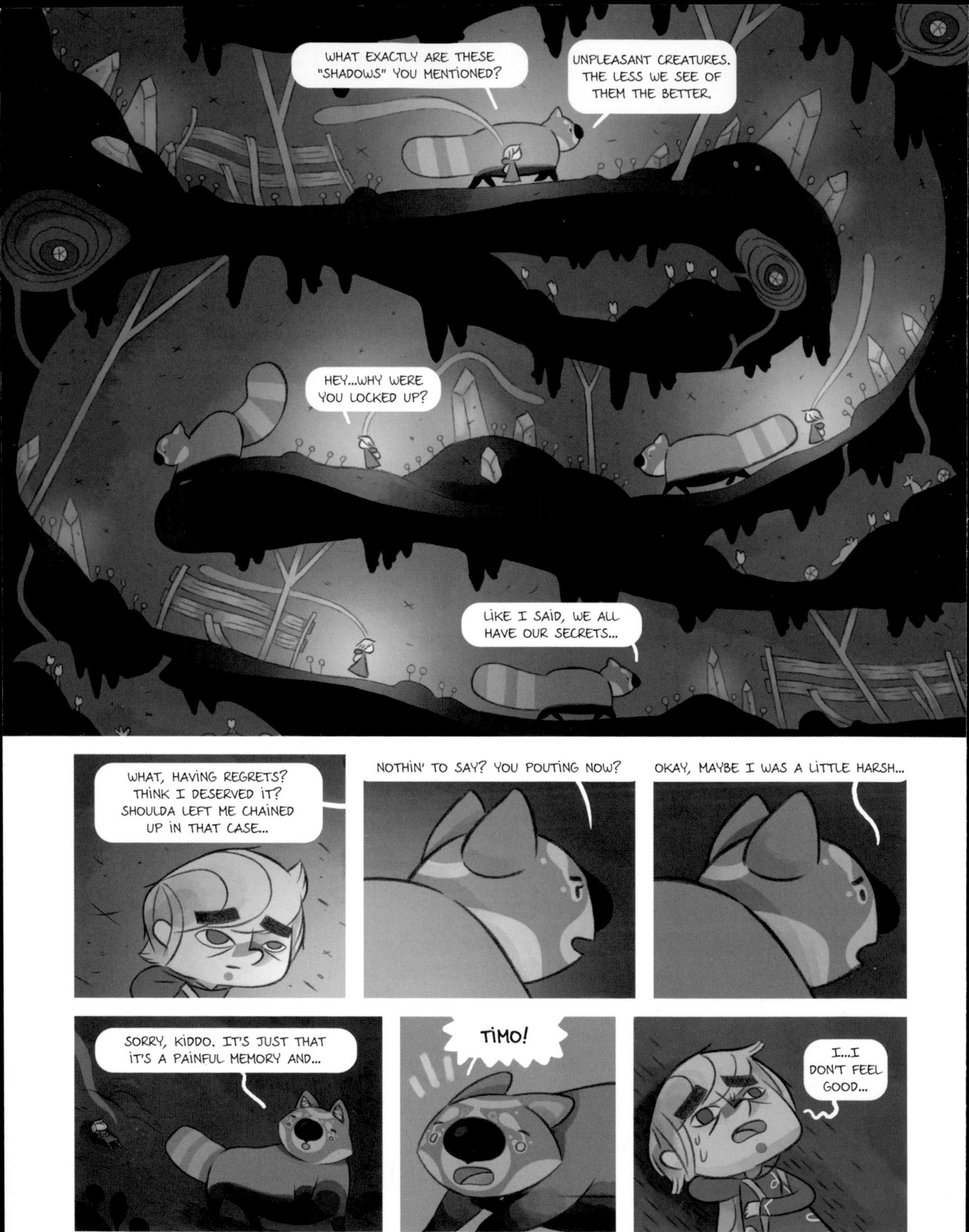
WHAT EXACTLY ARE THESE "SHADOWS" YOU MENTIONED?
UNPLEASANT CREATURES. THE LESS WE SEE OF THEM THE BETTER.
HEY...WHY WERE YOU LOCKED UP?
LIKE I SAID, WE ALL HAVE OUR SECRETS...
WHAT, HAVING REGRETS? THINK I DESERVED IT? SHOULDA LEFT ME CHAINED UP IN THAT CASE...
NOTHIN' TO SAY? YOU POUTING NOW?
OKAY, MAYBE I WAS A LITTLE HARSH...
SORRY, KIDDO. IT'S JUST THAT IT'S A PAINFUL MEMORY AND...
TIMO!
I...I DON'T FEEL GOOD...

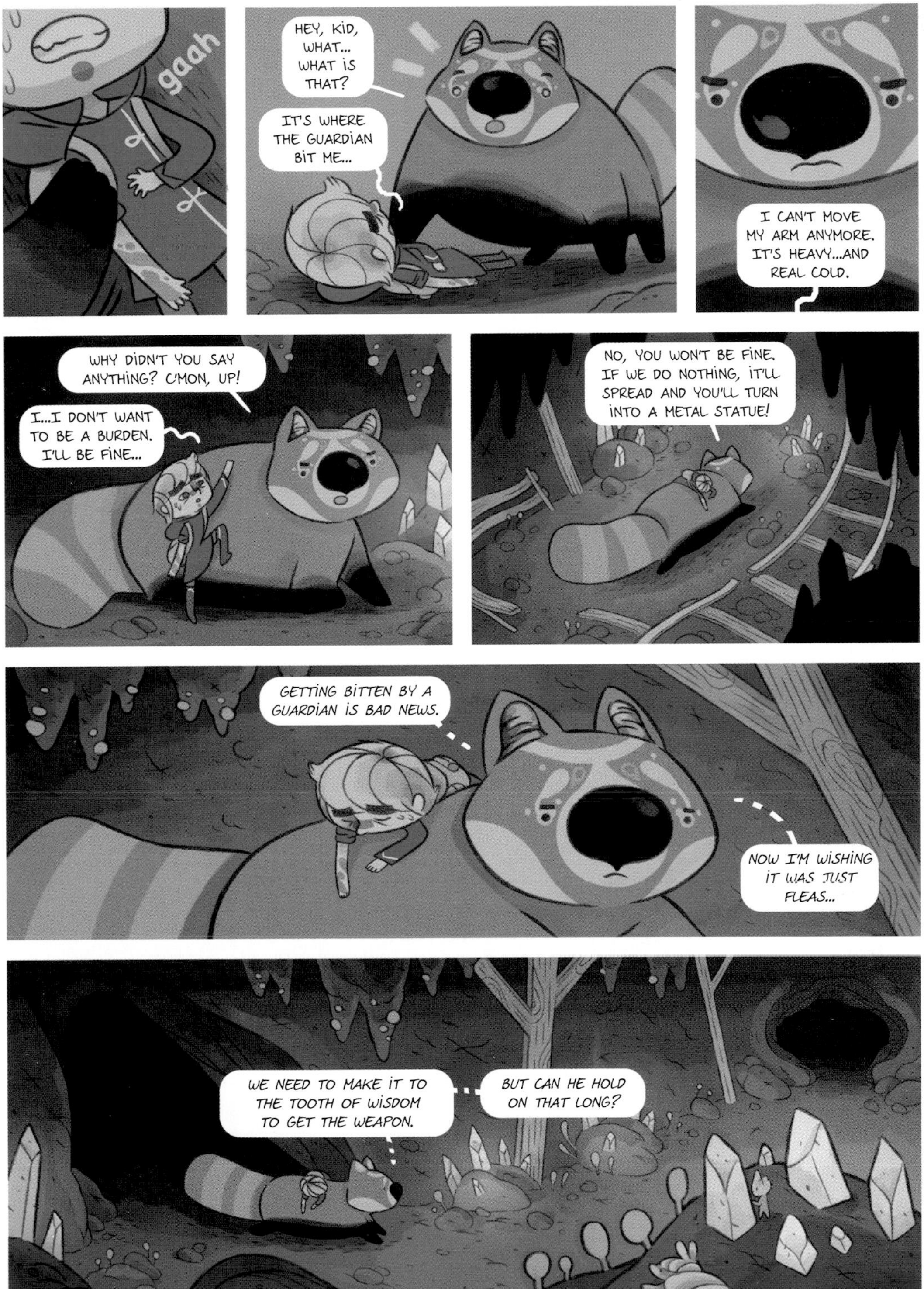
gaah
HEY, KID, WHAT... WHAT IS THAT?
IT'S WHERE THE GUARDIAN BIT ME...
I CAN'T MOVE MY ARM ANYMORE. IT'S HEAVY...AND REAL COLD.
WHY DIDN'T YOU SAY ANYTHING? C'MON, UP!
I...I DON'T WANT TO BE A BURDEN. I'LL BE FINE...
NO, YOU WON'T BE FINE. IF WE DO NOTHING, IT'LL SPREAD AND YOU'LL TURN INTO A METAL STATUE!
GETTING BITTEN BY A GUARDIAN IS BAD NEWS.
NOW I'M WISHING IT WAS JUST FLEAS...
WE NEED TO MAKE IT TO THE TOOTH OF WISDOM TO GET THE WEAPON.
BUT CAN HE HOLD ON THAT LONG?

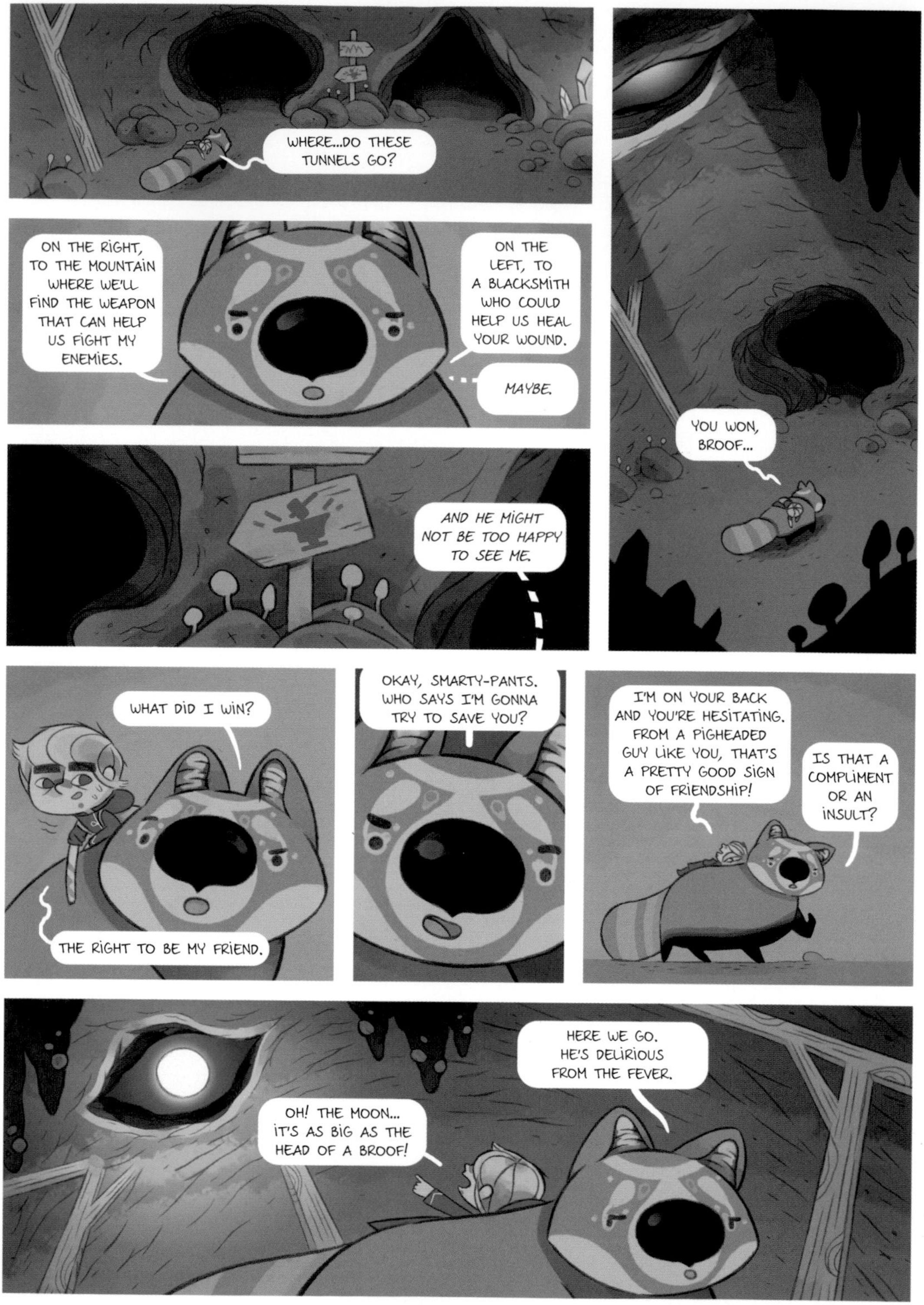
WHERE...DO THESE TUNNELS GO?
ON THE RIGHT, TO THE MOUNTAIN WHERE WE'LL FIND THE WEAPON THAT CAN HELP US FIGHT MY ENEMIES.
ON THE LEFT, TO A BLACKSMITH WHO COULD HELP US HEAL YOUR WOUND.
MAYBE.
AND HE MIGHT NOT BE TOO HAPPY TO SEE ME.
YOU WON, BROOF...
WHAT DID I WIN?
THE RIGHT TO BE MY FRIEND.
OKAY, SMARTY-PANTS. WHO SAYS I'M GONNA TRY TO SAVE YOU?
I'M ON YOUR BACK AND YOU'RE HESITATING. FROM A PIGHEADED GUY LIKE YOU, THAT'S A PRETTY GOOD SIGN OF FRIENDSHIP!
IS THAT A COMPLIMENT OR AN INSULT?
HERE WE GO. HE'S DELIRIOUS FROM THE FEVER.
OH! THE MOON... IT'S AS BIG AS THE HEAD OF A BROOF!

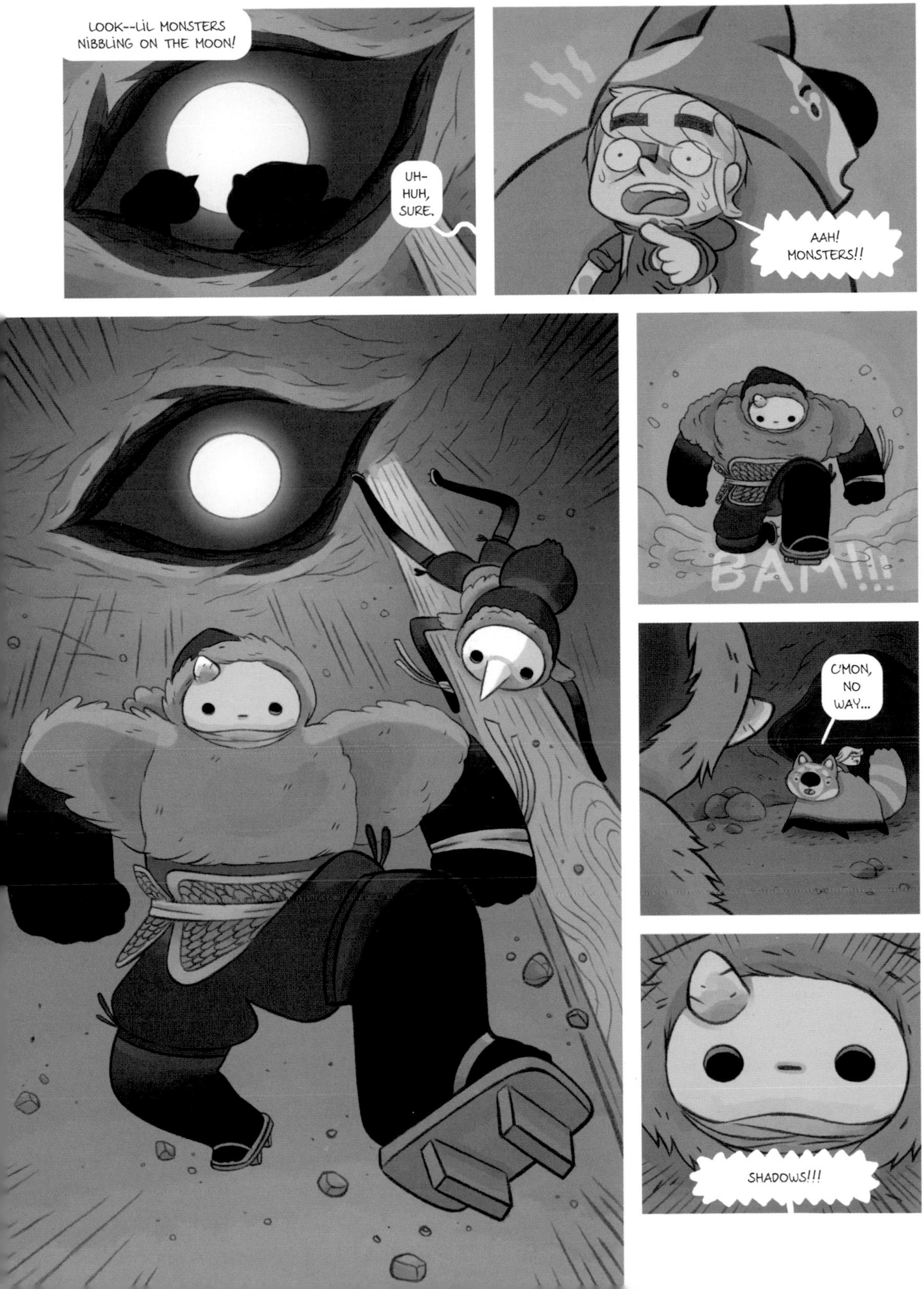
LOOK--LIL MONSTERS NIBBLING ON THE MOON!
UH-HUH, SURE.
AAH! MONSTERS!!
BAM!!!
C'MON, NO WAY...
SHADOWS!!!

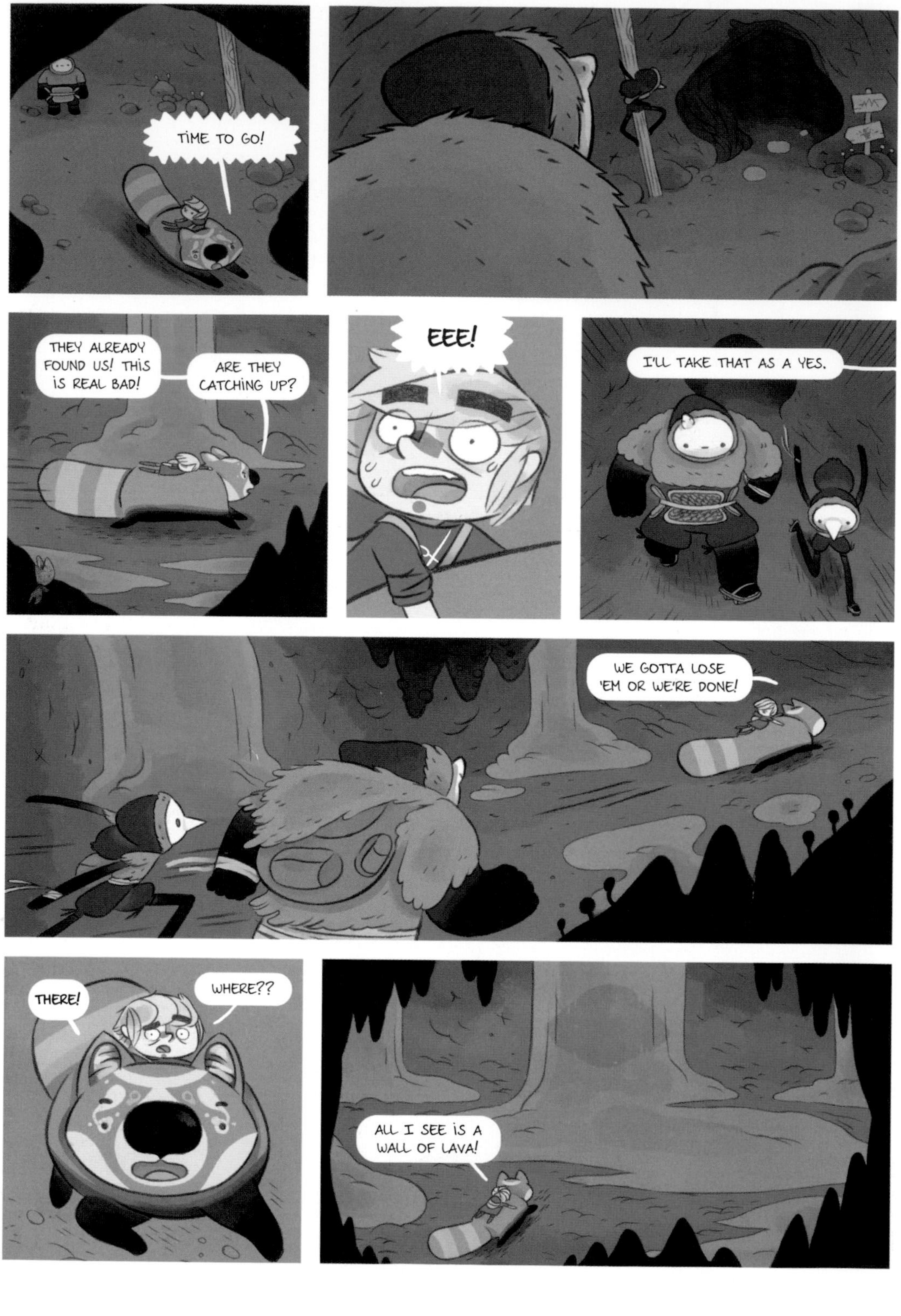
TIME TO GO!
THEY ALREADY FOUND US! THIS IS REAL BAD!
ARE THEY CATCHING UP?
EEE!
I'LL TAKE THAT AS A YES.
WE GOTTA LOSE 'EM OR WE'RE DONE!
THERE!
WHERE??
ALL I SEE IS A WALL OF LAVA!

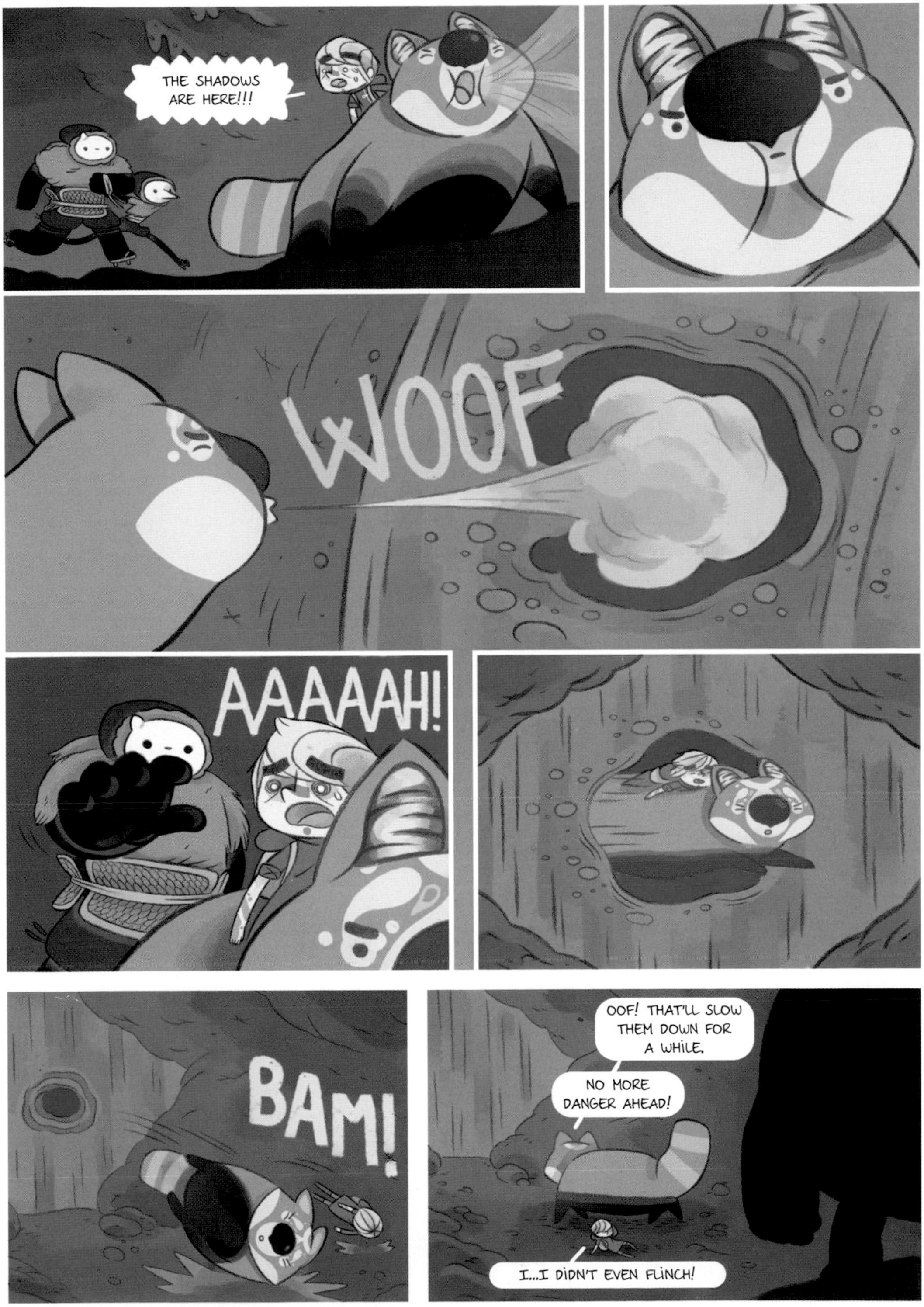
THE SHADOWS ARE HERE!!!
WOOF
AAAAAH!
BAM!
OOF! THAT'LL SLOW THEM DOWN FOR A WHILE.
NO MORE DANGER AHEAD!
I...I DIDN'T EVEN FLINCH!

HEY! YOU!

SHADOWS!

NOPE, I FLINCHED...

BOY, AM I POOPED...

I CAN'T EVEN TALK.

CLANG! CLANG! CLANG!

WHAT'S THAT NOISE?

WH-WHERE AM I?

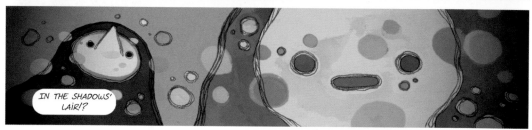

IN THE SHADOWS' LAIR!?

CLANG!

YOUR LIL FRIEND ISH FRAGILE, EH?

OH, A ROCK THAT CHITCHATS... A "CHATTER-ROCK"!

NOTHING TO BE AFRAID OF...

CLANG!

YEAH, HE'S IN BAD SHAPE AND HE'S FEVERISH.

CLANG!

HE'SH AWAKE BUT SHEEMS LIKE HE'SH IN A DAZE AND HISH ARM'S DONE-ZO.

WHAT ABOUT MY ARM? HEE HEE, IT'S SO SWOLLEN THAT I CAN'T FEEL IT.

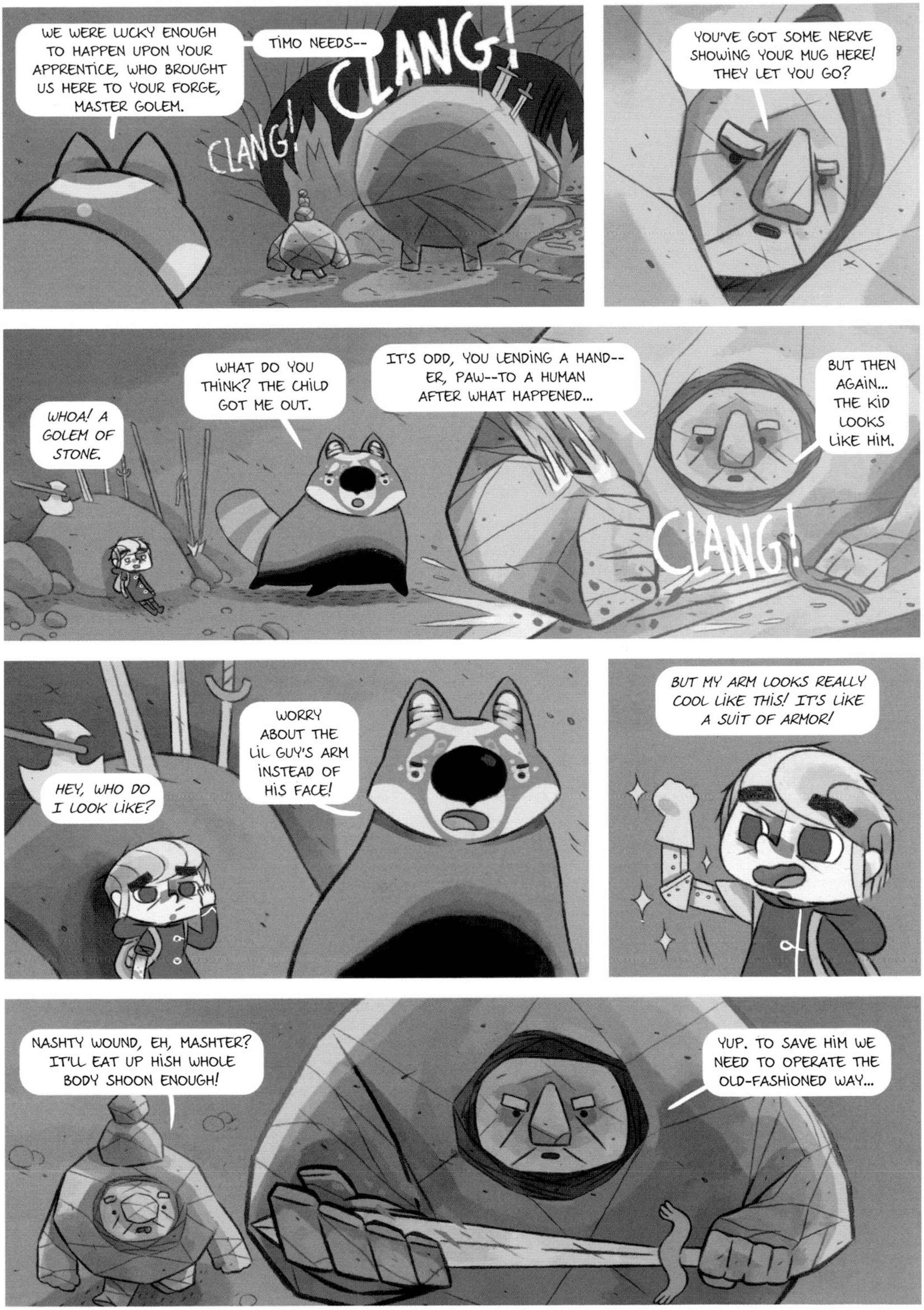
WE WERE LUCKY ENOUGH TO HAPPEN UPON YOUR APPRENTICE, WHO BROUGHT US HERE TO YOUR FORGE, MASTER GOLEM.
TIMO NEEDS--
CLANG!
CLANG!
YOU'VE GOT SOME NERVE SHOWING YOUR MUG HERE! THEY LET YOU GO?
WHOA! A GOLEM OF STONE.
WHAT DO YOU THINK? THE CHILD GOT ME OUT.
IT'S ODD, YOU LENDING A HAND-- ER, PAW--TO A HUMAN AFTER WHAT HAPPENED...
BUT THEN AGAIN... THE KID LOOKS LIKE HIM.
CLANG!
HEY, WHO DO I LOOK LIKE?
WORRY ABOUT THE LIL GUY'S ARM INSTEAD OF HIS FACE!
BUT MY ARM LOOKS REALLY COOL LIKE THIS! IT'S LIKE A SUIT OF ARMOR!
NASHTY WOUND, EH, MASHTER? IT'LL EAT UP HISH WHOLE BODY SHOON ENOUGH!
YUP. TO SAVE HIM WE NEED TO OPERATE THE OLD-FASHIONED WAY...

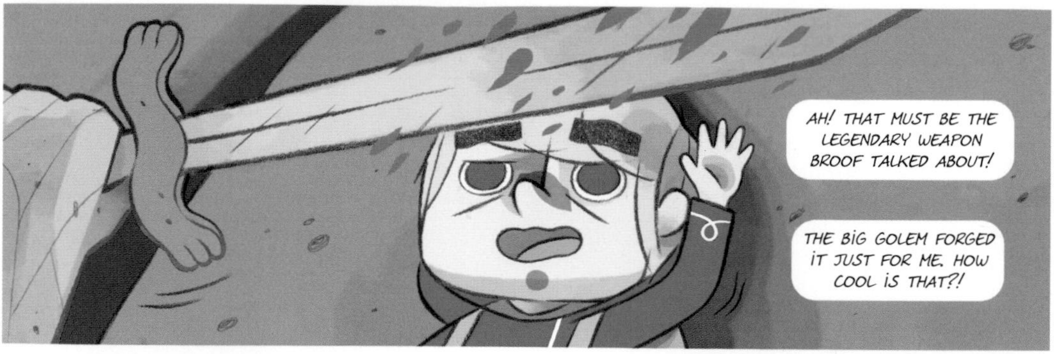
AH! THAT MUST BE THE LEGENDARY WEAPON BROOF TALKED ABOUT!
THE BIG GOLEM FORGED IT JUST FOR ME. HOW COOL IS THAT?!

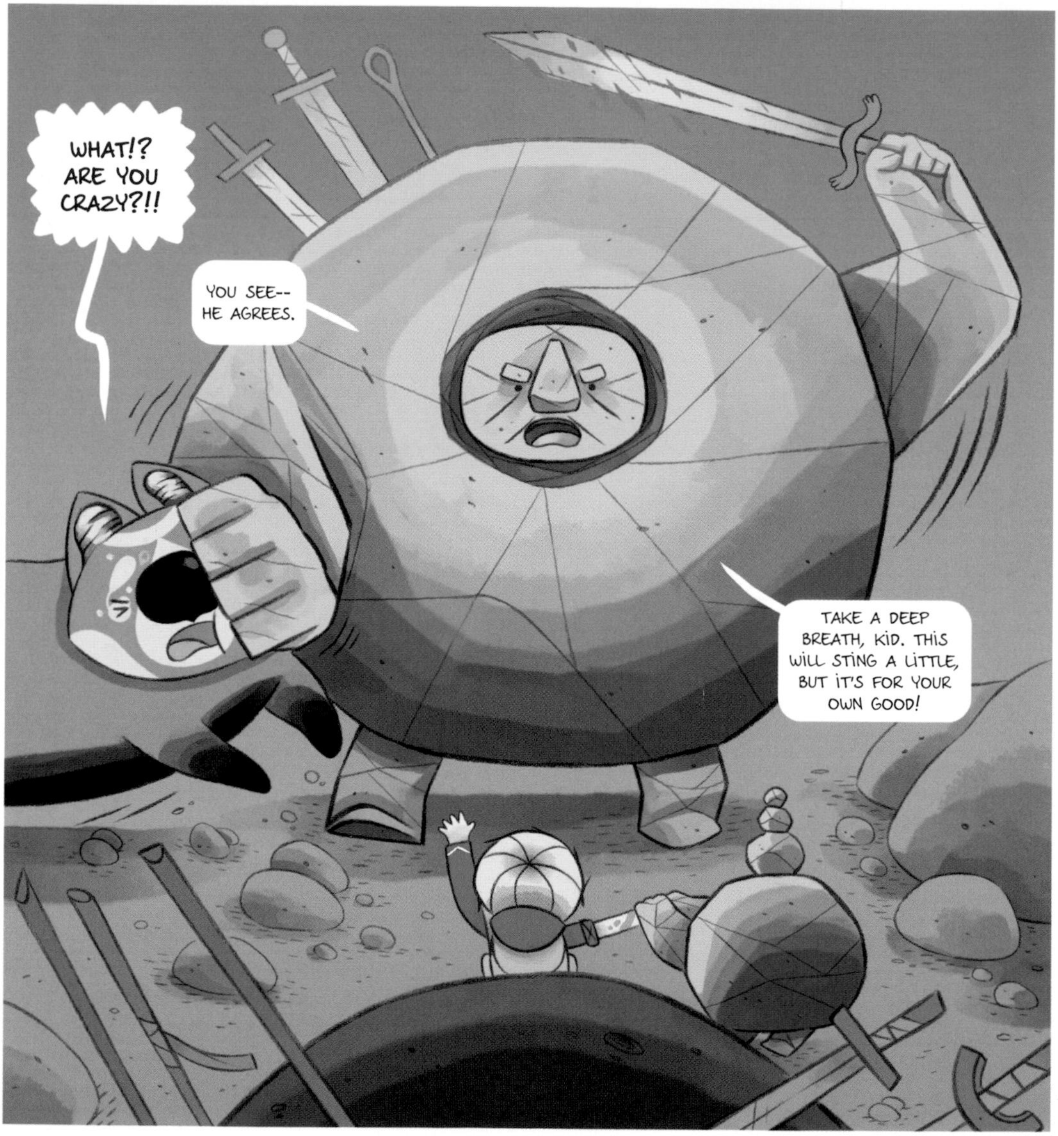
WHAT!? ARE YOU CRAZY?!!
YOU SEE-- HE AGREES.
TAKE A DEEP BREATH, KID. THIS WILL STING A LITTLE, BUT IT'S FOR YOUR OWN GOOD!

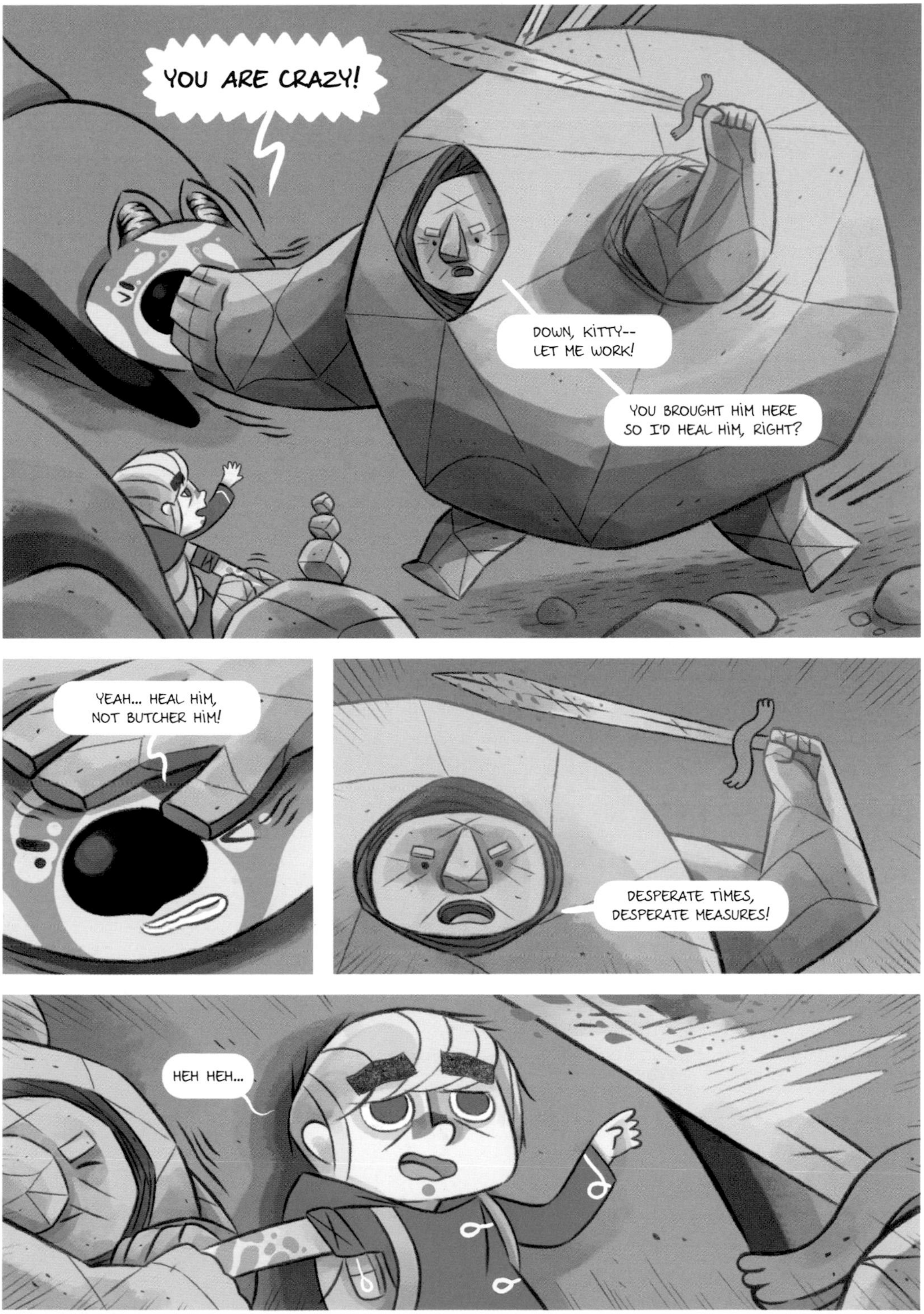
YOU ARE CRAZY!
DOWN, KITTY-- LET ME WORK!
YOU BROUGHT HIM HERE SO I'D HEAL HIM, RIGHT?
YEAH... HEAL HIM, NOT BUTCHER HIM!
DESPERATE TIMES, DESPERATE MEASURES!
HEH HEH...

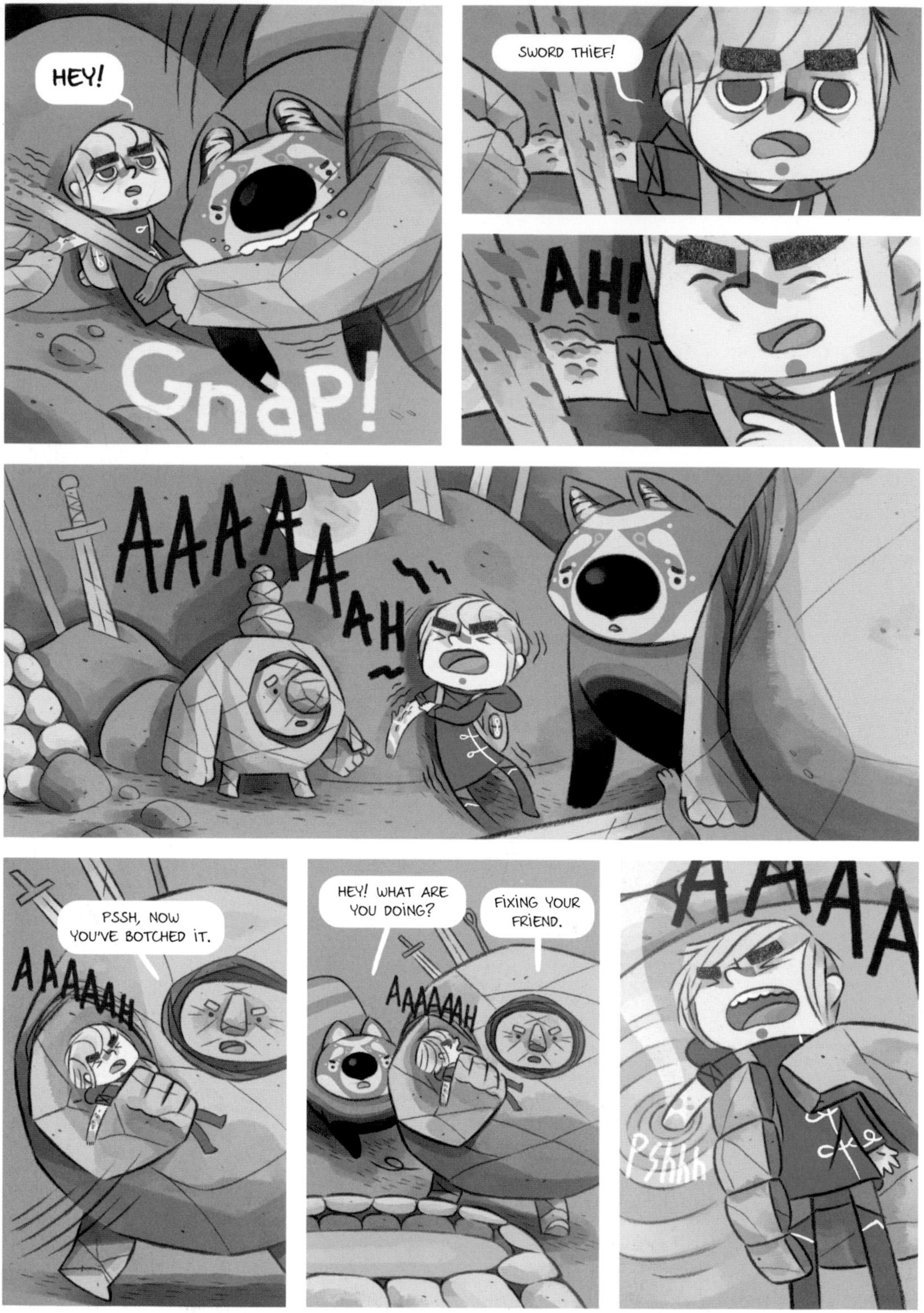
HEY!
Gnap!
SWORD THIEF!
AH!
AAAAAAAH
PSSH, NOW YOU'VE BOTCHED IT.
AAAAAH
HEY! WHAT ARE YOU DOING?
FIXING YOUR FRIEND.
AAAAAAH
AAAA
PShhh

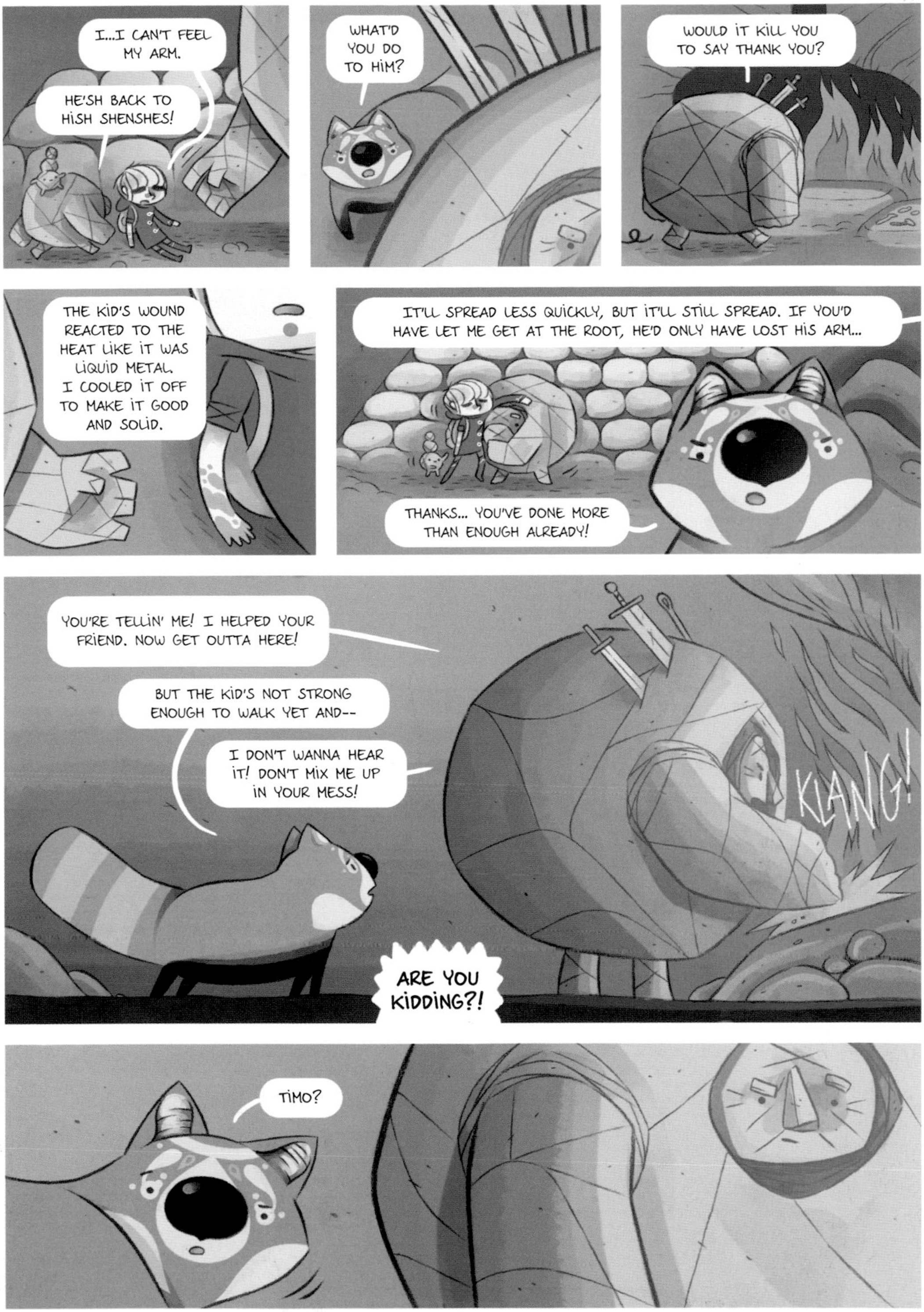
I...I CAN'T FEEL MY ARM.
HE'SH BACK TO HISH SHENSHES!
WHAT'D YOU DO TO HIM?
WOULD IT KILL YOU TO SAY THANK YOU?
THE KID'S WOUND REACTED TO THE HEAT LIKE IT WAS LIQUID METAL. I COOLED IT OFF TO MAKE IT GOOD AND SOLID.
IT'LL SPREAD LESS QUICKLY, BUT IT'LL STILL SPREAD. IF YOU'D HAVE LET ME GET AT THE ROOT, HE'D ONLY HAVE LOST HIS ARM...
THANKS... YOU'VE DONE MORE THAN ENOUGH ALREADY!
YOU'RE TELLIN' ME! I HELPED YOUR FRIEND. NOW GET OUTTA HERE!
BUT THE KID'S NOT STRONG ENOUGH TO WALK YET AND--
I DON'T WANNA HEAR IT! DON'T MIX ME UP IN YOUR MESS!
KLANG!
ARE YOU KIDDING?!
TIMO?

YOUR APPRENTICE TOLD ME YOU MADE ALL THESE WEAPONS!

IS IT TRUE?

YEAH. SO WHAT?

YOU'RE A GENIUS!

OH!

HOW 'BOUT I MAKE ONE FOR YOU?

A YOUNG HERO WITH SUCH GOOD TASTE MERITS MY HELP!

WAIT, FOR REAL?

SERIOUSLY? TWO MINUTES AGO, HE WAS KICKING US OUT.

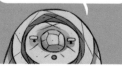

NOT TOO MANY FOLKSH SHTILL COME ROUND.

WHEN THE MASHTER MEETSH AN EXPLORER WHO COMPLIMENTSH HISH WORK, HE GETSH A LITTLE CARRIED AWAY.

KLANG

KLANG!

KLANG!

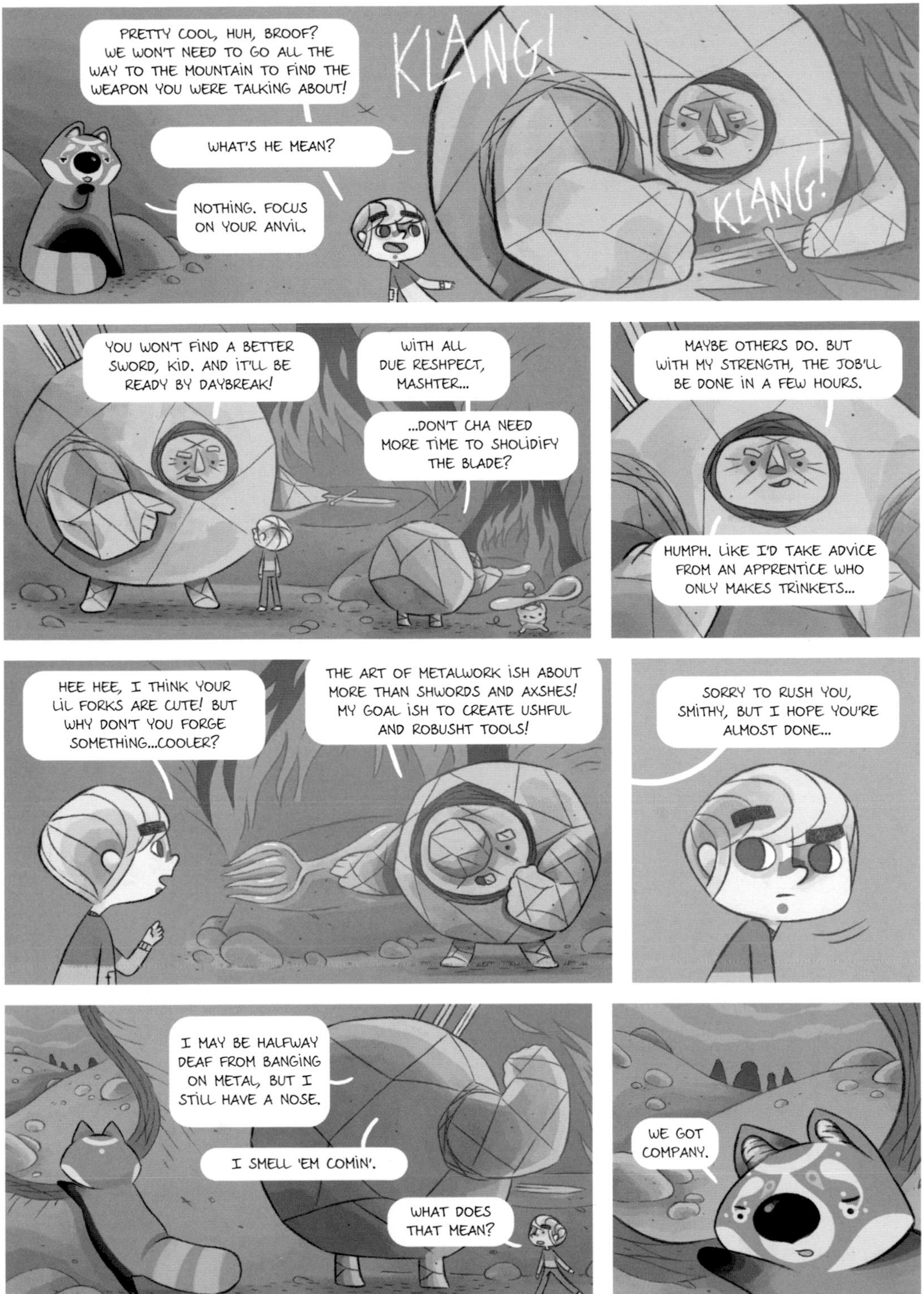
PRETTY COOL, HUH, BROOF? WE WON'T NEED TO GO ALL THE WAY TO THE MOUNTAIN TO FIND THE WEAPON YOU WERE TALKING ABOUT!
KLANG!
WHAT'S HE MEAN?
NOTHING. FOCUS ON YOUR ANVIL.
KLANG!
YOU WON'T FIND A BETTER SWORD, KID. AND IT'LL BE READY BY DAYBREAK!
WITH ALL DUE RESHPECT, MASHTER...
...DON'T CHA NEED MORE TIME TO SHOLIDIFY THE BLADE?
MAYBE OTHERS DO. BUT WITH MY STRENGTH, THE JOB'LL BE DONE IN A FEW HOURS.
HUMPH. LIKE I'D TAKE ADVICE FROM AN APPRENTICE WHO ONLY MAKES TRINKETS...
HEE HEE, I THINK YOUR LIL FORKS ARE CUTE! BUT WHY DON'T YOU FORGE SOMETHING...COOLER?
THE ART OF METALWORK ISH ABOUT MORE THAN SHWORDS AND AXSHES! MY GOAL ISH TO CREATE USHFUL AND ROBUSHT TOOLS!
SORRY TO RUSH YOU, SMITHY, BUT I HOPE YOU'RE ALMOST DONE...
I MAY BE HALFWAY DEAF FROM BANGING ON METAL, BUT I STILL HAVE A NOSE.
I SMELL 'EM COMIN'.
WHAT DOES THAT MEAN?
WE GOT COMPANY.

THE SHADOWS? NO WAY!!

THAT'S WHY I WANTED YOU TO CLEAR OUT!

I THOUGHT THOSE MANIACS MIGHT BE AFTER YOU.

NEVER SHEEN THE MASHTER SHO NERVOUSH.

WHAT ARE WE GONNA DO?

WILL YOU FINISH IN TIME?

I'M GONNA TRY...

KLANG!

KLANG!

KLANG!

KLANG!

KLANG!

KLANG!

KLANG!

KLANG!

KLANG!

KLANG!

GIVE 'EM UP!

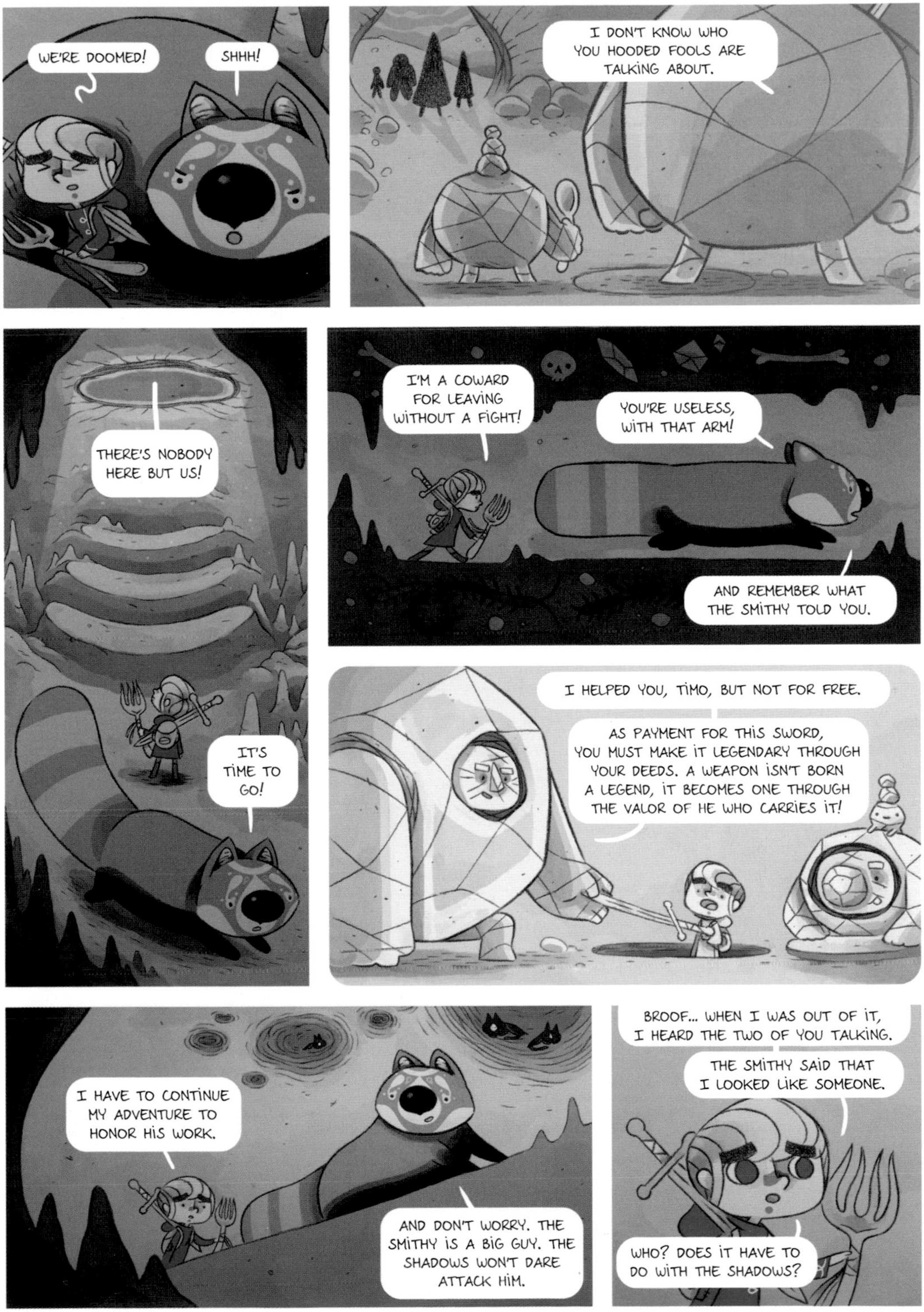

WE'RE DOOMED!
SHHH!
I DON'T KNOW WHO YOU HOODED FOOLS ARE TALKING ABOUT.
THERE'S NOBODY HERE BUT US!
IT'S TIME TO GO!
I'M A COWARD FOR LEAVING WITHOUT A FIGHT!
YOU'RE USELESS, WITH THAT ARM!
AND REMEMBER WHAT THE SMITHY TOLD YOU.
I HELPED YOU, TIMO, BUT NOT FOR FREE.
AS PAYMENT FOR THIS SWORD, YOU MUST MAKE IT LEGENDARY THROUGH YOUR DEEDS. A WEAPON ISN'T BORN A LEGEND, IT BECOMES ONE THROUGH THE VALOR OF HE WHO CARRIES IT!
I HAVE TO CONTINUE MY ADVENTURE TO HONOR HIS WORK.
AND DON'T WORRY. THE SMITHY IS A BIG GUY. THE SHADOWS WON'T DARE ATTACK HIM.
BROOF... WHEN I WAS OUT OF IT, I HEARD THE TWO OF YOU TALKING.
THE SMITHY SAID THAT I LOOKED LIKE SOMEONE.
WHO? DOES IT HAVE TO DO WITH THE SHADOWS?

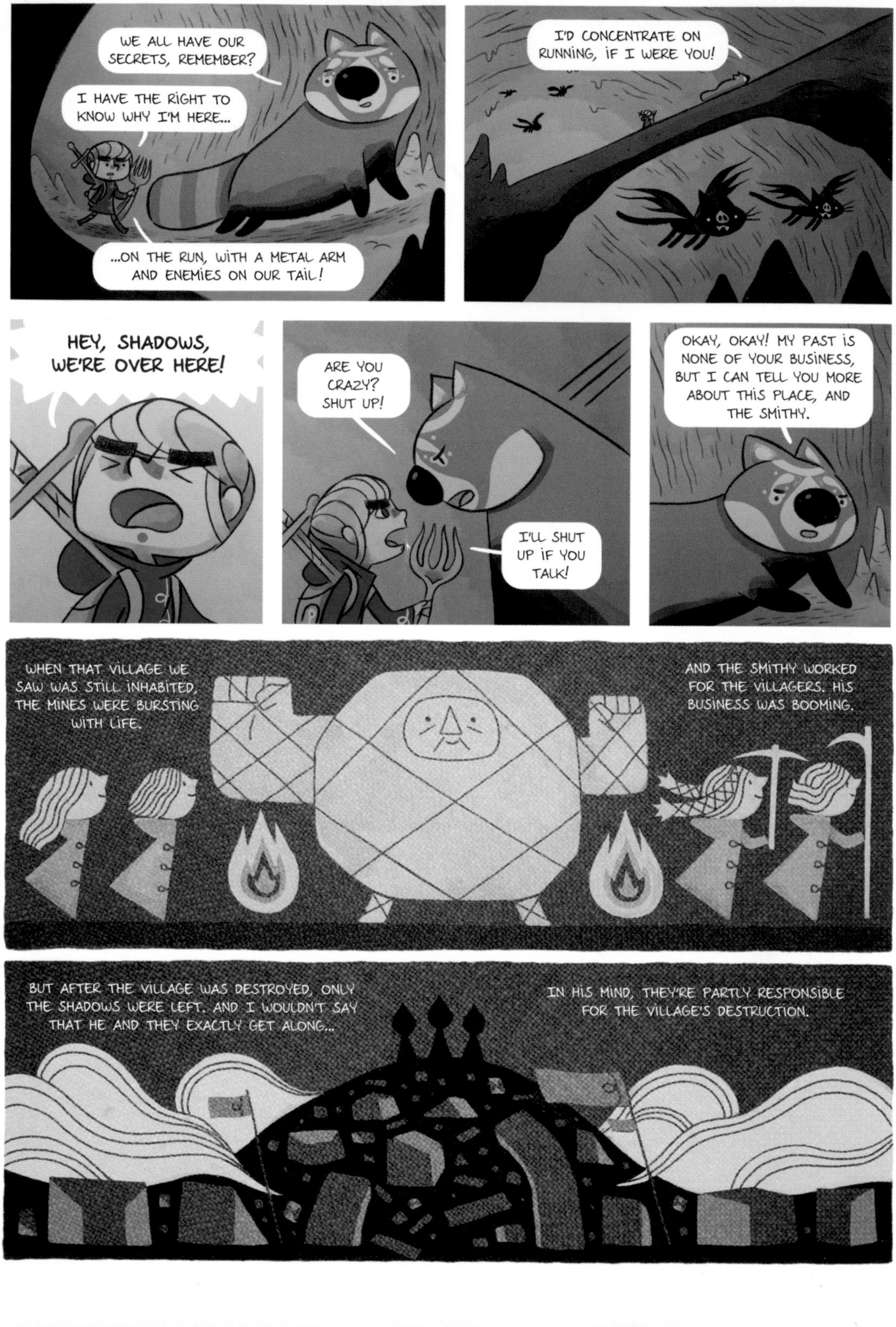
WE ALL HAVE OUR SECRETS, REMEMBER?
I HAVE THE RIGHT TO KNOW WHY I'M HERE...
...ON THE RUN, WITH A METAL ARM AND ENEMIES ON OUR TAIL!
I'D CONCENTRATE ON RUNNING, IF I WERE YOU!
HEY, SHADOWS, WE'RE OVER HERE!
ARE YOU CRAZY? SHUT UP!
I'LL SHUT UP IF YOU TALK!
OKAY, OKAY! MY PAST IS NONE OF YOUR BUSINESS, BUT I CAN TELL YOU MORE ABOUT THIS PLACE, AND THE SMITHY.
WHEN THAT VILLAGE WE SAW WAS STILL INHABITED, THE MINES WERE BURSTING WITH LIFE.
AND THE SMITHY WORKED FOR THE VILLAGERS. HIS BUSINESS WAS BOOMING.
BUT AFTER THE VILLAGE WAS DESTROYED, ONLY THE SHADOWS WERE LEFT. AND I WOULDN'T SAY THAT HE AND THEY EXACTLY GET ALONG...
IN HIS MIND, THEY'RE PARTLY RESPONSIBLE FOR THE VILLAGE'S DESTRUCTION.

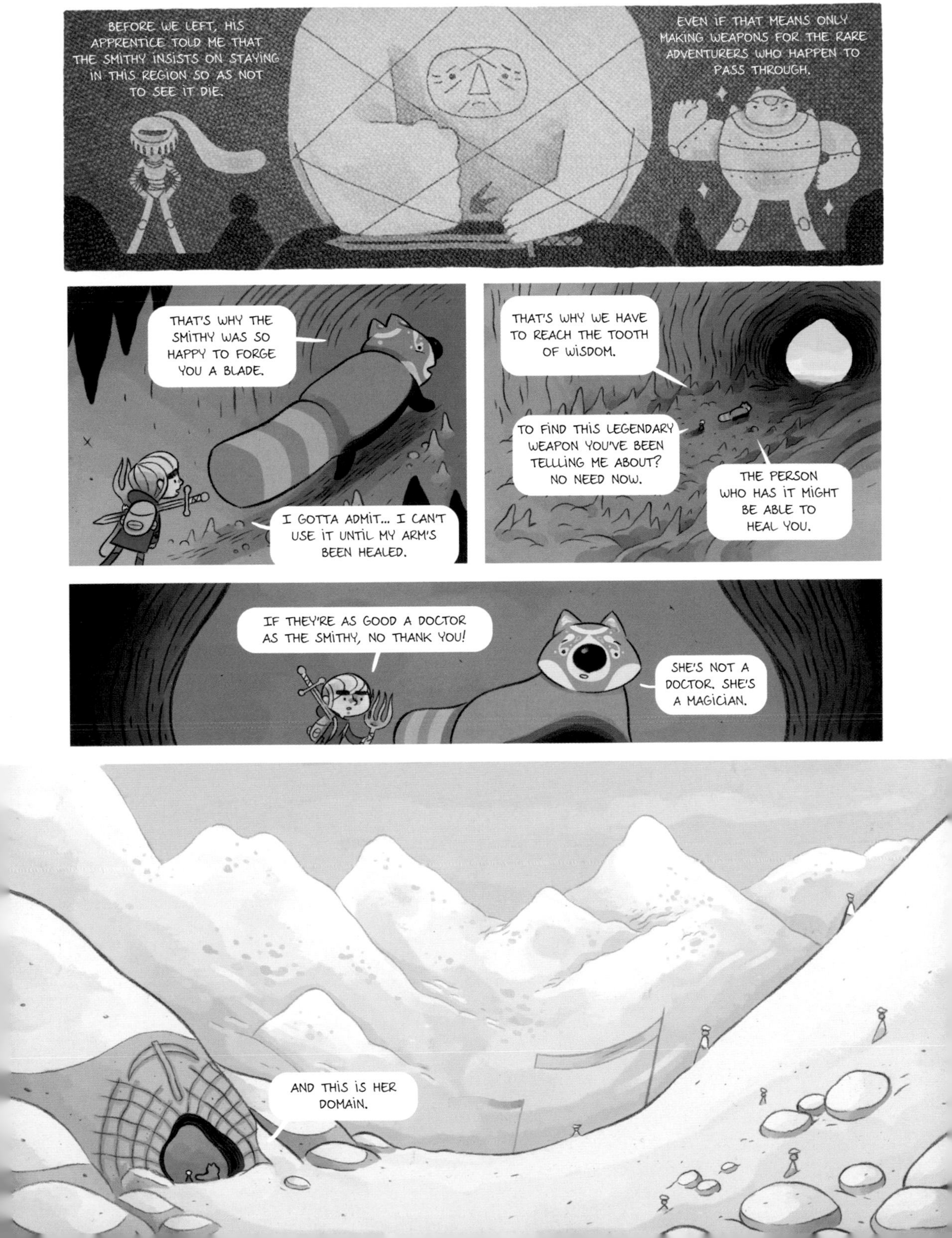
BEFORE WE LEFT, HIS APPRENTICE TOLD ME THAT THE SMITHY INSISTS ON STAYING IN THIS REGION SO AS NOT TO SEE IT DIE.
EVEN IF THAT MEANS ONLY MAKING WEAPONS FOR THE RARE ADVENTURERS WHO HAPPEN TO PASS THROUGH.
THAT'S WHY THE SMITHY WAS SO HAPPY TO FORGE YOU A BLADE.
I GOTTA ADMIT... I CAN'T USE IT UNTIL MY ARM'S BEEN HEALED.
THAT'S WHY WE HAVE TO REACH THE TOOTH OF WISDOM.
TO FIND THIS LEGENDARY WEAPON YOU'VE BEEN TELLING ME ABOUT? NO NEED NOW.
THE PERSON WHO HAS IT MIGHT BE ABLE TO HEAL YOU.
IF THEY'RE AS GOOD A DOCTOR AS THE SMITHY, NO THANK YOU!
SHE'S NOT A DOCTOR. SHE'S A MAGICIAN.
AND THIS IS HER DOMAIN.

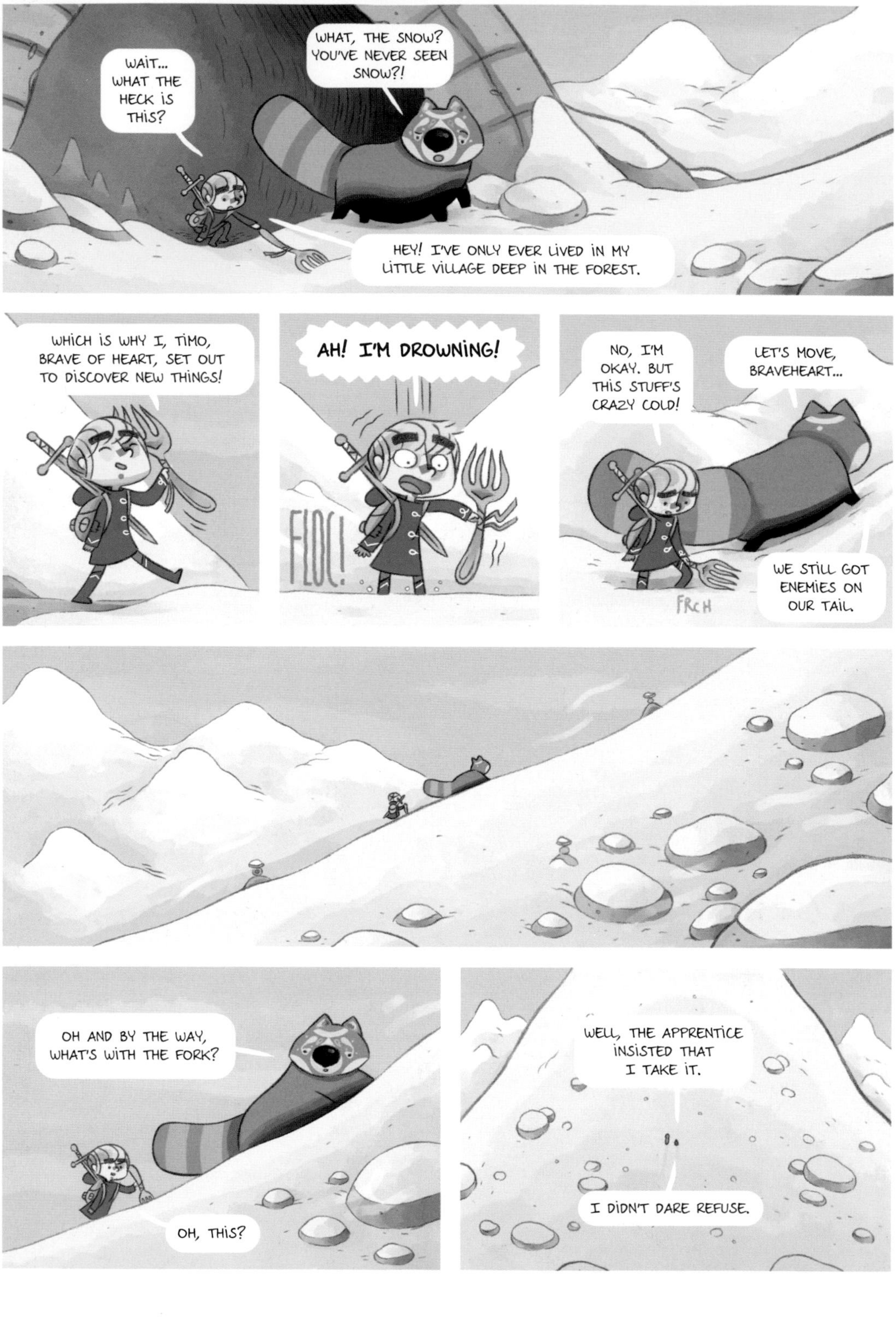
WAIT... WHAT THE HECK IS THIS?
WHAT, THE SNOW? YOU'VE NEVER SEEN SNOW?!
HEY! I'VE ONLY EVER LIVED IN MY LITTLE VILLAGE DEEP IN THE FOREST.
WHICH IS WHY I, TIMO, BRAVE OF HEART, SET OUT TO DISCOVER NEW THINGS!
AH! I'M DROWNING!
FLOC!
NO, I'M OKAY. BUT THIS STUFF'S CRAZY COLD!
LET'S MOVE, BRAVEHEART...
WE STILL GOT ENEMIES ON OUR TAIL.
FRCH
OH AND BY THE WAY, WHAT'S WITH THE FORK?
OH, THIS?
WELL, THE APPRENTICE INSISTED THAT I TAKE IT.
I DIDN'T DARE REFUSE.

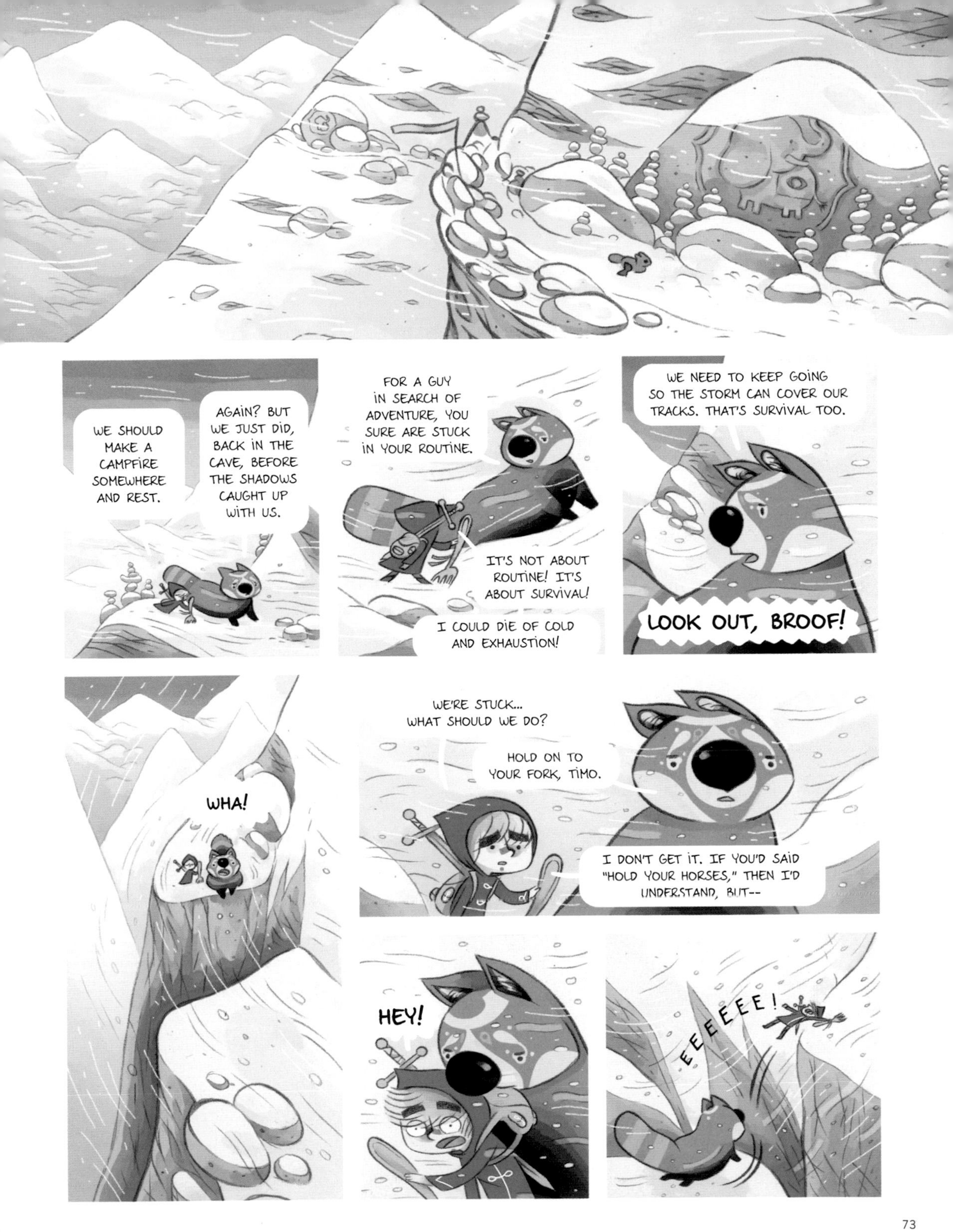
WE SHOULD MAKE A CAMPFIRE SOMEWHERE AND REST.
AGAIN? BUT WE JUST DID, BACK IN THE CAVE, BEFORE THE SHADOWS CAUGHT UP WITH US.
FOR A GUY IN SEARCH OF ADVENTURE, YOU SURE ARE STUCK IN YOUR ROUTINE.
IT'S NOT ABOUT ROUTINE! IT'S ABOUT SURVIVAL!
I COULD DIE OF COLD AND EXHAUSTION!
WE NEED TO KEEP GOING SO THE STORM CAN COVER OUR TRACKS. THAT'S SURVIVAL TOO.
LOOK OUT, BROOF!
WHA!
WE'RE STUCK... WHAT SHOULD WE DO?
HOLD ON TO YOUR FORK, TIMO.
I DON'T GET IT. IF YOU'D SAID "HOLD YOUR HORSES," THEN I'D UNDERSTAND, BUT--
HEY!
EEEEEE!

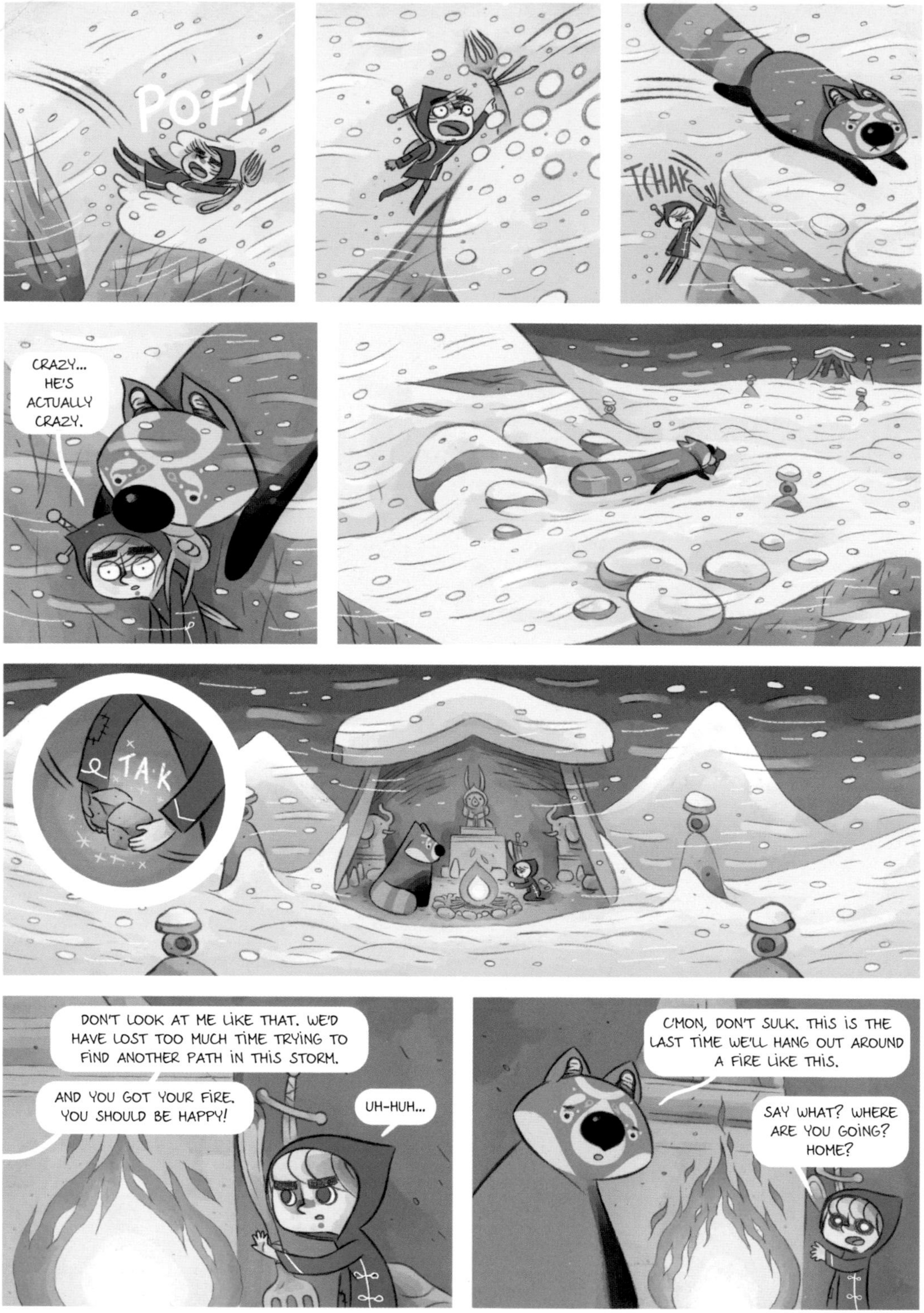
POF!
TCHAK
CRAZY... HE'S ACTUALLY CRAZY.
TAK
DON'T LOOK AT ME LIKE THAT. WE'D HAVE LOST TOO MUCH TIME TRYING TO FIND ANOTHER PATH IN THIS STORM.
AND YOU GOT YOUR FIRE. YOU SHOULD BE HAPPY!
UH-HUH...
C'MON, DON'T SULK. THIS IS THE LAST TIME WE'LL HANG OUT AROUND A FIRE LIKE THIS.
SAY WHAT? WHERE ARE YOU GOING? HOME?

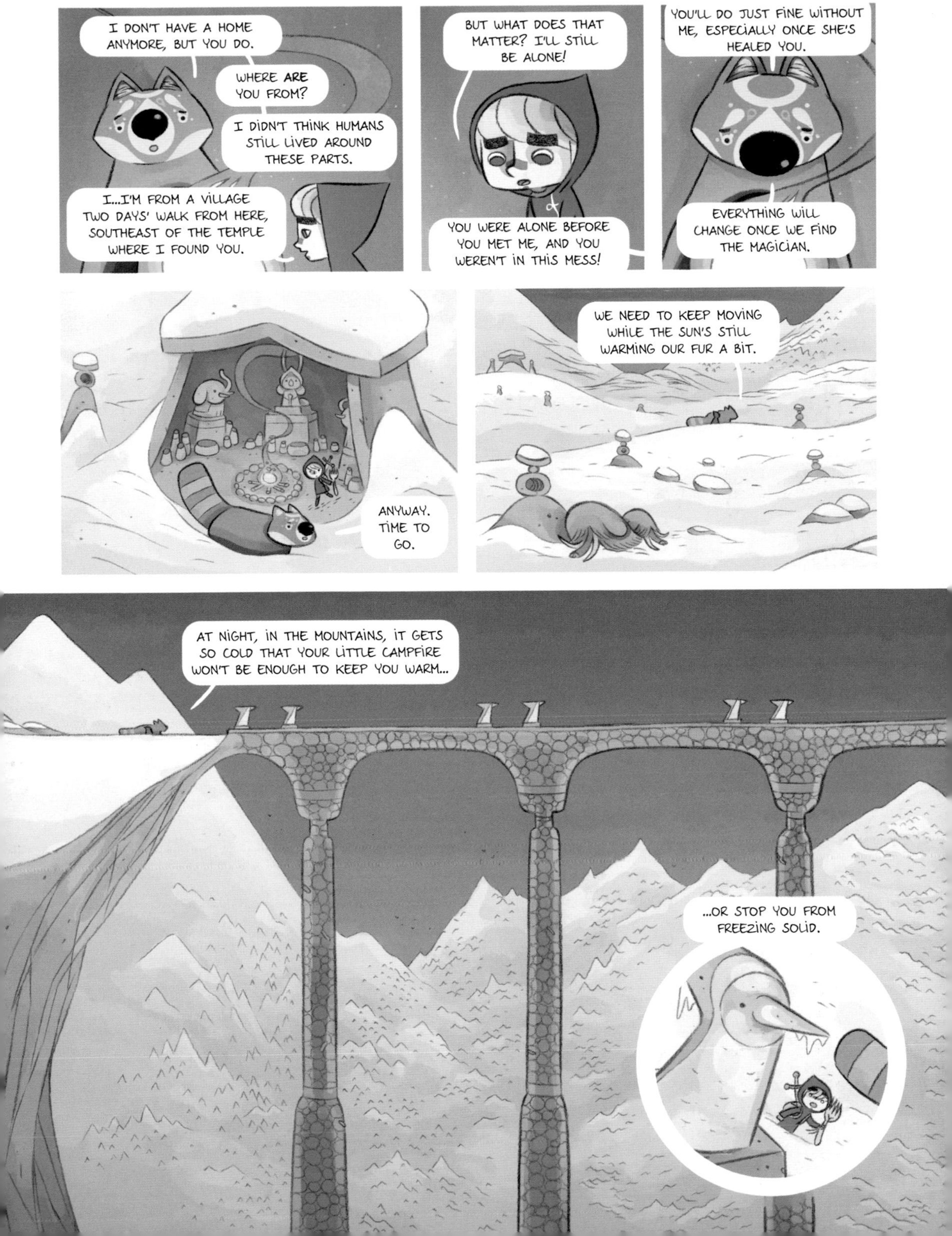
I DON'T HAVE A HOME ANYMORE, BUT YOU DO.
WHERE **ARE** YOU FROM?
I DIDN'T THINK HUMANS STILL LIVED AROUND THESE PARTS.
I...I'M FROM A VILLAGE TWO DAYS' WALK FROM HERE, SOUTHEAST OF THE TEMPLE WHERE I FOUND YOU.
BUT WHAT DOES THAT MATTER? I'LL STILL BE ALONE!
YOU WERE ALONE BEFORE YOU MET ME, AND YOU WEREN'T IN THIS MESS!
YOU'LL DO JUST FINE WITHOUT ME, ESPECIALLY ONCE SHE'S HEALED YOU.
EVERYTHING WILL CHANGE ONCE WE FIND THE MAGICIAN.
ANYWAY. TIME TO GO.
WE NEED TO KEEP MOVING WHILE THE SUN'S STILL WARMING OUR FUR A BIT.
AT NIGHT, IN THE MOUNTAINS, IT GETS SO COLD THAT YOUR LITTLE CAMPFIRE WON'T BE ENOUGH TO KEEP YOU WARM...
...OR STOP YOU FROM FREEZING SOLID.

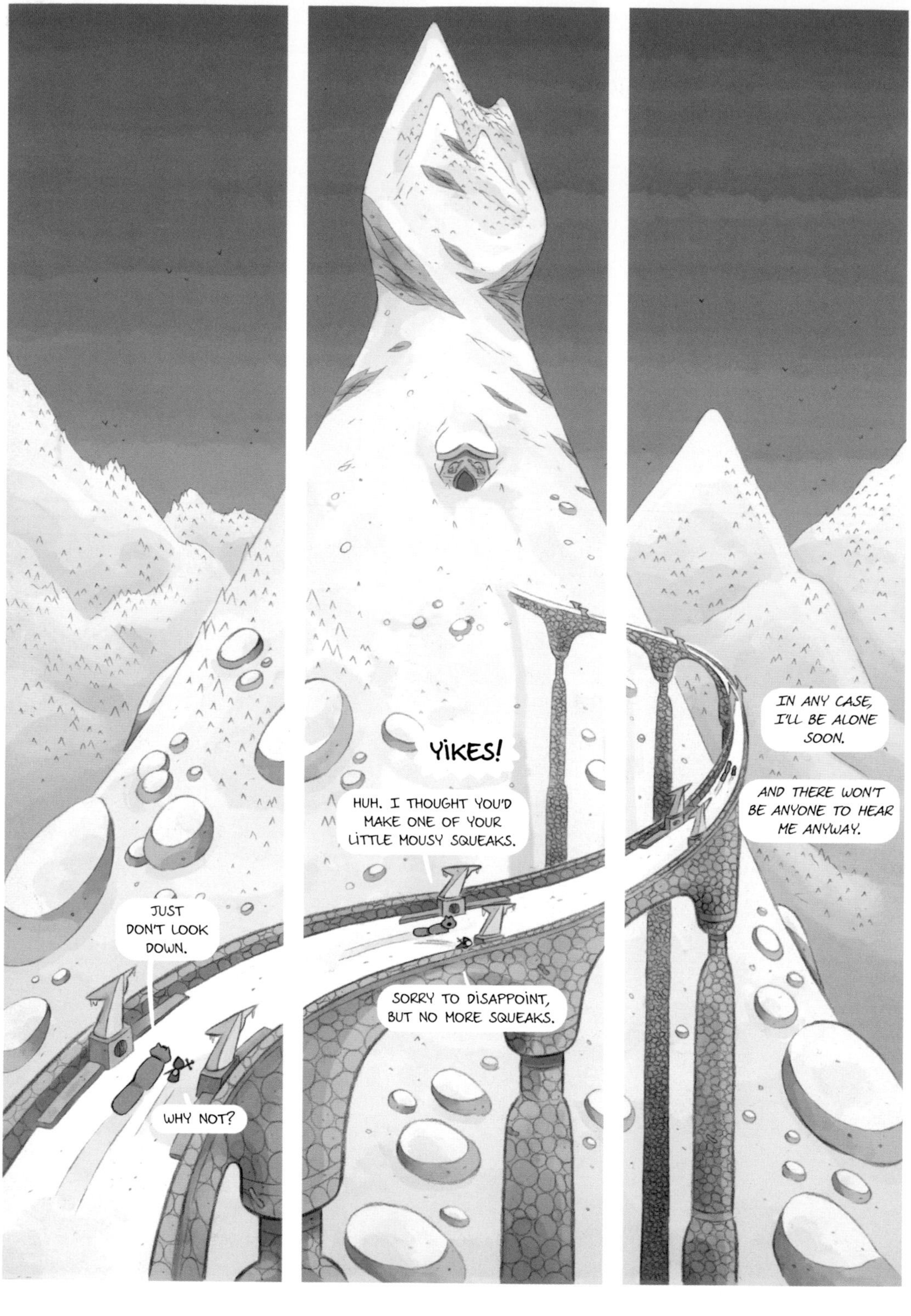
JUST DON'T LOOK DOWN.
WHY NOT?
YIKES!
HUH. I THOUGHT YOU'D MAKE ONE OF YOUR LITTLE MOUSY SQUEAKS.
SORRY TO DISAPPOINT, BUT NO MORE SQUEAKS.
IN ANY CASE, I'LL BE ALONE SOON.
AND THERE WON'T BE ANYONE TO HEAR ME ANYWAY.

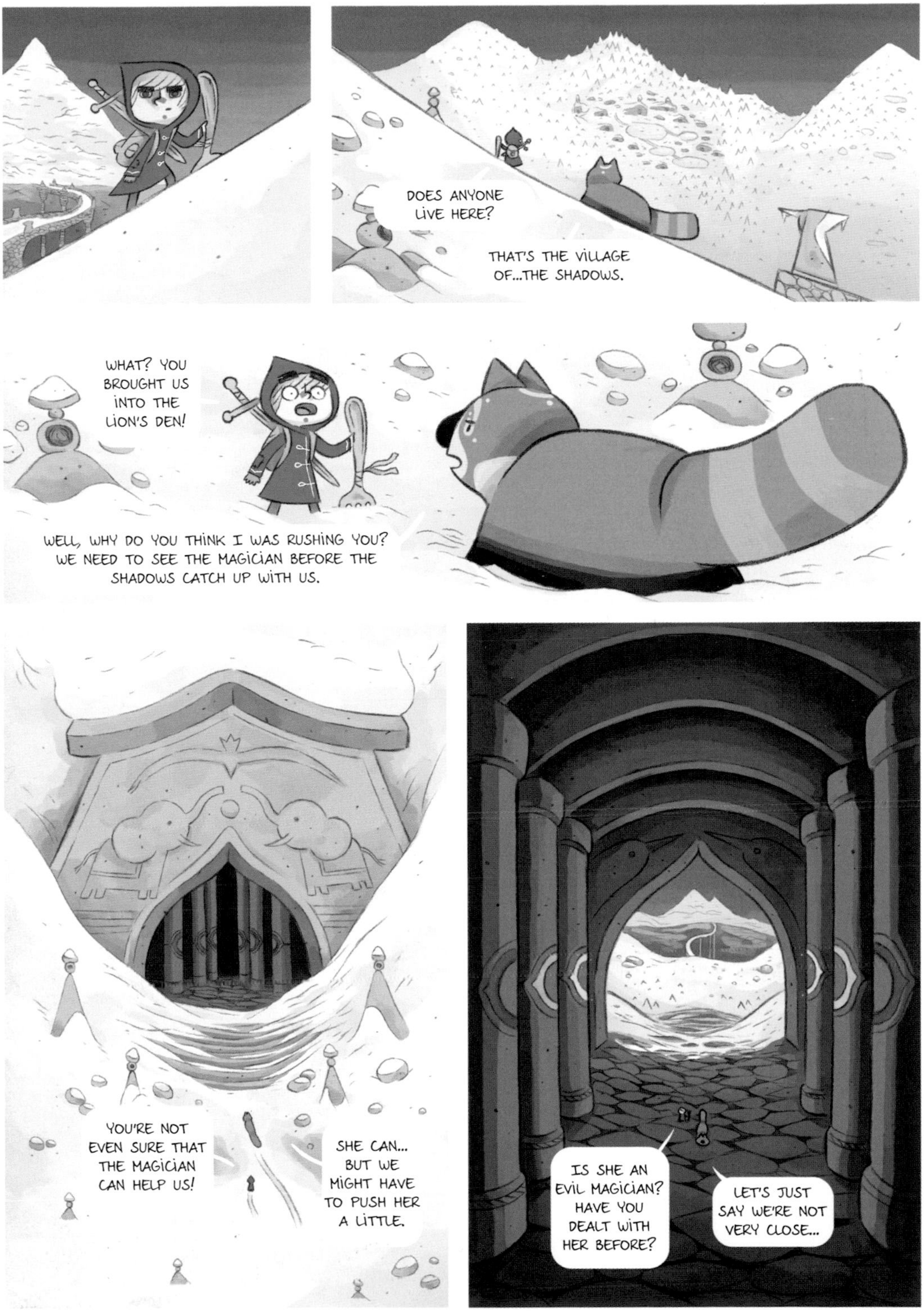
DOES ANYONE LIVE HERE?
THAT'S THE VILLAGE OF...THE SHADOWS.
WHAT? YOU BROUGHT US INTO THE LION'S DEN!
WELL, WHY DO YOU THINK I WAS RUSHING YOU? WE NEED TO SEE THE MAGICIAN BEFORE THE SHADOWS CATCH UP WITH US.
YOU'RE NOT EVEN SURE THAT THE MAGICIAN CAN HELP US!
SHE CAN... BUT WE MIGHT HAVE TO PUSH HER A LITTLE.
IS SHE AN EVIL MAGICIAN? HAVE YOU DEALT WITH HER BEFORE?
LET'S JUST SAY WE'RE NOT VERY CLOSE...

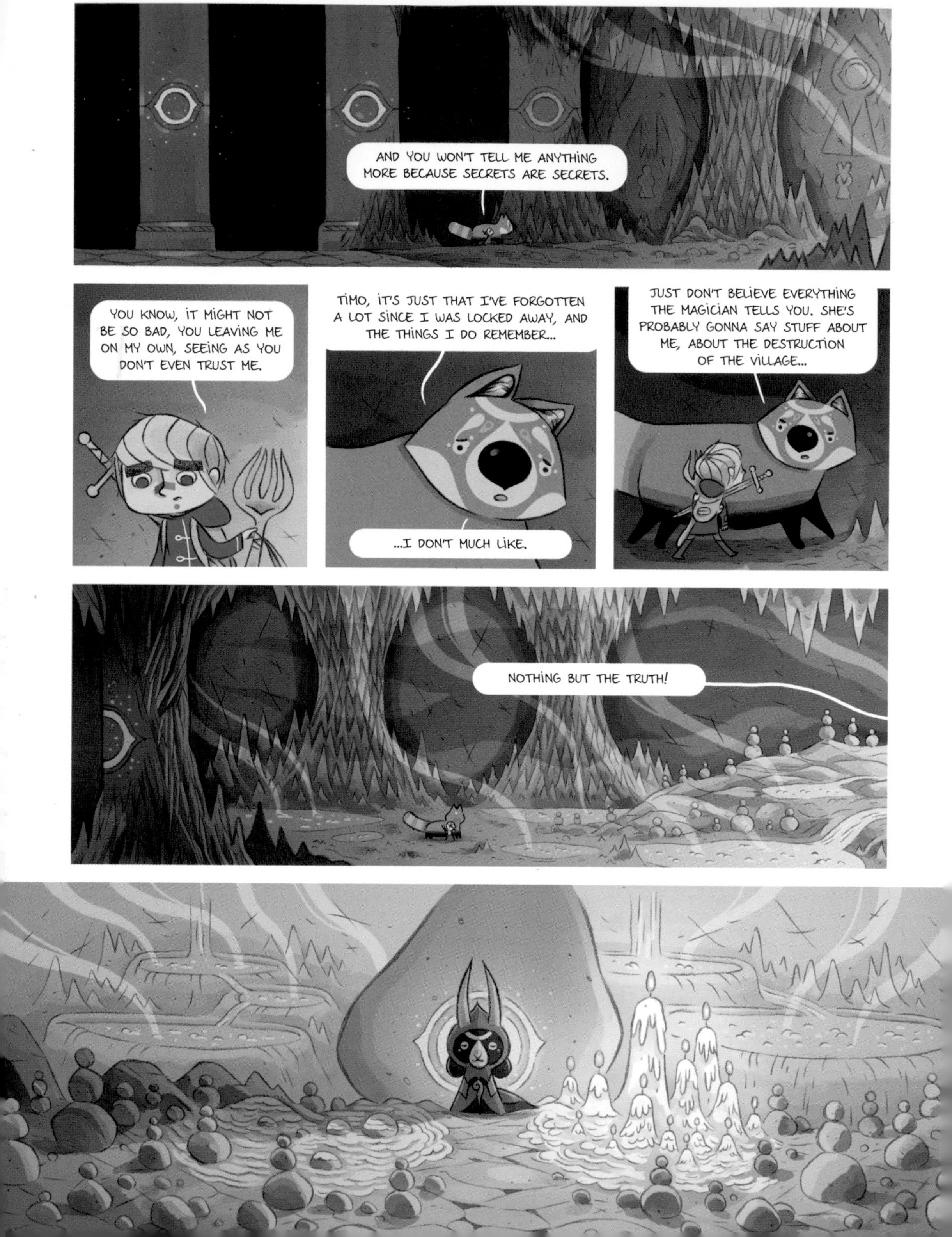

AND YOU WON'T TELL ME ANYTHING MORE BECAUSE SECRETS ARE SECRETS.
YOU KNOW, IT MIGHT NOT BE SO BAD, YOU LEAVING ME ON MY OWN, SEEING AS YOU DON'T EVEN TRUST ME.
TIMO, IT'S JUST THAT I'VE FORGOTTEN A LOT SINCE I WAS LOCKED AWAY, AND THE THINGS I DO REMEMBER...
...I DON'T MUCH LIKE.
JUST DON'T BELIEVE EVERYTHING THE MAGICIAN TELLS YOU. SHE'S PROBABLY GONNA SAY STUFF ABOUT ME, ABOUT THE DESTRUCTION OF THE VILLAGE...
NOTHING BUT THE TRUTH!

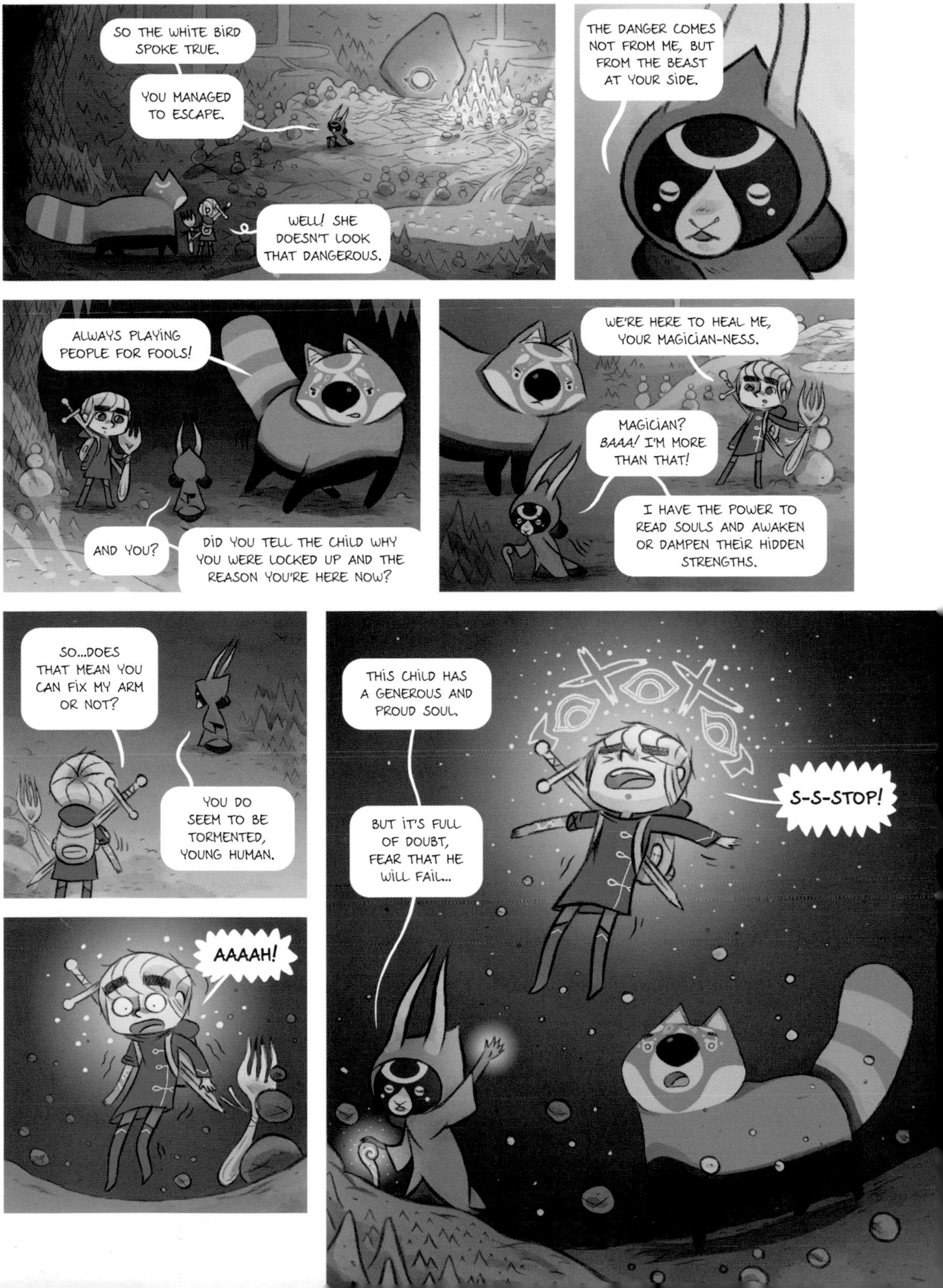
SO THE WHITE BIRD SPOKE TRUE.
YOU MANAGED TO ESCAPE.
WELL! SHE DOESN'T LOOK THAT DANGEROUS.
THE DANGER COMES NOT FROM ME, BUT FROM THE BEAST AT YOUR SIDE.
ALWAYS PLAYING PEOPLE FOR FOOLS!
AND YOU?
DID YOU TELL THE CHILD WHY YOU WERE LOCKED UP AND THE REASON YOU'RE HERE NOW?
WE'RE HERE TO HEAL ME, YOUR MAGICIAN-NESS.
MAGICIAN? *BAAA!* I'M MORE THAN THAT!
I HAVE THE POWER TO READ SOULS AND AWAKEN OR DAMPEN THEIR HIDDEN STRENGTHS.
SO...DOES THAT MEAN YOU CAN FIX MY ARM OR NOT?
YOU DO SEEM TO BE TORMENTED, YOUNG HUMAN.
AAAAH!
THIS CHILD HAS A GENEROUS AND PROUD SOUL.
BUT IT'S FULL OF DOUBT, FEAR THAT HE WILL FAIL...
S-S-STOP!

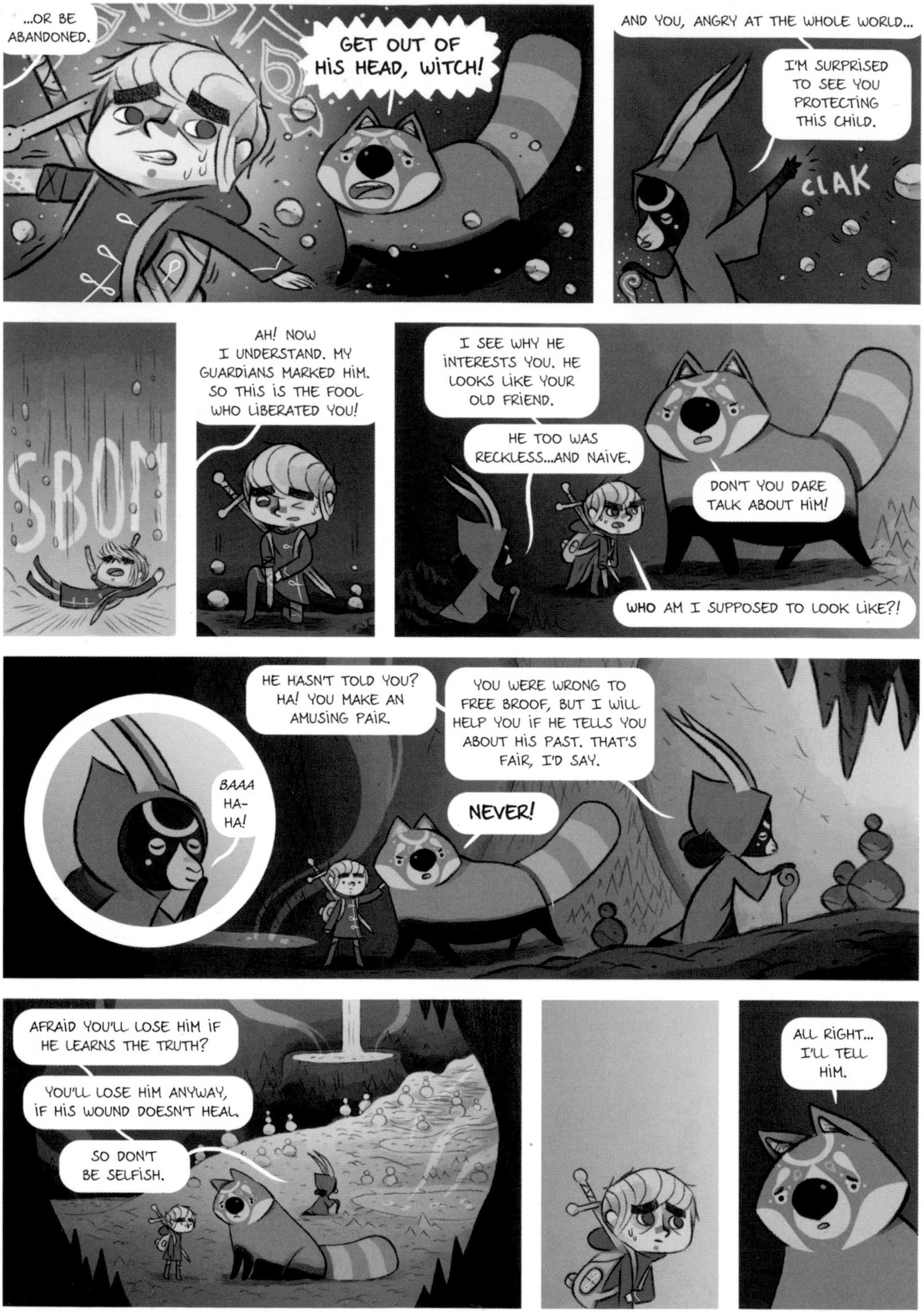

...OR BE ABANDONED.
GET OUT OF HIS HEAD, WITCH!
AND YOU, ANGRY AT THE WHOLE WORLD...
I'M SURPRISED TO SEE YOU PROTECTING THIS CHILD.
CLAK
SBOM
AH! NOW I UNDERSTAND. MY GUARDIANS MARKED HIM. SO THIS IS THE FOOL WHO LIBERATED YOU!
I SEE WHY HE INTERESTS YOU. HE LOOKS LIKE YOUR OLD FRIEND.
HE TOO WAS RECKLESS...AND NAIVE.
DON'T YOU DARE TALK ABOUT HIM!
WHO AM I SUPPOSED TO LOOK LIKE?!
BAAA HA- HA!
HE HASN'T TOLD YOU? HA! YOU MAKE AN AMUSING PAIR.
YOU WERE WRONG TO FREE BROOF, BUT I WILL HELP YOU IF HE TELLS YOU ABOUT HIS PAST. THAT'S FAIR, I'D SAY.
NEVER!
AFRAID YOU'LL LOSE HIM IF HE LEARNS THE TRUTH?
YOU'LL LOSE HIM ANYWAY, IF HIS WOUND DOESN'T HEAL.
SO DON'T BE SELFISH.
ALL RIGHT... I'LL TELL HIM.

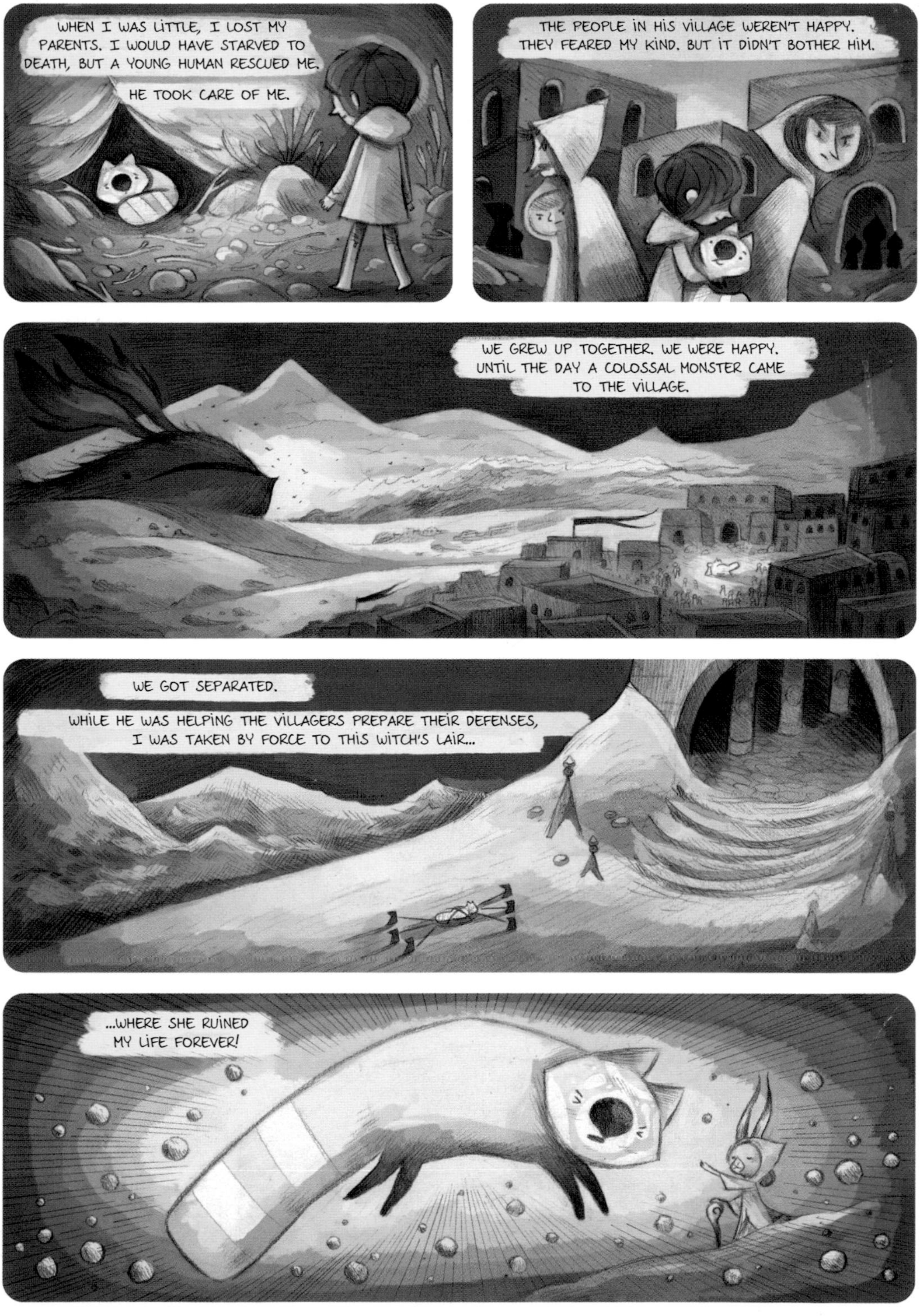
WHEN I WAS LITTLE, I LOST MY PARENTS. I WOULD HAVE STARVED TO DEATH, BUT A YOUNG HUMAN RESCUED ME.
HE TOOK CARE OF ME.
THE PEOPLE IN HIS VILLAGE WEREN'T HAPPY. THEY FEARED MY KIND. BUT IT DIDN'T BOTHER HIM.
WE GREW UP TOGETHER. WE WERE HAPPY. UNTIL THE DAY A COLOSSAL MONSTER CAME TO THE VILLAGE.
WE GOT SEPARATED.
WHILE HE WAS HELPING THE VILLAGERS PREPARE THEIR DEFENSES, I WAS TAKEN BY FORCE TO THIS WITCH'S LAIR...
...WHERE SHE RUINED MY LIFE FOREVER!

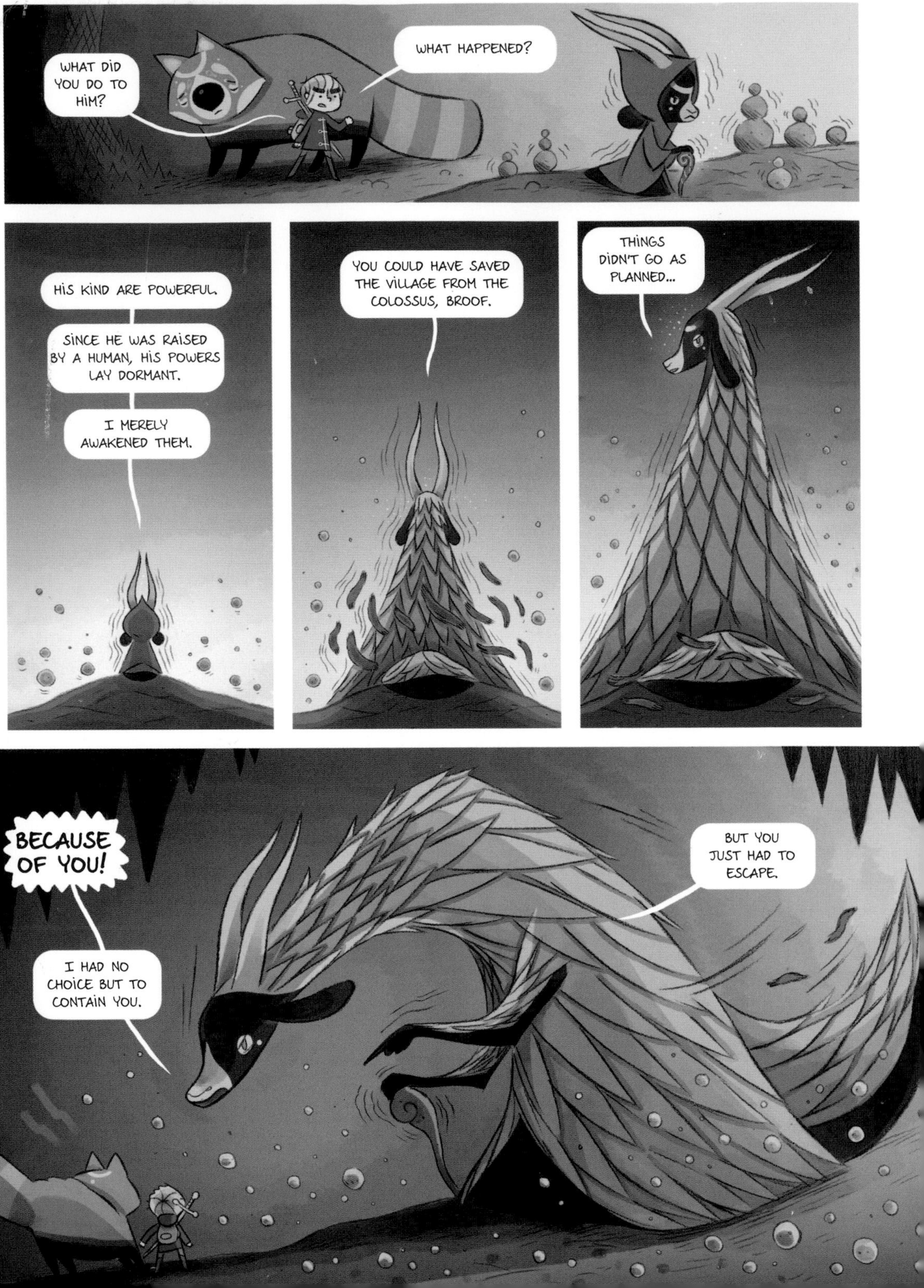
WHAT DID YOU DO TO HIM?
WHAT HAPPENED?
HIS KIND ARE POWERFUL.
SINCE HE WAS RAISED BY A HUMAN, HIS POWERS LAY DORMANT.
I MERELY AWAKENED THEM.
YOU COULD HAVE SAVED THE VILLAGE FROM THE COLOSSUS, BROOF.
THINGS DIDN'T GO AS PLANNED...
BECAUSE OF YOU!
BUT YOU JUST HAD TO ESCAPE.
I HAD NO CHOICE BUT TO CONTAIN YOU.

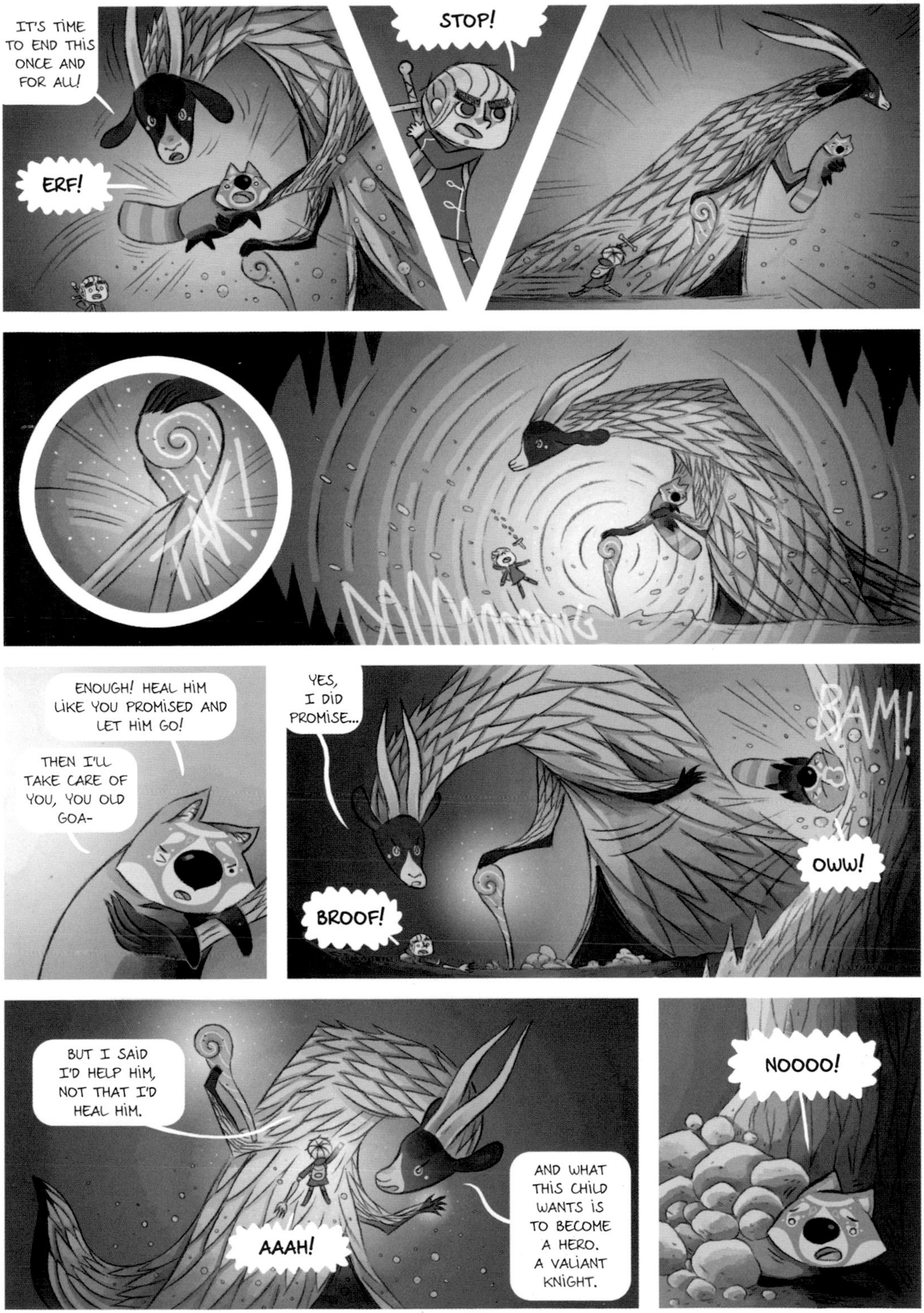
IT'S TIME TO END THIS ONCE AND FOR ALL!
ERF!
STOP!
TAK!
DOOOOOONG
ENOUGH! HEAL HIM LIKE YOU PROMISED AND LET HIM GO!
THEN I'LL TAKE CARE OF YOU, YOU OLD GOA-
YES, I DID PROMISE...
BAM!
OWW!
BROOF!
BUT I SAID I'D HELP HIM, NOT THAT I'D HEAL HIM.
AAAH!
AND WHAT THIS CHILD WANTS IS TO BECOME A HERO. A VALIANT KNIGHT.
NOOOO!

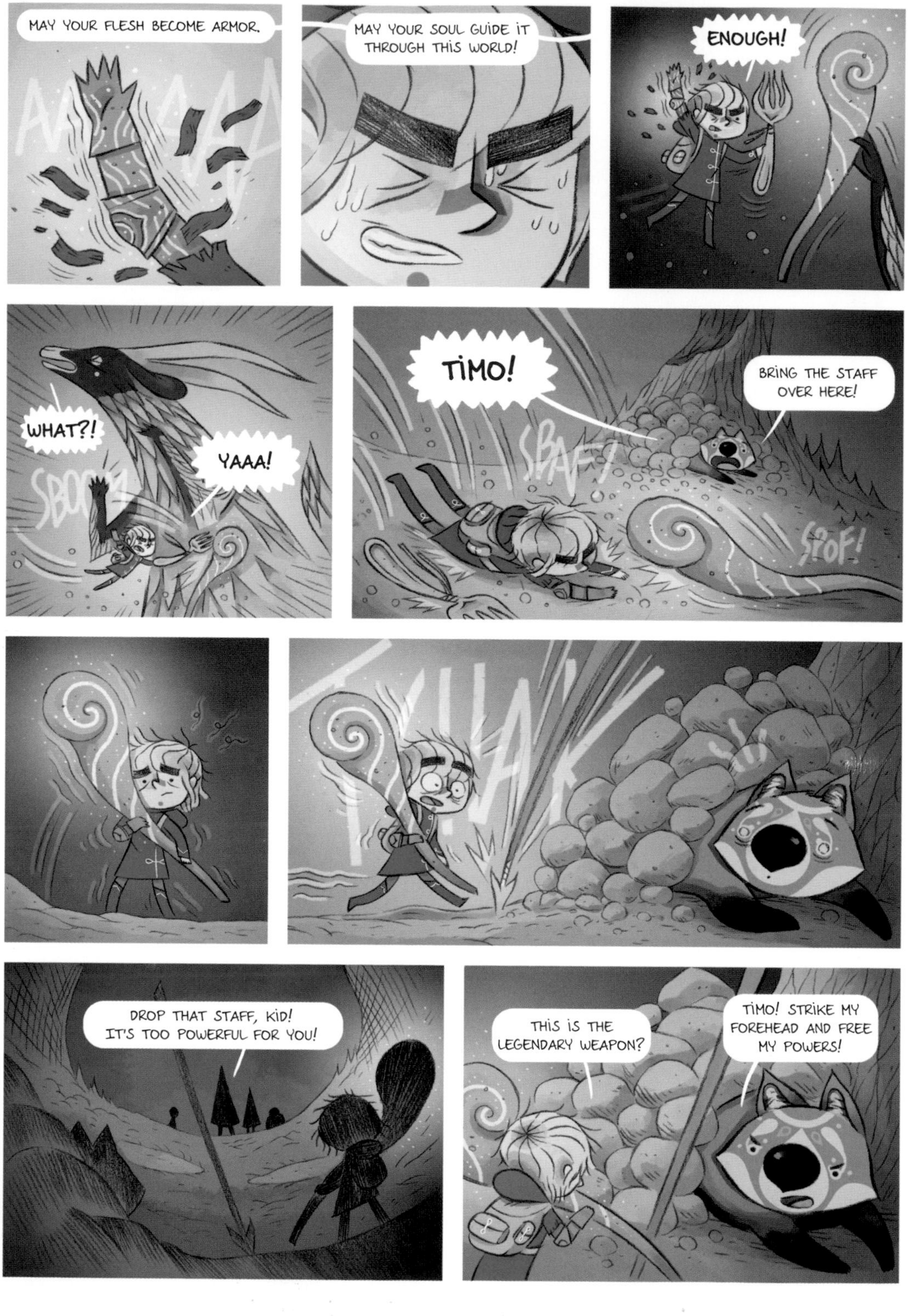
MAY YOUR FLESH BECOME ARMOR.
MAY YOUR SOUL GUIDE IT THROUGH THIS WORLD!
ENOUGH!
WHAT?!
YAAA!
SBOOM
TIMO!
BRING THE STAFF OVER HERE!
SBAF!
SPOF!
DROP THAT STAFF, KID! IT'S TOO POWERFUL FOR YOU!
THIS IS THE LEGENDARY WEAPON?
TIMO! STRIKE MY FOREHEAD AND FREE MY POWERS!

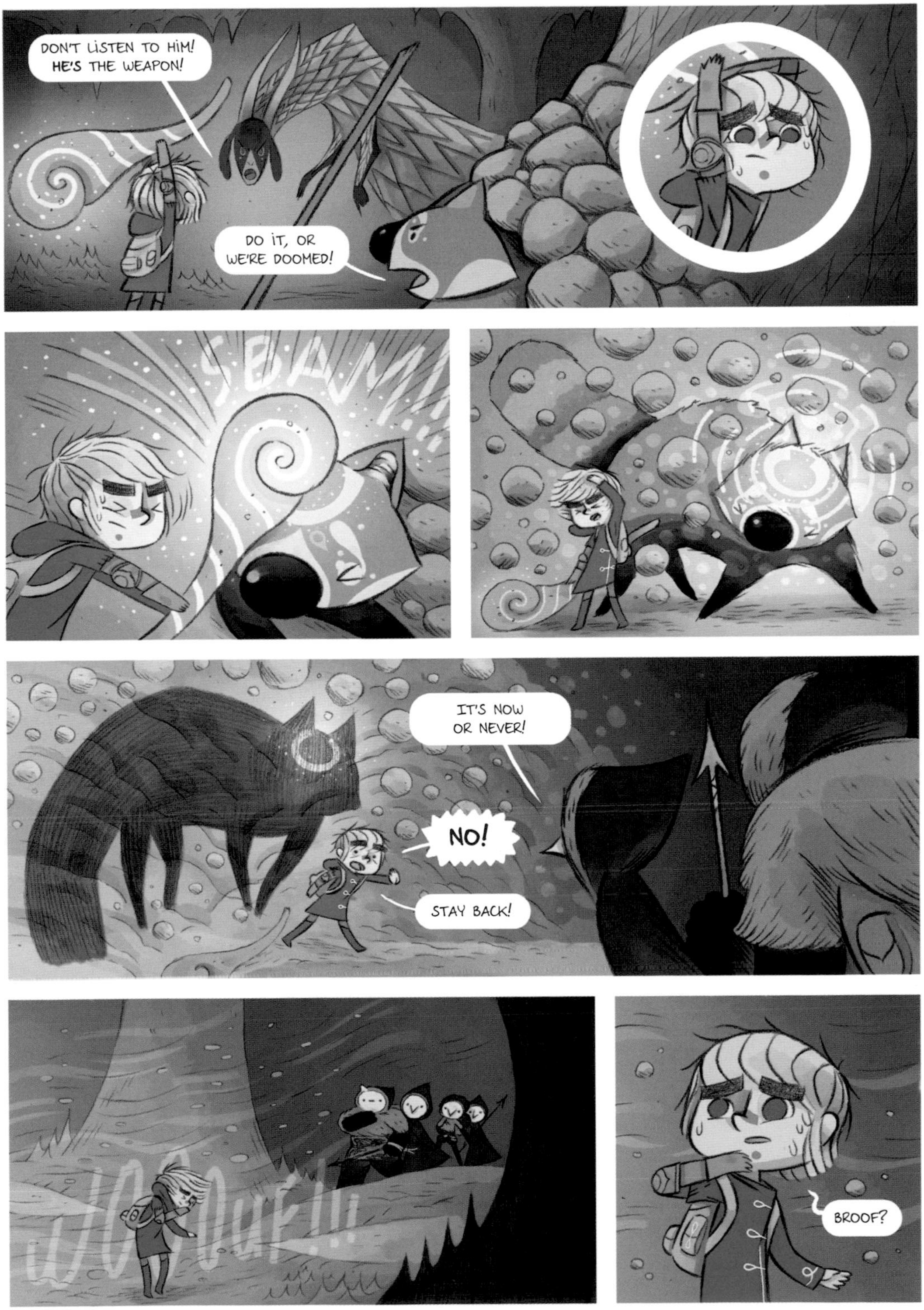
DON'T LISTEN TO HIM! HE'S THE WEAPON!
DO IT, OR WE'RE DOOMED!
SBAM!!
IT'S NOW OR NEVER!
NO!
STAY BACK!
WOOOUF!!
BROOF?

YOU THINK YOU CAN CONTROL ALL THAT POWER?!

I HAD TIME TO PREPARE WHILE I WAS YOUR PRISONER!

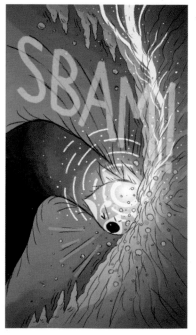

SBAM

NOW IT'S YOUR TURN TO BE IMPRISONED UNDERGROUND!

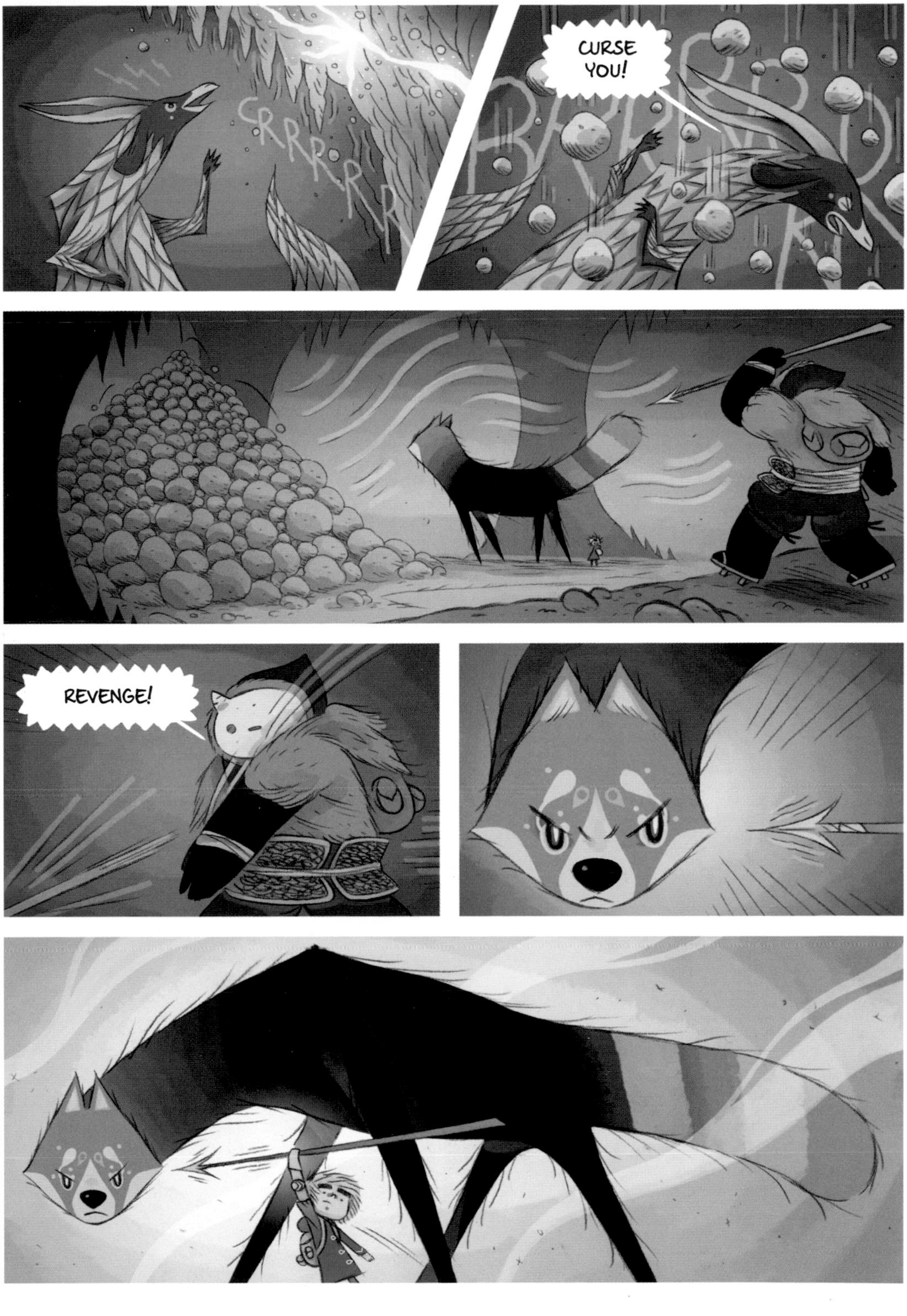
CRRRRRRR
CURSE YOU!
REVENGE!

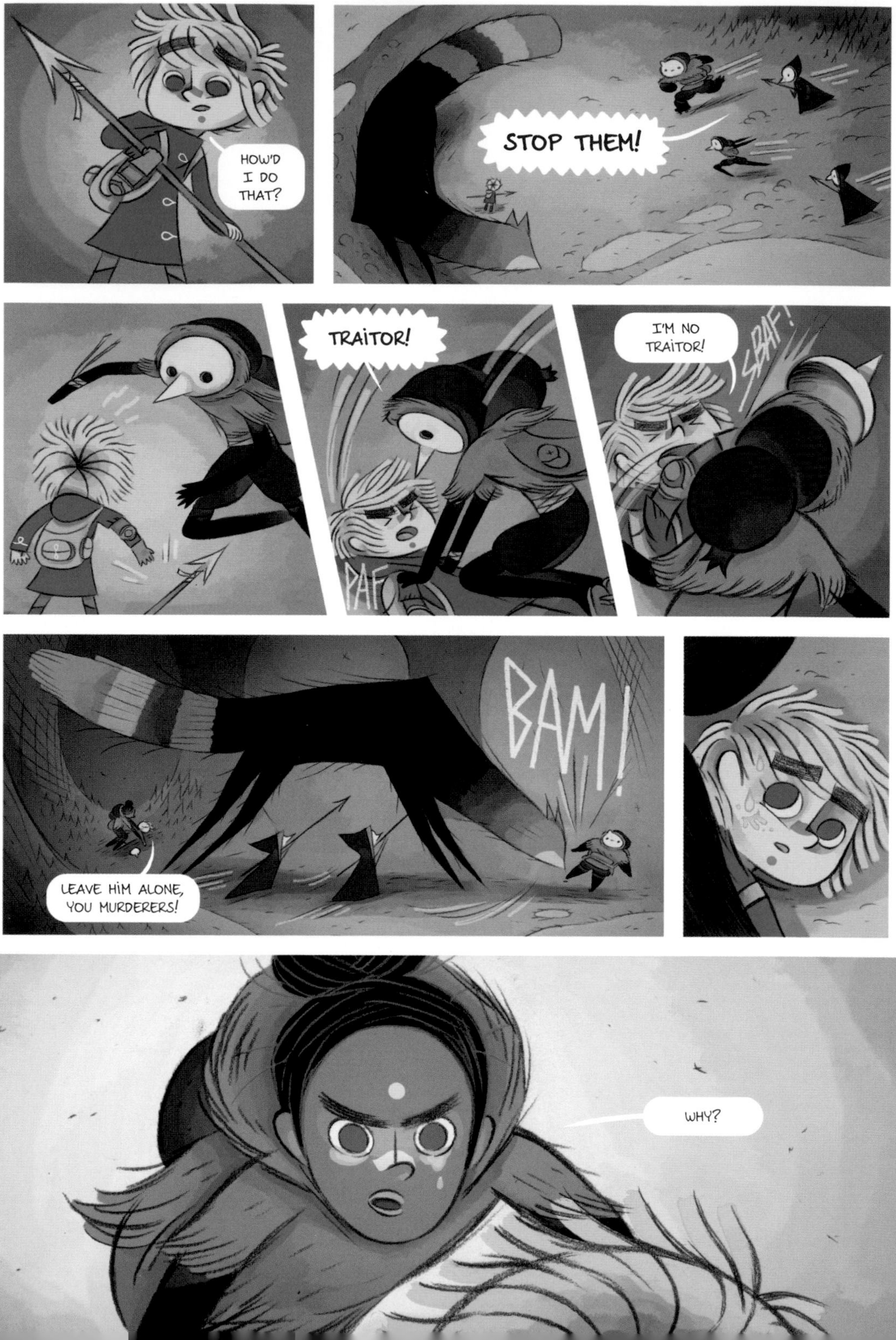
HOW'D I DO THAT?
STOP THEM!
TRAITOR!
PAF
I'M NO TRAITOR!
SBAF!
BAM!
LEAVE HIM ALONE, YOU MURDERERS!
WHY?

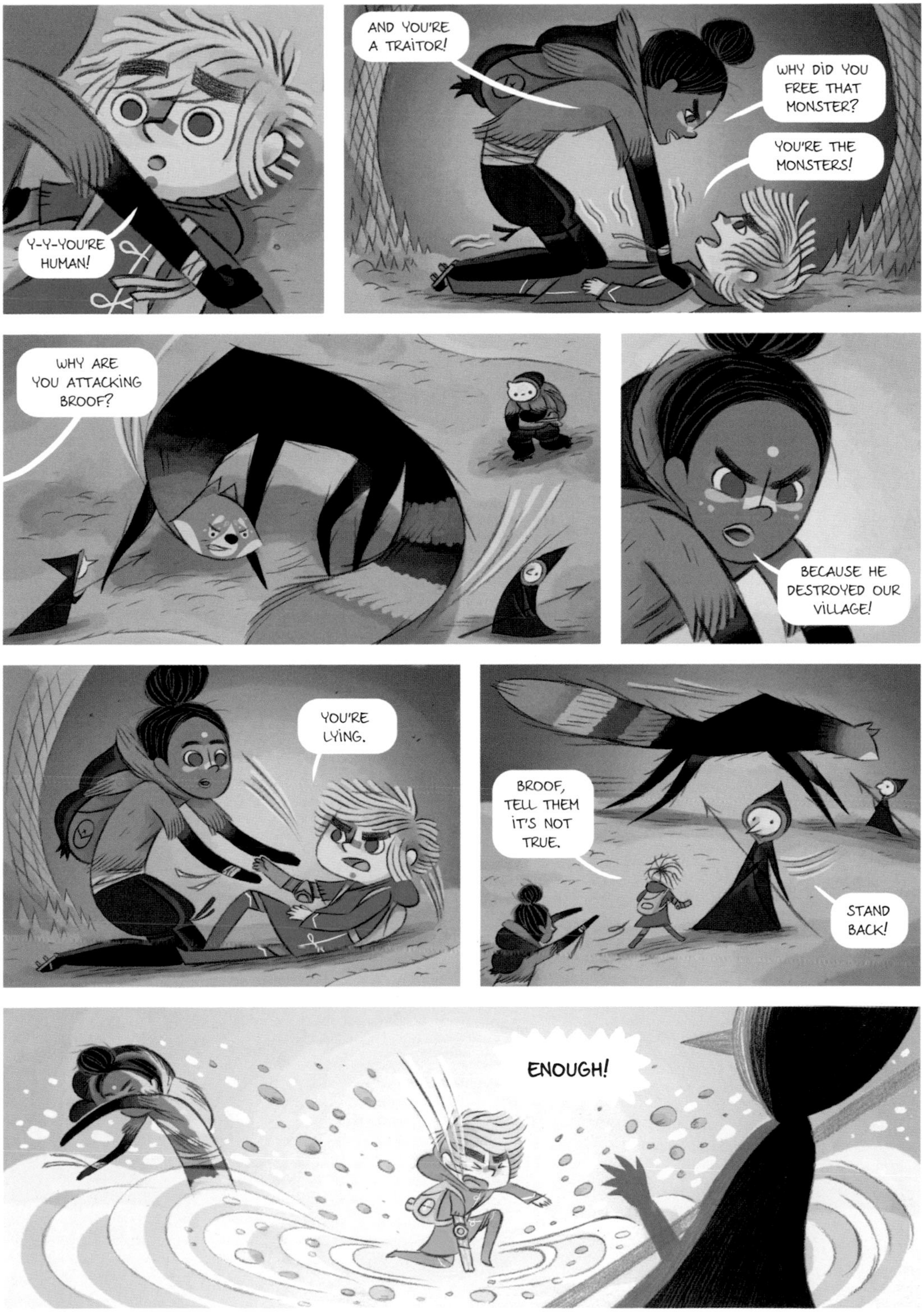

Y-Y-YOU'RE HUMAN!
AND YOU'RE A TRAITOR!
WHY DID YOU FREE THAT MONSTER?
YOU'RE THE MONSTERS!
WHY ARE YOU ATTACKING BROOF?
BECAUSE HE DESTROYED OUR VILLAGE!
YOU'RE LYING.
BROOF, TELL THEM IT'S NOT TRUE.
STAND BACK!
ENOUGH!

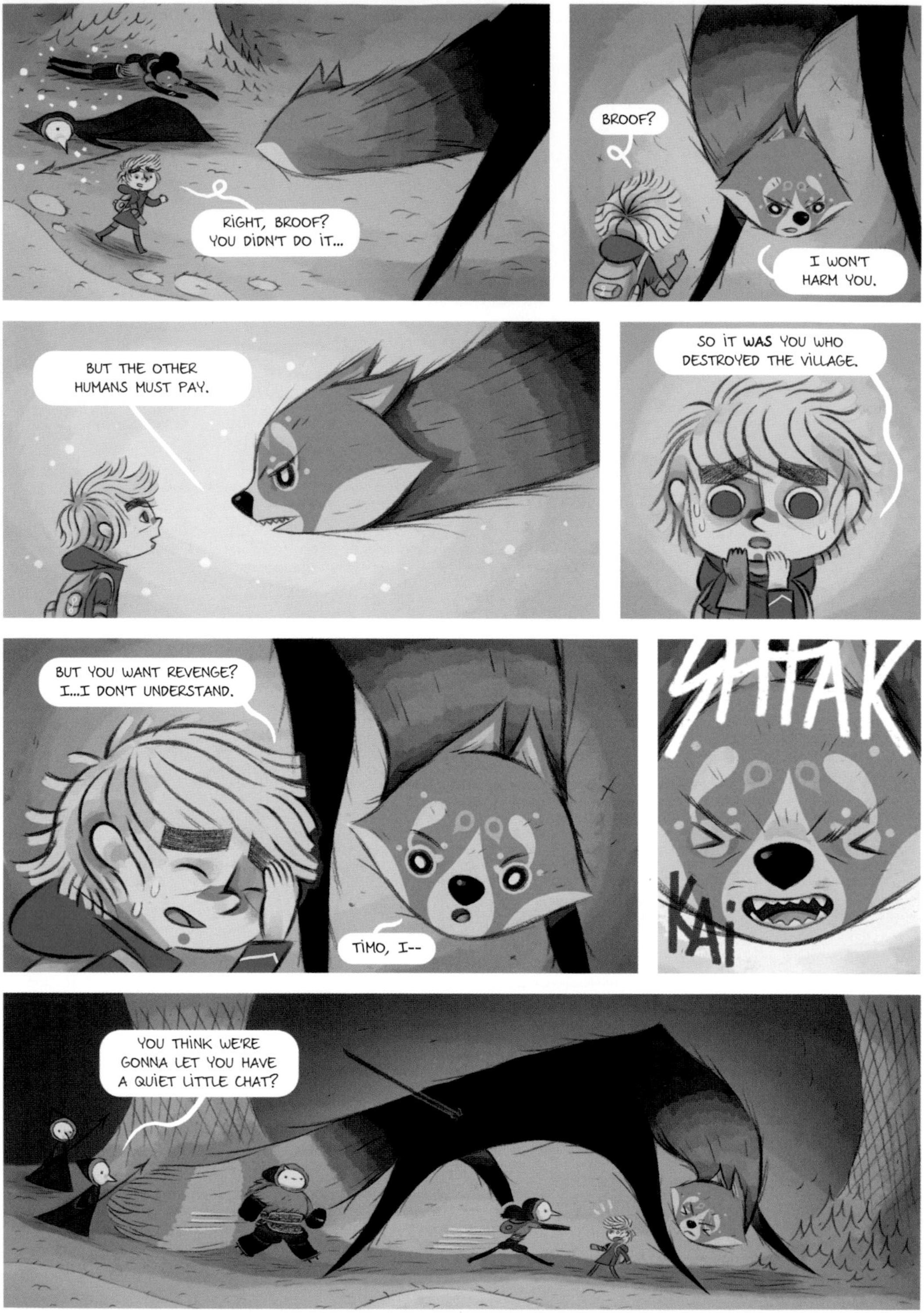
RIGHT, BROOF? YOU DIDN'T DO IT...
BROOF?
I WON'T HARM YOU.
BUT THE OTHER HUMANS MUST PAY.
SO IT **WAS** YOU WHO DESTROYED THE VILLAGE.
BUT YOU WANT REVENGE? I...I DON'T UNDERSTAND.
TIMO, I--
SHTAK
KAI
YOU THINK WE'RE GONNA LET YOU HAVE A QUIET LITTLE CHAT?

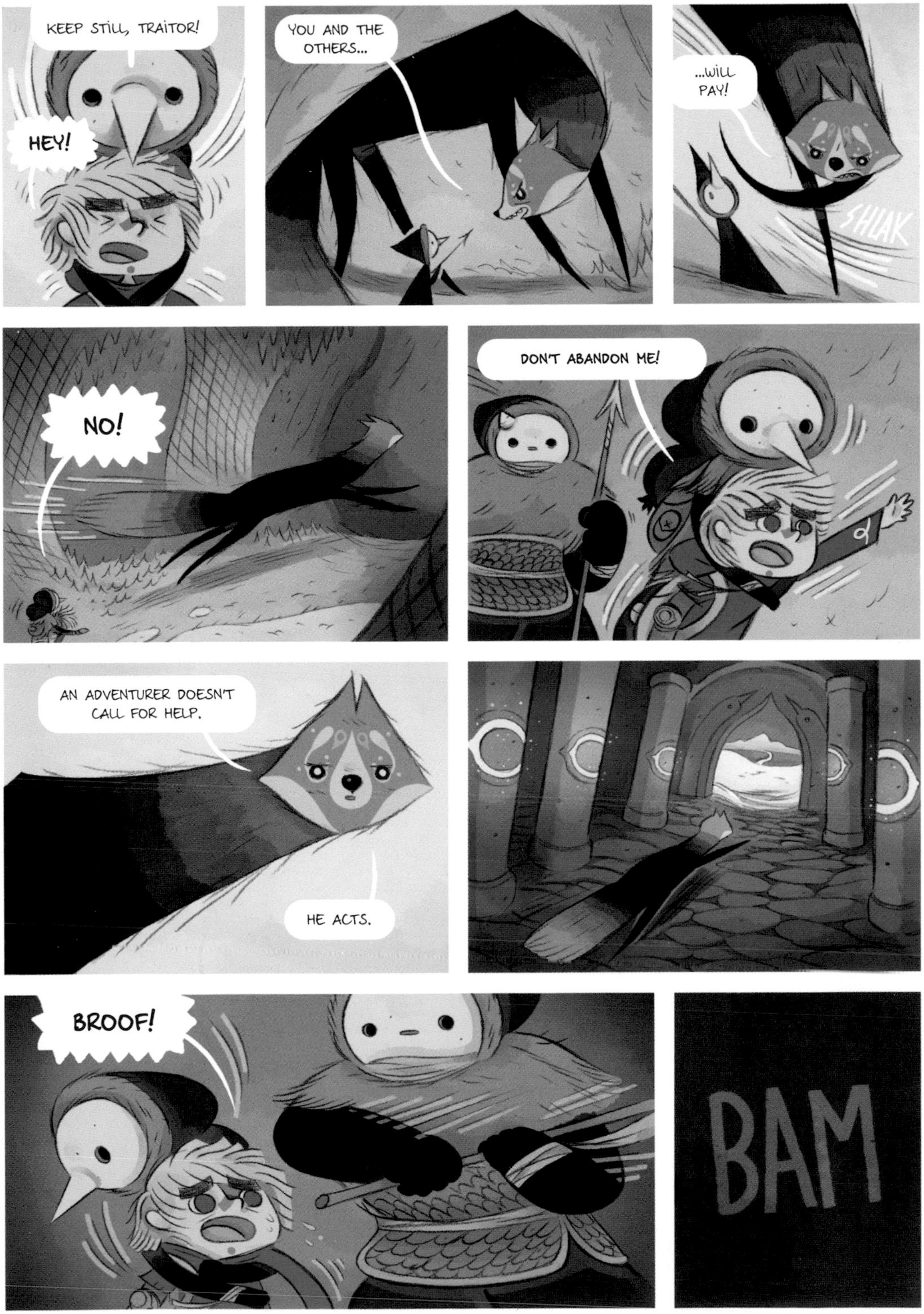
KEEP STILL, TRAITOR!
HEY!
YOU AND THE OTHERS...
...WILL PAY!
SHLAK
NO!
DON'T ABANDON ME!
AN ADVENTURER DOESN'T CALL FOR HELP.
HE ACTS.
BROOF!
BAM

IN MY HEAD

I left home to go on a great adventure, to discover an amazing world I'd never seen, to find a legendary weapon and brothers in arms, to vanquish dangerous beasts.

But the world hasn't turned out to be as wonderful as I thought... Far from it.

IN REAL LiFE

Temples and villages in ruins, caves that are either dank and clammy or stifling hot...
It hasn't exactly been all fun and games.

And the special sword the smithy forged for me...well it shattered at first impact.
It was thanks to a fork—a fork!—that I got away, even though I made fun of the
apprentice who gave it to me. It turns out he was the true master blacksmith.

But my fork couldn't protect my arm from the Magician.

She picked me up like a rag doll, and I almost ended up a living suit of armor. I try not to think
about it... I'm worried about my arm. It's all cold, and I can't feel much of anything with it anymore.
In fact, I can barely move it.

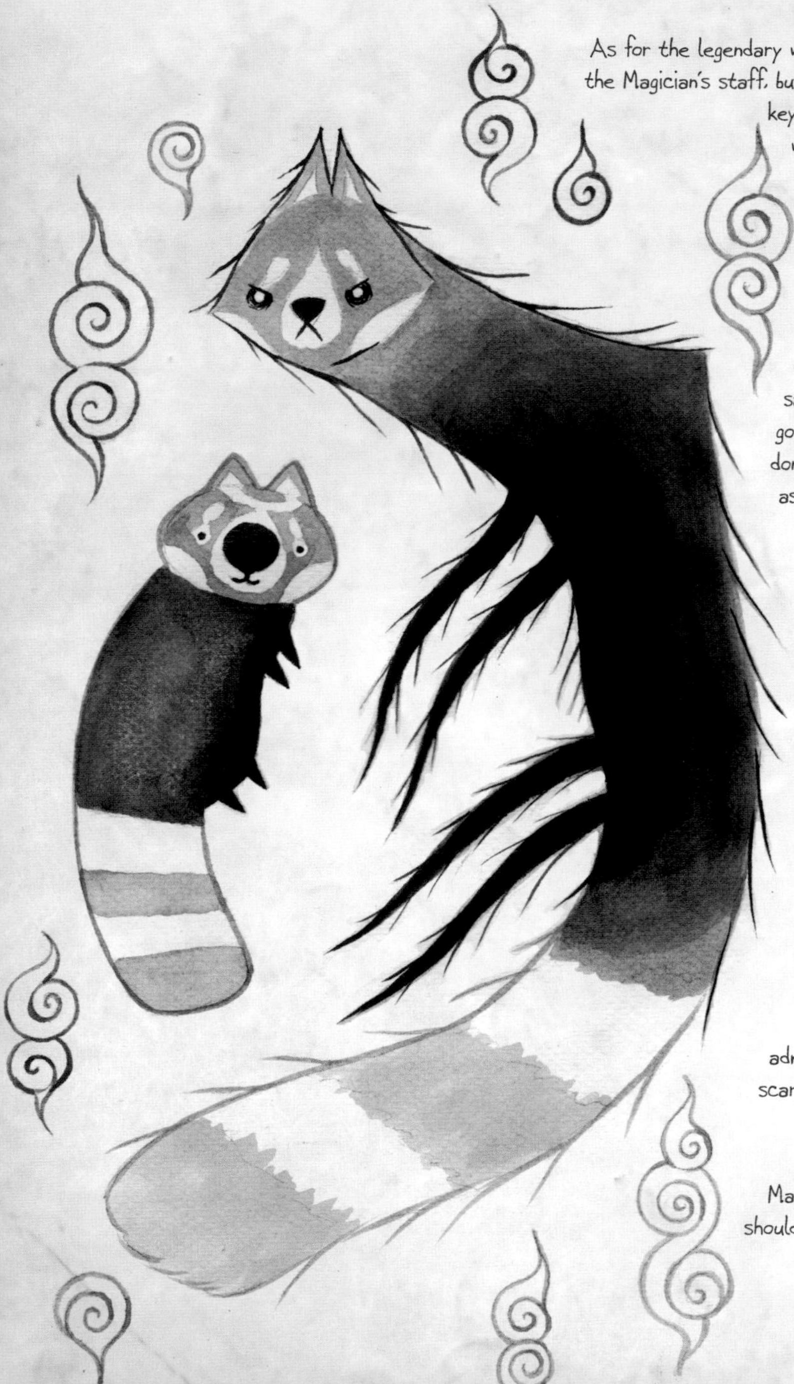

As for the legendary weapon, I thought it was the Magician's staff, but the staff was just the key that freed the true weapon—Broof.

Broof turned out to be a legendary weapon, a brother in arms, and a dangerous beast, all at the same time. And now he's gone. He abandoned me, and I don't know if I should see him as a friend...or an enemy.

To the Shadows, he's clearly the enemy. They locked him away because he supposedly destroyed the village we saw when we left the temple. Broof didn't deny it... But why is he angry at the Shadows?! Something must have happened that I don't understand.

In any case, I have to admit one thing: Broof looked scary after his transformation.

Maybe instead of freeing him, I should have left him locked up.

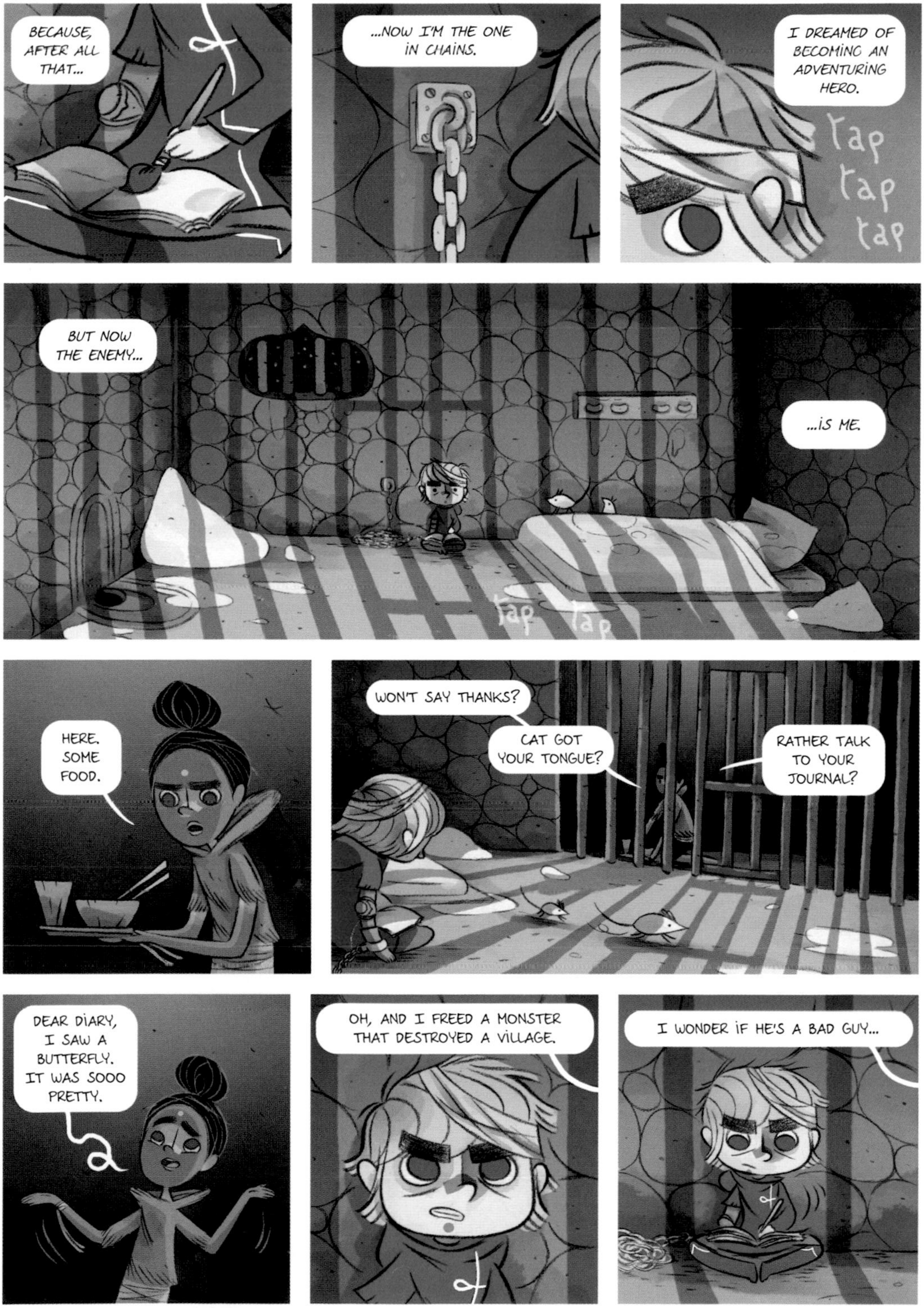
BECAUSE, AFTER ALL THAT...
...NOW I'M THE ONE IN CHAINS.
I DREAMED OF BECOMING AN ADVENTURING HERO.
TAP TAP TAP
BUT NOW THE ENEMY...
...IS ME.
TAP TAP
HERE. SOME FOOD.
WON'T SAY THANKS?
CAT GOT YOUR TONGUE?
RATHER TALK TO YOUR JOURNAL?
DEAR DIARY, I SAW A BUTTERFLY. IT WAS SOOO PRETTY.
OH, AND I FREED A MONSTER THAT DESTROYED A VILLAGE.
I WONDER IF HE'S A BAD GUY...

HEY! WHAT ARE YOU WRITING?
BETTER NOT BE BAD STUFF ABOUT ME!

Dear diary,

I met a girl... And she's really annoying!
She keeps calling me a traitor. I can't stand it!

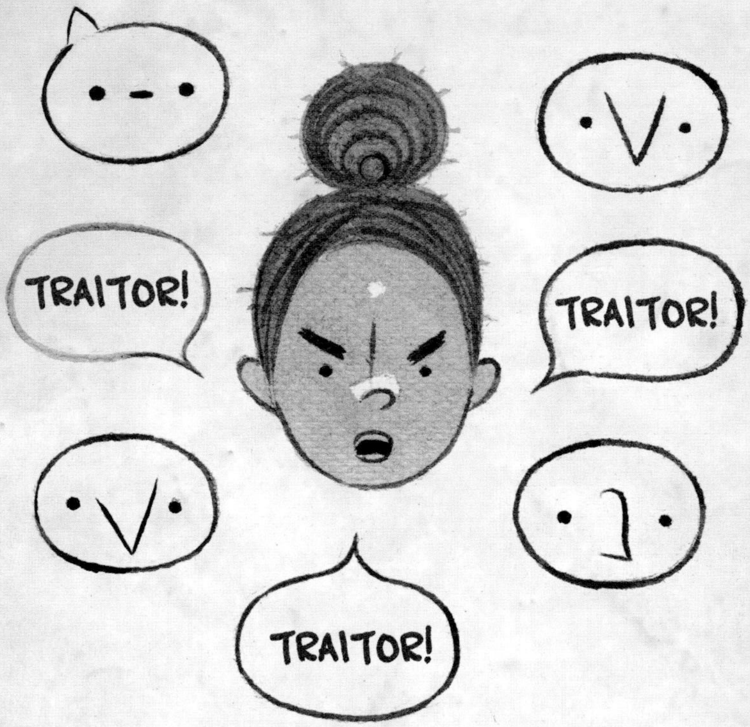
TRAITOR!
TRAITOR!
TRAITOR!

But what really bugs me is how she guessed right away that I'm still confused about Broof...

Am I dumb for not seeing him as an evil monster, despite what I've learned about him?

YOO-HOO! ARE YOU
EVEN LISTENING?

And what about the Shadows? What should I think of them?
I can't believe the freakiest masks I've ever seen had humans just like me hiding underneath.

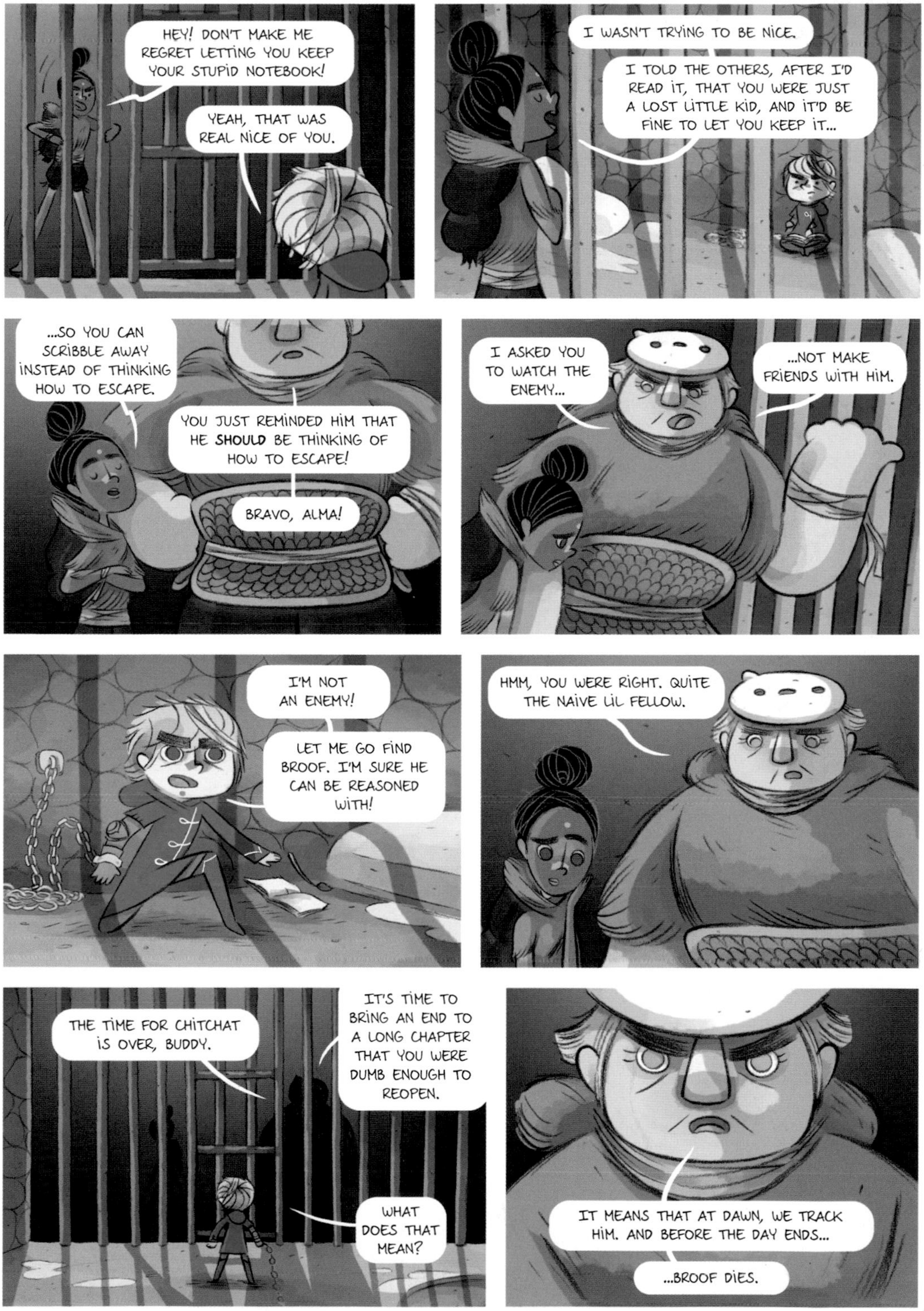
HEY! DON'T MAKE ME REGRET LETTING YOU KEEP YOUR STUPID NOTEBOOK!
YEAH, THAT WAS REAL NICE OF YOU.
I WASN'T TRYING TO BE NICE.
I TOLD THE OTHERS, AFTER I'D READ IT, THAT YOU WERE JUST A LOST LITTLE KID, AND IT'D BE FINE TO LET YOU KEEP IT...
...SO YOU CAN SCRIBBLE AWAY INSTEAD OF THINKING HOW TO ESCAPE.
YOU JUST REMINDED HIM THAT HE **SHOULD** BE THINKING OF HOW TO ESCAPE!
BRAVO, ALMA!
I ASKED YOU TO WATCH THE ENEMY...
...NOT MAKE FRIENDS WITH HIM.
I'M NOT AN ENEMY!
LET ME GO FIND BROOF. I'M SURE HE CAN BE REASONED WITH!
HMM, YOU WERE RIGHT. QUITE THE NAIVE LIL FELLOW.
THE TIME FOR CHITCHAT IS OVER, BUDDY.
IT'S TIME TO BRING AN END TO A LONG CHAPTER THAT YOU WERE DUMB ENOUGH TO REOPEN.
WHAT DOES THAT MEAN?
IT MEANS THAT AT DAWN, WE TRACK HIM. AND BEFORE THE DAY ENDS...
...BROOF DIES.

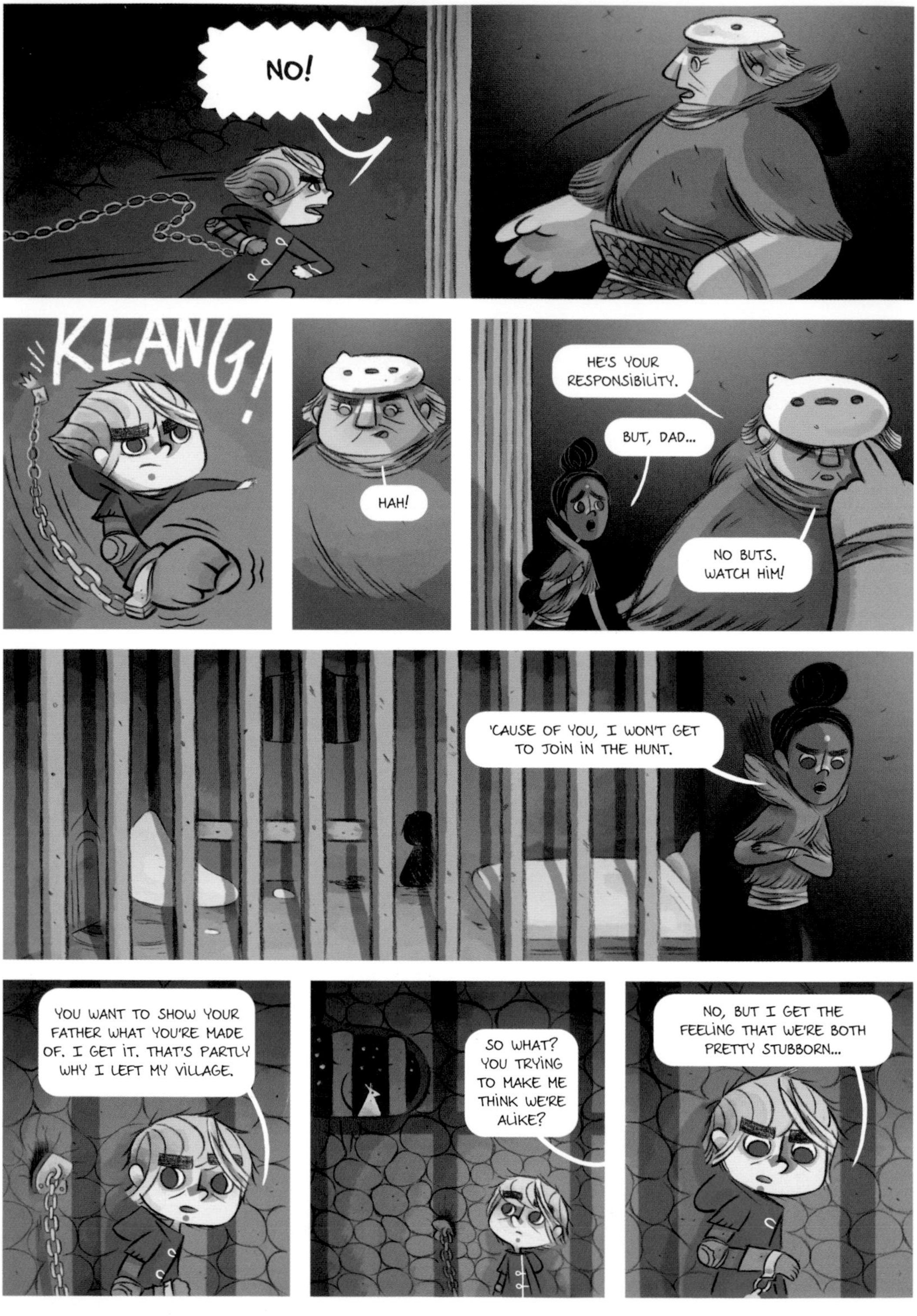
NO!
KLANG!
HAH!
HE'S YOUR RESPONSIBILITY.
BUT, DAD...
NO BUTS. WATCH HIM!
'CAUSE OF YOU, I WON'T GET TO JOIN IN THE HUNT.
YOU WANT TO SHOW YOUR FATHER WHAT YOU'RE MADE OF. I GET IT. THAT'S PARTLY WHY I LEFT MY VILLAGE.
SO WHAT? YOU TRYING TO MAKE ME THINK WE'RE ALIKE?
NO, BUT I GET THE FEELING THAT WE'RE BOTH PRETTY STUBBORN...

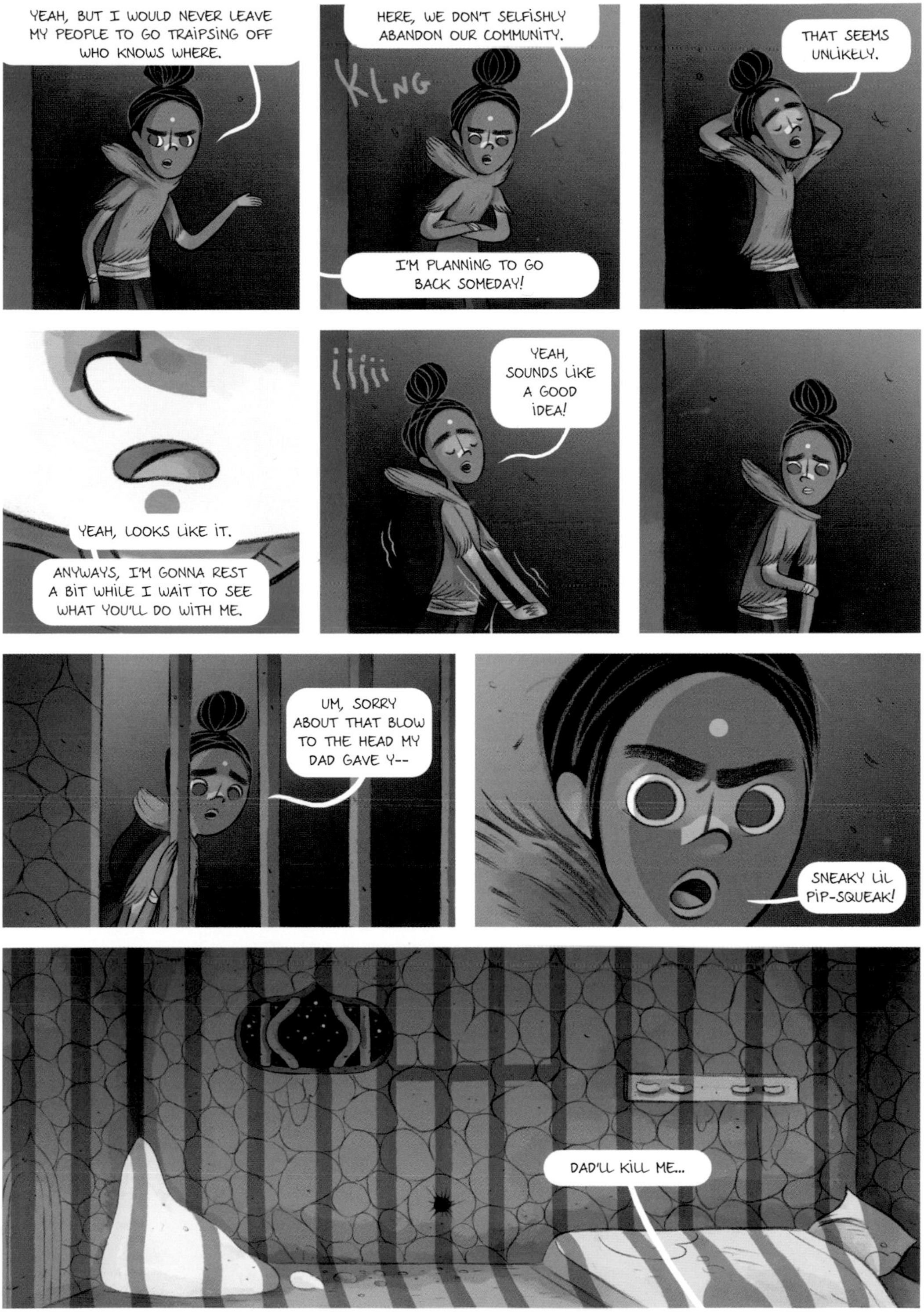
YEAH, BUT I WOULD NEVER LEAVE MY PEOPLE TO GO TRAIPSING OFF WHO KNOWS WHERE.
KLNG
HERE, WE DON'T SELFISHLY ABANDON OUR COMMUNITY.
I'M PLANNING TO GO BACK SOMEDAY!
THAT SEEMS UNLIKELY.
YEAH, LOOKS LIKE IT.
ANYWAYS, I'M GONNA REST A BIT WHILE I WAIT TO SEE WHAT YOU'LL DO WITH ME.
YEAH, SOUNDS LIKE A GOOD IDEA!
UM, SORRY ABOUT THAT BLOW TO THE HEAD MY DAD GAVE Y--
SNEAKY LIL PIP-SQUEAK!
DAD'LL KILL ME...

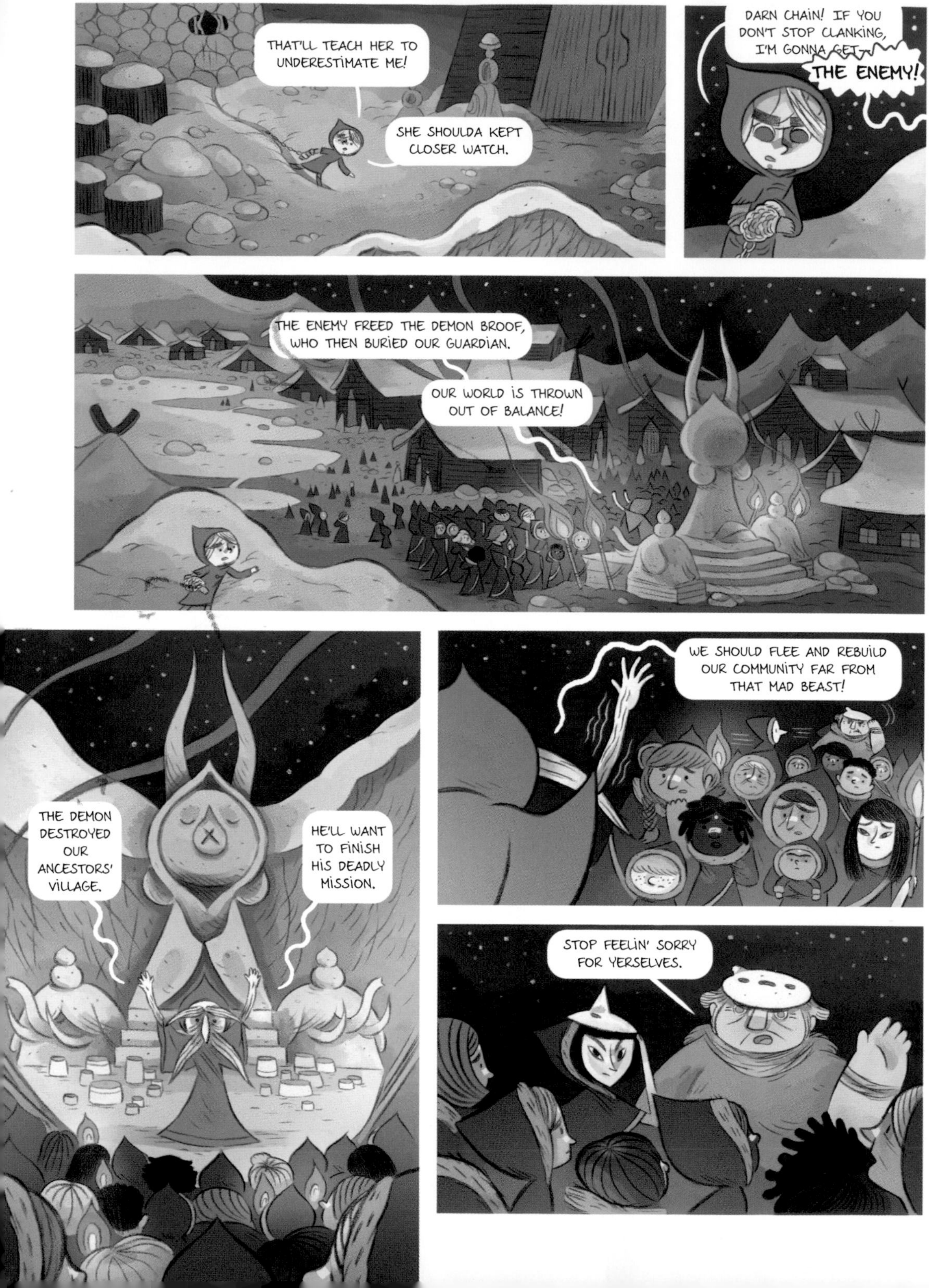

THAT'LL TEACH HER TO UNDERESTIMATE ME!
SHE SHOULDA KEPT CLOSER WATCH.
DARN CHAIN! IF YOU DON'T STOP CLANKING, I'M GONNA GET—
THE ENEMY!
THE ENEMY FREED THE DEMON BROOF, WHO THEN BURIED OUR GUARDIAN.
OUR WORLD IS THROWN OUT OF BALANCE!
THE DEMON DESTROYED OUR ANCESTORS' VILLAGE.
HE'LL WANT TO FINISH HIS DEADLY MISSION.
WE SHOULD FLEE AND REBUILD OUR COMMUNITY FAR FROM THAT MAD BEAST!
STOP FEELIN' SORRY FOR YERSELVES.

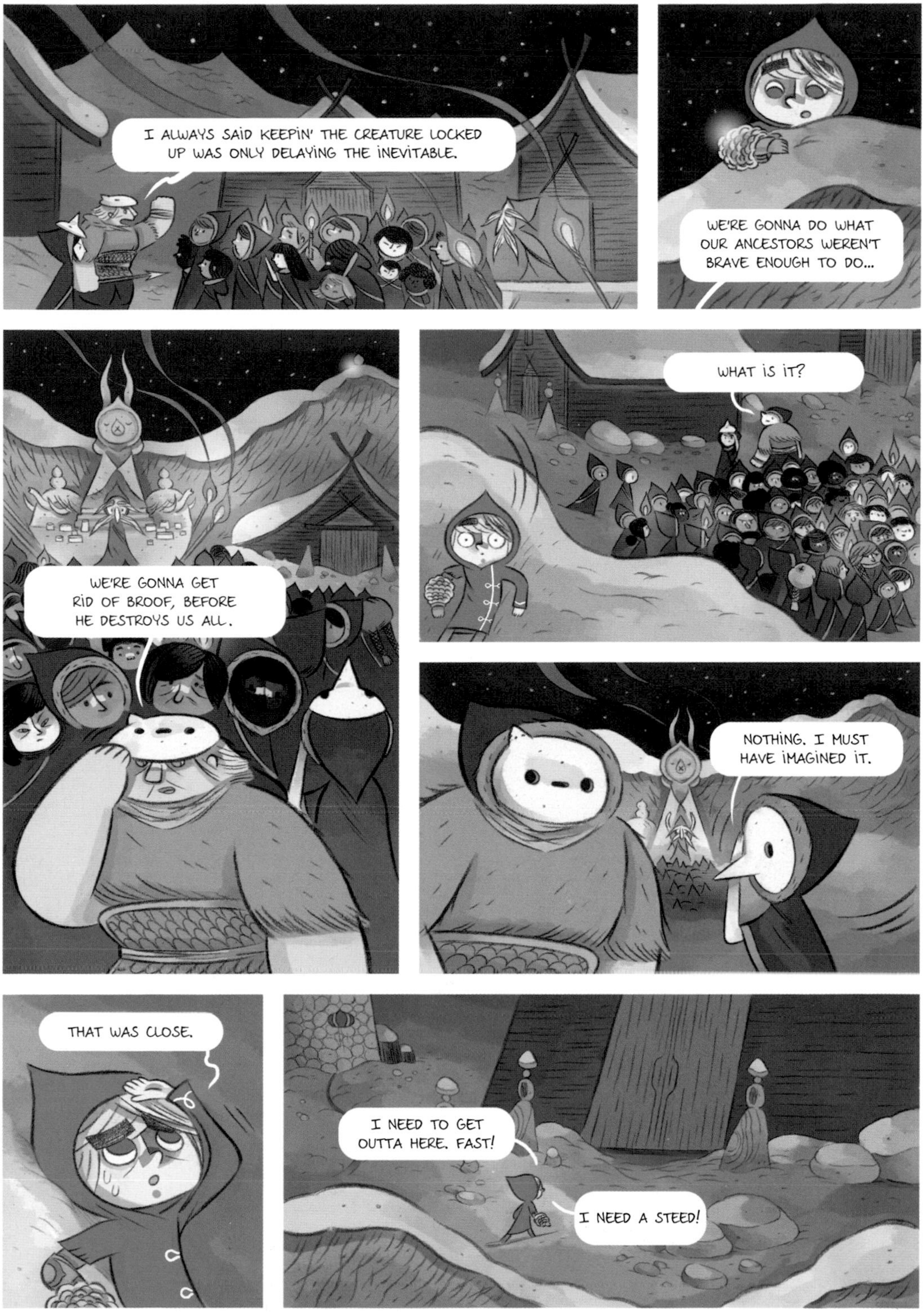
I ALWAYS SAID KEEPIN' THE CREATURE LOCKED UP WAS ONLY DELAYING THE INEVITABLE.
WE'RE GONNA DO WHAT OUR ANCESTORS WEREN'T BRAVE ENOUGH TO DO...
WE'RE GONNA GET RID OF BROOF, BEFORE HE DESTROYS US ALL.
WHAT IS IT?
NOTHING. I MUST HAVE IMAGINED IT.
THAT WAS CLOSE.
I NEED TO GET OUTTA HERE. FAST!
I NEED A STEED!

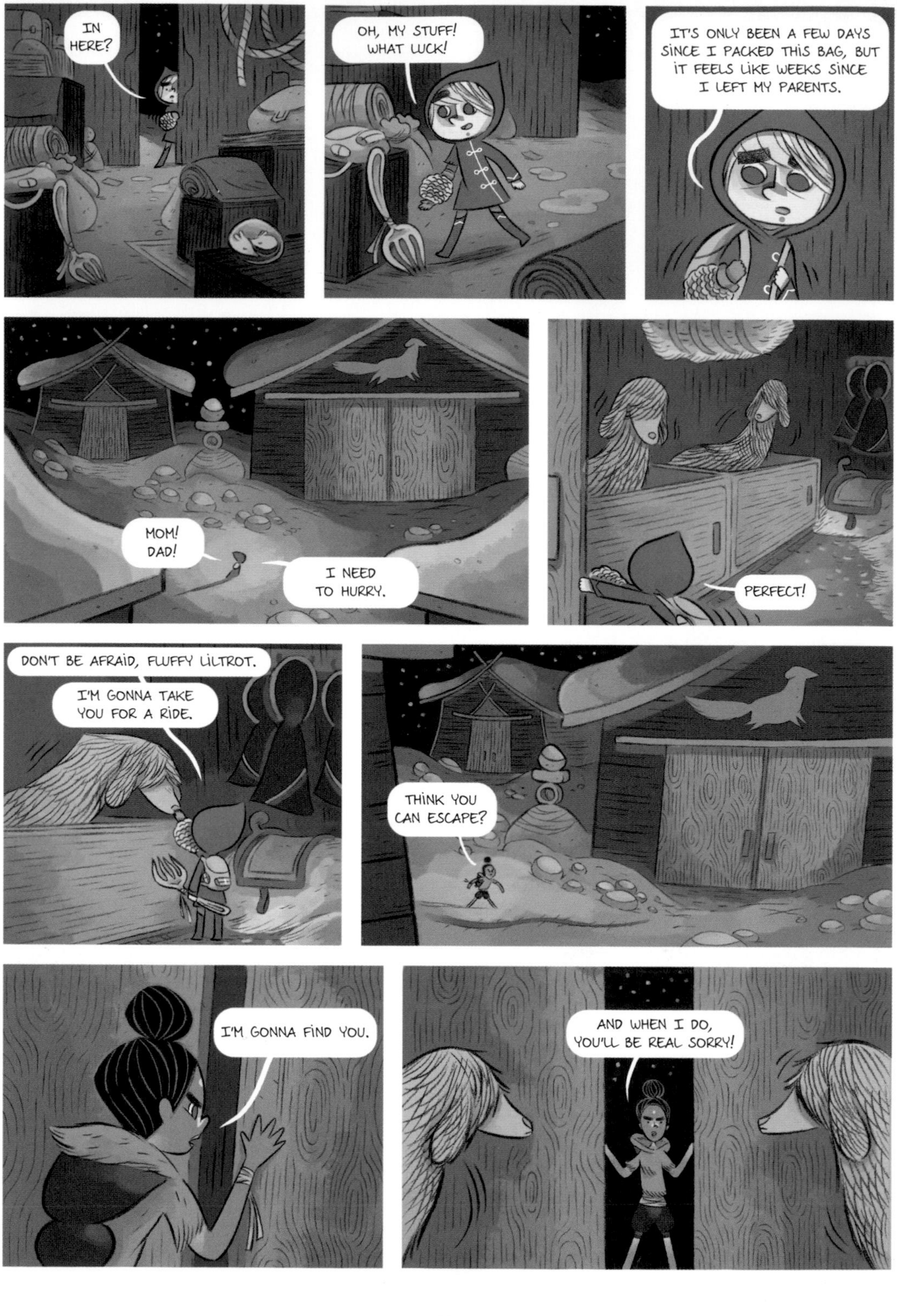
IN HERE?
OH, MY STUFF! WHAT LUCK!
IT'S ONLY BEEN A FEW DAYS SINCE I PACKED THIS BAG, BUT IT FEELS LIKE WEEKS SINCE I LEFT MY PARENTS.
MOM! DAD!
I NEED TO HURRY.
PERFECT!
DON'T BE AFRAID, FLUFFY LILTROT.
I'M GONNA TAKE YOU FOR A RIDE.
THINK YOU CAN ESCAPE?
I'M GONNA FIND YOU.
AND WHEN I DO, YOU'LL BE REAL SORRY!

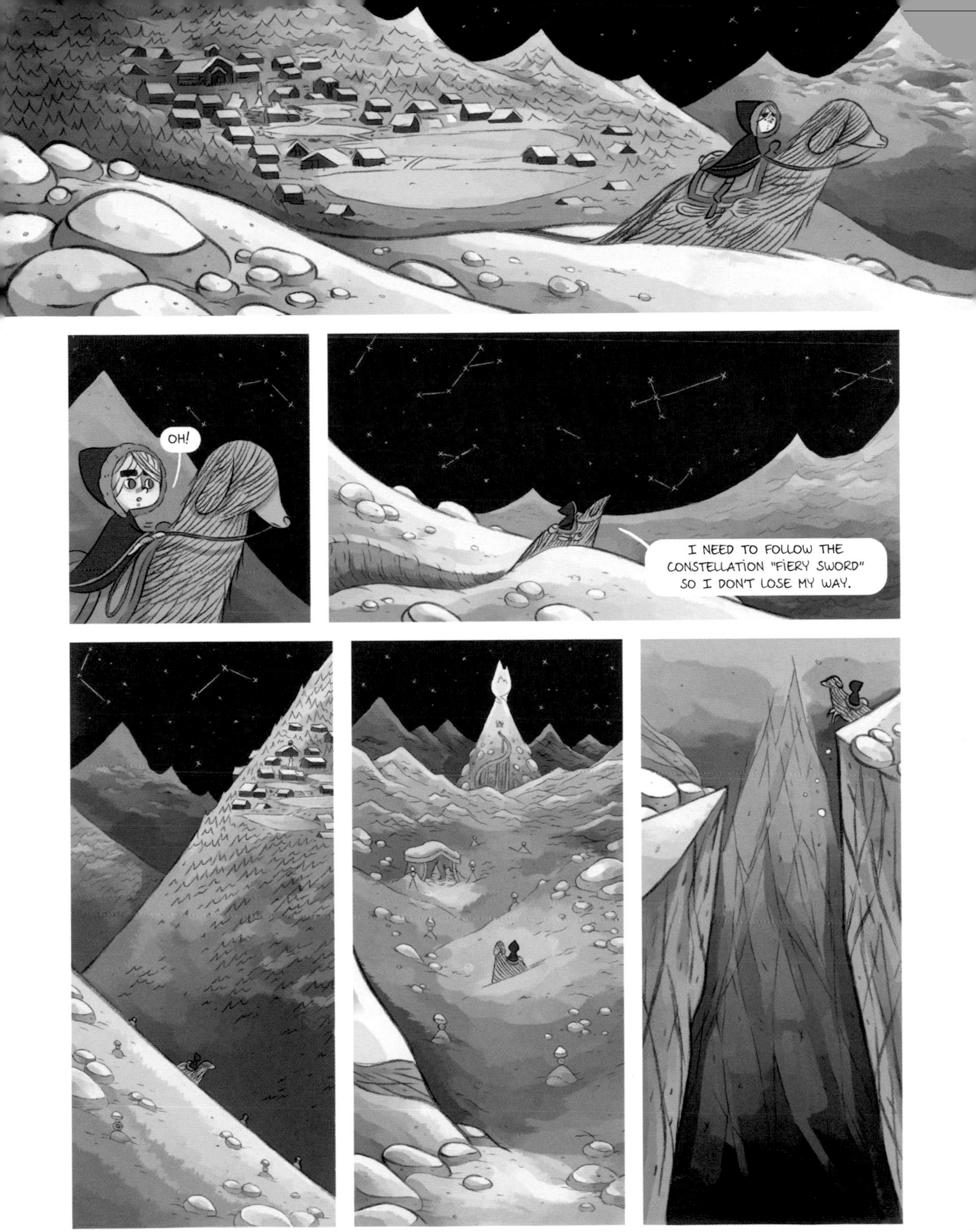
OH!
I NEED TO FOLLOW THE CONSTELLATION "FIERY SWORD" SO I DON'T LOSE MY WAY.

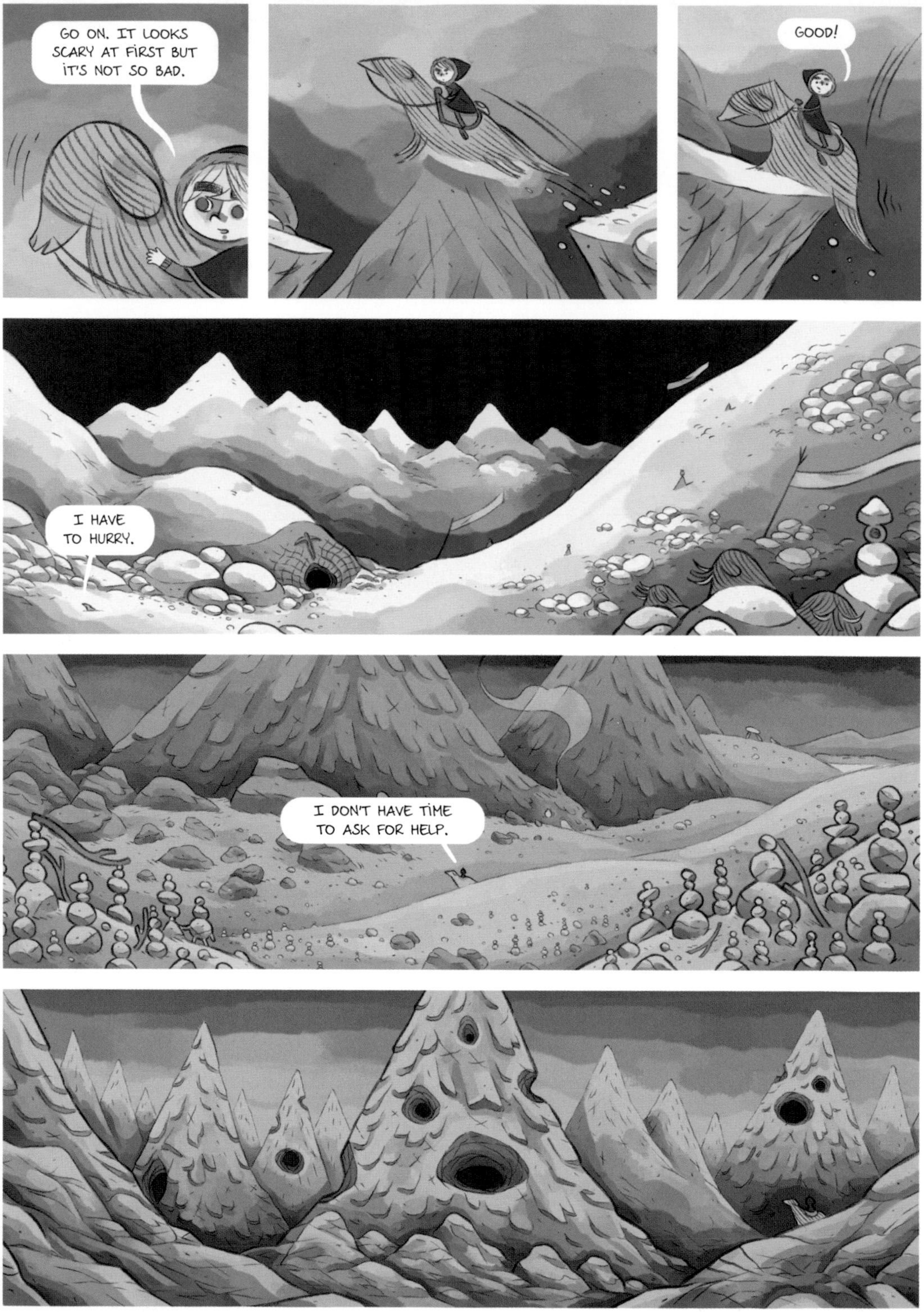
GO ON. IT LOOKS SCARY AT FIRST BUT IT'S NOT SO BAD.
GOOD!
I HAVE TO HURRY.
I DON'T HAVE TIME TO ASK FOR HELP.

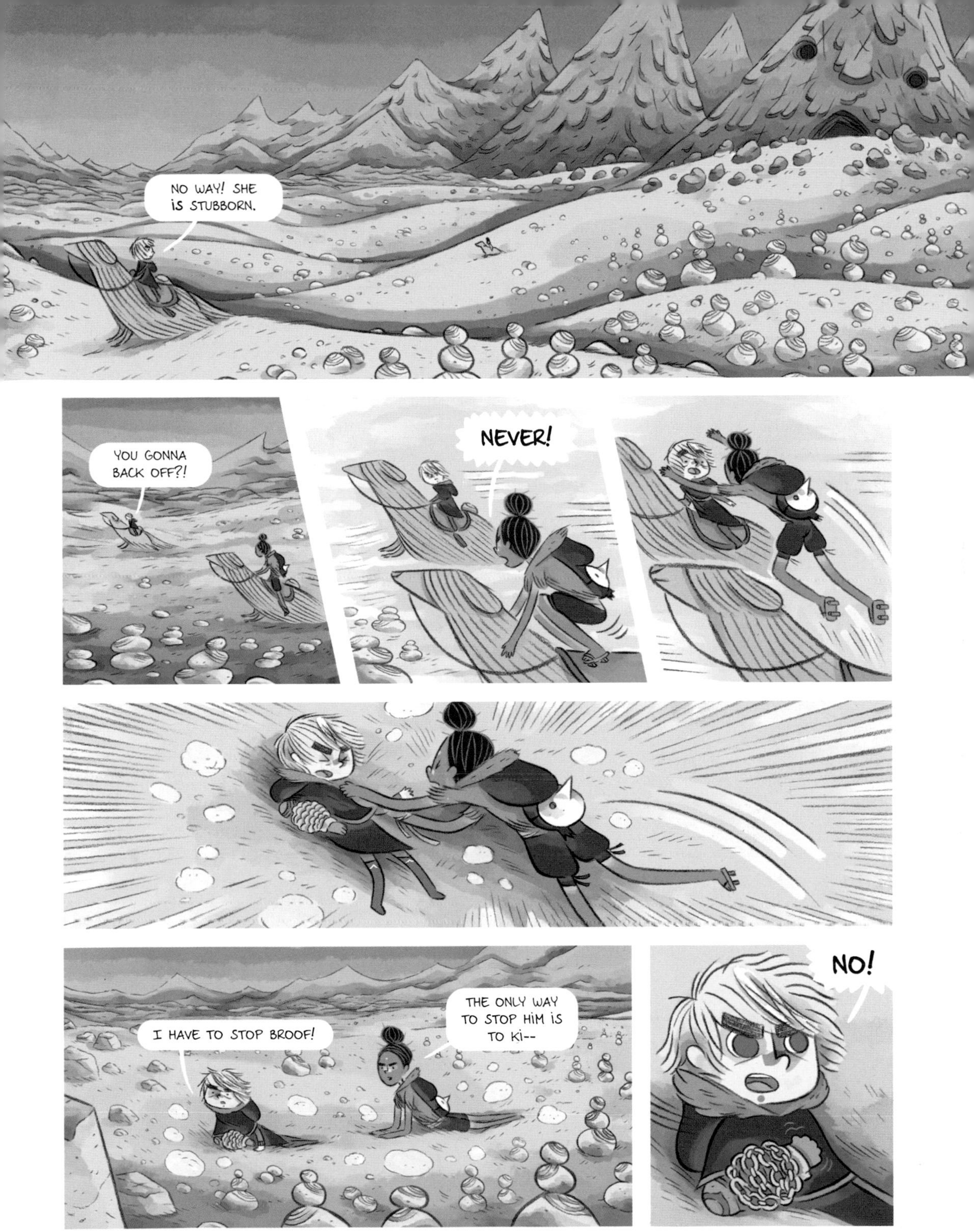
NO WAY! SHE IS STUBBORN.
YOU GONNA BACK OFF?!
NEVER!
I HAVE TO STOP BROOF!
THE ONLY WAY TO STOP HIM IS TO KI--
NO!

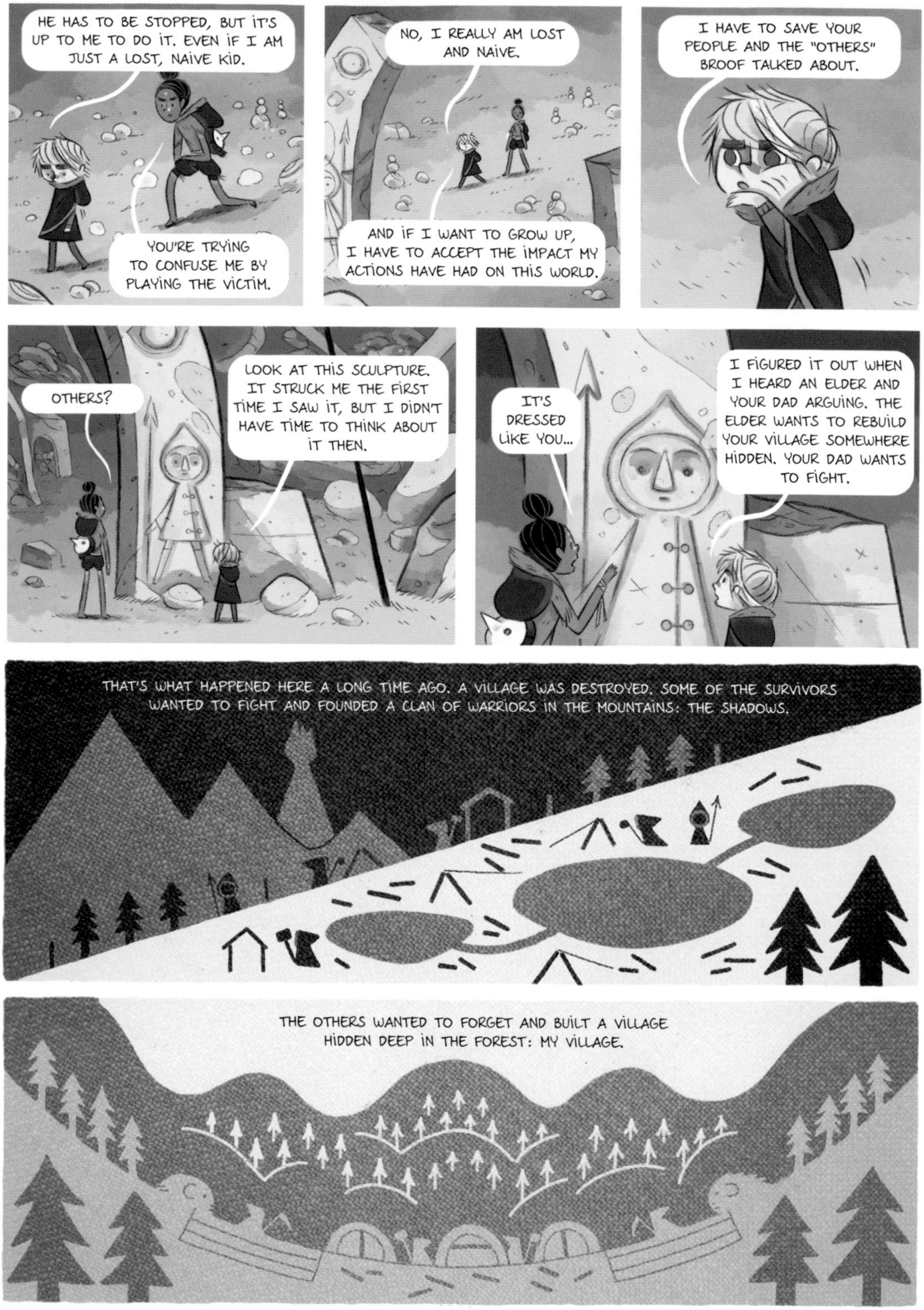
HE HAS TO BE STOPPED, BUT IT'S UP TO ME TO DO IT. EVEN IF I AM JUST A LOST, NAIVE KID.
YOU'RE TRYING TO CONFUSE ME BY PLAYING THE VICTIM.
NO, I REALLY AM LOST AND NAIVE.
AND IF I WANT TO GROW UP, I HAVE TO ACCEPT THE IMPACT MY ACTIONS HAVE HAD ON THIS WORLD.
I HAVE TO SAVE YOUR PEOPLE AND THE "OTHERS" BROOF TALKED ABOUT.
OTHERS?
LOOK AT THIS SCULPTURE. IT STRUCK ME THE FIRST TIME I SAW IT, BUT I DIDN'T HAVE TIME TO THINK ABOUT IT THEN.
IT'S DRESSED LIKE YOU...
I FIGURED IT OUT WHEN I HEARD AN ELDER AND YOUR DAD ARGUING. THE ELDER WANTS TO REBUILD YOUR VILLAGE SOMEWHERE HIDDEN. YOUR DAD WANTS TO FIGHT.
THAT'S WHAT HAPPENED HERE A LONG TIME AGO. A VILLAGE WAS DESTROYED. SOME OF THE SURVIVORS WANTED TO FIGHT AND FOUNDED A CLAN OF WARRIORS IN THE MOUNTAINS: THE SHADOWS.
THE OTHERS WANTED TO FORGET AND BUILT A VILLAGE HIDDEN DEEP IN THE FOREST: MY VILLAGE.

WAIT... SO WE COME FROM THE SAME PEOPLE?

I THINK SO. AND BROOF FLED SO HE COULD ATTACK THE OTHER DESCENDANTS OF OUR PEOPLE FIRST.

AND I'M THE ONE WHO TOLD HIM THEY EXISTED. I EXPLAINED WHERE HE COULD FIND THEM.

NOW DO YOU UNDERSTAND WHY I NEED TO FIND BROOF, AND STOP HIM?

REASONING WITH HIM WON'T WORK.

HEY, LET GO! WHY DON'T YOU TRUST ME?

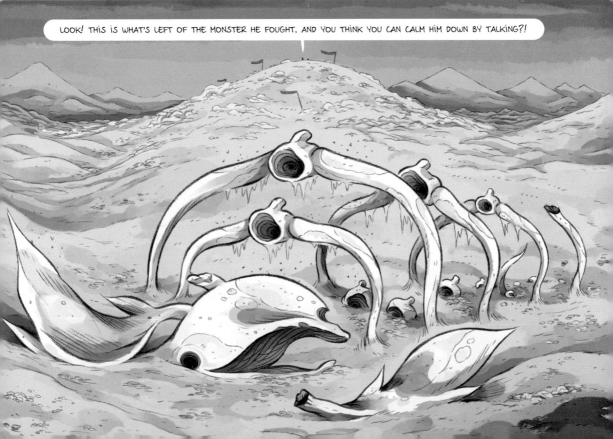

LOOK! THIS IS WHAT'S LEFT OF THE MONSTER HE FOUGHT. AND YOU THINK YOU CAN CALM HIM DOWN BY TALKING?!

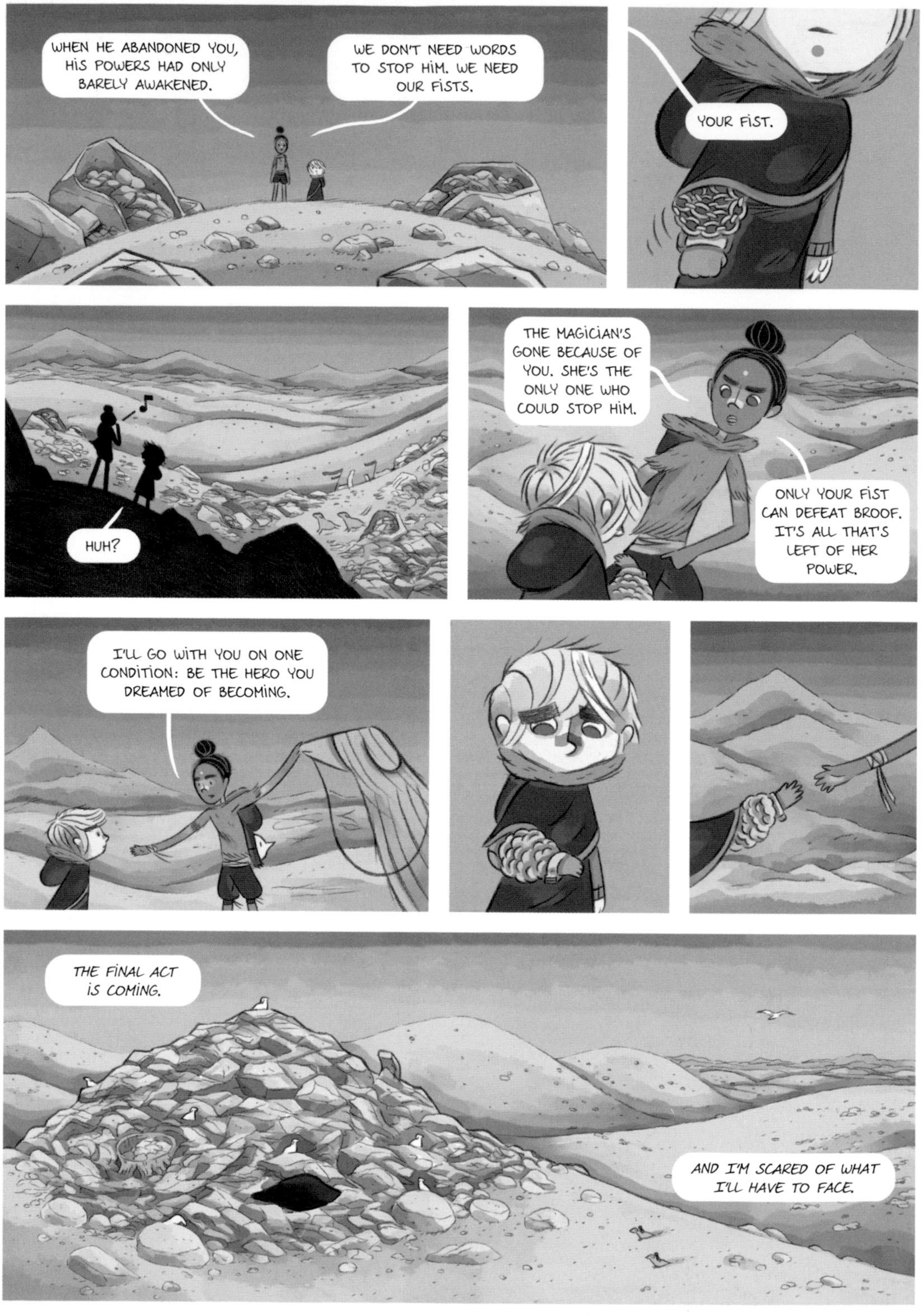
WHEN HE ABANDONED YOU, HIS POWERS HAD ONLY BARELY AWAKENED.
WE DON'T NEED WORDS TO STOP HIM. WE NEED OUR FISTS.
YOUR FIST.
HUH?
THE MAGICIAN'S GONE BECAUSE OF YOU. SHE'S THE ONLY ONE WHO COULD STOP HIM.
ONLY YOUR FIST CAN DEFEAT BROOF. IT'S ALL THAT'S LEFT OF HER POWER.
I'LL GO WITH YOU ON ONE CONDITION: BE THE HERO YOU DREAMED OF BECOMING.
THE FINAL ACT IS COMING.
AND I'M SCARED OF WHAT I'LL HAVE TO FACE.

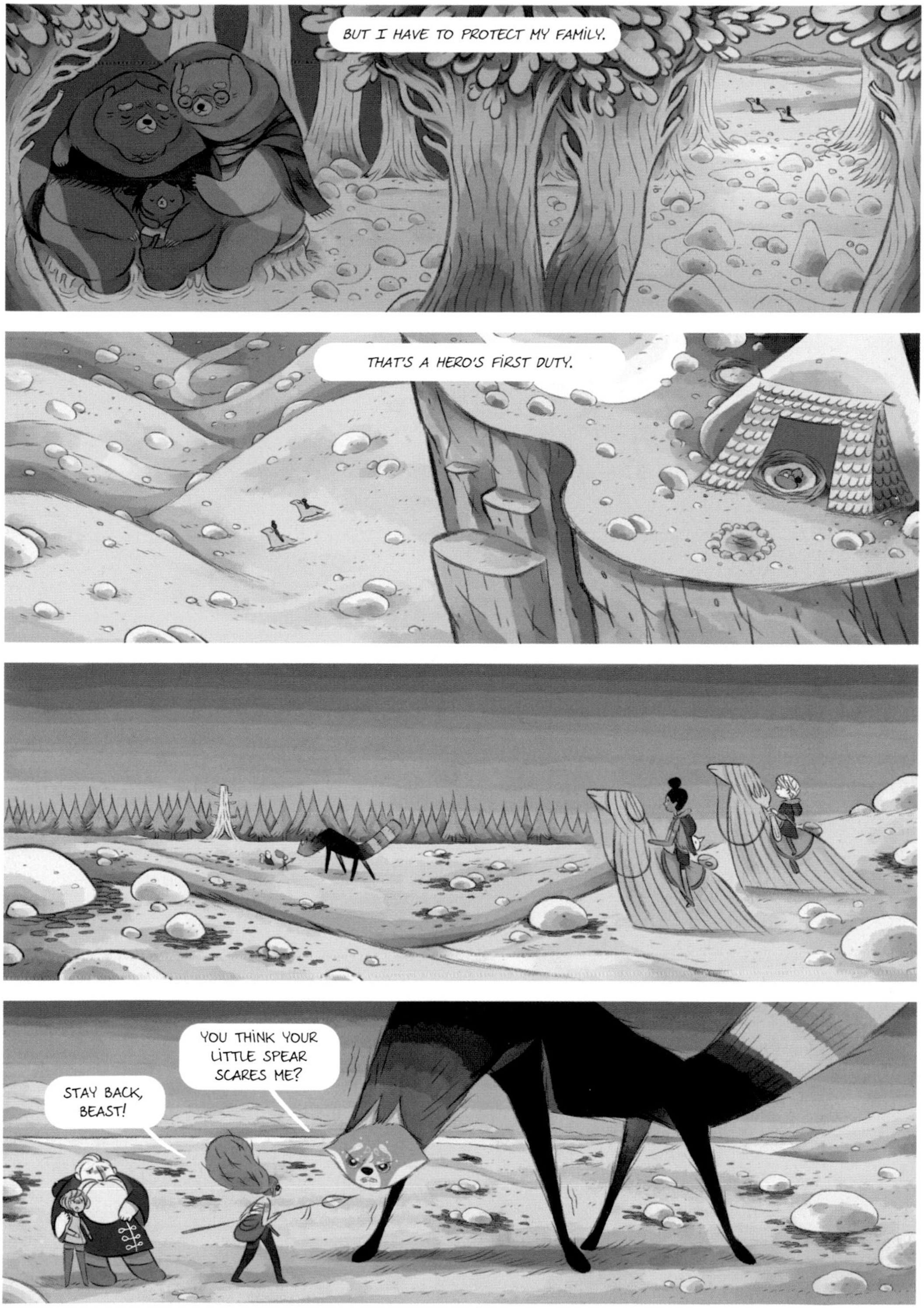
BUT I HAVE TO PROTECT MY FAMILY.
THAT'S A HERO'S FIRST DUTY.
STAY BACK, BEAST!
YOU THINK YOUR LITTLE SPEAR SCARES ME?

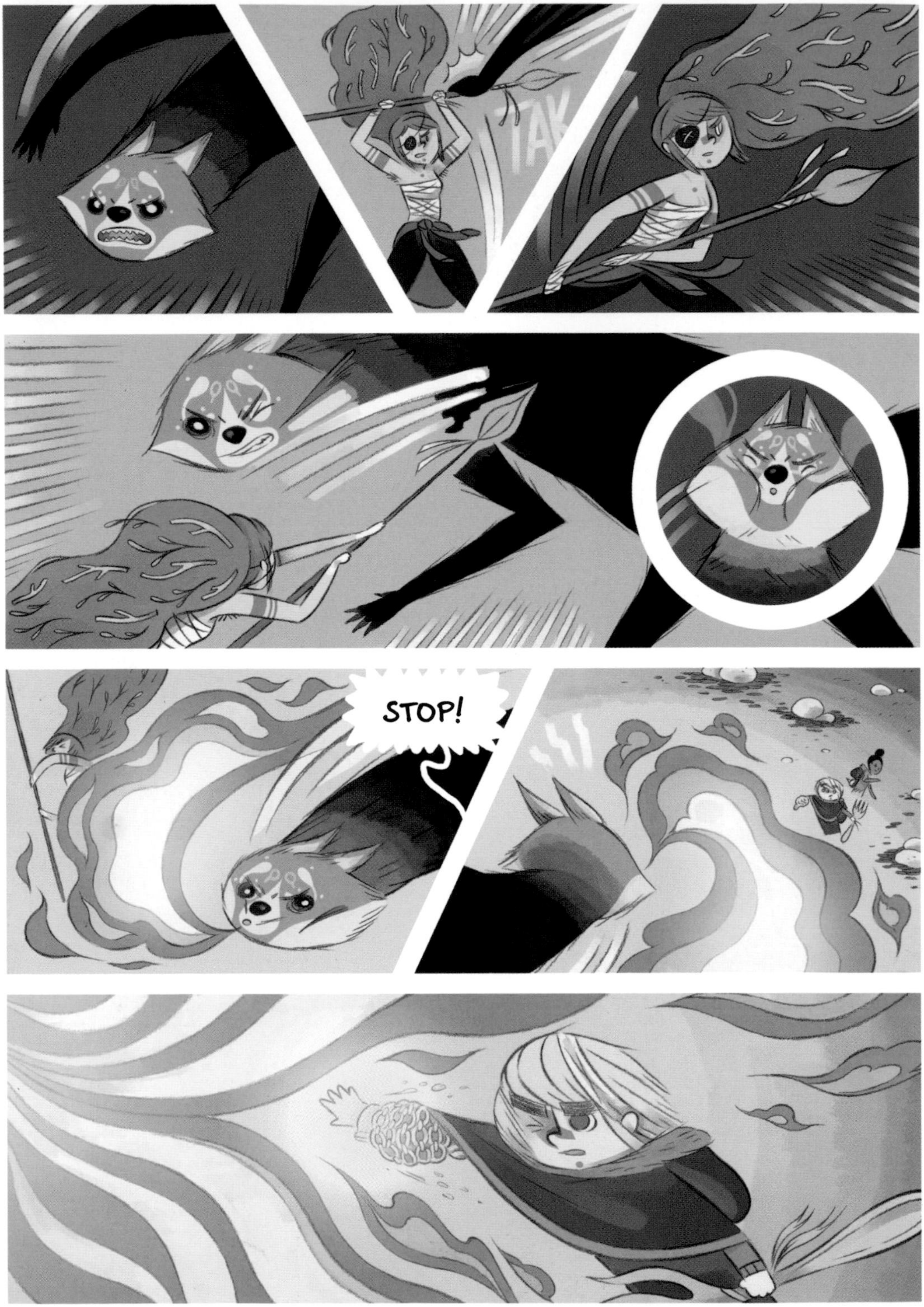
TAK
STOP!

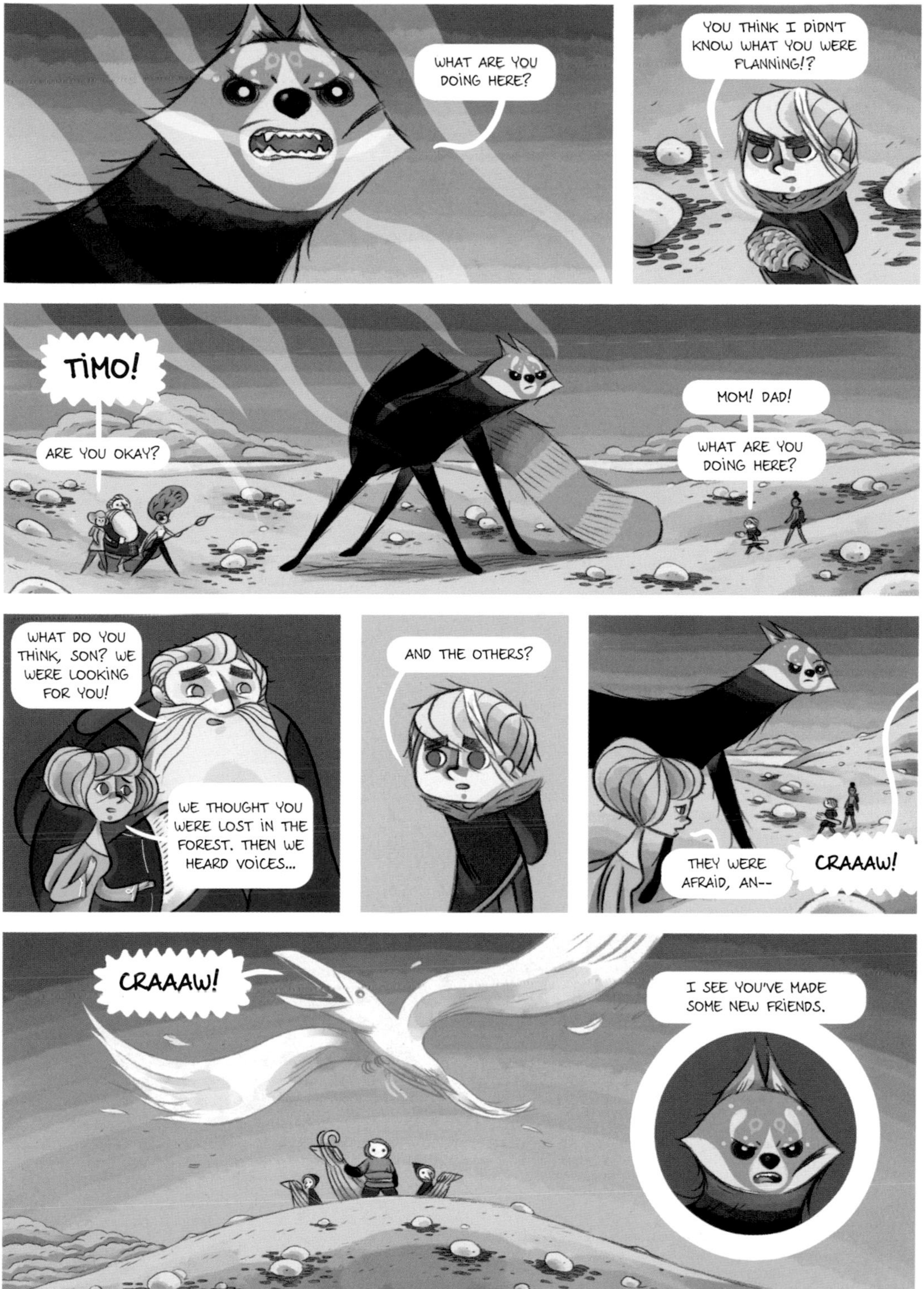
WHAT ARE YOU DOING HERE?
YOU THINK I DIDN'T KNOW WHAT YOU WERE PLANNING!?
TIMO!
ARE YOU OKAY?
MOM! DAD!
WHAT ARE YOU DOING HERE?
WHAT DO YOU THINK, SON? WE WERE LOOKING FOR YOU!
WE THOUGHT YOU WERE LOST IN THE FOREST. THEN WE HEARD VOICES...
AND THE OTHERS?
THEY WERE AFRAID, AN--
CRAAAW!
CRAAAW!
I SEE YOU'VE MADE SOME NEW FRIENDS.

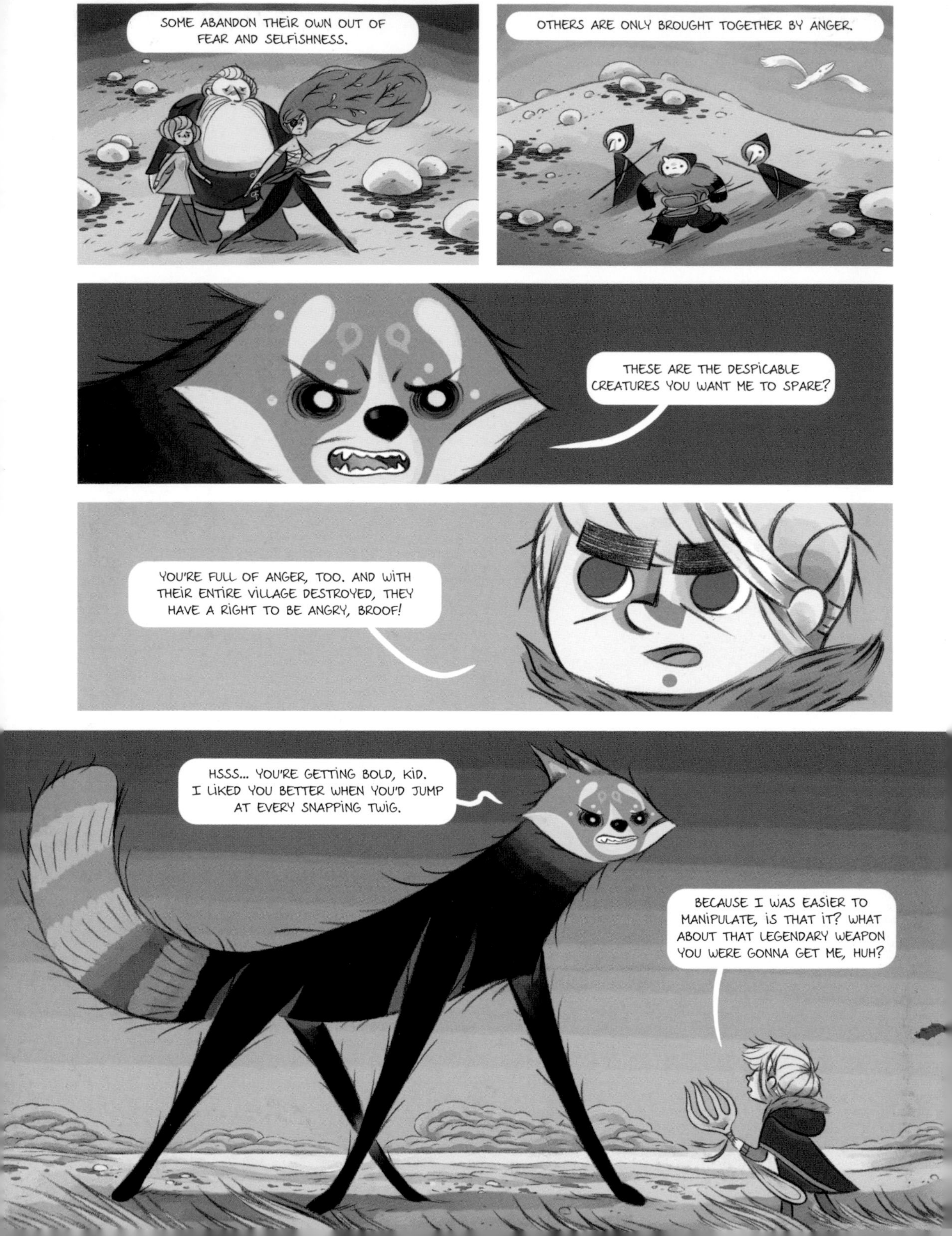
SOME ABANDON THEIR OWN OUT OF FEAR AND SELFISHNESS.
OTHERS ARE ONLY BROUGHT TOGETHER BY ANGER.
THESE ARE THE DESPICABLE CREATURES YOU WANT ME TO SPARE?
YOU'RE FULL OF ANGER, TOO. AND WITH THEIR ENTIRE VILLAGE DESTROYED, THEY HAVE A RIGHT TO BE ANGRY, BROOF!
HSSS... YOU'RE GETTING BOLD, KID. I LIKED YOU BETTER WHEN YOU'D JUMP AT EVERY SNAPPING TWIG.
BECAUSE I WAS EASIER TO MANIPULATE, IS THAT IT? WHAT ABOUT THAT LEGENDARY WEAPON YOU WERE GONNA GET ME, HUH?

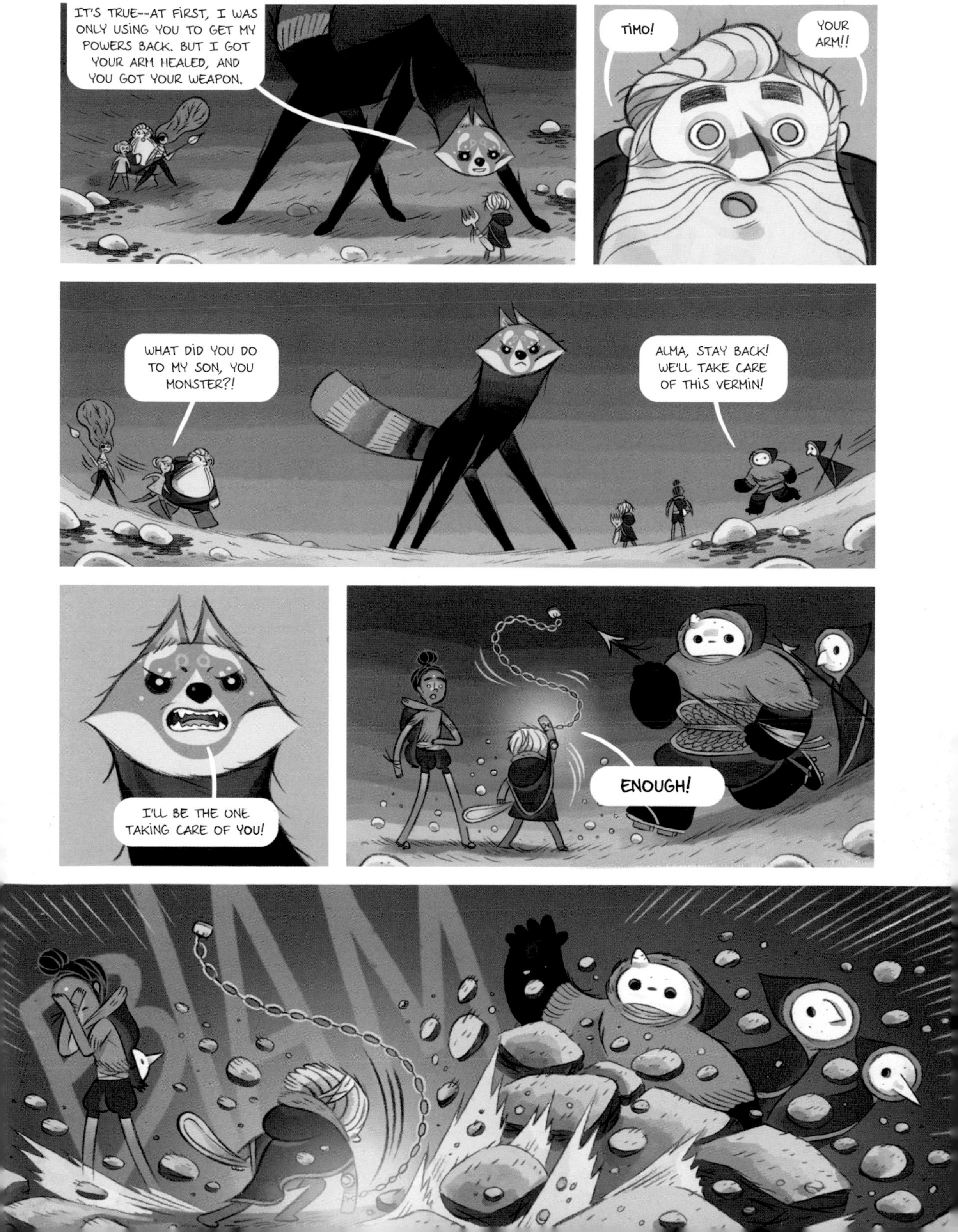
IT'S TRUE--AT FIRST, I WAS ONLY USING YOU TO GET MY POWERS BACK. BUT I GOT YOUR ARM HEALED, AND YOU GOT YOUR WEAPON.
TIMO!
YOUR ARM!!
WHAT DID YOU DO TO MY SON, YOU MONSTER?!
ALMA, STAY BACK! WE'LL TAKE CARE OF THIS VERMIN!
I'LL BE THE ONE TAKING CARE OF YOU!
ENOUGH!
BLAM

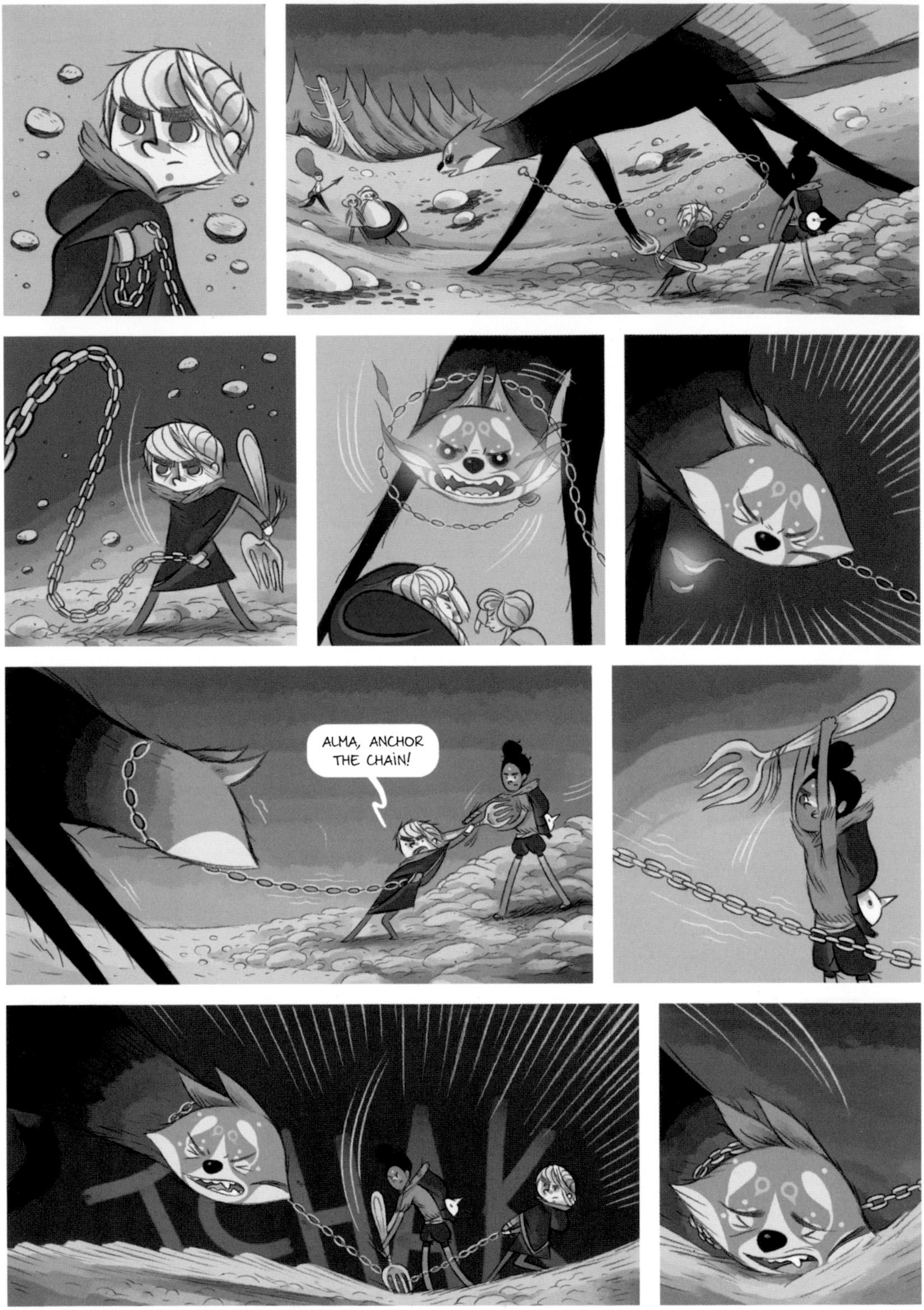
ALMA, ANCHOR THE CHAIN!
TCHAK

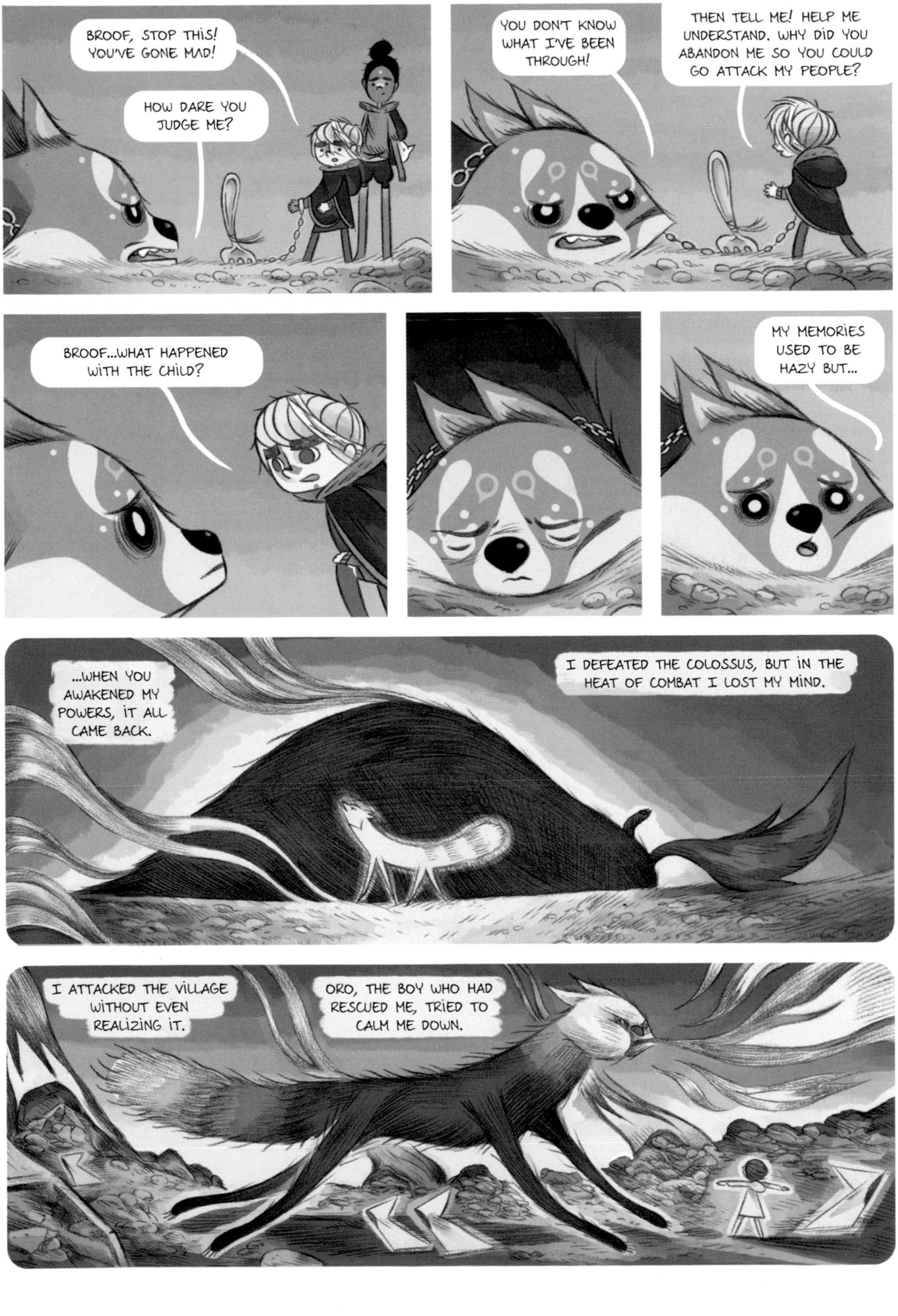
BROOF, STOP THIS! YOU'VE GONE MAD!
HOW DARE YOU JUDGE ME?
YOU DON'T KNOW WHAT I'VE BEEN THROUGH!
THEN TELL ME! HELP ME UNDERSTAND. WHY DID YOU ABANDON ME SO YOU COULD GO ATTACK MY PEOPLE?
BROOF...WHAT HAPPENED WITH THE CHILD?
MY MEMORIES USED TO BE HAZY BUT...
...WHEN YOU AWAKENED MY POWERS, IT ALL CAME BACK.
I DEFEATED THE COLOSSUS, BUT IN THE HEAT OF COMBAT I LOST MY MIND.
I ATTACKED THE VILLAGE WITHOUT EVEN REALIZING IT.
ORO, THE BOY WHO HAD RESCUED ME, TRIED TO CALM ME DOWN.

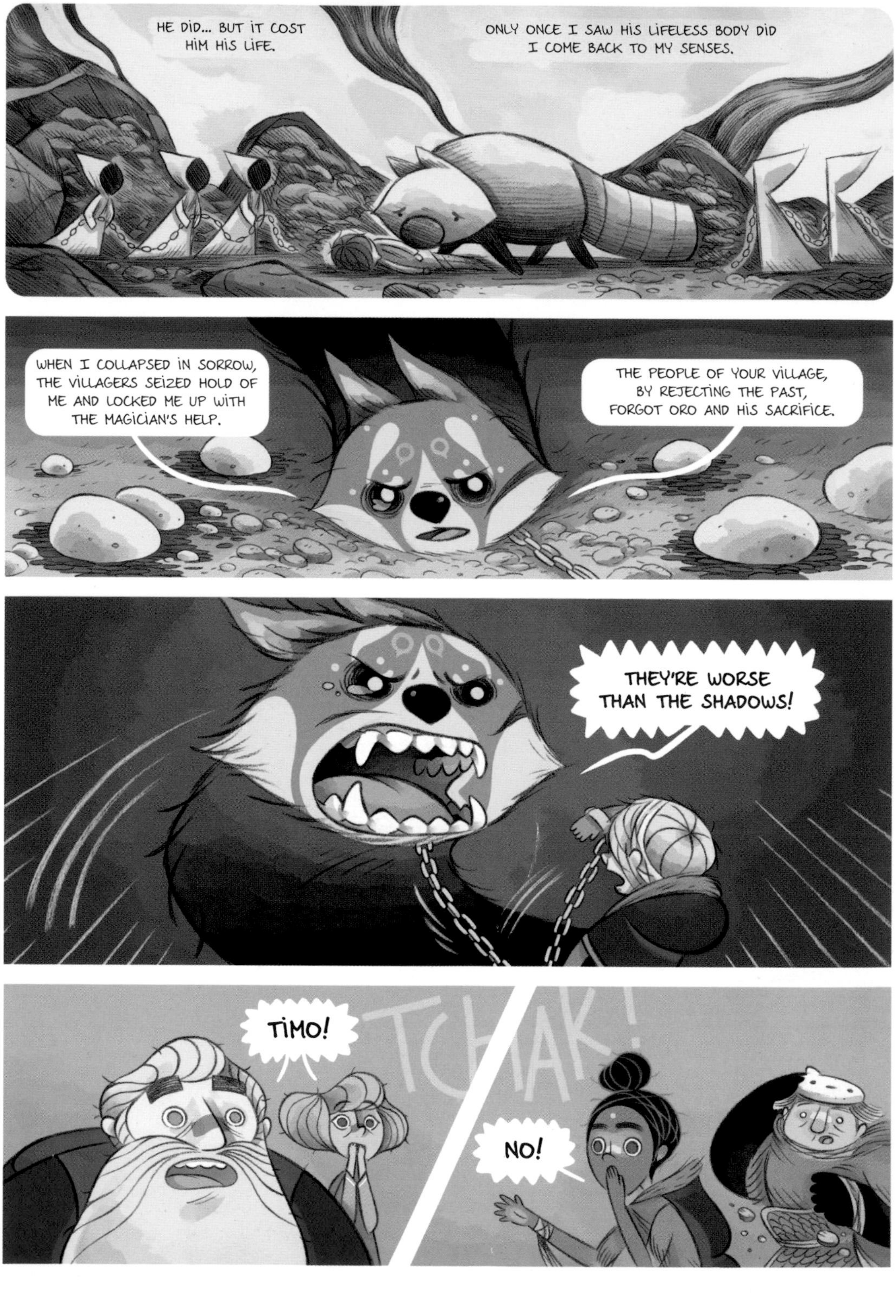
HE DID... BUT IT COST HIM HIS LIFE.
ONLY ONCE I SAW HIS LIFELESS BODY DID I COME BACK TO MY SENSES.
WHEN I COLLAPSED IN SORROW, THE VILLAGERS SEIZED HOLD OF ME AND LOCKED ME UP WITH THE MAGICIAN'S HELP.
THE PEOPLE OF YOUR VILLAGE, BY REJECTING THE PAST, FORGOT ORO AND HIS SACRIFICE.
THEY'RE WORSE THAN THE SHADOWS!
TIMO!
TCHAK!
NO!

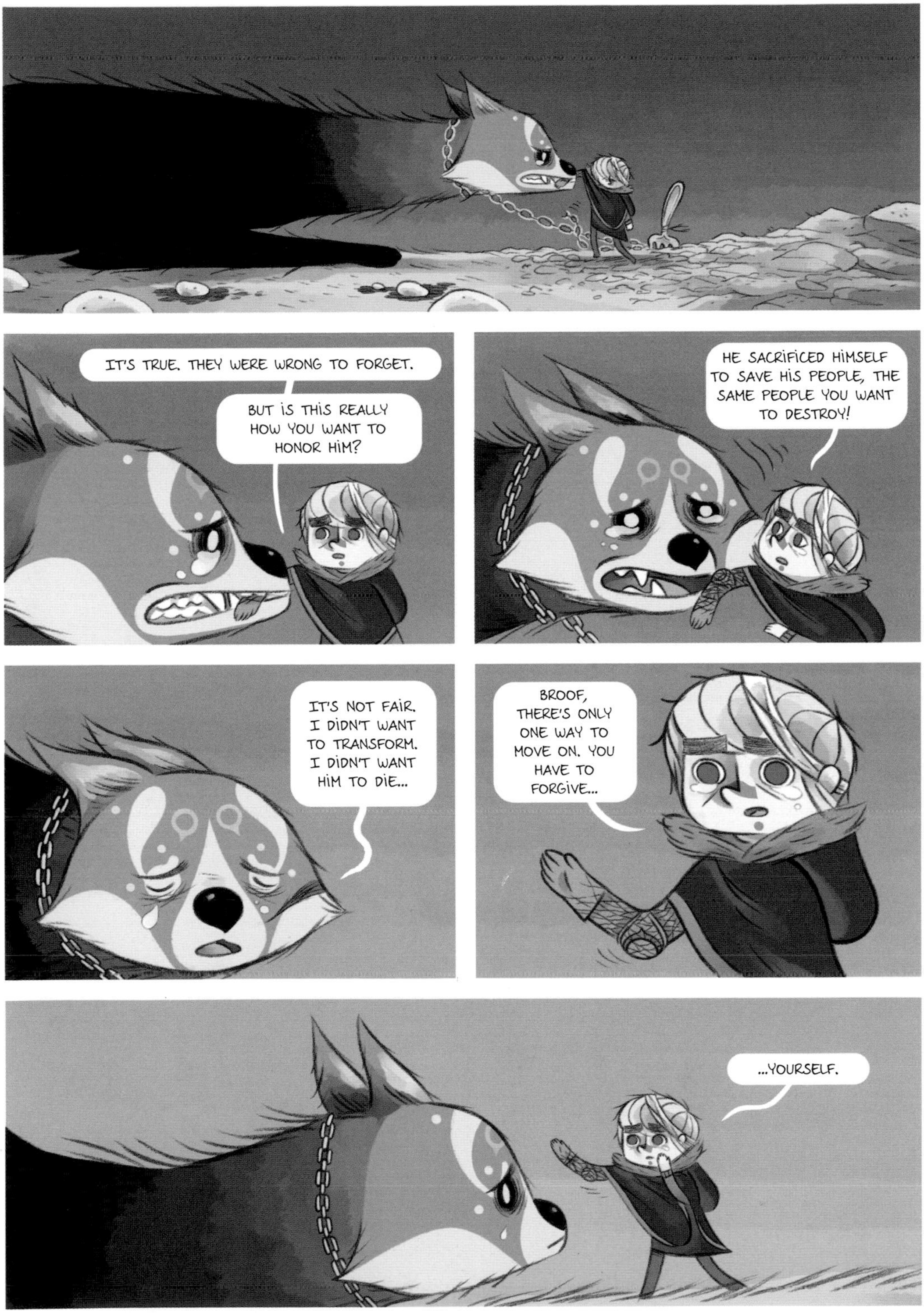
IT'S TRUE. THEY WERE WRONG TO FORGET.
BUT IS THIS REALLY HOW YOU WANT TO HONOR HIM?
HE SACRIFICED HIMSELF TO SAVE HIS PEOPLE, THE SAME PEOPLE YOU WANT TO DESTROY!
IT'S NOT FAIR. I DIDN'T WANT TO TRANSFORM. I DIDN'T WANT HIM TO DIE...
BROOF, THERE'S ONLY ONE WAY TO MOVE ON. YOU HAVE TO FORGIVE...
...YOURSELF.

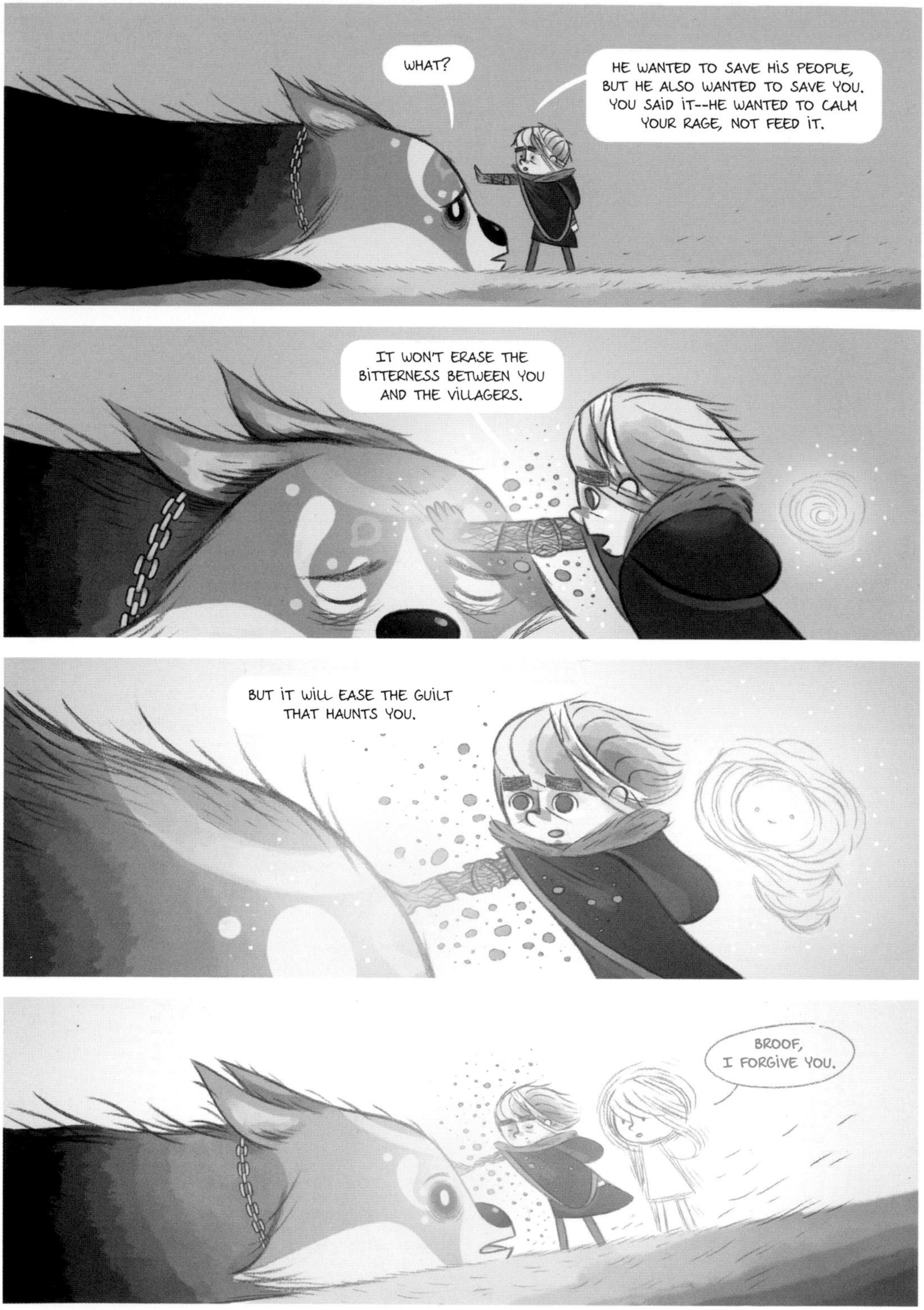
WHAT?
HE WANTED TO SAVE HIS PEOPLE, BUT HE ALSO WANTED TO SAVE YOU. YOU SAID IT--HE WANTED TO CALM YOUR RAGE, NOT FEED IT.
IT WON'T ERASE THE BITTERNESS BETWEEN YOU AND THE VILLAGERS.
BUT IT WILL EASE THE GUILT THAT HAUNTS YOU.
BROOF, I FORGIVE YOU.

ALL'S WELL THAT ENDS WELL?

Alma was right. I was the only one who could stop Broof, thanks to my arm, which had become the super-powerful weapon I'd always dreamed of. But I disagreed with her about one thing: I wasn't going to use force to stop him.

If being a hero meant destroying your enemy, if owning a weapon that powerful was supposed to help me strike down a living creature, then I didn't want to be a hero or own that kind of weapon.

I don't understand exactly what happened when I put my hand on Broof's forehead, but I think that the power the Magician had awakened in me reacted to what I was thinking. I wanted to calm Broof down, and I felt the power spread around us like a big, warm bubble. And in the end, he did calm down.

And I lost my arm...
    It disintegrated.
But I'm not complaining. That was the price I had to pay to make up for my mistakes, and it's nothing compared to Oro, who gave his life to save the people of his village, including my ancestors.

I lost my arm, but I was able to free Broof from his anger, probably because I wanted to save him more than I wanted to fight him.

Would you have been happy if the story ended and I said "all's well that ends well" because I'd defeated Broof, the big raging beast, by bashing his head in? No, because you've read my story, so you know that Broof wasn't bad deep down.

What I've learned from all this is, you have to put yourself in someone else's shoes to understand them and not judge them too quickly.

I also learned that holding a sword or having big muscles doesn't make you a hero. The real heroes are the scampermunk who'd stop at nothing to feed its family; the blacksmith's apprentice, who gave away the fruits of his labor; Alma, who took the time to listen to me and gave me her trust...and my parents, who set out to find their adventurer son even though the rest of the village was too scared to help them.

And me? I just feel like a kid who's a little less dumb and naive,
thanks to everyone I met during my adventure.

And as for Broof?

Everyone made it sound like all he did after I freed him from the temple was manipulate me so he could get revenge on the Shadows. Even I thought so for a while... But I wonder if he didn't sincerely want to help me so he could make up for what he did to Oro.

In the end, I forgave him, and I don't think I was the only one...As my arm disappeared, I felt a presence take shape next to me. I'm convinced that it was Oro. His old friend appearing to him must have helped Broof come to peace with himself.

The Magician had the power to awaken hidden strength in the people she bewitched, but she also had the power to make it lie dormant. At that moment, the spell that had transformed Broof was reversed.

When the white light disappeared, I found a baby Broof in front of me, surely the same one that Oro had discovered: abandoned and lost and only looking for one thing—a new family. All he'd really wanted was to turn back into the innocent little Broof he'd been before the tragedy. To start over, and not make the same mistakes again.

Start over, avoid making the same mistakes... That's what we all decided to do.

The people from Alma's village and mine came together and built a new village.
This time, they didn't plan on hiding or fighting—they planned on just living together
and learning from one another.

And that's a good thing, because forgetting the past, pushing it aside,
is the best way to end up making the same mistakes over and over.

Okay, that's the last piece of advice I'm gonna give to whoever is reading
this book. Now it's up to you to explore the world and go on an adventure.
Just make sure you don't make the same mistakes I did!

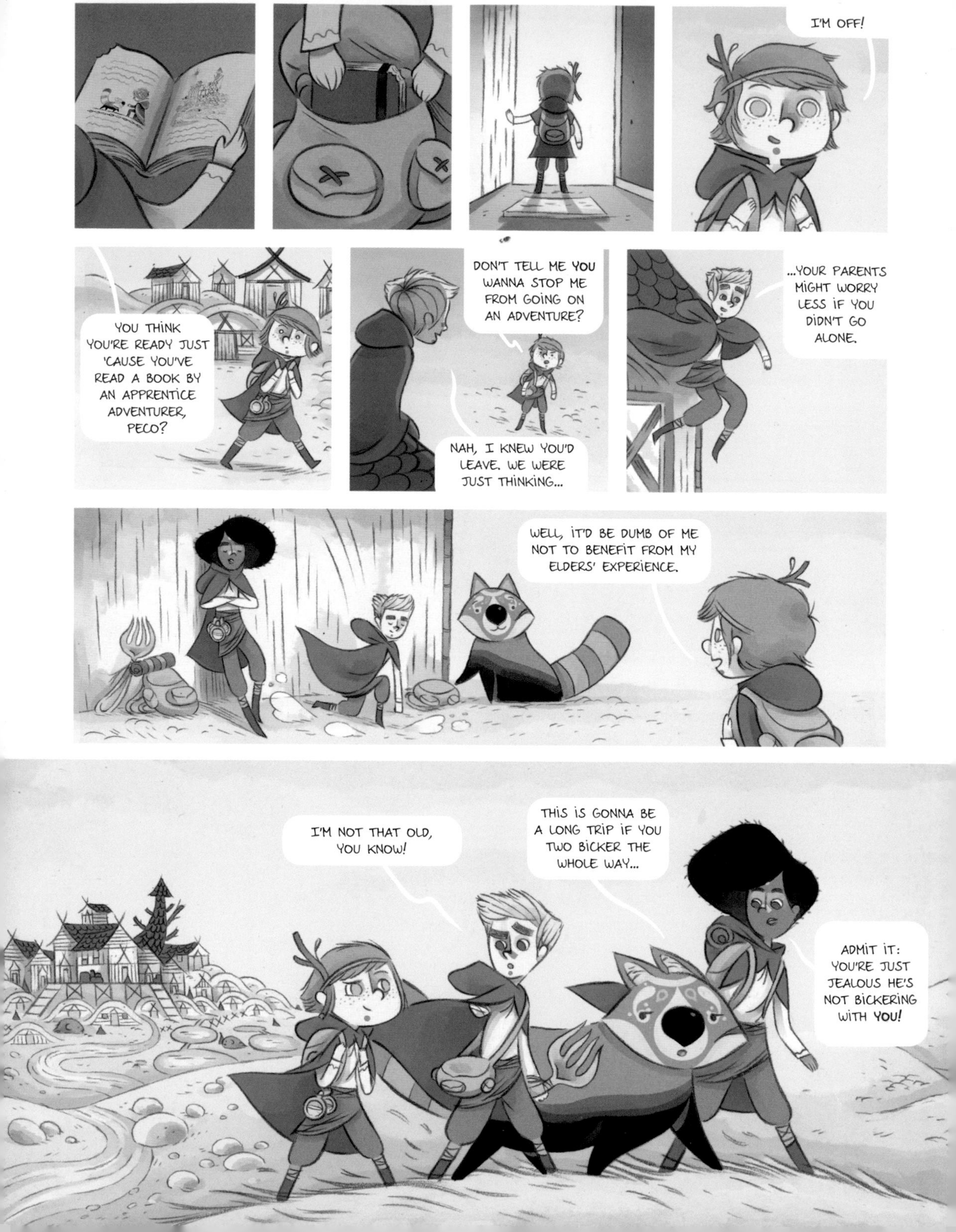
I'M OFF!
YOU THINK YOU'RE READY JUST 'CAUSE YOU'VE READ A BOOK BY AN APPRENTICE ADVENTURER, PECO?
DON'T TELL ME YOU WANNA STOP ME FROM GOING ON AN ADVENTURE?
NAH, I KNEW YOU'D LEAVE. WE WERE JUST THINKING...
...YOUR PARENTS MIGHT WORRY LESS IF YOU DIDN'T GO ALONE.
WELL, IT'D BE DUMB OF ME NOT TO BENEFIT FROM MY ELDERS' EXPERIENCE.
I'M NOT THAT OLD, YOU KNOW!
THIS IS GONNA BE A LONG TRIP IF YOU TWO BICKER THE WHOLE WAY...
ADMIT IT: YOU'RE JUST JEALOUS HE'S NOT BICKERING WITH YOU!

The End

Thanks to Amélie for her constant support.
Thanks to Pico the cat for the lovely company during my late night work.
Thanks to:
Yohan for sharing this adventure with me,
Nathalie for her energy during the launch of this project,
Elise and Louise for the follow-up,
Gauthier and the entire Lombard team for their work.
Welcome to Pénélope, the little adventuress! —JONATHAN

To Anaïs who makes me live beautiful adventures.
Thanks to Jonathan, Nathalie, and to the Lombard team for this journey.
Without all of you this story wouldn't exist.
Congratulations to GRISFX and to BXL FUN for being the best!
To Nathan and Sarah, the new explorers.
To Canine, Super, and Mothra.
As Timo would say: "Mommy, Daddy, you'll be proud of me!" —YOHAN

Timo l'Aventurier 1 © ÉDITIONS DU LOMBARD (DARGAUD-LOMBARD S.A.) 2018, by Sacré, Garnier
Timo l'Aventurier 2 © ÉDITIONS DU LOMBARD (DARGAUD-LOMBARD S.A.) 2019, by Sacré, Garnier
www.lelombard.com
All rights reserved.

First published in the United States in 2020.

Etch and Clarion Books are imprints of Houghton Mifflin Harcourt Publishing Company.

hmhbooks.com

The text was set in Mathieu and GFY Brutus.
Book design by Andrea Miller

Library of Congress Cataloging-in-Publication Data is available.

ISBN: 978-0-358-36012-4 (paper over board)
ISBN: 978-0-358-36011-7 (paperback)

Manufactured in China
SCP 10 9 8 7 6 5 4 3 2 1
4500799930